# A
# LEGACY
## OF
## *LOVE*

THANK YOU FOR SHARING IN
THIS MINISTRY TO WIN SOULS
FOR THE KINGDOM OF GOD

*Victoria Burks*

# A LEGACY OF *LOVE*

## Victoria Burks

TATE PUBLISHING & *Enterprises*

Scriptures taken from the *Holy Bible, New International Version*®, NIV®. Copyright © 1973, 1978, 1984 by Biblica, Inc.™ Used by permission of Zondervan. All rights reserved worldwide. www.zondervan.com

This novel is a work of fiction. Names, descriptions, entities, and incidents included in the story are products of the author's imagination. Any resemblance to actual persons, events, and entities is entirely coincidental.

The opinions expressed by the author are not necessarily those of Tate Publishing, LLC.

Published by Tate Publishing & Enterprises, LLC
127 E. Trade Center Terrace | Mustang, Oklahoma 73064 USA
1.888.361.9473 | www.tatepublishing.com

Tate Publishing is committed to excellence in the publishing industry. The company reflects the philosophy established by the founders, based on Psalm 68:11,
*"The Lord gave the word and great was the company of those who published it."*

Book design copyright © 2010 by Tate Publishing, LLC. All rights reserved.
*Cover design by Blake Brasor*
*Interior design by Nathan Harmony*

Published in the United States of America

ISBN: 978-1-61663-952-5
1. Fiction / Christian / Romance
2. Fiction / Christian / General
10.08.19

# DEDICATION

*T*his book is dedicated to the love of my life, my best friend, and my greatest advocate—my husband, William C. Burks.

# ACKNOWLEDGMENTS

*I* would like to extend a special thank you to my family and friends who supported me in this new journey, especially to my daughter-in-law, Tammy, and my friends Sue, Kay, and Glenda, whose faith in me prompted the courage to take the next step toward accomplishing my dream. And the biggest of hugs to Lauren, my twelve-year-old granddaughter, who said, and I quote, "Grandma, I had no doubt your book would be published." No one could ever articulate what those words meant to me.

# THE LETTER

*D*ani blinked back the tears that threatened to mingle with the cold, autumn drizzle stinging her face. Her hands shaking, she retrieved her mail from the mailbox near the door of her condominium. She rushed inside to escape the deluge from a sudden cloudburst. She wished she could just as quickly flee the memory of Lance Carter's vicious remarks, his words, the hour before, whirling in her thoughts like a tornado.

The amiable greeting from her snowy, blue-eyed kitten, usually a delight, failed to lift her spirits. His back bowed in a sleepy arch against her leg; she scooped the mewling pet from the floor with her free hand and buried her cheek into the long, soft fur. "Oh, Percy, what am I to do about Lance?" Releasing the kitten a moment later, Dani slipped the straps of her briefcase from her shoulder, tossing it onto the sofa. She ignored the clutter as contents from the leather tote spilled onto the floor.

Dani cringed, the reaction from her co-workers a vivid memory. The pace to their respective vehicles outside Pendergraff Accounting had slowed at the sound of Lance's raised voice. Mortified by their curiosity, she'd tried to sidestep the confrontation in the parking lot, but he'd blocked the way. Dani had stiffened. Lance had gone too far with that last retort, something about "the high and mighty Miss McKinnon no longer finding it feasible to associate with the lower staff."

A tear slid from her eye and dripped onto the unopened correspondence in her hand. How could he have been so thoughtless? Dani sighed as a smidgeon of compassion blended with her indignation. She knew his anger had erupted from more than just a broken date. He'd smoldered like embers all week, his obnoxious attitude beginning the moment their employer had announced his choice for the vacant manager's position. With Lance's desire to wear the prestigious title a known fact, she'd expected a reaction from him. But public degradation? Had their friendship over the years mattered so little to him?

She recalled their first date. They'd talked for hours over dinner. He'd seemed so lonely, needing a kind ear, yet an attentive listener when she'd told of her own loneliness. Dani choked back her tears. A relationship with Lance had seemed so promising. Yet in time she'd realized he just wasn't her knight in shining armor. She touched her cheek, recalling the feel of his heated words as he'd stood inches from her face, his eyes glaring and formidable. If only she'd listened to her heart weeks ago and ended their romantic relationship altogether, perhaps today could have been avoided.

Laying her mail aside, she bent to retrieve the fallen items from her briefcase. She reached for the file her secretary, Peggy Owen, had stuffed into her hand just before she left the building. Her chest tightened. What if that stranger hadn't walked up at that moment to hand over some papers that had slipped from the file onto the concrete? Recalling the sight of Lance's fist in the air, she shuddered. Had he intended to strike her as his stance imposed?

Too upset with Lance at the time to scrutinize the kind gentleman's features, she couldn't avoid notice of his apparel. Pendergraff Accounting catered to a variety of clients but seldom modern-day cowboys. A disturbing thought wrinkled her brow. At least she'd assumed him to be a late-scheduled appointee. What other reason would prompt his appearance near the firm at the close of the day?

With a start, she remembered that he'd spoken her name upon his approach. Dani's full lips straightened to a hard, thin line. Well, who wouldn't know it by now if they'd been within fifty feet of the scene? Consumed with relief when Lance had darted away, she'd turned to thank the man for his interference, but he'd disappeared. With a sigh, Dani massaged her temples, hoping it would somehow ease the pain in both her head and heart.

Her briefcase intact once more, Dani thumbed through her mail. A legal-sized envelope caught her eye. She read the return address: Harcourt, Harcourt, & Paine, Attorneys at Law. Dani pulled a tissue from a box nearby and wiped her face, thoughts of Lance receding. "Why would a lawyer from Atlanta, Georgia, write to me?" she muttered. *Probably nothing more than a bogus company using a law firm to announce a one in a billion chance to win a sweepstakes*, she thought, dismissing its importance. She started to trash the envelope along with the other missives bearing third class symbols, but something she couldn't explain stayed her hand.

Deciding she needed a strong cup of tea to settle her nerves, Dani stepped into her small kitchen and reached for the teakettle, surprised she still held the letter from Atlanta. Believing her suspicion would be affirmed once she broke the seal, Dani adjusted the temperature on the stove.

While she waited for the water to heat, Dani moved toward the sofa, switching the knob on the thermostat to a higher setting, hoping the effect would stifle the sudden chill rumbling down her spine. She glanced about the room, aware that the warm, beige undertones of the fashionable décor did nothing to minimize the dankness that had crept into the room and encircled her thoughts. Dani picked up the cat to salvage her ankles from its playful attack before she sank deep into the overstuffed couch, settling Percy into her lap.

She studied the bold, black script in the upper left hand corner of the envelope. Was it possible the correspondence concerned the recent deaths of her paternal grandparents, who'd died within months of each other? She frowned. She could think of nothing worse to end her disastrous day than having to recall unpleasant memories of life in the elderly McKinnon household. If only—

Dani bolted upright, Percy leaping from her lap to cower beneath a chair. *Could it be? But that's been over twenty years.*

Like a javelin centering its target, the recollection of her parents' death stabbed at her heart. Again, moisture formed behind her eyelids and then scudded down her cheeks.

The years since hadn't dispelled the bereavement that washed over her on occasion. Lifting her head, she stared out the window, seeing, yet not mindful of her well-manicured suburban neighborhood. A few moments later, Dani dried her tears, her attention returning to the letter. She sighed. One thing was certain; she'd never know the contents if she didn't open it.

Her breath in her throat, she slipped her fingernail beneath the seal. Seconds later, her lips parted in disbelief, the irony of Lance forgotten. She reread the short message.

> Dear Miss McKinnon,
>     This is to inform you that you've been named primary beneficiary in the estate of your deceased great-grandaunt, Mathilda Danielle Thorndike.

Dani's eyes widened. She knew of no one by that name, least of all a relative. The letter ended:

> Please contact my office as soon as possible regarding this matter.
>     Respectively yours,
>     Phillip J. Harcourt, Attorney at Law

She swept her shoulder-length, strawberry-blonde hair behind her ears, a furrow of concentration nestled in her brow. Something about the woman's name nettled Dani. It was more than just the fact that she and the deceased shared the same middle name. All at once a bittersweet memory filled her mind.

Her seventh birthday had arrived at last. She and her parents were about to travel from her hometown, Augusta, Maine, to the not too distant Atlantic coastline to celebrate the special day. Sailing in the sparkling, blue-green bay had been Dani's favorite childhood pastime.

Just prior to their departure, the postman had delivered a package addressed to Dani. "Why, it's from my great-aunt Mattie in Georgia," her mother had explained. "Don't you remember? We spent part of our vacation at her home a few years ago." At her young daughter's perplexed look, Mrs. McKinnon had added, "Of course, you were only four at the time."

At that moment, her father's summon to embark to the coast prevented additional inquiry about the mysterious person. Furthermore, Dani never gained the opportunity to continue the conversation. Two days later on their return trip, her parents died in an automobile accident involving an intoxicated driver. She had managed to escape the tragic affair with minor injuries. Following the funeral, her father's parents had whisked her away from the only home she'd ever known to live with them in Hartford, Connecticut, where she'd grown to adulthood and now resided. Her vision blurred once again. *Oh, God! Why did You let them die!*

The sound of the doorbell jarred Dani back to the present. She took a few deep breaths to regain her composure. A sigh of relief escaped from her lips when she glanced through the peephole. Opening the door, she pulled the petite, dark-haired Valerie Grant inside.

"You'll never guess what came in the mail!" Dani said after she'd seated her long-time best friend. Dani ignored the concerned look on Valerie's face.

A moment later, Valerie held the mysterious letter, soon afterward exchanging it for the hospitable cup of tea in Dani's hand. Valerie laughed, her expression filled with amazement. "Wow! What do you suppose you've inherited?"

Lifting her shoulders, a look of doubt crossed Dani's features. "I can't imagine. I do wish Mr. Harcourt had been more specific." Glancing at the letterhead, Dani sighed. "I admit I'm curious. It's too bad I won't be able to phone his office until next week." She smiled. "Undoubtedly, this will be the longest weekend of my life."

Laying the letter aside, Dani faced her friend once again. "What do you say to a fast food dinner at the mall food court? Shopping is just the therapy I need right now to take my mind off Lance's despicable behavior this afternoon and the news of unknown relatives." Dani paused. "I just thought of something … perhaps in a week or so … " Her eyes twinkled. "How about a road trip to, say, California?"

Valerie laughed then glanced at Dani's face. "Oh, my, you're not kidding." Valerie shrugged her shoulders. "I'm game if you are. You know we both have some vacation time we need to use before the end of the year."

"Hey, you're right." Dani's expression grew thoughtful. She tapped her finger against her chin. "A long trip might be just the answer to cure my head and heart of Lance. Let's pick up some West Coast brochures at that travel agency in the mall."

Valerie picked up her coat from the sofa, her large, brown, doelike eyes full of questions. "I knew something was wrong the moment you answered the door. What happened with Lance?"

Dani's mouth turned downward. "Let's go. I'll explain on the way. Once we get home we can plan our trip.

Dani arrived at Pendergraff Accounting on Monday morning a little out of breath. Entering the three-story brownstone, she glided toward her office. She'd pick up her messages later, she decided, swishing by her secretary's desk with a brief hello. The letter from Atlanta inside her blazer pocket crinkled beneath her fingers. She brushed off the questioning look on the secretary's face. Her usual morning chat with Miss Owen would have to wait until another day, the call to Mr. Harcourt too important to delay.

Seated at her desk a moment later, Dani reached for the phone, but a sudden spark of misgiving caused her to pull back her hand. At that moment a voice from the doorway startled her. She looked up, forcing herself to speak in a tone far more courteous than she felt.

"Oh! Lance. I didn't hear you knock."

"Uh … Good morning, Dani. Look, I owe you an apology."

Dani lowered her lashes to hide the anger that flashed in her eyes. After a moment she again peered at the tall, slender man leaning against the doorframe, his wire-rimmed glasses somewhat askew.

He stepped inside to stand between the chairs near her desk. "I should have realized you were too beat for a night on the town." He leaned forward. "Forgive me?"

Dani battled the urge to deny the request, his harsh retorts the previous Friday a stinging reality. She scrutinized his expression. His penance seemed genuine. She supposed they must share a congeniality of sorts. They still had to work with each other, no getting around that. Dani hesitated another moment and then waved away his contrition.

"Apology accepted." With the sound of her words, she felt her ire drain away. What would it benefit to hold a grudge anyhow? She'd give him the benefit of the doubt. After all, the week before had been unusually stressful for him.

His gray eyes brightened. "I know how much you enjoy Shakespeare, so I purchased two tickets for *A Midsummer Night's Dream* playing this weekend at the Civic Center. I managed to get great seats. How about it?"

Dani eyed his stylish blond hair, his handsome features displaying a boyish eagerness hard to resist. However, it was high time he realized a personal relationship between them held no future. But how could she refuse his invitation without hurting him? Dani fumbled with the papers on her desk, the letter from Atlanta catching her eye. She breathed easier. "It sounds entertaining, but I'm afraid I have to beg off. I've some personal business to untangle before I can make any definite plans." Lance observed her movements as she set the correspondence aside.

His eyes darkened. "Sure, Dani, I understand. Maybe some other time."

She glanced away, unable to lift her eyes after viewing the disappointment on his face. Dani picked up a file. "Sorry, Lance," she said, softening her tone. "Duty calls. As you know, the Classen audit is a stickler. The corporation has threatened to pull its business unless we can complete the audit today."

A sneer distorted his angular features. "Oh, I'm sure it won't take you long to finish it. We're all familiar with your accounting agility," he said, casting a pointed glance toward the new sign on her door.

Dani threw him a look that promised to wilt a last-standing, end-of-summer daisy. Would it be like this from now on, one moment his affectionate friend, the next moment his worst enemy? She forced her lips to stay closed. She couldn't allow personal conflict to interfere with job performance. Years of school sports that had netted a full scholarship to Connecticut University had taught her the value of teamwork. Her muscles grew taut. She'd never allowed life's challenges to deter her from her responsibilities in life, and Lance Carter would not be the exception to the rule.

Dani watched his hasty retreat. Twinges of regret nipped at her conscience. If only he'd been more understanding of her goals and aspirations—a husband, children, a place to call home. "You know I didn't have a single clue I'd be given this job," she declared under her breath, aware he probably wouldn't have believed the fact had he heard her reply.

Dani took the phone in hand. A wisp of a smile touched her lips. Hopefully she still held a good rapport with her secretary. "Peggy, see if you can schedule me a few moments with Mr. Pendergraff this morning, please."

While she waited for the response, Dani recalled her secretary's first day at the firm, a week after her graduation from high school. Peggy, loaded down with an armload of files to deliver to various offices, had collided with Dani in the corridor, scattering papers in all directions. The young woman had burst into tears, frightened that she'd lose her job. Dani had calmed Peggy, helped restore the paperwork to order, and then escorted her throughout the building, aiding the girl's endeavor.

Earning a vocational degree for secretarial training in night school, she had worked hard in the secretarial pool, her accomplishments well known throughout the agency. When Dani learned that her promotion would include a private secretary, she at once thought of Peggy, who'd jumped at the opportunity to fill the position. Dani smiled. She couldn't have found a more competent or faithful assistant.

Two hours later, the Classen feat accomplished, Dani sat in William Pendergraff's spacious office. She waited patiently while he examined the missive from Atlanta. She smothered a laugh. Some of her fellow employees often felt intimidated by their self-confident, dignified employer. However, he'd just been lovable Uncle Bill to her for as far back as she could remember.

"Well, what do you think?" she asked when he'd finished reading the correspondence.

Pushing his glasses upward to rest on his thick, iron gray hair, his steel blue eyes grew warm with tenderness as he beheld his protégé. "I've heard of Harcourt, Harcourt, and Paine. They're a reputable firm. However, I can't recall your parents mentioning a Mathilda Thorndike."

"Neither can I, unless..." Dani relayed the memory of her seventh birthday and Aunt Mattie.

Leaning back in his chair, Mr. Pendergraff tapped his fingers together a moment before he spoke. "I believe it's safe to conclude that the deceased Mrs. Thorndike and your mother's aunt could be one and the same."

Dani nodded in agreement. "It's too bad I didn't remember about her until now. I wonder if she tried to contact me after my parents' death."

Mr. Pendergraff shrugged his shoulders. "I'm sure your grandparents would have informed you if she had. But it's my guess Mrs. Thorndike wasn't acquainted with your father's family or else you'd have heard from her before now." He studied the letter for a moment and then gave it to Dani. "Would you like me to give Harcourt a call?"

She laughed. "Really, Uncle Bill, I think I can handle it. Remember your oath. You promised to let me grow up several years ago. I'm pushing thirty, you know."

Smiling, he held up his hands as though to ward off a spirited attack. "Okay, I give up."

She stood to leave. "Thanks for putting my fears to rest. I'll get back with you after I've spoken with the attorney."

In her office once again, Dani noted the time. *Darn!* The call to Georgia would have to wait until after her luncheon engagement with friends in Wholesale Accounting.

Dani collected her handbag and closed the door. She looked up to see Lance hurrying toward her.

"Here is the inventory you requested last week," he said, his manner cool.

Ignoring his clouded expression, she replied, "Thanks. Just drop it on my desk. We'll go over it after lunch." Skirting around him, she made her way to the elevators.

Striding along the corridor an hour later, Dani intended to telephone Atlanta the moment she reached her desk. But as she rounded the corner, she saw Lance waiting outside her door. As she drew near, Dani's steps faltered when she beheld his expression, the fresh glow of malice in his eyes ruthless enough to halt an infantry regiment en route to war. A harsh winter wind seemed to drift into the room when she ushered him into her office.

"Okay, Lance," she said, anxious to create an achievable atmosphere for their project. "Don't you think we should clear the tension between us? It would make our work this afternoon go a lot smoother."

His expression turned cold and hard like ice. "Red, you know we shouldn't discuss personal vendettas on company time."

Anger choked back the lump that rose to her throat at hearing the affectionate title he'd bestowed on her sometime ago, the nickname due to her liking for Red Hots. When stressed with a particular work project, she would munch on the cinnamon candies, believing they stimulated her thought processes. Tossing sentiment aside, she leaned forward, glaring. "When did you become so corporate minded? If I recall correctly, a few hours ago we were discussing Shakespeare. The last I heard, his talents had little to do with accounting."

His mouth tightened. "Not now, Dani. We'll settle our problems another day."

Dani met his cold, hard eyes stare for stare. "*What* problems, Lance? The fact that I abhor your lack of professionalism lately or your belief that I stole this job right out from under you? Or is it that continuing to see you on a personal basis has now lost its appeal? Which is it, Lance? A, B, C, or all of the above?"

Lance rose halfway from his chair, his fingers gripping the chair arms so tight his knuckles paled to a near incandescent glow. "I said not now."

Stunned, Dani recoiled within at the black look on his face. She sat down quickly. What had she done this time to merit his hostility? Neither her recent attempts to withdraw discreetly from their romantic relationship nor their employer's decision to name her manager of retail accounting had provoked him to this state of mind.

She fell back against her chair, a look of resignation stealing across her face. Dani bowed her head. She rubbed the wrinkles from her brow as though the action might rid her mind of the situation at hand. After several moments, she spoke. "You're right. Shall we get started?"

She watched a string of emotions dance across Lance's face as he concentrated on the portfolio he removed from her desk, the tension so thick in the room, Dani felt sure a tangible sculpture of ire could be carved in the air within minutes.

Eyeing his efforts to force calmness into his demeanor before they began their work, a burst of regret fluttered within her heart. Where had they lost touch? Dani drew a long, deep breath, recalling the beginning of the end of their romantic involvement. Her affection for him had grown cold when he'd expected more from her than she'd felt at liberty to give—his desire for their relationship falling far short of her dream for a lifetime commitment.

Much later that afternoon, her timepiece displaying four o'clock, Dani watched Lance depart her office without a word. A slight, sardonic smile touched her mouth.

Inventing ways to discourage his attentions wouldn't be a problem now. Whatever previous devotion he'd held for her had vanished. How long before she discovered the reason behind his alienation only Lance knew.

Out of the corner of her eye, Dani glimpsed the letter from Phillip Harcourt. She lifted it from the desk. A heady breeze of curiosity stifled the sudden icy sensation that flitted across the back of her neck. She dismissed the impression of danger, believing it to be nothing more than emotional aftermath from the conflict she'd endured the previous few hours. Forcing the issue with Lance out of her thoughts, she dialed the attorney's number.

# THE INHERITANCE

*D*ani reread the letter from Atlanta while she waited for her telephone call to be answered. She felt her stomach grow taut at the sound of the feminine voice on the other end of the line.

"Harcourt, Harcourt, and Paine."

"Phillip Harcourt, please."

"May I ask who is calling?"

"Yes. Danielle McKinnon from Hartford, Connecticut."

"One moment, please."

Dani's heart skipped a beat and then slowed in rhythm when the attorney spoke her name, his deep, mellow voice soothing her apprehension.

"Miss McKinnon, Phillip Harcourt here. Thank you for your prompt response to my letter."

"You're welcome. Although I'm not sure you've contacted the right person. I can't recall a Mathilda Thorndike in my genealogy."

"Please be assured, Miss McKinnon, the detective agency we engaged to discover your whereabouts supplied ample accreditation of your kinship with my former client. With that in mind..."

Three days later, Dani boarded a plane to Atlanta, hoping her scant knowledge of Mathilda Thorndike would soon be clad with facts. Other than mentioning her aunt had insisted upon Dani's presence at the reading of her last will and testament, Mr. Harcourt had yet to explain the details of the inheritance. Her later phone call acquainting him with her trip itinerary still had offered no clue as to the nature of her bequest. Dani had since experienced an uncertainty she couldn't shake. And her experience the evening before, she recalled with a shudder, only added to the anxiety.

Leaving the office later than usual, she'd just stepped outside the building when she sensed that danger lurked nearby. Hastening toward her Lexus, she could have sworn another's footsteps echoed her own, but a look over her shoulder had revealed nothing. Once she'd locked the doors of her car, she'd laughed off the incident, blaming her suspicions on the deserted building and her passion for late-night mystery flicks.

Now, as she observed the white fluffy clouds outside the window of the plane, the thought of the incident drifted away as she beheld the beauty of the sky.

The scene seemed to draw her to its depths. Fleeting memories of Sunday school, church attendance, and the God her parents had loved and worshiped traipsed across her mind. An indefinable wistfulness erupted within—a deep-seated hunger she experienced on occasion for something she couldn't explain. Could it be she needed to reacquaint herself with the God of her childhood? In her grandparents' care, she'd been taught to be self-sufficient, moral, and crown her endeavors with personal dignity, which she attempted to apply to her life each day, but a relationship with God had never been an issue. Dani stiffened in the seat. Just as well, she decided. She'd discovered how much God cared for her twenty years ago. No child should suffer the desolation and loneliness she had endured in her youth. Yes, Lucille and Bill Pendergraff had been wonderful to her, but their love hadn't been enough to compensate for her loss.

Her godparents often encouraged her to seek help from her Creator. They believed He was the answer for her quest to vanquish the ache in her heart. But how could she serve a God that had torn her childhood to shreds?

As the plane leveled out to cruise along the skyway, Dani noticed the quizzical look on the face of the passenger across the aisle as he gazed at her features. Dani settled back in her seat, her face tinged with red. She decided the legacy awaiting her in Georgia would be a much safer subject on which to steer her thoughts.

After a few moments, a smile sneaked into her eyes. It was possible the ambiguous bequest might be nothing more than the responsibility to care for a pet left behind in the wake of her aunt's demise. At the thought of Percy's response to a roommate, Dani stifled a chuckle. Closing her eyes, she hoped the cat wouldn't cause any trouble while in Valerie's care.

An hour later, the captain's voice cracking over the intercom woke Dani from her short nap. Soon they'd be landing. Her fingers trembled as she straightened her hair. A moment later, she snapped the seatbelt into place. Soon they taxied toward the terminal.

Once inside the airport, Dani paused at the arrival waiting area to look around, her eyes falling upon an incredible sight. Striding toward her, his eyes bright with recognition, was one of the most handsome men she'd ever seen. He stood several inches above six feet, his well-tailored suit disguising his almost too slender frame in comparison to his height. But still, his raven hair, impeccably styled, and large blue eyes framed by long, dark lashes seemed only a beginning token of his good looks. Once Dani realized she was the object of his attention, she pressed her lips into a professional smile.

"Miss McKinnon? Justin Harcourt at your service." He shook his head. "I'm sorry, but this photograph taken by our detective during the investigation of your whereabouts doesn't do you justice at all." Smiling, he lifted the carry-on bag from her shoulder, offering the printed image for her perusal.

She started to speak, but her voice seemed stuck in her throat. To hide the color crawling into her cheeks, she glanced at the snapshot. His opinion was understated. Clothed in sweats, her plaited hair loosened by a vigorous jog in the park near her home, the detective couldn't have chosen a more inopportune moment to snap her picture.

"Uh, I don't mean to be rude, but I expected an older gentleman to meet me."

"You're referring to my father, Phillip Harcourt, of course. Unfortunately, he gives me all the *unpleasant* tasks," Justin said, his charming Southern accent accompanied by an infectious grin that weakened her knees.

Dani returned his smile. Gazing up into his tanned, finely chiseled face, her five-foot-six-inch frame seemed diminutive beside him.

He took hold of her arm. "Shall we collect your luggage? Dad is expecting us at the office within the hour."

Her mouth grew dry at his touch. "S ... sure," she said, straightening to her full height. *Dani McKinnon, get hold of yourself.* As they moved forward, she whittled her reasoning to more businesslike thoughts, although she couldn't help admire his chivalry.

"I hope you enjoy our celebrated Southern hospitality while you're in Atlanta. Matter of fact, I've been commissioned by Dad to see that you do."

Sneaking a glance in his direction, Dani found that she wasn't at all disturbed by his father's injunctions. "I'm sure my stay will be a memorable one."

"We shall do our best to make that happen," he replied, his bewitching eyes twinkling with mirth.

Once outside, Justin guided her toward a sleek, white Cadillac stationed next to the curb. The chauffeur stowed her luggage while Justin helped her into the automobile.

The ride downtown proved difficult for Dani. The aroma of Justin's expensive cologne seemed to spirit her thousands of miles away. A vision of them together in a gondola drifting down a Venetian canal came to her mind.

Justin's husky laugh shattered the illusion. "I see the enchantment of our glorious South has found a target. You haven't heard a word I've spoken since we left the airport."

Dani's face flamed. "I'm sorry. This is all a bit overwhelming."

Justin edged closer to her, stretching his arm along the back of the car seat. A smile played at the corners of his mouth. "Just remember, taking advantage of an unexpected opportunity can often enrich one's life in a most delightful way."

All at once the memory of Lance's expression the moment she received her new job title appeared in her mind. "Maybe for you, but I'm afraid I've experienced the opposite of late."

"Oh?"

She looked toward the car window. "It's nothing, really, just a few complications at work." Dani forced herself to relax against the seat.

Stepping from the automobile a few minutes later, Dani breathed deep, hoping the fresh air would clear her thoughts for what lay ahead. Once inside the swank office complex Justin referred to as Peachtree Center, he escorted her past the receptionist, who all but swooned at the sight of Justin, and knocked on a large door, entering the office without waiting for official permission. An older, more sedate gentleman stood with a smile of welcome on his face just inside the doorway. After Justin introduced his father, Phillip Harcourt stepped forward. "Miss McKinnon! It's wonderful to meet you at last."

She concealed her surprise behind a smile when he raised her extended hand close to his lips for no more than a split second before releasing her fingers. His wavy, silver streaked hair seemed to cap his tall, slender build with a dignity that spilled over into the surroundings. When he straightened, Dani realized that Justin's eyes mirrored his father's—flint blue and cool like a mountain stream yet without the lifetime of wisdom reflected in the elder Harcourt's gaze.

Phillip seated her in one of the burgundy leather chairs near his massive mahogany desk. Justin waited until she appeared comfortable and then sat in the chair next to her.

While the senior Harcourt settled himself behind his desk, Dani resisted the temptation to remove her pumps and bury her feet in the plush ivory carpet. At the same time, she noted how the rich, contemporary, wine-colored window dressings added a touch of elegance to the otherwise masculine setting.

After a few moments of polite exchange among them, Phillip cleared his throat. "Miss McKinnon, what I have here is your aunt's last wishes regarding her estate." In a respectable tone, he began to read. "I, Mathilda Danielle Thorndike, being of sound mind..."

Dani could hardly hear the sound of the attorney's voice over the pounding of her heart. At the mention of her name, she straightened.

"To my great-grand niece, Gwendolyn Danielle McKinnon, I bequeath..."

The reading of the will complete, Dani sat speechless, her face bathed with a look of shock. It just couldn't be. This sort of thing only happened in movies. Yet she now owned considerable monetary assets, plus "the land and buildings known as Stratford Hall, provided she maintains residence at said estate. Should she not elect to claim the property and furnishings, they are to be sold, the receipts donated to the Carroll County Children's Home, Evansville, Georgia."

It seemed her aunt had held regard for underprivileged children as well. The image of Moriah, the child Dani now mentored as a volunteer in the national Brothers and Sisters organization, came to mind. Life had in nowise been fair to the eleven-year-old girl, the daughter of a single parent recovering from drug addiction. But Dani tried to give the preadolescent hope for a better future each time they were together.

Sensing the Harcourts' expectant gaze upon her, she glanced first at Phillip and then Justin, pointing to the document still held by Mr. Harcourt. "Incredible. I can't believe it."

Phillip gave Dani a smile of encouragement. "But you must!" Justin reached over and gave Dani's hand a quick squeeze, causing her heart to skip a beat.

"Miss McKinnon," Phillip continued. "Your aunt also bequeathed an endowment to the live-in housekeeper, Mrs. Annie O'Brien. A devoted companion to Mrs. Thorndike, Mrs. O'Brien can remain at Stratford Hall until her death, should you decide to accept the manor. Mrs. O'Brien is aware of the provisions of the will concerning her. She opted to forego her presence here today to prepare Stratford Hall in case you wanted to visit the estate during your stay in Atlanta."

"I see. There seems to be no end to my list of surprises today."

Justin handed Dani a sheaf of papers. "As soon as we have your signature on these, we'll finalize the process for you to receive your inheritance. Please take as much time as you need to examine them."

A few minutes later, she handed the signed documents to Phillip. When he'd finished inspecting them, he lifted a sealed envelope from a drawer in his desk and held it momentarily before presenting it to Dani. "This is a personal letter from your aunt to be given to you in the event she died before we found you. Perhaps it will help clarify any misapprehension you may still have about your relationship to her."

A whiff of gardenia drifted toward Dani when she took the embossed blue envelope from his hand. She started to open it, but Justin's voice stopped her.

"Dad, perhaps Miss McKinnon would like to read Mrs. Thorndike's letter in private."

Dani smiled at Justin. "Yes, I would. Thank you." Dani rose to her feet. "Now that our business has concluded, I won't take up anymore of your time. Would you mind asking your secretary to phone a taxi for me?" She pulled a fax she'd received from Mr. Harcourt from her purse. "I have the confirmation and address of the hotel you reserved for me right here."

"Now, Miss McKinnon," Justin said, his expression serious, "we can't allow you to traipse about the city alone." He winked at his father. "You're forgetting that as Dad's proxy, it is my responsibility to be at your beck and call while you're in Atlanta."

Dani leaned forward. "Please, I don't want to be an inconvenience."

Justin held up his hand in protest, his eyes crinkling with merriment. "It's not an imposition to be in the company of such an attractive heiress, Miss McKinnon," he said, rising to his feet.

Phillip frowned at his son. "Miss McKinnon, please forgive Justin's flamboyance. I'm afraid he tends to forget himself in the presence of one so gracious."

Dani tilted her head sideways. "How could I dare not, sir, when you've placed the world in my hands?"

A short time later, Dani and Justin stepped from the complex into the warm, bright sunlight of a Georgia Indian summer. He left her for a moment to confer with his chauffeur. As Dani scanned the scenery around her, the same frightful awareness she'd experienced the night before in Hartford stole over her.

She turned slowly, eyeing her surroundings. A man standing nearby scowled at her, his features etched with venomous scorn. Horrified, she turned away. Sneaking a look behind her, her eyes widened in surprise. The man had vanished. Was her vision playing tricks on her?

Dani, lost in the moment, failed to note Justin's return to her side.

"Miss McKinnon, are you okay?" Justin asked, his brow knit with concern as he assisted her into the car.

Dani looked up, desiring the warmth of the Southern sun to chase away the chill that embraced her. "Of... of course. Why do you ask?"

"For a moment I thought someone had frightened you."

She tilted her lips upward to force a smile. "Sorry. I'm an emotional wreck right now and, yes, a little afraid. It's not every day one becomes an heiress. I'll be fine once I put everything into perspective."

Justin nodded. "I understand."

Inside the car, Dani rubbed her cold, moist palms down the length of her skirt. Should she tell him about the incident? But what could she say? That a stranger glared at her? It would make as much sense to him as it did to her.

As the chauffeur drove away from the building, Justin turned to her, a lazy smile ambling across his face. "I've made reservations for dinner at the Towers, an exclusive restaurant in the city for this evening. I hope you don't think me too presumptuous, but I want you to enjoy the best of Atlanta."

"Sounds terrific. What time should I expect you to pick me up?

"Seven sharp."

"Agreed. I'll be ready." She lowered her head. Had she detected more than just friendly interest in his actions? She'd noted the absence of a wedding ring before leaving the airport. After all, every single woman knew the first criterion when introduced to a potential candidate for romance: check out his eligibility status!

Hesitant to acknowledge her growing fascination with him, she diverted her thoughts to the letter in her lap. She clutched it tighter. Would life ever be sane again? Problems with Lance now seemed elementary compared to seething strangers, wealthy relatives, and much too handsome lawyers. Her breath sharpened as the Cadillac crawled to a stop beneath the hotel canopy. Soon she'd be alone and would have the chance to sort the events of the past few days into some type of explicable continuity.

Her luggage in the chauffeur's hands, Justin escorted Dani inside the five-diamond establishment. He handled the check-in preliminaries, Dani clutching the key to her suite within moments.

Justin's voice interrupted her thoughts. "I hope the accommodations will be suitable to your taste.

She glanced around the impressive lobby. "No less than perfect, I'm sure. Thank you."

"The pleasure is all mine, Miss McKinnon." He reached out his arm to shake her hand. Once he had her fingers in his grasp, he held them a moment longer than necessary, his gaze lingering upon her face. Dani felt her mouth grow dry. Her face tinted with a mixture of delight and chagrin, she eased her fingers from his grip. "Well, Miss McKinnon, I must leave to keep an appointment in half an hour, but if there's anything I can do to make your lodging more comfortable, just let me know."

"Th ... Thank you, but you've done quite enough already."

"I'm off then. See you at seven."

Once inside her suite, Dani leaned back against the door, the hard, cool exterior helping to bolster her reserve. Her heartstrings were playing far too many fanciful tunes to suit her. Eyeing the Victorian antique replicas amidst the turn-of-the-century décor, her breath caught as she took in the luxurious surroundings. A moment later, she walked across the colorful, lush floral carpet to the sliding patio door. Opening it, Dani stepped onto the small balcony to view the attractive grounds below. She brushed aside a lock of hair from her forehead, the movement interlocking with a mental decision to sweep away the allure this man had imposed upon her. Why, Justin Harcourt might be nothing more than a modern-day fortune hunter. *Stop it*, she thought. *You are reading way too much into his gallantry.*

Stepping back inside the room, she snatched up the blue envelope propped against her handbag. Her suitcase needed to be unpacked, but the task would have to wait. Her aunt's words were too important to delay the scrutiny of her letter.

# AUNT MATTIE

*D*ani sat down at the table near the window. She opened Mathilda Thorndike's letter, taking a moment to switch on the lamp nearby to better view the spidery penmanship. Settling once more into the cushioned armchair, Dani began her journey into the past.

My dear Danielle,

On many occasions I've recalled your visit to Stratford Hall. You were like golden rays of sunshine bursting through the clouds at the end of a storm. You were so intrigued, a fountain of curiosity bubbling over each time you entered a different room within these ancient walls. How pleased I was to behold your childish esteem for my beloved home. Then, alas, the time for your departure came.

After waving a last good-bye to you, I climbed the stairway to the gallery to look upon my ancestors' portraits. I felt that, if alive, their sentiments would equal my belief that our destinies entwine—mine nearing sundown, yours just dawning.

Only recently, through the detective agency my attorney engaged to find your mother, have I learned of your parents' death. I often wondered why your family had ceased to correspond with me, my letters over the years returning with no forward address available. When my husband, Silas, became terminally ill, all my thoughts turned to him. Following his death, I wrote to your mother to inform her of his demise, but again the letter was returned to me.

I know my days on this earth are short. It is my prayer that you will be located soon. Not only are you the last descendent in my lineage, but I desire greatly to see you again before I go to my eternal reward. However, as the days unfold and we have yet to receive word of you, my hope grows bleak.

My earnest desire is that you accept your birthright, this antebellum landmark held in reserve for future generations by God's mercy and sheer determination. Your inheritance, my dear, is not just a house and land but a legacy of love handed down to you from those whose lives were enriched by the generosity and traditions of the people bred and nurtured on Southern soil.

Should our reunion on this earth fail to transpire, I pray that we will meet in heaven. Please know this, dear child: my love for you never ceased. God be with you!

With highest regards,
Mathilda D. Thorndike

Dani hugged the letter against her chest. With her fingertips she wiped away the moisture gathering at the corners of her eyes. *How sad that our paths never crossed again*, she thought, marveling at the affection she felt for the aunt she'd never had the chance to know and love.

A shadow fell across the table. Dani glanced out the window, the setting sun casting the last of its heat for the day in her direction. She savored the streaming warmth dousing her cheeks, the doubt and apprehension regarding their kinship melting away in the glow of the sun. She took in her aunt's words once more. Obviously a lot of decisions had to be made in the near future. Noting the time on her watch, she thought of Scarlett O'Hara's famous line in the movie *Gone with the Wind*. "I won't think about that now. I'll think about it tomorrow."

Dani sprang from the chair. There wasn't a moment to waste if she was to be ready on time for her dinner engagement with Justin.

A few minutes before seven, Dani scrutinized herself in the full-length mirror on the closet door, glad that she'd thought to pack the little black dress at the last minute. Satisfied that her stylish accessories made the outfit conducive for any occasion, she gave her hair one last pat before she answered the knock.

Dani smothered a gasp when she opened the door. *No one should be allowed to look this good*, she thought as she admired Justin's superb black-tie physique.

"A sudden case of laryngitis, Miss McKinnon," he asked, sauntering into her suite.

Mortified that she'd been caught staring, she shut the door just short of a slam, wincing when she heard him chuckle beneath his breath. Dani tightened her grip on the wrap in her hand. "Shall we be off?"

Before Dani could utter words of protest, Justin had the shimmering stole in hand and sheathed about her, his palms resting lightly on her arms. "May I say that your loveliness this evening is enough to disarm any man, Miss McKinnon? By the way, do your friends call you Gwendolyn or Danielle? Miss McKinnon sounds much too formal to address a friend, and I do believe that we are destined to become the best of friends. Agreed?"

Dani found it difficult to swallow against the catch in her throat. She moved toward the door, his touch too appealing to her senses. "My friends call me Dani." *Good grief! I'm attracted to a man I've just met. I must maintain some sort of equanimity*, she thought, searching her mind for ways to combat his roguish wiles. "Mr. Harcourt, I believe you said our reservations are for eight o'clock."

"Right you are, Miss ... uh ... Dani." A grin spread across his face as he rushed past her to open the door. "After you, mademoiselle."

When they arrived at the Towers, the maitre d' led them to a table near a large window that sported a fabulous view of Atlanta's nightlife. After ordering the finest repast on the menu, Justin pointed out interesting landmarks amidst the array of colored lights. Dani took a deep breath, exhaling slowly. She felt the tension ease from her shoulders, grateful that at least for now he had adopted a more professional stance.

Justin smiled at her, turning the conversation to personal issues. "Have you adjusted to your new title of heiress?"

"No. But after reading the letter from Mrs. Thorndike, I'm convinced she was indeed my mother's great-aunt. When would be a good time to visit Stratford Hall?"

"Unless you think tomorrow is too soon, Mrs. O'Brien is expecting us for lunch."

"That's wonderful. What's she like, this venerable housekeeper?"

Justin grinned. "There's no one quite like Mrs. O'Brien."

"What do you mean?"

"Well, she's rather indescribable. I think I'll let you draw your own conclusions."

"Please, Mr. Harcourt! Don't keep me in suspense."

Justin made a pretense of glancing around the restaurant as though searching for someone and then smiled. "Do you mind not referring to me as Mr. Harcourt? I keep expecting my father to materialize. It's Justin to my friends."

Dani returned his smile, a look of resignation tiptoeing onto her countenance. "As you wish, so it shall be. I do hope we'll be friends. I've always considered genuine friendships priceless treasures—wealth that no one could acquire regardless the amount of monetary riches available to him." Dani took note of Justin's expression. "Sorry. I didn't mean to sound so philosophical. I hope I'm not boring you."

"No. I just never thought of friendship in those terms." Justin smiled in a way that made it difficult for Dani to hold onto her fork, the look in his eyes revealing an attraction for her that far exceeded ordinary friendship. He winked at her. "How could one be bored when surrounded by such beauty?" He waved his hand back and forth as though speaking of their surroundings, the elegant pristine décor in Old New Orleans style reflecting Louisiana's distinctive addendum to Deep South splendor and charm.

Dani looked away. Did he think her naïve? His statement, although true, was only a guise to camouflage what he really had on his mind. She felt warmth steal across her cheeks, the compliment reaching its target regardless of her oath to not be affected by his charisma. A new wealth of determination nudged within her. She had to watch her step. If not, she'd fall prey to his ploy and be totally smitten with him before the evening drew to a close. Dani blew a mental kiss to the waiter who approached the table at that moment with their food. Asparagus had never looked so appetizing before.

Justin forked a bite from the plate set before him. "Mmm. Chef Bordeaux has outdone himself tonight." He grinned. "Such serious thoughts should never be discussed at the expense of delicious cuisine. We wouldn't want the chef to think his fare less than enjoyable."

Dani laughed. She had to agree. Her meal superb as well, she maneuvered their conversation toward Justin, hoping to learn more about her escort. "How long have you worked with your father?"

"Since I graduated from law school. My father granted me a full partnership this past year. Dad and I still collaborate on certain cases—yours, for example. But my own practice, in addition to another business interest or two, keeps me busy. What about you? Have you always been employed by Pendergraff Accounting?"

"Yes. I joined the corporation fresh out of college. Mr. Pendergraff, a family friend, assured me the company couldn't survive without my expertise." She smiled. "Back then I was too inexperienced and immature not to believe him."

Justin passed the rolls to Dani, covering her hand with his when she took hold of the basket. "It seems we have a lot in common."

Dani quickly withdrew her hand, ignoring the bemused look in his eyes. It would take every feminine wile she possessed to keep this overconfident Southern bachelor in line. She pretended to smother a yawn. "At least in respect to our careers. What time did you say we would leave for Stratford Hall in the morning?"

He smiled as though conscious of her stratagem. "I didn't, but we should be on the road by at least ten o'clock."

Later, after Justin had used his cell phone to inform his chauffeur, Isaac, that they were ready to depart the restaurant, he turned to Dani. "I know some terrific night spots. Would you like to take in a show? Or perhaps dance the night away?"

Before she could answer him, Isaac arrived. Once inside the car, Dani turned toward the window to conceal her thoughts. The last thing she needed was intimate atmosphere in the company of this particular gentleman if she were to survive the emotional roller coaster ride she'd experienced since meeting him.

"Well, how about it, sweet Dani? Want to take in the town?" Justin asked as they drove away from the Towers.

Dani stiffened and then decided to ignore the intimate endearment. "Thanks for the offer. It sounds like fun, but it's been a long, awe-inspiring day, and my energy level is at zero. Besides, I want to be fresh for our trip tomorrow. I'm so looking forward to the visit at Stratford Hall."

Justin nodded. "Your fatigue is understandable. We'll plan it for another time."

Dani glanced at him through her eyelashes. Did his words mean he wanted to see her socially, or was he just being cordial? Had his flirtation been genuine after all? And, if so, did she want to begin a liaison with him? She sighed. She couldn't deny her attraction for him, no matter what wisdom inspired. However, thus far in her life, she'd scored few points in the game of love.

An image of Lance Carter formed in her mind. Yes, he was angry with her over the job promotion, no doubt, but she knew in time his ire would subside as with incidences in the past. He always sought reconciliation with her. Dani breathed deeply. And, as before, she would forgive him. Was it worth the pain she might endure to risk another romantic relationship? Dani's thoughts were interrupted by their arrival at her hotel.

Once inside, Dani started toward the elevators, but Justin, taking her arm, guided her toward the open lounge in the center of the lobby.

She frowned at him. "Justin, it really is quite late."

"But I'm not quite ready to let you out of my sight, dear, sweet Dani."

She flinched at the endearment, his forwardness all evening a constant pecking at her restraint. Deciding no harm could come from either a nightcap or his informality at the moment, Dani allowed Justin to escort her to one of the tables. Soon afterward, she sat next to Justin, taking pleasure in the aroma from a cup of steaming cappuccino. With a sigh, she realized the mocha-flavored coffee was the perfect finale to the day.

She glanced around the cozy area. They were the only occupants, save for one other gentleman seated at the bar. Although he had his back to her, she noticed a familiarity about him. She studied him closely. Seeming to sense her scrutiny, he turned around. Dani blinked in disbelief. It was the same man she'd seen outside Justin's office.

The stranger's olive-skinned face grew ugly with rage. Rising from the barstool, he almost collided with the waitress bringing Justin a fresh drink. He hurried to exit the establishment. Dani stared after him. There was something about his demeanor, or was it the look in his eyes? It was as though she'd known him before today. But when? Where?

Justin finished stirring his drink and then glanced at her. His smile faded. "Dani, what's wrong?"

"That man!" she said, nodding her head in the direction of the retreating figure.

Justin studied the stranger as he exited the building through the entrance to the hotel. "What about him?"

Her hand shaking, Dani shared her frightening experience earlier that day as well as her strange notion the previous evening in Hartford, the fear she felt reminding her of the incident.

His face etched in perplexity, Justin curled his fingers over her clenched fist resting atop the table. "Do you know anyone who'd want to harm you?"

Dani shook her head. "No, no one. The thought is preposterous."

Justin's voice softened. "Maybe it's a matter of mistaken identity."

Unaware that Justin still clasped her hand, Dani swallowed a sip of her hot drink, hoping the strong coffee would assuage her taut nerves. She spoke, her voice seeming far away. "What other possible answer could there be?"

Her earlier trepidation lingering, she didn't protest when Justin put his arm around her shoulders as they stepped out of the elevator onto the fourteenth floor a short time later. Near her suite, she pulled the key to the room from her purse. Handing it to Justin, she spied a small envelope taped to the door. Who would leave her a message in this manner? Not the hotel staff, she was certain. They used more sophisticated methods to deliver messages. The image of the man in the lounge filled her mind. Could he have been responsible for the note? As Justin unlocked her door, Dani tore open the envelope.

"Oh, my God!" she said a moment later, her body swaying toward Justin. As he enclosed her in his arms, the note with its torn cover floated to the carpet.

# THE MESSAGE

*J*ustin held Dani close to him, oblivious to the stares of other hotel occupants returning to their rooms. "Dani! What is it?"

"It … it …" She buried her head deeper in Justin's chest.

When she raised her head, his face paled at the terror visible on her face. He led Dani inside the suite and settled her trembling form onto the sofa. Suddenly she stiffened. "Justin! The note!"

Retracing his steps, he picked up the papers from the corridor floor. His brow darkened with anger as he read the newspaper lettering pasted on plain white paper.

Stay away from Stratford Hall unless you want to die.

Dani watched Justin struggle with his thoughts. His face seemed to mirror her perception of the horrid event; it must be some kind of cruel joke!

Justin threw off his coat onto the nearest chair and sat beside Dani, cupping her clenched fists into his hands. "Dani, I'm not sure how to interpret this situation as yet, but I think we need to notify the police right away. Dad too."

She nodded slowly. "This is bizarre! Who's responsible? And why?"

Justin strode over to the desk and picked up the phone, his eyes glowing with determination. "I don't have a clue, but I intend to find out!"

While Justin made his calls, Dani rose from the couch and walked over to the window. She felt estranged, as though she observed the scene from a distant place. She glanced at the message in Justin's hand and shuddered.

Joining Dani, Justin turned her around, his hands tightening on her shoulders. "Dad said for you not to worry; we'll get to the bottom of this soon. Also, Sergeant Hagerman from the police department is en route to the hotel to take our statements." Justin studied her features. "You look like you could use a drink." He glanced about the room. "Anything stronger than water here?"

Dani shook her head. He left her side, returning momentarily with a glass of water in his hand. She accepted the drink with gratitude, the liquid cooling her parched lips. After a moment they returned to their positions on the sofa to await the arrival of the policeman.

A measure of calm overtaking her, Dani grew thoughtful. "Justin, do you think it's possible I'm not my aunt's only descendant as she supposed? I mean, what if there is another relative who has learned of her death and is trying to scare me away in order to claim my inheritance?"

He shrugged his shoulders. "Our records indicate otherwise. However, anything is probable, I guess." Justin grew thoughtful. A few moments later, his face brightened. "If anyone knows about the family relationships, it would be Mrs. O'Brien. Tomorrow we'll ask her about it."

Justin slid close to Dani, embracing her. "Nothing is going to happen to you, I promise."

She probed his expression as though searching for evidence that what he said was true. "If only I could believe it!"

At that moment an insistent rap sounded on the door. Justin admitted the men standing beyond the threshold. The taller of the two stepped forward, holding up his badge. "Miss McKinnon? I'm Sergeant Dan Hagerman, Atlanta PD. And this is Mr. Anderson. He's in charge of hotel security."

Dani greeted the men, introducing Justin as she motioned the burly, sandy-haired policeman and his companion toward the two wing-backed chairs opposite the couch. "Won't you be seated?"

"Could I please see the note?" the sergeant asked Justin after heeding Dani's invitation.

Justin collected both pieces of stationery from the table where he'd tossed them earlier. Meanwhile, Sergeant Hagerman withdrew a handkerchief from his inside coat pocket, wrapping it around the papers before he accepted them. After examining the threat, he handed the note to Mr. Anderson, the man's solemn expression turning dour after scrutinizing the contents.

"Now then, Miss McKinnon, when I spoke with Mr. Harcourt on the phone earlier"—the policeman nodded toward Justin—"he indicated there might be other incidences associated with this threat. Would you tell me about them, please?"

Following her statement, a look of helplessness shaded her features. "I just can't believe this is happening to me."

"Yes, ma'am, I understand. Can you describe this fellow who seems aggressive toward you?"

"Well, he's about six feet tall, has dark brown hair and eyes, his build wiry, slender." She glanced at Justin. He gave her an encouraging smile.

"Anything more?" the detective asked, jotting down her comments.

"Yes. His face was wrinkled, leathery, as though he spent too much time in the sun. Also, he looked slightly unkempt—hair a bit shaggy, rumpled clothes, that sort of thing. I'm not positive about the color of his suit though. Gray, perhaps?"

"Mr. Harcourt also informed us regarding your recent inheritance. Do you know anyone who'd profit from your demise?"

"No."

The sergeant focused his attention on Justin. "Did Mrs. Thorndike have other descendants?"

He shook his head. "We know of no one at this moment. However, we intend to check into the matter beginning tomorrow."

"Good. Let me know if you come up with a name." Finished with taking their statements, Sergeant Hagerman stood, Mr. Anderson likewise. The sergeant handed Dani a business card. "If you need me, I can be reached day or night."

Dani and Justin accompanied the two men to the door. Mr. Anderson turned and smiled at Dani. "As a guest in our hotel," he said, shaking her hand, "you can depend on our staff to take every precaution to ensure your safety."

Dani smiled at the thin, balding man. "Thank you."

Hagerman pocketed the note and then studied Dani's expression. "In the meantime, I'll send this to the lab. Mr. Harcourt, would you mind escorting Miss McKinnon to the station in the morning? We'll have the police artist draw up a composite from her description. Then you two can peruse the mug files. We might get lucky."

"Thanks, Sergeant. We'll see you tomorrow morning," Justin said, easing the door shut behind them.

All at once the events of the day took their toll on Dani. She sank to the sofa, at the same time reaching for her purse. She pulled a bottle of aspirin from the bag, washing a couple of them down with the rest of the water Justin had brought her earlier.

Justin's expression full of sympathy, he lifted her hand to his lips. "You've had quite a day. First you became an heiress; then someone threatens to kill you, and you've even managed to turn the head of a prominent bachelor. What more could a woman desire?"

Dani looked astonished. "Justin, you think a threat on my life is something to joke about?"

His grin faded. "Sorry. Bad timing, I'm afraid," he said, standing a moment later to retrieve his coat from the back of the chair. "I was just trying to lift your spirits." He glanced at his watch. "I'd best get out of here so you can get some sleep. We have to get an early start. Mrs. O'Brien is adamant about serving meals at the proper hour."

Dani stood up to see him to the door. "I'm not positive I want to go anywhere near the place now."

He cupped his hand beneath her chin. "You owe it to your aunt to at least see the hall. Besides, you'll be safe as long as I'm around. Trust me."

*Trust him?* Dani thought. *Never in a million years! Not with those beguiling eyes.*

At the door, he leaned over to brush his lips against her cheek, the look of concern in his eyes axing away every reservation she'd had toward him like a lumberjack felling a forest one tree at a time.

Raising his hand in a mock salute, he stepped out into the corridor. "Good night, sweet Dani. I'll see you in the morning, early. We need to be at the precinct by eight."

Dani thought sleep would come the moment her head hit the pillow. But when she closed her eyes, the fearsome visage of the dark-skinned stranger appeared in her mind, crowding out thoughts of Justin. What she'd believed to be a dream come true hours before had turned into a nightmare. The temptation to take the first available flight to Hartford and forget she ever heard of Mathilda Thorndike struck her like a stone. What good was a bountiful inheritance if it meant losing her life in the meantime?

The confusion in her mind grew idle when an item of vital importance sneaked into her thoughts. If her mother had lived, she would have been the beneficiary of her great-aunt's estate. The thought bolstered Dani's courage. Her innate reserve of strong determination snapped into place. She wasn't about to run before she viewed the ancestral home. After all, didn't she have an obligation to her mother's heritage?

"Mommy, Mommy! I'm scared! Mommy, help!"

"Shhh. You're okay. It's just a thunderstorm." Dani's hysteria calmed at the sound of her mother's voice. "God has an angel watching over you. He'll protect you." The young Dani snuggled in her mother's arms, reassured by the soft-spoken words.

Later, when Dani awoke, daylight peeped from the edges of the heavy drapes holding back the entrance of morning into the bedroom. Her skin clammy, she glanced at the tangled mass of covers. She lifted one hand to her cheek. It was as though her mother's touch had been real, not a dream. Dani wiped away the tears that clung to her eyelashes.

Fully awake now, she realized the prayerful vigil during her dream could do nothing to prevent the storm brewing about her now. Angelic security hadn't spared her parents' lives, so how could she dare hope that God would shield her from the danger that threatened her life? Dani raised her fist toward the ceiling. "They believed in You! And You let them down. In fact, just where were their guardian angels the night they died? Vacationing on the high seas?"

Dani glanced at the radio, the clock reading half past six. Reining in her frustration, she thrust the bedclothes aside and padded toward the shower. Would she ever be able to put the past behind her?

A few hours later, Sergeant Hagerman abandoned his efforts to identify her alleged stalker. No fingerprints, other than those of Dani and Justin, had been found on the note. Also, the attempt to match the composite with the face of a known criminal had proved unsuccessful.

The beautiful sunny day greeting the couple as they emerged from the precinct failed to cheer Dani. "The police sure don't give us much hope, do they?"

"No. It's not a crime to express angry feelings toward someone. Unless they can prove the man we saw in the hotel lounge assembled the note, the most the police can do is circulate his composite throughout Georgia law enforcement and then bring him in for questioning once he's identified. If this fellow is actually stalking you, more than likely, he'll confront you again soon."

"Oh, that's a comforting thought."

Justin laughed as he helped her into his red Jaguar convertible. Soon they skirted in and out of traffic. Dani relaxed, noting his adeptness for driving in heavy traffic. Once they drove onto the interstate, however, she couldn't contain her curiosity any longer. "When will we arrive at Stratford Hall?"

Justin grinned. "I see the dawning of the day has sparked a change of heart concerning our trip." A wry smile touched her lips.

Satisfied with his promise they would arrive at the estate within the hour, she turned her attention to the scenery outside the car. Her breath caught at the loveliness of the fall foliage intermingling with the tall, stately pines aligning both sides of the highway. The beauty inspired a sense of serenity she hadn't felt in several weeks. First, she'd had to deal with Lance's issues and then with the notification of her relationship to Mrs. Thorndike from Phillip Harcourt. Had just a mere week passed since she'd received his letter?

Once outside the city, Dani inhaled the fresh air, deciding to enjoy the trip in spite of the danger that haunted her. She had to believe the perpetrator would soon be captured and just punishment received for his misdeeds. Fury gripped her as the events of the previous evening replayed in her mind. Her eyes filled with fortitude. God help his poor soul should she encounter that dreadful man again! A moment later a slight smile touched her lips, draining away her anger. *Isn't it strange?* she thought. *I can believe in heavenly aid for that individual yet not for myself.*

Dani turned to focus her attention on Justin. Seeming to be lost in his thoughts, she took the opportunity to observe him from the corners of her eyes. His high, smooth cheekbones, accentuated by thick, curling eyelashes, gave him a boyish look. All at once she longed to swoop back the lock of hair the wind had shoved onto his brow, the ache so strong she entwined her fingers, forcing her hands to remain in her lap.

Seeking to divert her mind-set, she asked, "What do you usually do on weekends when you're not pinch-hitting for your father?"

His eyes crinkled into a smile. "Oh, just the norm—fighting off the latest crop of eligible debutantes determined to allay my confirmed bachelorhood."

*I just bet you do!* Dani adjusted her sunglasses to smother the burst of laughter in her throat. "Yes, it must be such a trial to have so many women grappling for your attention. You probably drive your shrink to madness."

Justin laughed and then sobered, his serious expression erasing Dani's smile. "Actually, I prefer more mature women."

Dani's heart seemed to leap into her throat. Discouraging his attentions wasn't going to be easy. She turned toward the passenger window. Her face aflame, she realized she didn't mind his pursuit at all, even desiring his engaging remarks. What had come over her? She aborted her thoughts. It was too soon to dive into another romance. Momentarily, Justin veered toward an exit ramp. She breathed deep, thankful that the change in driving prevented a reply.

Dani resumed their former conversation. "Have you always maintained your present opinion on the holy state of matrimony?" she asked once Justin had maneuvered the car off the interstate and onto the state highway leading to their destination. He remained quiet for so long she began to regret her flippancy.

Justin drew a deep sigh. "No. I planted myself in the institution some years ago, but it didn't work out."

Dani bit her lip. "I didn't mean to bring up unpleasant memories."

"No problem. I married my college sweetheart, but soon afterward I found the initial marital bliss had disintegrated. One afternoon I came home early from work to find my wife in bed with a state congressional candidate. I walked out and never looked back."

Dani reached over and touched his arm, her face a vision of compassion. "I'm sorry."

With his free hand, Justin clasped her fingers, lifting them to his lips. "You're quite a woman, Dani." He let go of her hand to concentrate on his driving.

Her heart lurched at his almost inaudible words. She lowered her eyelids. Dubious of how to respond, she leaned back against her seat and gazed at the rolling countryside. Every few miles tucked in between closely-knit spans of trees a small farm could be seen, the autumn-plowed fields on the hillsides grabbing her attention. She marveled at the clay-red color of the fallowed ground, so different from the black soil in the agriculture community surrounding Hartford. She looked at Justin. "Can farmers actually produce crops from that red dirt?"

Justin smiled. "Yes, quite a number, in fact." She turned away to glimpse more of the scenery.

"The landscape is fascinating, so inviting, soothing to the soul," she said, her eyes wide with amazement.

"Gets to you, doesn't it? Other than the cultivation, not much has changed since the Creek Indians owned this land. Dad told me that one of your ancestors, Louis Danielle, a French trapper, purchased the original grounds of Stratford Hall from a Creek Indian chief after migrating to the Georgia territory following the Revolutionary War. Later on, Danielle married one of the chief's daughters."

"Intriguing. Who would have thought I could trace my maternal family that far back? All Grandmother McKinnon knew about my mother was that she'd been the only child of missionaries in South Africa. While attending college in New England, she met and married my father. I never saw my grandparents. They were martyred during a native uprising soon after my entry into junior high school."

"That's too bad." Justin braked to allow a motorist to pass before driving onto a concrete lane cracked many times from age yet not in disrepair. The driveway, like a curling ribbon, wound its way upward through the trees, narrowing until it curved out of sight. Halfway up the incline, he slowed the car to a stop. She glanced at him, a puzzled frown on her face.

"I just wanted you to get a feel for the place," he said smiling. "But I see you're captivated already."

She looked around, mesmerized by the serenity of the forest bordering the lane. Only the sound of the idle motor beneath the hood of the car could be heard within the seclusion. Tilting her head, she gazed up at the tall timber surrounding the whisper of sky, the branches intertwining like ancient, outnumbered warriors' shields interlocked to protect the army from an advancing enemy. She marveled at the array of colors riding on the sunbeams that filtered down through the native Georgian wood. A sacred aura seemed to fill the air as Dani allowed the magic of the moment to embrace her.

Finally, a scolding squirrel broke the spell. Justin put the car into gear and advanced toward the bend in the road. "Those intertwining trees are known as Live Oaks. The South is famous for them. Now, Dani, close your eyes."

"What?"

"Please shut those gorgeous emerald eyes and don't open them until I say you can."

"Okay," she said as a look of bewilderment spread across her face.

Justin drove the car around the curve. Dani felt his gaze upon her when he killed the motor.

"Now you can open your eyes."

# STRATFORD HALL

*O*nce Justin helped Dani from the car, she stood transfixed, breathing in the sweet, dense aroma of honeysuckle that filled the air. "Justin, I never dreamed…" Her eyes wide, she stared at the magnificent, life-sized portrait of history looming before them. She determined only an artist of the highest repute would be able to capture its exquisiteness.

Dani took in the scene, little by little, absorbing every detail. The red brick mansion sat on a carpet of deep green grass that spilled downward to rest at the foot of the surrounding forest. Towering above the porch were four white Grecian columns rising upward to hug the red-tiled roof. A balcony protruding from the second story shaded the porch. A smaller, semicircle, third-floor portico, like its counterpart below, brandished black wrought-iron railing, the French doors beyond each terrace hovering like ladies-in-waiting, ready to open at the queen's command. The entrance to the dwelling consisted of a massive wooden door, which seemed to embolden the ornate Palladian window above, the intricate carving in the wood like fine lace.

Justin smiled at the shock written on Dani's face. "Now you can understand Mrs. Thorndike's desire for your presence in Georgia.

She believed that once you laid your eyes on Stratford Hall, you'd have to think twice before resisting its charm."

"Talk about not playing fair."

Dani's gaze rested on the collie barking near the bay window. The sunbeams frolicking on the panes seemed to keep time with the dog's consistent yapping.

A moment later, the English ivy splayed against the east and west wings caught her attention. The creeping trails wended upward to nip at the white-shuttered windows above, the rebellious vines finally climbing onto the roof to encircle the three chimney tops.

Dani stepped forward a few paces as though some magnetic force willed her toward the house. "I've never witnessed anything more enchanting."

"I have," Justin said, taking her hand.

Neither his gesture nor his words registered in Dani's mind as she took notice of the vivid chrysanthemums hugging the front of the house. Similar blossoms cuddled two huge trees in the midst of the circle drive, the ageless oaks positioned like giant soldiers guarding the manor from the enemy of time.

All at once a burst of breeze dipped the majestic limbs, the wind spraying the air with an array of leaves and acorns. "Oh my! Just look at those brilliant colors."

He laughed. "Are you ready to go inside? Mrs. O'Brien is eager to meet you."

Dani turned away from the view to look at him, her brow furrowed from her thoughts. "You know, if we're right about another relative of Mrs. Thorndike desiring to have this estate, I can understand his use of desperate measures to get ownership of it."

"Even his willingness to commit murder?"

A teasing glint appeared in her eyes. "I've heard it said that in everyone a dark side crops up now and then. The person who wrote the note threatening my life had best keep one eye over his shoulder now that I've witnessed this gorgeous creation."

Mock horror contorted Justin's features. "You surprise me, Miss McKinnon. I had no idea such thoughts could weave their way into your mind, although I can't think of a more pleasant way to die than at your lovely hands."

She chuckled. "I believe that's the nicest compliment I've ever received." Dani knew the situation of the note to be serious, but in this peaceful setting, their lightheartedness made the matter seem somehow remote, as if it had happened to someone other than herself.

Taking her arm, Justin urged her toward the house. "Let's go. The best is yet to come." As they strolled up the pathway, a skylark trilled a song overhead. *Was it a melody of love?* Dani wondered as Justin's touch sent a thrill along her spine.

Stepping onto the porch, Justin stroked the collie's fur to quiet the canine, its tail wagging in a friendly manner as though it recognized Justin's voice. Before he had time to ring the doorbell, the door opened with a flourish. Startled, Dani stared at the short, stout, pleasant-faced woman who stood before them attempting to tuck an escaped tendril of gray-streaked auburn hair into a bun at the back of her neck.

"Top of the morning to ye, Mr. Justin. My, 'tis good to see ye again." Not waiting for a return greeting, her blue-green eyes widened as she focused her attention on Dani.

"Saints be to heaven! 'Tis Miss Mathilda home again. Come in, lass. Come in."

Justin leaned against the walnut banister supporting the spiral staircase that rose from the foyer to the second floor. Laughter teased the corners of his mouth as he listened to Dani's hearty welcome.

"I'm Annie O'Brien. I suppose Mr. Harcourt told ye about me? My, my! You sure turned out to be a pretty thing. Miss Mathilda always said ye would. She talked of you often, especially those last weeks before she died. God rest milady's soul.

Dani opened her mouth to greet the housekeeper, but before she could get a word in edgewise, the lady prattled onward. "Now, ye just follow me. It turned out to be such a beautiful day I thought the veranda would be the perfect place for your lunch. The summer roses are still in bloom among the fall flowers, just awaiting to be admired."

Overwhelmed, Dani glanced back at Justin, who merely winked and shrugged his shoulders. Opening the double doors at the end of the polished, pine-floored hallway, the housekeeper escorted them outside.

"Breathtaking," Dani said, admiring the English garden a few steps below the brick patio. Although she longed to explore the cobblestone pathways leading to various locations on the grounds, she was most impressed by the fountain in the center of the garden. A Greek goddess poured water from an urn into a brick base at least five feet cubed in dimension. The obvious focal point of the garden, the sculpture had the markings of seasoned, well-preserved art. Dani assumed the structure to be as old as the house itself.

Justin seated Dani on one of the wicker chairs plastered with floral cushions and then sat opposite her. Meanwhile, Mrs. O'Brien bustled about, placing their lunch amidst colorful outdoor tableware. After setting the breadbasket on the table, she stood back to survey her handiwork, a slight nod indicating her satisfaction.

"Now, if ye'll excuse me, I'll attend to me duties in the kitchen." Mrs. O'Brien gestured toward the wall near the table. "Should ye need anything at all, just push that button. I'll be here quick as a wink. As soon as lunch is over, we'll get on with the tour."

The meal proved to be both sumptuous and plentiful, the freshly squeezed lemonade the perfect thirst quencher for the warm day. Dani grinned as she watched Justin devour the last piece of Southern fried chicken. "Does Mrs. O'Brien also do the gardening?" she asked, leaning back in her chair to observe her surroundings. "No. Clive Morgan, who lives a mile or so down the road, takes care of the grounds. Besides his notoriety as the best gardener in the county, he's descended from one of the original slaves of Stratford Hall Plantation."

"Interesting."

"When I was a boy, I often accompanied Dad when he called on Mrs. Thorndike. Once I'd greeted your aunt, I would seek out Clive. He entertained me with stories of past generations that had resided at the hall. I think the most intriguing was the tale of your grandmother, three or four times removed, Clarissa Kingsley. The Civil War had just ended. Her husband had returned from the war with only one arm and a broken spirit, leaving the fate of Stratford Hall to his wife.

"Not willing to give up her home to carpetbaggers or Southern scal-awags, she sacrificed her dignity and pride to become a washwoman for the Union soldiers stationed in nearby Evansville. Also, she became a seamstress for their wives, who ridiculed and despised Clarissa. She had what they desired most—the inbred qualities of a true lady.

"With the aid of her daughter, Sara, and a few loyal slaves who'd remained at the plantation, Clarissa planted a cotton crop the next year. Although she battled insurmountable odds, iron will and strength of character conquered her enemies, the goal to save Stratford Hall for Sara intact."

A silence filled the air as both Dani and Justin seemed lost in thought. Finally, she spoke. "I can see Mr. Morgan instilled in you a love for this estate I've yet to acquire.

"Watching you, I could almost believe you'd been sharing a story about your own heritage instead of mine." She smiled. "I think I'm a little jealous of your regard for the hall."

Justin laughed. "Your observation is not far from the truth. Devoted Southerners do share a distinct camaraderie. We're bound together by our loyalty to the past, and we resent anyone's effort to infringe upon our creed."

Dani detected a hint of anger in his eyes. "Is that why you seemed so upset after I found the note?"

"Perhaps to a degree." He hid a look Dani couldn't perceive behind a smile. "However, one of our responsibilities as a law firm is to provide protection for our clients any way we can. And," he said, his smile deepening, "as a gentleman, I'm duty-bound to see that no harm befalls your charming self, whose company I'm beginning to crave even more than Mrs. O'Brien's delectable fare."

Dani laughed. "Of whom shall I fear when I'm surrounded by such gallantry?"

Pushing back his plate, Justin reached over to press the bell the housekeeper had pointed out earlier. Within moments, she scuttled through the door, her face bright with a pleased smile. "Now that's what I like to see! People with a hearty appetite makes me day worthwhile," she said, beginning to clear the table.

Dani offered to help but was waved aside. "Ye and Mr. Justin take yourselves a pleasant jaunt in the garden. I'll be through with this chore in a flash, and then we'll get on with the business at hand."

Dani rendered Justin a helpless look and then took his out-stretched arm. The path they chose ended at the outskirts of the garden overlooking the spacious south lawn. To the west, a winding brook snaked across the perimeter of the land, the stream dividing the deep forest edging the grass-covered slope. In the distance, Dani spied a small fenced graveyard.

"Let's go take a look," she said, nodding toward the cemetery.

Complying with her wishes, Justin led her down the walkway and ushered her through the squeaking spiked, iron gate. At once an up-to-date granite marker amongst the older tombstones drew her attention. Dani grew quiet as she gazed at the names of Mathilda and Silas Thorndike. Most of the family history on her maternal side had been buried with her mother. Was it possible knowledge of her ancestry was about to be uncovered? Dani turned to Justin, smiling sadly. "I've a feeling I missed out on a great deal in life by not having known my aunt and uncle."

"Are you ready to return to the house?" he asked softly.

"Yes," she said, following him through the gate after glancing at the names on the other grave markers. "Wouldn't it be interesting if we could go back in time and get to know our ancestors—see how they lived, how they thought, how they responded to life situations?"

"I never considered the idea. But for the most part they probably reacted to life pretty much as we do. Even though our generation experiences multiple advantages over those of the past, I don't think people in general have changed much over the years."

Dani pondered his words. "But I wonder, though, if in some respect they had the advantage over us. Our generation seems to have lost some of the qualities revealed in prominent people of the past—character, integrity, thinking of others before ourselves." Dani drew a deep sigh.

Justin threw a look over his shoulder. "I think, sweet Dani, the sight of the graveyard has made you melancholy."

Dani smiled. "I suppose." She glanced upward, allowing the image of the beautiful garden to brighten the despondency she'd encountered in the cemetery.

Once inside the hall, they noticed that Mrs. O'Brien stood at the front door dismissing a visitor to the hall. At that moment, the color drained from Dani's face. Justin, noting her reaction to the stranger, took a second look, recognizing him as the very man suspected of stalking Dani. Justin rushed down the hall, but as he stepped onto the porch, the man sped away in a blue sedan, smoke pouring from the tailpipe.

When Justin returned to Dani's side, he found her sitting on the bench in the foyer, Mrs. O'Brien fanning her new mistress's cheeks with her apron. "Now, now, Miss Danielle. Whatever could be troubling ye, lass? Ye're as pale as the spirits of me ancestors."

"You're not going to faint, are you?" Justin asked, his face darkening with concern.

"No. I'll be okay in a minute," she said, wiping perspiration from her brow with the back of her hand. *Okay?* She wondered if the term would ever apply to her again. What she'd give to turn back the clock. She didn't know how long she could endure this topsy-turvy world.

Justin turned to the housekeeper. "Mrs. O'Brien, did you know that gentleman?"

She shook her head, her mouth twisting in distaste. "Gentleman? Bah, he wasn't a gentleman at all, not with those shifty eyes. He claimed to be a real estate salesman interested in arranging a sale for the hall. But he became real nervous when I asked him if he'd care to discuss the matter with you or Miss Danielle. He stammered something about a late appointment and then took off like a scared varmint."

"Did he mention his name?"

"Aye. Jules Davenport. I know 'cause I thought he sure didn't appear to be no gem to me, kinda glassy around the edges in me opinion."

Dani and Justin exchanged looks. The terror of the moment hung suspended in the air and then plummeted in their gales of laughter. Mrs. O'Brien stared at them, the couple finally restraining their mirth at the quizzical look on her face. Dani nodded her head at Justin's silent inquiry. Within moments Mrs. O'Brien knew the details of Dani's recent plight.

The housekeeper bristled. "Ye just let that scoundrel try to harm Miss Danielle! He'll have to reckon with me first."

Justin laid his hand on her arm. "We're not positive how much danger is involved at this point. But if you see this man prowling about the place, please notify the county sheriff. I'm sure by now he's aware of the all points bulletin the Atlanta police have issued on this fellow. Please don't take any unnecessary risks."

Once again Justin searched Dani's face. Seeming reassured, he excused himself to phone Sergeant Hagerman.

Once they were alone, Mrs. O'Brien put her arm around Dani. "Now, Miss Danielle, no need for ye to worry. I've known Mr. Phillip for years; ye can count on him to abide by Miss Mathilda's wishes to look after ye. And I hear tell that Mr. Justin is afollowing in his father's footsteps."

At that moment, Justin returned to their side, assuring the women the police were aware of the situation and had been told the description of Davenport's car.

"Mrs. O'Brien," Justin said, turning to the housekeeper, "did Mrs. Thorndike have any other relatives other than Miss McKinnon?"

Mrs. O'Brien shook her head. "Nary a one to me thinking. If she had other relation, she never spoke of them, outlived them all except Miss Danielle would be me guess." Mrs. O'Brien stood from the settee. "Now if ye be ready, we'll see the house.

"No one loved this house more than Miss Mathilda. Somehow I feel like she's awaiting in the wings to tour with us." Mrs. O'Brien inclined her ear. "I can still hear the sound of her walking stick upon these old floors. Did Mr. Justin tell you me mistress died at the age of one hundred and two years? A whole century of living. Perky and sharp as a tack clear up to the day she died. Just before she passed on, she quoted her favorite scripture in the Bible: 'I will bless the Lord at all times. His praise shall continually be in my mouth.' Then she was gone." The housekeeper dabbed at her eyes with the corner of her apron. "How I loved that woman!"

Dani shook her head. "No, he didn't. However, in the cemetery a few moments ago, I read that information on her tombstone. That is quite a feat to live that many years in our society. A phenomenon, really, when you think about all the changes she witnessed in our world during her life."

Mrs. O'Brien led them down the wide hall to a dark-paneled room smelling of lemon oil. Once they were inside, the housekeeper's expression softened to reveal a hint of her comeliness in years past. Dani wondered what fond memory accounted for the wistfulness on the older woman's face.

"This library was known as the gentleman's parlor in your aunt's day. Milady told me that as a child she often sneaked down the back stairs late at night to hide in the shadows outside the door and eavesdrop on her father and his guests. She said the gentlemen's conversations were much more interesting than the tête-à-tête heard amongst the ladies."

Dani walked over and touched the Chippendale secretary. Early 1800s, she guessed, thinking that if the rest of the house compared to this room, they were in for a intriguing journey into the preceding two centuries. At that moment Dani wished she could hug her Grandmother McKinnon for all those tedious trips to various antique shops and seminars on antiquity that Dani had been forced to attend with her grandparents. McKinnon's Antiques had been a thriving entity in Hartford for many years, her grandmother selling the business soon after the death of her husband.

Dani's thoughts were interrupted at the sound of the housekeeper's voice. "Mr. Silas was the last person to use that desk. On the evenings he worked late, I'd bring him tea brewed just the way he liked it. He'd take a sip, look up and say, 'Annie, I don't know anyone who can brew a cup of tea the way you do.' 'Tis not the tea ye favor so much,' I'd say, 'but the fresh-baked crumpets alongside.'"

Noting Mrs. O'Brien's sad countenance, Dani sympathized with the housekeeper, realizing how difficult it must be for her to relive these memories. How long did Justin say she'd worked for the Thorndikes? Since age sixteen?

Dani eyed the leather-bound books that lined three of the four walls from ceiling to floor. Squelching the temptation to scan the titles right away, she followed Justin and their guide across the hall to another part of the house.

They entered what Mrs. O'Brien called the gathering room, the spacious tasteful room adorned with both modern, comfortable-looking furniture and a few dated furnishings. The dominating fireplace stood ready to welcome anyone who might enter therein.

Mrs. O'Brien made a sweeping motion with her arm. "Miss Mathilda said her fondest childhood memories included time spent around this old hearth with her brothers, Elijah and Matthew, your great-great-grandfather."

Dani edged closer to a nineteenth century Victrola housed in a corner. A display of seventy-eight records occupied the slanted shelf beneath the early phonograph. "Does this still play music?"

"Yes, indeed! Would ye like me to show ye how to operate it?"

"Please."

Within a few moments, the matron sparked to life the melodious rhythm of a drawing room waltz.

Justin walked over to Mrs. O'Brien, bowing low before her. "Mrs. O'Brien, may I have the pleasure of this dance?"

The housekeeper's ruddy complexion deepened as she held up her hand to prevent Justin's attempt to put his arm around her. "Now, Mr. Justin, whatever could ye be thinking, asking an old woman like me to step about when ye've got the likes of Miss Danielle in the room? Thank ye kindly, but I'm afraid my feet have forgotten how to prance about."

"Nonsense." Justin lifted her hand. "You just follow me. Dancing is like riding a bicycle; you never forget how to do it."

Mrs. O'Brien's face glowed with pleasure as he glided her around the room. When the music ended, Justin bowed over her hand, thanking her for the dance in a most sophisticated manner. Her eyes shining, Mrs. O'Brien closed the record player and then ushered them through a doorway at the far end of the room.

Dani gasped for breath when she caught sight of the gilded ballroom. All four walls were paneled in brocade satin and donned cushioned built-in seating. At one end of the room, a spindled balustrade enclosed an orchestra box high above the parquet-tiled floor, the wood reflecting the soft light from the sparkling twin chandeliers.

"Oh, 'twas a grand time we had those many years ago," Mrs. O'Brien said in a hushed tone. "Miss Mathilda would hire extra help, and we'd clean till the old place shone like a summer sun exploding upon a frosty morn. And food, why, ye've never seen the like of the dishes we prepared to feed the folks that attended a Thorndike ball."

The housekeeper paused at the sound of the phone. "Excuse me," Mrs. O'Brien said. "I'll be right back."

Dani stepped through a pair of French doors onto a cobblestone courtyard, seating herself on a stone bench beneath a rose-covered arbor. She gazed toward the gazebo she'd seen earlier from the backyard. "Can't you just imagine the excitement of a ball—beautiful dresses swirling about the room, starlit nights, air thick with romance?"

Justin sat beside her. "Any particular romance in mind?"

Dani wasn't about to tell him he bore a striking resemblance to the man whirling her around the floor in her fantasy. "No. Just fanciful musings."

He picked up her hand. "May I say, Miss McKinnon, that whoever you had in mind is a very lucky man, indeed."

Dani's pulse quickened. Had he read her thoughts? Did he suspect her interest in him? She turned away, frowning. Why couldn't she resist him? She had to do something fast before her priority was lost, although at that moment she desired nothing more than to yield to her traitorous emotions. But she'd dealt once too often with a broken heart and had no desire to face one again. She frowned, lifting her hand from his. "You don't waste any time seeking life, liberty, and the pursuit of your own happiness, do you, Mr. Harcourt?"

Shrugging his shoulders, he laughed. "I just believe that when a person finds something he wants, he should pursue it. And, sweet Dani, my desires as of yesterday afternoon seem to include you. Perhaps the old adage, 'love at first sight,' has merit after all."

She gazed momentarily at his face, the hint of smugness in his eyes irritating to say the least. Dani's eyes deepened in color to the hue of a stormy sea. "Has it ever occurred to you, Mr. Harcourt, that you're not Sir Galahad to every female you meet?"

Justin leaned toward her. "Are you trying to deny the chemistry between us, or is it guilt you feel because you're spoken for already?"

Her face grew hot. "Of all the conceited—"

"Oh, Miss Danielle, Mr. Justin?"

Dani stood quickly, grateful for the interruption. "Out here, Mrs. O'Brien." Dani threw Justin a look that told him he needed to cool his ardor.

Momentarily, Mrs. O'Brien appeared in the doorway. "I apologize. The phone call took longer than I expected. Shall we continue?"

"Yes, of course," Dani said, ignoring the bemused twinkle in Justin's eyes. Suddenly, she felt a sting of chagrin, aware that her irritation originated more from her inability to quench her fascination for him than his untimely romantic blitz.

Mrs. O'Brien escorted them through the door at the opposite end of the ballroom. Dani surveyed the blue and gold decor enhancing the Queen Anne furnishings in the room Mrs. O'Brien referred to as the formal parlor. Dani spied the grand piano situated near the bay window and moved forward to run her fingers over the gleaming ivory keys, at once regretting her inattentiveness to childhood music lessons.

"Miss Danielle, there's something I've been awanting to show ye since yer arrival." Mrs. O'Brien focused her eyes above the fireplace. "'Tis rather extraordinary, don't you think?"

Dani glanced upward in the direction the housekeeper indicated. "Oh!" Dani said, grasping her chest, her annoyance with Justin lost in the revelation of the moment.

# THE THORNDIKES

*D*ani stared at the woman's portrait above the mantel. Had it not been for the 1940s hairstyle and clothing, the image could have been that of Dani herself. But she guessed it to be a painting of Mathilda Thorndike when she was close to Dani's present age.

Justin turned to Mrs. O'Brien. "Now I understand your reaction when you first met Miss McKinnon. The likeness is remarkable."

Dani shook her head. "Uncanny, I'd say. I feel I've come face-to-face with a long lost twin or been transported to a previous time." She stared at the portrait, feeling as though she floated back and forth between fantasy and reality. If she pinched herself, would she awaken in Hartford, safe and rational, ready to tackle the challenges her job often incurred?

Justin took Dani's arm, startling her. He frowned at the look on her face. "Is all this excitement too much for you?" Glimpsing the concern in his eyes, her annoyance toward him vanished. *It could be,* she thought, *that he only desires a mild flirtation, not a serious love affair.*

Again, she eyed her aunt's likeness. "No, I'm just a bit disoriented." With a mild shake of her head, Dani turned to listen to the housekeeper, who pointed out an English tea set displayed atop a dated Pembroke table near the Victorian sofa.

"It is reputed that General Marquis de Lafayette drank from one of these cups when he arrived for the wedding of Aimee Little Fawn Danielle, the daughter of Louis Danielle, the original owner of this land. Aimee wed the son of an English nobleman, George Kingsley, who'd migrated to northwestern Georgia to grow cotton. Years later, in 1835, Mr. Kingsley, along with his four sons and their slaves, built this house. Before long, the whole South had heard of the prosperous Stratford Hall Plantation."

Dani smiled. "Justin told me the story of my Indian heritage on our way to the hall today. But I didn't realize my ancestors had hobnobbed with historical figures as well."

The housekeeper laughed. "'Tis true, me lass, on more than one occasion. When milady's illness finally kept her abed for the most part, she filled me in on as much family history as she could remember, afraid she wouldn't live long enough to tell ye the tales herself. I wrote most of them down so I wouldn't forget in case ye might be interested."

Mrs. O'Brien pushed open another set of pocket doors and led them across the opposite end of the hall to the dining room. Dani eyed the furnishings, the tall mahogany china hutch arresting her interest. She examined it closer. Unlike the freestanding Queen Anne buffet, the hutch recessed into the wall a few inches, showing only a portion of its depth. She soon forgot the oddity, though, her mind becoming engrossed in the housekeeper's words. She joined Mrs. O'Brien and Justin beside the colonial dinette set.

"According to Miss Mathilda, General Lee once graced this table. And I'll never forget the night a Turkish prince set his feet upon that rug." Dani glanced down at the Persian carpet woven in shades of brown and deep blue.

"His Highness had been invited to the hall by Mr. Silas to discuss the purchase of a large quantity of steel from the Thorndike Steel Mills. I thought I'd die when Betsy, the serving maid, nearly spilled soup in the prince's lap. Of course, Miss Mathilda had things smoothed over in no time at all. I always said she could charm a bear outta his coat when needed."

Dani suppressed a giggle and then exchanged a smile with Justin.

Following Mrs. O'Brien's exhibit of the immaculate kitchen and laundry, both rooms containing every convenience known to modern man, the housekeeper paused inside the kitchen before continuing the tour. "Miss Danielle, a few months before milady passed on, she hired a decorating crew that specializes in historic homes to update the hall to me mistress's specifications. She wanted you to see the hall at its best."

Dani's eyes grew misty. To conceal her emotion, she turned toward the window. The east lawn lay before her peppered with trees, their amber and red bows stretching skyward as though in hope of touching the sun. As she watched two squirrels scamper across the lawn and skitter up a tree, a convoy of feelings riddled through her—disbelief, pleasure and gratitude, all mixed with perplexity. Dani turned and smiled at the housekeeper. "It's difficult to imagine Mrs. Thorndike's devotion to me. I was only a child when we met."

Mrs. O'Brien shook her head. "'Tis not hard to understand me mistress at all. Why, she had enough love in her heart to cover the whole world. 'Twas even hard for her to swat a bee. 'Annie,' she'd say, 'God made all things for some purpose.' 'Course I'd agree with her, but sometimes me old brain couldn't figure out just what the good Lord had in mind when He made certain creatures, especially some of the human species. Once, when I mentioned this to milady, she said, 'Look for the best in things and especially people. Then life won't have near as many disappointments.'"

Brushing a tear from her eye, Mrs. O'Brien escorted them back to the foyer. "We'll see the upper floors now. The master suite and the conservatory occupy the west wing while the guest bedrooms and the children's quarters are housed in the east wing. My apartment, plus two smaller bedrooms, are on the third floor."

When they reached the landing, Dani took a few moments to view the portraits lining the walls of the upper foyer. This had to be the gallery her aunt had written about in her letter to Dani.

"I thought Miss Mathilda would grieve herself to death when Mr. Silas died." Mrs. O'Brien motioned them toward the corridor that led to the master suite. "But one morning while I straightened her room, she threw back the bedclothes, saying, 'Silas wouldn't want me to mope around like this. From now on we'll have laughter in this house.' She gathered up her mourning clothes and marched straight down to the incinerator, burning the black garments one at a time. The next day she drove into town to volunteer her services at the Carroll County Children's Home."

An hour later, the young couple followed Mrs. O'Brien to the third floor to view her modest, contemporary quarters. Soon afterward, Dani and Justin climbed the steep curving staircase that led to the attic, Mrs. O'Brien deciding to wait for them below. Still elated from discovering some of her aunt's childhood toys stuffed in a dated Pennsylvania Dutch toy chest located in the nursery, Dani marveled at all she'd seen. Like the main floor, the second floor boasted treasured antiques, but it was up to date in all other respects. And the conservatory with all its species of plants, Dani recalled. What a delight!

"Oh, Justin." Dani's eyes began to sparkle like a Christmas tree. She gazed at the old relics in childish wonder. A wicker perambulator along with several trunks and other ancient paraphernalia below the slanted ceiling seemed to huddle together like lost children waiting to be discovered.

"What I'd give to spend a rainy day in here. Look at all this."

"Yeah, a fortune in disguise," Justin answered, carefully surveying each item. Dani frowned at the implication in his voice.

She watched him brush a cobweb from his coat sleeve, noting the cut of his clothes. His taste for the finer things in life apparent; he must realize the value of these treasures far exceeded their monetary worth. What about the Southern loyalty to the past he'd spoken of earlier? Had they just been words to impress the Yankee newcomer?

She followed him down the stairs a moment later, her mind filled with questions. Who was this enticing interloper that threatened to invade her heart? Was he all that he appeared to be? Should she be wary of him or follow her aunt's advice and give him the benefit of the doubt? Dani recalled the previous weeks, updating her resolve to allow precaution to precede her steps in the days to come. Romantic disillusionment often came wrapped in a painful adjustment to life.

❧❧❧

"Are you still upset with me, Dani?" Justin said on their way to Atlanta following a refreshing afternoon tea with the housekeeper. "You haven't said a word since we left Stratford Hall." He reached out to take her hand, but she moved it away.

"I don't like it when a man comes on too strong," she said softly.

The fine lines at the corners of his eyes crinkled. "Does that mean I've struck out?"

A ghost of a humorless smile touched her lips. She had the feeling he'd continue to bat even after the umpire had called the last strike.

"What do you think about your new home?" he asked when she didn't respond.

Dani waved her hand in midair. "It's all so surreal, like a work of fiction that's been made into a movie. And I've been cast as the heroine."

"Trust me. It's no figment of your imagination. You own Stratford Hall, lock, stock, and barrel. And, I might add, all the responsibility that goes along with it as well. It won't be easy to manage alone, but your expertise in finances will enable you, and you can count on Mrs. O'Brien and Clive to assist in other matters. Of course, Dad or I are available as well."

Dani twirled a ring on her right hand. "I'm undecided about the hall. I'm not sure I'm going to accept that part of my inheritance."

Justin took his eyes off the road a second to stare at her in bewilderment. "You're kidding, right? The net worth of that prized piece of property is a fortune in itself."

Dani's eyes danced with anger. "I'm not ignorant, Justin. However, in case you've forgotten, there's more at stake here than mere monetary value. It's the price attached to the acquiescence of the estate that concerns me. I know you believe this to be an once-in-a-lifetime opportunity; and you're right, but at this point I'm not willing to take the risk. The note, remember?"

A contrite look raced across his features. His voice softened. "Forgive me. Sure, you have a right to be concerned, but as I mentioned before, we'll do whatever it takes to keep you safe."

"I'm convinced you and your father have my best interest at heart; however, there are other things to consider as well."

"Such as?"

"For one thing, to my employer and his wife, I've been the child they never had. My godparents helped raise me when my parents died. I owe them a lot. It would be difficult to leave them, not to mention the promising career they established for me. Two, I'm happy with my life and work. But thanks to the stipulation in my aunt's will, I'm forced to choose between Hartford and Stratford Hall. I'm not ready to do that."

Justin flashed an engaging smile toward her. "For whatever it's worth, managing the hall and Mrs. O'Brien will be a challenging career in itself."

Dani couldn't help but laugh. "No doubt about it." She rubbed the back of her neck. "That brings up another aspect of the situation. Within a matter of hours I've become bonded to a family I never knew. I don't understand how it happened. Perhaps the saying, 'Blood runs thicker than water,' is true after all."

Justin nodded. "And now a part of you feels obligated to bear the responsibility of your heritage."

"Exactly. No, it won't be an easy choice to make."

"You're saying then that without Davenport's intervention, if indeed he's the one that sent you the note, you'd still have reservations?"

"Yes. Leaving Hartford..." Dani grew quiet for a moment. "I'm not sure I can."

Occupied by her thoughts, Dani didn't see his baffled expression or the quizzical shake of his head. "Well, Dani, if it were me, I'd not let anything keep me away from Stratford Hall, no matter how great the risk."

Dusk had descended by the time they reached the hotel. "Dani, would you join me for dinner this evening?"

She hesitated a moment before answering. "If you don't mind, I prefer to dine alone tonight. I've a lot to consider."

Entering the hotel suite, Justin made sure that nothing was amiss before he allowed Dani beyond the hallway. She crossed the room and opened the drapes enclosing the sliding door. She stepped onto the lanai, breathing deep of the cool air. Her heartbeat quickened as Justin drew near. He took hold of her shoulders and turned her toward him.

"Dani, about this afternoon. I overstepped my bounds, and I'm sorry."

The depth of his gaze was overpowering; she puzzled at the message she read in his eyes. Did he have genuine feelings for her, or was she just another conquest? Justin lowered his head. Before she had a chance to protest, she felt the touch of his lips. The image of a soft, gentle rain falling on a spring morning floated in her mind. A moment later, the faint sound of an orchestra tuning up for a concert on the hotel lawn drifted upward from the plaza below, breaking the spell.

Justin smiled as he ran his fingers along her cheekbone. "Dani, sweet Dani. What am I to do about you?"

Turning from his embrace, her lips tingling with warmth, Dani reentered the room. Like a challenged general amassing his troops at the threat of war, Dani gathered her wits about her. The last thing she needed this evening was romantic thoughts of Justin conflicting with her intent to ponder the future. She strode toward the door, tossing him a smile over her shoulder. "Why, nothing, nothing at all. Thank you for today. I'll remember it all my life. But you must excuse me. I need to check on things at home."

Justin joined her at the entrance to the suite, his expression puzzled. "Well, Miss McKinnon, since you've refused my company tonight, what about my showing you the sights around our illustrious city tomorrow afternoon? Perhaps a good rest tonight will help you better access all that transpired today."

She smiled at him. "I hope so. Thank you for your understanding. And, yes, I'd love to go sightseeing. It sounds like a lot of fun."

"Good. I'll bring tourist brochures, and you can decide what interests you the most."

"Is one o'clock okay?"

"Perfect."

She closed the door behind him, the scent of his cologne lingering in the air, as did the memory of his kiss. She pulled in a long breath, slowly releasing it. *You've got it backward, Justin Harcourt. The question is: What am I going to do about you?*

Dani ordered her dinner from room service. But when it arrived, she found she could swallow only a few bites. She put the dishes aside, her mind too preoccupied with indecision to concentrate on her palate. How could she leave what she'd known and loved all these years? Dani frowned. Mrs. Thorndike's expectations were too high. But yet how could she turn her back on her mother's heritage?

Dani rubbed her temples to ward off the increasing ache in her head. She reached for her cell phone. Uncle Bill had always given her good advice in the past, she recalled, and she needed him now. *Whose council will you seek when he's no longer around?*

Startled, Dani glanced around, the still, small voice within her heart seeming audible. She leaned back against the chair. *But that's silly*, she thought, ignoring the unction. Her godparents weren't that old. About to punch in his number, Dani let the phone slip from her fingers. She couldn't let them know about this now, she decided. Aunt Lucille would be too distraught at the thought of Dani departing Hartford.

Dani took a sip of water from the glass on the tray. *When the Pendergraffs have important decisions to make*, she thought, *they rely on council from God*. A moment later, Dani spurned the notion of doing likewise. When had she given Him any reason to help her? All at once exhaustion seized her. Closing her eyes, she succumbed to the drowsiness blotting out her thoughts.

The jarring of the telephone woke Dani. Once alert, she realized that night had fallen over Atlanta. "Hello?" she said, smothering a yawn. Seconds later, she arose from the sofa and stood stock-still, her eyes widening with terror as she listened to the words the caller hissed in her ear.

# THE DECISION

*S*tunned by the caller's words, Dani tightened her grip on the receiver. "Wh...Who is this?" The only answer she heard was a distinctive *click* at the opposite end of the line.

She debated her next move. *Justin!* He'd know what to do. Dani switched on the table lamp and then grabbed her purse, dumping the contents onto the sofa. In seconds, she located the business card he'd given her the day before. With trembling fingers, she dialed his number.

"Justin! This is Dani. A man just called and threatened to kill me."

"Good Lord! What did he say?"

"Something about my last warning to stay away from the hall or I'd die."

She heard his sharp intake of breath. "I hoped that once he'd discovered you weren't subdued by his message last night he'd leave you alone. Apparently I was wrong. If the theory of another relative proves otherwise, we have no choice but to investigate the orphanage."

Dani frowned. "The orphanage?"

"Yes, the Carroll County Childrens' Home."

"Oh, I remember now…the one mentioned in my aunt's will. I can't believe they'd be involved in something so evil."

"Neither can I. However, if financial distress is involved, the thought of gaining control of a fortune might encourage desperate measures. I can't imagine, though, how the knowledge of the forfeiture clause in your aunt's will became available to the staff at the home."

Dani felt her body go limp. "I think the best thing for me to do is board the next plane to Hartford."

"Look, Dani, I know how you feel, but don't panic. I'll phone Sergeant Hagerman. Let's give the police a chance to do their job before you make any rash decisions." He paused. "Besides, we have a date tomorrow."

Dani drew a deep breath. "Yes, I know."

"That's the spirit. I'll see you then."

The next morning, Dani rode the elevator to the first floor planning to partake of a hearty breakfast. Near the entrance to the restaurant, she stopped short, her eyes narrowing. Jules Davenport stood less than five feet away. Dani began to tremble, anger meshing with the fear that gripped her throat. She intended to clarify his interest in her right this minute.

"Mr. Davenport." He turned at the sound of her voice. His surprised countenance melting as fury leaped into his eyes, he whisked past her, sidestepping the other customers in line for a table. Knotting her fists, Dani turned to follow him, but the hostess's voice detained Dani from acting on her impulse.

"Smoking or non?"

Oblivious to the glances sent her way from others around her, Dani faced the woman holding a stack of menus in her arms. "Wh…What? Oh, nonsmoking, please."

By the time the waitress recorded the order, Dani had her emotions in check, even relishing the surge of courage that had initiated her response to Davenport. How dare that obnoxious brute or anyone else try to stop her from receiving Aunt Mathilda's generosity!

Later, back in her suite, Dani phoned the police to report her encounter, Sergeant Hagerman stating he'd send a unit out to case the area for Davenport immediately. A few minutes later, at the sound of Justin's arrival for their date, she rushed to open the door.

"Did the guy do anything, say anything?" he asked when Dani informed him of the chance meeting with Davenport.

"No. He just stared at me with his cold, cruel eyes and then hurried away." Dani lifted her chin, a determined look in her eyes. "I was so angry; I wasn't even afraid of him. No longer will I allow him to intimidate me. My mind is set. Aunt Mathilda meant for me to live in Stratford Hall, and I plan to see that her desire comes to pass just as soon as I can make the arrangements."

Justin smiled and then stepped forward, taking her into his arms before she could prevent the action. "You won't regret it, sweet Dani, and neither will I."

Her heart raced. She couldn't decide if the accelerated beat was from her emphatic resolution or the feel of Justin's arms. Tearing her gaze from his enticing lips, she moved away, reaching for her jacket and purse. If they didn't leave this moment, she'd be back in his arms, their plans falling by the wayside. Dani glanced at him, the look in his eyes causing her knees to feel like melting rubber. Maybe now was the time to throw aside her resolution to keep him at bay. After all, she wasn't getting any younger. Someone once said, "Life is full of chances." If she gambled on love again, would she win this time?

Justin ushered her into the corridor, dispelling her thoughts. "Oh, I almost forgot. Sergeant Hagerman said to tell you that all your incoming calls are now monitored."

Dani shivered. "I hope I never hear that horrible voice again."

Once in the car, Dani read the tourist information he'd brought for her perusal. "Is Stone Mountain State Park as interesting as it sounds?"

"I guarantee you won't be disappointed."

Within the hour, they drove through the park gates.

Back in the city much later that day and dressed for the evening, Justin escorted Dani to a concert at the Memorial Arts Center. Following an outstanding performance by the Atlanta Symphony, he treated her to a delicious meal at Gepetti's Villa Italia near the center. They had almost finished their dessert when an elderly gentleman accompanied by a much younger woman approached their table. Dani couldn't help but notice that Justin grew pale at their intrusion.

"Good evening, Justin, my boy. Who may I ask is this delightful-looking belle in your company? Pray introduce me, please."

Dani tucked a grin behind her napkin as Justin stood to greet the couple.

"Hello," he said, turning to introduce Dani. "May I present Miss Danielle McKinnon from Hartford, Connecticut. Miss McKinnon, meet Miss Marguerite Van Buren and her father, the distinguished Albert Van Buren."

Despite the cool, distant look she received from Marguerite, Dani shook hands with the woman, smiling warmly at her. Mr. Van Buren leaned back on his cane to study Dani a moment before again addressing Justin.

"Well, I say, dear boy, you know how to pick la crème de la crème. I've always considered the South to produce the finest belles, but I see I've been mistaken."

"Thank you, sir." Dani could understand his partiality if all the women in the South compared to the dark-eyed brunette by his side.

"How long do you plan to visit our fair city, Miss McKinnon?" his daughter asked.

Turning to answer Marguerite, Dani's friendly smile faded for a split second and then sweetened when she noted the woman's features turn granitelike as she observed Justin's smile toward Dani. This particular Yankee wasn't about to be put off by such discourteous behavior. "I'm afraid I have to return to Hartford tomorrow, much to my displeasure." She laid her hand on Justin's arm. "Justin has taught me so much about your Southern culture in my short visit." Dani had trouble containing her laughter at his attempt to smother a sudden cough.

Marguerite lifted her chin. "Father, we must go and let Justin and Miss McKinnon finish their dinner." She threw a grim look over her shoulder. "Have a safe journey home. And, Justin," she said with a murderous gleam in her eyes, "I'm sure we'll see each other soon."

"Uh, of course, Marguerite. Have a good evening. You too, Albert."

With a puzzled frown, Dani watched Justin quickly down his drink and then motion for the waiter to bring him another one. She lowered her eyes, a warm glow appearing on her cheeks. Maybe he didn't like her cattiness toward Marguerite. Dani had to admit she wouldn't receive a reward for the greatest act of kindness shown to a stranger.

She broke the silence that had resonated since the parting of Justin's friends. "Mr. Van Buren is charming. I take it you know him well?"

"The Van Burens are close family friends. Marguerite and I were childhood playmates, even dated some in high school. We lost touch with each other, though, after I entered college. Since my divorce, we've renewed our friendship."

Dani thought he stammered somewhat over the word *friendship*. "Do I detect a Mediterranean origin in her exceptional looks?"

"Yes. Her mother, Carmen San Miguel, came from a lineage that can be traced back to an era long before the Spanish acquisition of Georgia. The family's life hasn't been the same since an incurable disease confined her to a nursing home."

"How sad."

The waiter approached their table with the check for the meal, interrupting their discussion. As Justin paid the tab, Dani noticed his relieved expression. Did Marguerite mean more to him than he'd stated? If not, he must be aware of her interest in him. Miss Van Buren showed every mark of a woman who'd staked a claim and intended to keep it.

A short time later, Dani and Justin entered her suite, a glance at the phone reminding her of the malevolent call the night before. She stretched out her hand, inviting Justin to sit at the sofa. A moment later, Dani sat beside him, worry lines marring her complexion. "Do you think Davenport is the man who called me last night?"

"He's definitely a suspect in my book. But he also could be a run-it-down." He smiled at the confusion written on Dani's face. "Police slang for a person who does all the legwork for another. Let's hope he follows you to the airport tomorrow."

Her eyes registered shock. "Why?"

Justin tapped the end of her nose with his forefinger. "Because, my sweet Dani, when he sees you board that plane, he just might think you're returning to Hartford for good." He leaned close to Dani. "Let's forget about Davenport for now. I can think of more pleasant things to talk about, for instance, the vivacious woman beside me."

Her protest died in her throat as his lips claimed hers, affirming the thoughts portrayed in his eyes. A short time later, when Dani closed the door behind him, she realized her double-crossing heart had overridden her resolution to keep him at arm's length.

❧

The next morning, ready to leave for the airport sooner than expected, Dani decided to browse in the gift shop for suitable tokens to take back to her friends. While waiting for the clerk to wrap their gifts, a familiar sensation gripped her. She glanced around the room.

Yes, there he stood! Like an evil omen, Jules Davenport glowered at her through the glass enclosure facing the street. A moment later, he walked down the sidewalk, the sight of him soon lost in the pedestrian traffic. She stood motionless until the attendant's voice broke the silence.

"Excuse me, ma'am. I have your packages ready." Dani turned toward the clerk. The woman's features took on a quizzical look. "Is something wrong?"

"No, no, I'm just fine." Dani paid for her purchases and then hurried out of the boutique, breathing much easier when she stepped into her suite and heard the lock snap, securing her safety. Soon afterward she answered Justin's knock.

His exuberant greeting stilled when he saw her face. "Dani, what happened?"

Without thinking, she threw herself into his arms. Relating the details of the episode involving Davenport, the tears she'd held back the last two days streamed down her cheeks. Between sobs she spoke her thoughts. "I just don't know if I can go through with my decision to inhabit the hall. I'm not the invincible woman the song artist sang about several years ago. Inheriting a fortune and a fabulous estate, stalking, life threats, and mysterious strangers just don't fall under the category of Dani McKinnon, ordinary working girl."

Justin thumbed away her tears. "I know it may sound trite, but believe me, justice will be served if we give it time."

Drying her eyes on a handkerchief he produced from his pocket, she asked, "Did you talk to your father about my aunt's family?"

"No. I didn't get a chance to. Dad left early to take a deposition from a client in a nearby town. When he returns later today, I'll discuss it with him." He leaned his cheek next to hers and spoke softly in her ear. "Sweet Dani, although I regret to say so, we must go. You don't want to miss your plane." Laughing, he pulled her close again. "On second thought, that might not be such a bad idea."

"Justin, stop," she said, laughing and slapping at his hands. "If I don't go home today, the move to Georgia will be delayed even longer." The words bolstered her courage.

He reached for her bags. "Well, that won't do at all. Out the door, fair lady."

Once inside the Cadillac, Justin turned to her, an apologetic expression on his face. "Dani, as you once proclaimed, I've come on a little strong these past few days."

Her mouth curved in a wan smile. "You think?"

"What I'm trying to declare is that I've never met anyone like you. I'm afraid you've stolen my heart."

"From what I observed last night, you're spoken for already." Dani cringed inside. Jealously was the last thing she wanted him to believe of her.

Justin had the grace to look guilty. "Oh, that. Don't worry about Marguerite. She's a good friend, but I'm not in love with her. She knows where she stands with me."

Dani studied his features. Did he think the woman would give him up just like that? He looked as though he wanted to say more, but at that moment, Isaac stopped the car near the section of the airport that accommodated Delta Airlines.

Just before she went through security, Justin took Dani apart from the other passengers for a more private good-bye. "Call me tonight so I'll know you arrived home safe."

"I will. Thank you again for your kind hospitality."

Dani glanced backward for one last look at Justin, smiling in response to the wave of his hand. Were they destined to find happiness together?

Fastening her seatbelt minutes later, she pushed aside the reservation creeping into her thoughts—the reminder that in the past she'd shied away from suitors who used savoir faire to win a girl's heart, favoring instead the company of men who were steady and more reserved. And she'd never believed in "love at first sight," the term Justin had mentioned when they were at the hall.

Dani leaned back against the seat, closing her eyes. The image of herself in Justin's arms caused her heart to skip a beat. She made a mental note that perhaps along with the other changes about to take place in her life maybe, just maybe, her romantic ideology could stand an alteration too.

# HOME AGAIN

*D*ani drove to her office the next day, confident that her return to Connecticut soil would restore the sense of security she'd taken for granted prior to her trip to Atlanta. In the familiar surroundings, the harrowing experiences of the past three days and the churlish image of Jules Davenport now seemed nothing more than a bad dream. However, the portfolio she'd added to her briefcase before embarking to work told a different story.

Inside the complex a few minutes later, she stopped by her secretary's desk to scan the calendar for the day, hoping that a full schedule would restore her life to order once again. "Good morning, Peggy. How's everything?"

"Just fine, Miss McKinnon. Welcome home. Did you enjoy your time away?"

Dani laughed. "Well, yes and no."

"Pardon me?"

Dani gave Miss Owen a reassuring smile. "Oh, nothing. Any messages?"

"Yes. I laid them on your desk, along with some correspondence requiring your signature. Also, Mr. Pendergraff wants to see you right away."

"Thanks. I'll let him know I'm here."

As Dani started toward her office, a voice from behind detained her. "Hello, Dani." She turned to face Lance's cool, polite smile.

"Good morning," she answered, surprised yet grateful for his attempt at friendliness. "I trust you kept everyone in line while I was away?"

"Business progressed as usual."

"Good. I knew I could count on you, Lance." She touched his arm. "Can we talk later? Mr. Pendergraff is waiting to see me."

Anger sparked in his eyes for a split second and then vanished behind a sedate smile. "Sure. We'll catch up later."

She paused to watch him stride toward his office, his spine rigid. She knew he had issues with their employer, his decision not to give Lance a promotion at this time a major addition to Lance's string of grievances against the man. Dani had on occasion tried to discuss with Lance his dislike of their boss, hoping to help sort out the problem, but to no avail. Lance, knowing of the relationship between the Pendergraffs and Dani, felt her interference would be biased and refused to talk about it.

She closed her office door, glad he had been congenial toward her. If his attitude remained constant, it would make her final days at Pendergraff Accounting much easier to bear.

Sitting down at her desk, she dialed her boss's extension. "Hi, Uncle Bill. Peggy said you wanted to see me."

A few minutes later, Dani walked into Mr. Pendergraff's office unannounced and plopped into the nearest chair. "What's so urgent?"

"Nothing. I just wanted to hear the outcome of your trip. But I can tell by the cat-in-the-cream expression on your face it was worthwhile."

"I'd say so." She handed him a large envelope. "See the proof for yourself."

He opened the manila folder, his eyes widening with disbelief after careful scrutiny of its contents. "My word, Dani. Once Lucille hears about this, she'll insist you buy the company right out from under me and then immediately phone the nearest travel agent." He rolled his eyes toward the ceiling. "God forbid. I just can't imagine hopping about the world throughout my twilight years."

Dani giggled. "You're such a lovable, old teddy bear. Aunt Lucille and I both know that nothing, not even an eight-ton truck, could drag you away from this place until you are good and ready."

He grinned. "I guess you're right at that."

Returning the documents to Dani, a shadow of pain appeared in his eyes. "What do you intend to do about Stratford Hall?"

Dani hesitated. She needed time to gather the courage to share her plans. "Oh, Uncle Bill! You should see the place. If you and Aunt Lucille are free this evening, I'd like to come out to the house and tell you about it."

"You bet. Come for dinner too. You know how Lucille loves for you to critique her new recipes."

"You don't have to ask me twice." Dani stood. "In the meantime, I'd best earn my wages. See you at seven."

Seated at the Pendergraff dining table hours later, Dani waved away the offer of dessert. "Thanks but no thanks." Dani patted her stomach. "Another bite and I'll be in agony. That roast duck was awesome."

Lucille smiled. "Thank you. I've wanted to try that recipe for some time. I'm glad you liked it." She darted a glance toward her husband. "Dani, why don't you tell us about your trip to Georgia while my husband indulges in his *second* slice of pie?"

Bill paused between bites, his fork in midair, grinning at his wife. "You know you make the best apple pie on the East Coast. How can I resist?"

She threw up her hands. "You're impossible! Just don't start complaining to me the next time you have to *squeeze* into one of your suits."

Dani laughed. "Hey! I thought you wanted to hear about Stratford Hall."

Lucille gave her husband a light kiss on his cheek and then seated herself at the table once again. "Of course we do, Dani," she said, pointing at her husband. "You're out of the hot seat for now."

For the next half hour, Dani described Stratford Hall to them, including a delightful description of Mrs. O'Brien. Dani opted for the time being to spare them the dangerous acts of her journey. No need to cause them unnecessary alarm, she decided. Toward the end of her narrative, she paused to take a sip of water. All at once a sense of sadness swept the room, stilling her excitement. Dani glanced first at Lucille and then Bill. It was as though each of them in that instant anticipated the unpleasant change about to occur in their lives.

After Dani helped Lucille restore her kitchen to order, they joined Bill in the family room, where, after a short silence, Dani made her announcement.

"I guess this moment had to come. You both know how much I love you and that I'd never hurt you." Dani drew a deep breath. "Before I knew about Mathilda Thorndike, the thought of leaving Hartford never crossed my mind. But after visiting Stratford Hall and discovering my maternal heritage, I find I can't say no to my aunt's wishes." She appealed to each of them for understanding with her eyes. "The hall has been in my family for generations. How can I let it be sold to an outsider?"

For several minutes, the only sound heard in the room was the crackling logs blazing in the fireplace. Lucille toyed with the lapel on her blouse as she stared off into space. Finally, Bill spoke, his voice raspy with emotion. "I believe I speak for us both when I say it won't be easy to see you go. I know how capable you are, but I wonder if you realize the full extent of what's ahead of you."

*If only they knew!* Dani cast a look in his direction. In her youth he'd often been aware of troubles in her life almost before she was. Had he perceived the present peril she faced?

"The Harcourts have promised to assist me whenever I need help, and of course I know I can count on you for advice when necessary." Shrugging her shoulders, she grinned. "How could I ask for more?"

At the look on Lucille's face, Dani sobered. She moved to sit beside her beloved friend, enclosing her in an embrace. "Please don't worry about me. You and Uncle Bill have trained me well."

While answering their questions, Dani skirted any reference to her relationship with Justin or the malicious attempts to scare her away from the hall. An acute awareness of guilt made eye contact with them hard for her to manage. During the course of their conversation, she felt Bill's intense gaze upon her several times. She folded her hands together in her lap to still the slight tremble in her fingers, hoping he hadn't detected her evasiveness. If so, eventually she'd have to confess all.

Eventuality came sooner than Dani expected. When she arrived at work the next morning, she found her employer seated in her office. He waited until she appeared comfortable behind her desk before he spoke. "Okay, Dani. Now I'd like to hear the details you so carefully omitted last night."

Peering at his unsmiling face from under her eyelashes, she sighed. It wouldn't do any good to argue with him, not with his jaw set that way. Within minutes he'd been told all about Jules Davenport, the threatening note, and the anonymous phone call. However, she couldn't bring herself to tell him of her budding romance with Justin.

Frowning, Bill pondered the distressing news. "I assume the young Mr. Harcourt notified the police of these dreadful occurrences."

"Yes. A Sergeant Hagerman is handling the case. Justin assures me the police are doing everything possible to find Davenport."

Bill's eyebrows lifted at her use of the lawyer's given name. Crimson warmth spread across her face. She couldn't hide anything from him.

"Dani, in light of what you've said, do you think it wise to inhabit the estate?"

"To be honest? No. However, Justin has assured me I'll be protected."

"And what are his plans to accomplish the task?"

Dani straightened a stack of papers. "He didn't elaborate, but he seems trustworthy, and you told me yourself their law firm has a sound reputation."

"Yes, that's true."

"I know my decision is hard to understand. I'm not sure I comprehend it myself. Although reason dictates otherwise, an inner force I can't explain compels me forward. It's something I have to do. And don't you think I owe this to my mother? I know she would have wanted me to have her legacy no matter what."

"Even at the risk of your life?" he said softly.

An eternity seemed to pass before Dani could answer. "Uncle Bill, you told me once that some goals in life require a certain amount of risk in order to attain them. Besides, I have the power of justice working in my behalf."

A look of frustration bordering on disapproval appeared on his face. "You might do well to put your trust in the power of a few prayers also if you plan to follow through with your decision."

Dani looked away. How could she convince him that God wasn't interested in her prayers? If so, he would have listened to them on that long ago night her mother had died in Dani's young arms.

At her silence, a sigh of resignation escaped his lips. "Although Lucille and I are hesitant to give you our blessing, we won't interfere." A smile lifted the corners of his mouth, dispelling the morbid friction in the room. "That streak of strong determination down your spine has gotten you out of tough spots before, along with more than a few prayers from our lips, I might add." He paused and then spoke. "May God be with you, dear one."

Dani's throat constricted with tears. At least they were willing to support her although they disapproved. How could she tell him the misgiving she read in his eyes mirrored her own reservations? Suddenly, an urgency to obtain the same confidence in the all-knowing God he exemplified daily overwhelmed her. Before she could grasp the full implication of what the desire could mean for her, Bill stood to his feet.

"Should you change your mind or if things don't work out in Georgia, you're welcome to return to the firm. I can't tell you how much you'll be missed. As you've probably guessed, Lucille will cry for days. Please keep in touch."

She arose from her desk to give him a generous hug. "You know I will. I don't deserve it, but I'll be forever grateful for the love you've given me all these years. I can't imagine the turns my life would have taken had you not offered your home to me when Grandfather's illness finally claimed all of Grandmother's time and energy. It was a relief to them. I don't think they ever forgave me for surviving the accident rather than my father. I can't count the times I heard the remark, 'If only you hadn't asked to go sailing.'" Dani lowered her head, the old guilt hammering at her self-esteem.

"Now, Dani, you know the accident wasn't your fault. The McKinnons just couldn't stop grieving for their only child. It was hard on all of us. Michael and I had been best friends since grade school." Mr. Pendergraff reached out to take her hand. "As for the other," he said, a smile tugging at the corners of his mouth. "We couldn't shirk our responsibility as your godparents, now could we?"

Dani laughed. "No, I guess you couldn't. And who knows? The life of an American country heiress may prove less engaging than I first thought. You may find me on your doorstep once again sooner than you expect."

Two weeks later, Dani sat in the conference room observing Lance's reaction to their employer's announcement of her replacement upon her departure from the company. The angry scowl on his face told the story. But she had to hand it to him; he recovered with aplomb, even offering a congratulatory handshake to David Thatcher, promising to aid him in every way possible.

As she started to exit the room after the meeting, she felt a touch on her shoulder. She turned to see Lance's smile. "I'm sorry to see you go, Dani."

She couldn't hide her surprise. "Why, thank you, Lance. You don't know what that means to me."

He looked down. "I apologize for my loutish behavior of late. I was angry at Mr. Pendergraff and took it out on you. Forgive me?"

"Gladly."

"I take it the reason for your leaving the firm is a better job offer?"

"More like an opportunity to expand my horizons." She stretched her height to kiss him on the cheek. Good luck to you, Lance."

"Yeah, thanks."

At home that evening, Dani smiled when the phone rang. Justin had telephoned her every night since her return to Hartford.

"Well, it won't be long now," he crooned after their initial greetings.

"No. Just a couple more days and I'll be at Stratford Hall."

"I can't wait to see your sweet face."

Dani felt her skin tingle. "It will be great to see you again too, Justin. Uh, any word from Sergeant Hagerman?"

"Not a sign of Davenport in the whole state. Had I not seen the guy myself, I'd be tempted to think him a figment of your imagination."

"Justin!"

"Come on, Dani. I'm kidding. Look, I've got to go. I have a dinner engagement with a business partner in fifteen minutes."

"Male or female?"

He chuckled. "Female. Jealous? I hope so. 'Til tomorrow night, sweet Dani."

"Yes. Good-bye."

Before leaving her apartment for the last time, Dani paused to take a final look at the condo that had been her home for eight years. "Well, Dani McKinnon, this is it. You can't back out now." Justin's laughing face appeared in her mind, erasing her dejection. Humming a well-known love song, she drove away.

Valerie's warm welcome a few minutes later tempted Dani to adhere to those last-minute reservations she'd had since signing the sublease on her home.

"Gosh," Valerie said, following the superb dinner she'd prepared for Dani's last night in town. "It's not going to be the same around here." Her eyes filled with tears.

Dani put her arms around her friend. "Please don't cry or we'll both become blubbering idiots. It isn't like I'm moving to the North Pole."

Valerie nodded. "I know. It's just that we've always been here for each other."

"That won't change. I promise. Now let's hurry and get these dishes done so we can have an old-fashioned gabfest. I don't want to be too late arriving at the Pendergraffs tonight. You know how they worry about me. Also, I have to stop by Alexander's Studio, remember? My backside still aches from all those hours I posed for him. I hope Aunt Lucille and Uncle Bill will like the finished product."

Two hours later, Dani drove toward the studio. She had intended to give the portrait of herself to the Pendergraffs for Christmas but decided the morning of her departure to Georgia would be a better time to present the painting to them. She hoped the gift would make her leaving less difficult for them.

Dani drove into the parking garage, anticipation mounting as she hurried toward the entrance to the building. All of a sudden, uneasiness gripped her. She glanced around but saw nothing. Hearing the descent of the elevator, she breathed easier. A moment later, a sound from behind frightened her anew. She whirled around. Her eyes grew wide at the horror standing within an arm's reach.

# THE ATTACK

*A* man dressed in dark clothing, his face covered with a black ski mask, towered over her. Screaming, Dani turned to flee. Too late. He lunged at her, his arm snaking around her neck. Gasping, she fought the death grip with every ounce of strength she possessed.

Twisting her arm behind her back, he dragged Dani to a darkened corner of the garage, slamming her against the concrete wall. Pain exploded in her head as the roughly textured barrier spurred deep into the side of her face.

Thrusting his knee against her back, he buried the muzzle of a gun in her ribs. "You just won't listen, will you? Stratford Hall belongs to me! Do you understand?" he said through clinched teeth.

Too terrified to speak, her vigor drained from her body, she sagged against his chest.

At that moment, lights flashed across them from a car entering the garage. With a violent shove, he flung Dani away from him then sprinted out of sight. She crumpled to the floor, her head striking the concrete. Slipping into unconsciousness, she had a vague awareness of squealing tires in the background.

Beginning to rouse a short time later, she heard laughter close by. Lifting her head, she attempted to speak, but only a hoarse whisper escaped into the air. The merry couple drew nearer. Her voice stronger this time, she called out to them. "Help me! Please help me!"

The footsteps ceased. Within seconds the couple scurried to her side. "Oh, dear God! George, phone the police. I'll see if I can tend the poor child." Dani tried to thank the woman, but her words were swept into merciful darkness.

Dani struggled to open her eyes, but the bright overhead light forced them shut again.

"She's coming around, Doctor."

Doctor! The memory of the attack rushed into her thoughts like a screaming locomotive. Once again she heard the assailant's vicious retort, felt his arm around her throat. She had to get away!

Two gentle hands clasped her shoulders. "Miss McKinnon! You're safe now."

Dani felt the prick of a needle in her arm. Her breath slowing, she gazed through squinted eyes into the face of a man in medical attire.

He smiled. "I'm Dr. Neilson. Your friends are waiting just outside the door. Would you like to see them?"

"Yes," she said through swollen lips, the medication slurring her words.

"Nurse, have them step inside for a moment."

"Oh, darling!" Lucille said, scurrying to Dani's side. "We're here."

Dani opened her eyes, a sigh of relief escaping her lips as Bill stroked her hand. "Yes, dear. We're right here."

Valerie, her eyes brimming with tears, said nothing but observed her friend from the foot of the hospital bed.

Dr. Neilson moved forward when he saw Dani begin to tremble with emotion. "I'm sorry. We have to move Miss McKinnon from Emergency to her own room. She'll feel more like talking in the morning."

Lucille, observing the alarm visible in her godchild's eyes, leaned close to Dani's ear. "Don't worry, darling. I'll stay with you."

When Dani awoke the next day, sunlight streamed through the window. Looking around, she saw Lucille seated in one corner of the private hospital room, a smile on her lips.

"Well, it's about time you woke up, Miss Rip Van Winkle."

"How long have I been asleep?"

Lucille glanced at her wristwatch. "Over twelve hours. How do you feel?"

"Like some wayfarer who has been beaten and left stranded in a desert with no oasis in sight. Do you suppose you could round me up a glass of water?"

"Sure thing, sweetheart."

Dani downed several swallows of the ice water and then asked, "How did I get here?"

Lucille smoothed Dani's hair back from her face. "The police phoned for an ambulance when they received a phone call from a man notifying them of the attack. They contacted us after locating a list of emergency numbers in your wallet while they searched for your identity. I, in turn, telephoned Valerie."

The door swished open. "Good afternoon, Miss McKinnon," said a cheerful nurse preparing to read Dani's vital signs. The doctor will be glad to know you're awake. Also, there's a Lieutenant Masterson who's been bothering the nurses all morning asking for an interview. Do you feel up to it?"

"I guess I have to talk to him sometime."

Within a few minutes, a plain-clothes police officer stood beside her bed. "Hello, Miss McKinnon. I'm Lieutenant Charles Masterson. I realize how difficult this is, but I must ask you some questions."

With his prompting, Dani described the horror of the night before, as well as the events leading up to it, the officer recording her statement on a small notebook he retrieved from his coat pocket. As Dani disclosed the details of the attack, Lucille's deeply tanned complexion paled. She hurried to place a tissue in Dani's hand, seemingly unmindful of the tears streaming down her own cheeks.

Lieutenant Masterson waited until Dani had composed herself before he continued. "I'll contact Sergeant Hagerman right away and inform him of the assault. At least now we know there are two men involved."

"Oh?"

"Yes. The man who called the police, along with his wife, saw the rapid departure of a dark, late-model sedan from the garage and the passenger pulling something from his head just before they drove onto the street. However, the dimly lit area prevented a close view of the men themselves."

A sympathetic look appeared on the lieutenant's face when he noted Dani's wary countenance. "Don't worry, Miss McKinnon. We've unraveled crimes with less evidence than this."

"Thank you, Lieutenant. I hope you solve this one right away."

He paused in his retreat to the doorway. "It's my job to do just that."

Valerie's form appeared from behind the policeman's shoulder, her face breaking into a radiant smile. "May I come in?"

"Please do. This gentleman is Lieutenant Masterson from the Hartford Police Department. Lieutenant, Valerie Grant."

She shook the officer's hand, and after nodding a greeting to Lucille, Valerie hurried to the bedside. Amused, Dani watched the officer. He couldn't take his eyes off her petite friend. With a slight shake of his head, he said, "Miss McKinnon, do you still intend to move to Georgia once you've passed this crisis?"

Lucille stood from her chair. "Not if I have anything to say about it."

Dani took in the tight-lipped expression on the older woman's face. "I really can't say right now, sir."

Without further comment, his eyes lingering on Valerie a moment longer than necessary, Lieutenant Masterson bade them adieu.

Lucille picked up her handbag. "I think I'll grab a quick bite to eat while you two visit."

"Aunt Lucille, you don't need to stay. You've been here all night as it is. Why don't you go home and get some sleep?"

"We'll discuss it after the doctor makes his rounds." With a wave of her hand, she left the room, easing the door shut.

Valerie turned to Dani, her eyes full of love and concern. "Do you want to talk about it?"

Dani's eyes spilled over with fresh tears. "Oh, Val. I've never felt so helpless or afraid in my whole life."

Later that day, Dani awoke to find the doctor conferring with Lucille about Dani's injuries. "She's got a nasty contusion, multiple bruises, and a slight concussion. We'll keep the pain at bay with medication and time will take care of the bruises."

Turning, Dr. Neilson observed his patient. "Good afternoon, Miss McKinnon." He leaned over to examine the lacerations on her cheek. "You're healing as expected. But I want to keep you at least another twenty-four hours for observation. Also, I've asked Doctor Wade to stop by this evening to chat with you. He's a psychologist whose specialty is treating victims of violent crimes. He's also in charge of a support group that meets on Tuesday nights here at the hospital. I suggest you follow through with any recommendations he deems necessary. It will speed your recovery."

Dani sighed. "Whatever you think is best, Doctor."

Dr. Neilson patted her on the shoulder and then smiled. "I'll see you tomorrow. We'll know by then how soon you can go home."

After he'd gone, a look of hopelessness shrouded Dani's features. "Home! What home?"

Lucille planted a kiss on Dani's temple. "Darling, you know you can stay with us as long as you like. When you're ready, we'll find a new place for you to live. All you need think about now is getting well."

Groaning, Dani shifted her position. She touched the bandage on her cheek. "I wonder if I'll ever be able to close my eyes without visualizing that dreadful night."

"In time, darling. I promise." Lucille turned to gather up her jacket and purse. "I've decided to take your earlier advice. Bill will be by to check on you soon." She planted a kiss on Dani's head. "See you later tonight."

Early that evening, Lance strode into the room with a bouquet of red roses in one hand and a book in the other. "Hello, Dani."

Her facial expression registering mild shock, she replied, "Hi yourself. How did you know I was in the hospital?"

"Why, you're the talk of the office." He handed her the newspaper tucked under his arm. Dani stared at the front-page coverage of the attack, shuddering as she gazed at the photograph of the parking garage.

Lance took her hand in his. "I'm really sorry, Dani. You hear about this sort of thing all the time but never expect it to happen to someone you know."

Dani turned her face toward the wall, tempted to tell Lance the reason for the attack but decided to heed Justin's advice to let as few people know about her inheritance as possible for the time being. "I can't talk about it now."

He touched her uninjured cheek with the back of his hand. "I understand. It must have been awful for you." He picked up the novel. "Maybe this will help occupy your time during your convalescence."

"Thank you. For the flowers too. Roses are my favorite, as you know."

A wistful look appeared on his face. "Yes. I'd know a lot more if you'd but give me a chance. I care a great deal about you."

"Please, Lance, let's not even go there," she said, tugging the blanket closer to her chin.

He sighed. "Okay, Dani. I just thought I'd try once more to win your heart before I make other plans."

"What do you mean?"

"Some weeks ago I applied for a position at a Midwestern oil company; then in my absence from work last week I flew to Oklahoma for a scheduled interview. Well, today I received an e-mail stating I'd been accepted for the job."

"You can't be serious! You're one of Mr. Pendergraff's most valued employees. Have you discussed this with him?"

Lance's face grew dark. "No! Regardless of your opinion, I've discovered just how much I'm valued at Pendergraff Accounting. I've been passed over twice for a promotion I'm quite capable of handling. He's fortunate I plan to give him a two-week notice."

The sudden awareness of another presence in the room startled them both. Neither of them had heard the door open. "Did you ever stop to think that had I promoted you to an administrative position, your expertise in the field would have been lost? Your salary should have been proof of your worth to me."

Bill's soft-spoken voice didn't fool Dani at all. She shrank back against the pillows, dreading what might come next. Her intuition proved to be correct.

"Lance, I think you've made a wise decision about seeking other employment. A formal notice of resignation is unnecessary. I'll have payroll draft you a final check first thing in the morning. You can clear out your office then."

Lance opened his mouth to speak but seemed to change his mind after further observance of his ex-employer's face. Instead he turned and marched out the door without additional comment.

Bill sat down beside Dani. "I'm sorry you had to witness that. I have to say, though, I saw it coming weeks ago. In fact, I'd planned to discuss his poor job performance of late with him this week.

"Maybe he'll be more satisfied in his new job." She glanced toward the door, amazed that she could dismiss him from her life without the tiniest regret.

Mr. Pendergraff nodded his head. "Perhaps. Enough about Lance Carter. How are you feeling?"

"About as well as I look."

He drew back in mock concern. "Let's hope better than that. I wouldn't encourage your nomination for the Miss America Pageant any time soon."

She groaned. "That bad, huh?"

"Dani," he said, his expression turning serious. "I promise I'll do everything in my power to see that the person who did this to you is put behind bars for a long time."

Dani turned away, her countenance stricken with anger mixed with grief. "Why me, Uncle Bill?"

"Only God knows the answer," he said, taking her hand. "However, the good news is He's known for turning tragedies into triumphs. God doesn't cause destruction in our lives, but sometimes He uses the situation to get our attention, a sort of wake-up call. Perhaps now would be a good time to renew your relationship with Him."

Dani sighed. Was God indeed vying for her attention? *For some time now, Miss Dani McKinnon.* She opened her eyes. *Who said that? Is Uncle Bill playing a trick on me?* she wondered. "I'm sorry, I didn't catch what you said."

"I just thought now might be a good time for you to renew your relationship with Christ. He's been waiting for your return to his presence a long time."

"But where do I start?" She might not be ready to forgive and forget just yet, but it might be good to know how to become reacquainted with Him just in case she decided the time was right.

"A prayer of forgiveness for your assailant might be a good beginning."

She choked back her tears. "Sorry. I'm not sure I can do that." Dani realized the word *forgiveness* hadn't been in her vernacular where God was concerned for years. Could years of stored-up bitterness be erased with a few sincere words? It just couldn't be that simple, could it?

"Ask God to show you how. He knows the subject backward and forward." Mr. Pendergraff stood to leave the room. "We'll talk of this another time. You need to rest."

She received his affectionate kiss with a smile. "Good night, Uncle Bill." At that moment, Lucille arrived to spend another night with her godchild.

Early the next morning, Dani roused from her slumber, reluctant to leave her dreams of Justin. His featherlike kiss on her lips seemed real, as did the woodsy scent of his aftershave. She could almost hear him whisper her name. Dani opened her eyes to discover she hadn't been dreaming at all.

# STARTING OVER

"*J*ustin! What are you doing here?" She glanced around the room. "And where is Aunt Lucille?"

Smiling, he pointed back over his shoulder. "She stepped out for a moment. Said if you woke up to tell you she'd return in a few moments. As to your first question, Miss Inquisitiveness, I just thought I'd stop by to see if you were receiving proper care from these people."

"Who told you about the assault?"

"Dad phoned me in Albany."

"As in New York?"

Justin held up his hand. "To continue. Your friend Valerie phoned the house late last evening to inform me about the attack. But when she learned I'd flown to New York on unexpected business, she gave the details to Dad, who later telephoned my hotel. After speaking with him, I booked a flight to Hartford, and here I am." He glanced up to see a nurse bearing a breakfast tray enter the room. "My company about to be abandoned for an infamous hospital meal."

Dani raised the lid, eyeing the too wet scrambled eggs and the dried-out bacon. With a groan she replaced the cover and pushed the food aside, opting to dine on coffee and toast alone.

She lifted her hand to smooth her tangled hair. "I must look a fright."

Justin's eyes twinkled. "I admit your appearance is somewhat altered from the lovely creature I met in Georgia. Perhaps Cupid blinded me during your stay in Atlanta, and I'm now surveying your true likeness." Justin picked up her hand and held it against his face. "Please tell me I'm wrong."

"Oh, you!" Dani said, pulling her fingers from his clasp.

When Dani had finished eating, Justin kissed her on the cheek, his eyes glowing with compassion. "I know it's been rough for you, sweet Dani. Somehow, someway, we'll catch the fink that did this."

Dani placed her hand on his arm. "Please make it soon." Her breath caught and held when he raised her fingers to his lips.

During a lull in their conversation a short time later, Justin picked up his coat from the chair in the corner of the room. "Uh, Dani, a friend of mine is in Hartford on assignment. When I phoned him earlier, I promised we'd get together this morning to discuss a business project. But I'll be back this afternoon to spend a couple of hours with you before I return to Albany. His gaze lingered on the nurse who stood nearby assembling the utensils for Dani's bath. "From what I can gather, I'd only be in the way around here."

She smiled. "I understand. 'Til later then."

He blew her a kiss just before he walked out the door.

By the time Justin returned that afternoon, quite a change had occurred in Dani, thanks to her dear friends. Lucille, after her luncheon engagement with her husband, had entered Dani's room within moments of Valerie, each of them toting supplies guaranteed to transform even the most unattractive person into an alluring beauty.

Justin paused just inside the door. "Excuse me, ma'am. I seem to be in the wrong room."

Dani laughed. "Justin. Do come in and meet my friends."

Following the introductions, the two women excused themselves, promising to return in a while. When they'd gone, Dani motioned toward a chair beside her bed. "Please sit down, Justin. Did your time with your friend go well?"

He hesitated a moment before answering, a faraway look appearing in his eyes. "Yes. If the venture is a success, I'll be able to disconnect myself from an unwise business merger I made a few years back."

Dani waited for him to explain further, but when he didn't, she changed the subject. "Have the police discovered any leads?"

"Not so far. Nevertheless, they are pursuing your theory of an unknown relative, if that's any consolation. Dad is at this moment searching the office archives for any Thorndike papers that might reveal a name.

"Also, I've asked Mrs. O'Brien to check out the library at Stratford Hall just in case Mrs. Thorndike had failed to mention one of her distant relations. Mrs. O'Brien's answer, and I quote, 'Why, I'd be glad to look for the name of the blackguard who'd do something like that to me lass. I'll start clearing the cobwebs from the family genealogy right away. You tell Miss Danielle I expect to see her as soon as she's well.'"

Dani laughed at Justin's attempt to mimic Mrs. O'Brien's Irish brogue. Momentarily, her expression sobered. The thought of the risk involved if she were to heed Mrs. O'Brien's entreaty pressed upon her soul.

A glimpse at Dani's countenance washed the smile from Justin's face. "Dani, look at me." She turned a woeful glance his way. "You haven't changed your mind about the hall, have you?"

Self-doubt devouring her previous courage, she couldn't meet his gaze. "I...I want to, but I'm afraid. I fooled myself into believing I could take anything Davenport threw at me." Dani paused, her next words ending on a rueful sigh. "Not comprehending I'd have to contend with maniacs."

Justin shifted his weight from the chair to the edge of the bed where he enfolded Dani in his arms. "Dani, please forgive me. I promised to protect you, yet you became prey to a human animal. I should have insisted you move to Georgia days ago."

Pulling back to look into her eyes, he shook his head at the fear projected in her gaze. "No, Dani. Don't let this jerk scare you off. I swear you'll be safe from now on."

Her look changed to one of disbelief. "How can you promise that? Do you intend to guard me night and day?" As much as the idea might appeal to her, she knew it to be absurd.

Justin grinned, his expression turning seductive. "Now *that's* an engaging thought."

Dani shrugged out of his grasp, not at all impressed with his humor. The pain was too real.

"Besides," he continued, grinning, "once you arrive in Georgia, you'll be in Mrs. O'Brien's safekeeping. I can't imagine even Davenport wanting to tangle with her."

Dani laughed in spite of her disapproval regarding his banter. "I certainly wouldn't want to wager any stakes against her."

Their laughter subsided at the sound of a knock on the door. "Come in," Dani called.

Lance entered the room. "Good afternoon, Dani," he said, turning a curious glance toward Justin.

"Hello, Lance. I don't believe you know my friend, Justin Harcourt. Justin, Lance Carter, a former colleague of mine from Pendergraff Accounting." Lance's jaw tightened at the word *former*.

"My pleasure, Carter." Justin stretched out his arm to shake Lance's hand.

"Likewise," Lance said, his acknowledgement of the friendly gesture accompanied by a chilly, detached smile.

Dani watched the two men size each other up like two boxers prancing about the ring just before the first punch. As she noted their silent sparring, all of a sudden an evil image spun like a carousel in her head. Her eyes widened. No! Impossible! Yet their physiques didn't lie. Either of them could have been the man who attacked her.

Dani turned her attention to Justin, paying no mind to his conversation with Lance as another ugly thought quickened her heartbeat. Didn't Justin say just this morning that he had a friend residing in Hartford for a short time? Could that friend be Jules Davenport? Oh, dear God!

Both men turned to stare at the sound of alarm erupting from her throat.

"Is something wrong, Dani?" Justin said, coming to her side.

She felt her cheeks burn from more than her injuries. "No! I ... I just ... I mean, it's painful when I try to change positions." *What could I be thinking? Besides, what possible interest could Justin have in Stratford Hall?* Refusing to allow any more absurd imaginings, she listened to Lance's comments while Justin adjusted her pillows, doing what he could to make her more comfortable.

When Dani settled back against her pillows, Lance spoke. "I just thought I'd drop in to say good-bye on my way to the airport. I leave for the Midwest in a few hours."

Dani picked up her glass of water and held it toward Lance, smiling. "Here's to your new job. I wish you lots of luck."

Lance returned her smile. "Thanks. I've discovered, though, that the goals I hope to attain will be more of a challenge than I anticipated."

She gave him an encouraging look. "With your aptitude, I'm sure you'll conquer any obstacles that get in your way in no time at all."

He turned his head toward the window. "That's what I'm counting on." Lance averted his gaze back to Dani, smiling. "And I do appreciate your vote of confidence. Now, if you you'll excuse me, I need to run along."

Justin stepped forward to open the door. "Although it's been good to make your acquaintance, we certainly don't want you to miss your plane."

Dani raised her hand in salute. "So long, Lance. The next time we see each other, you'll probably be dressed in jeans and cowboy boots." As she drew a mental picture of him in western apparel, a veiled image of the cowboy she'd seen outside Pendergraff's the day of her vicious encounter with Lance came to her mind. She wished she could recall his features. *Oh well,* she decided. *That incidence is best forgotten. Besides, I probably won't ever see the man again anyway.*

Dani's comment seemed to be lost on Lance. "What? Oh…oh, of course. Oklahoma *is* quite different from the East. I may even learn to ride a horse." He leaned down to give her a good-bye kiss. "See ya, Red. You'll be in my thoughts."

When the door closed behind Lance, Justin returned to Dani's side, brushing his palms together as though to rid his hands of unwanted dirt. "Now that we're alone…"

Later that day, the doctor dismissed her into Lucille's capable care. Upon leaving the hospital, Dani realized she looked forward to convalescing at the Pendergraff home. She hoped the peace she often experienced there would spill over into her soul to abate the mental anguish she'd endured since the attack.

The days passed quickly. One night while in her room, she gazed at her image in the dresser mirror, noting with pleasure that the only visible reminder of the attack was a tiny scar on her cheek. *It's time to put all this behind me,* she thought, recalling the counsel of Doctor Wade and the Violent Crime Support Group. Dani groped for an answer to her future. Should she remain in Hartford and return to Pendergraff Accounting or follow Justin's urging to become the new proprietor of Stratford Hall? *Justin!* How she missed him. His arguments for her to return to Georgia sounded more convincing each time she spoke with him. Yet climbing into bed moments later, doubts lingered in her mind. Could she face what might lie ahead?

The next afternoon, Dani drove into Hartford to exchange a dress she'd purchased a few days before. Her shopping complete, she stopped by Valerie's apartment to see how Percy fared. The pet had remained with Valerie while Dani recuperated.

"Have your weeks at the Pendergraff's seemed like old times?" Valerie asked once the two friends were comfortable amongst the sofa cushions and sipping cups of Earl Grey tea.

"As you know, my godparents are wonderful to me, but it's time to make other arrangements. Sometimes I feel a bit smothered by Aunt Lucille's mothering. It's not that I don't appreciate their care—you know that—I just need to get on with my life so they can resume their previous routine."

Valerie nodded her head. "Have you made any specific plans?"

"No. I hoped you could help me decide what to do. I know I should jump at Uncle Bill's generous offer of a position at his company, but my heart is no longer at the firm. I keep visualizing myself seated in the gazebo at Stratford Hall admiring the setting sun. Oh, Val! What should I do?"

Valerie hugged her friend. "You know I can't make that choice for you. But I know you well enough that you'll never be content if you don't follow your heart."

"But that could mean my demise in the end."

The jarring of the phone took Valerie's response from her lips. "Hello? Oh, hi, Lieutenant."

The word *lieutenant* piqued Dani's curiosity. Not wanting to eavesdrop, she thumbed through a magazine. However, she couldn't help but realize it wasn't a professional call.

"That was Charles Masterson," Valerie said, her complexion deepening in color at the look on Dani's face. "You know, he's the police officer who took your statement at the hospital?"

"Yes, I remember."

"The other night he dropped by to ask if I knew anything pertinent to the case that you might have forgotten."

Dani straightened the smile that formed on her lips. "And?"

"He left after a few minutes of polite conversation. That's all."

Dani couldn't hide her grin any longer. "And now?"

Valerie's eyes danced with delight. "He asked me to dinner on Saturday."

Both women burst into giggles.

In control once again, the friends hugged each other. Dani glanced at her watch. "I hate to leave good company," she said, removing Percy from her lap, "but I must go. I'm surprised Aunt Lucille hasn't called to scold me for not arriving home before dark. By the way, did you pick up the portrait from Alexander's Studio?"

"Yes. I'll get it for you. You don't have to worry. He did an excellent job."

A moment later, Valerie held up the painting for Dani to inspect. She gave her friend a warm smile. "Thanks for the favor. I just couldn't go back to that parking garage."

On her way home, Dani glanced often in her rearview mirror to watch the vehicle that kept pace with her own car. Could the driver be following her? She breathed a sigh of relief when the automobile turned onto a street a block before her own. Yet the thumping in her chest didn't slow down until she'd closed the door to her room.

Seated at her vanity after preparing for bed, she noticed a letter from Mrs. O'Brien propped against the lamp stand. Scanning the housekeeper's words of encouragement, Dani felt something akin to homesickness overwhelm her. She *did* belong at Stratford Hall. She'd known it the moment she'd seen the place. But fear had restrained the weapons she'd used against life's adversities in the past—her inner strength and strong determination. Why, she'd fought for one cause or another from the time she'd entered grade school. Dani smiled. Once, while in second grade, she'd used her fists to keep Timothy Sparks, the second grade bully, from teasing a handicapped student. And her recent efforts included contending for the protection of women's rights in the workforce.

Dani glanced down at the scripture verse Mrs. O'Brien had written at the end of her note.

> Joshua 1:9: "Have I not commanded you? Be strong and courageous. Do not be terrified; do not be discouraged, for the Lord your God will be with you wherever you go."

Could she take this at face value? Did God really care enough to keep her from danger? Dani bowed her head. Could she find the courage to forgive both her assailant and the man who'd killed her parents?

What about God Himself? All these years she'd turned her back on Him, refusing to acknowledge His existence in her life. Dani believed if God had loved her with the depth her mother had proclaimed, He wouldn't have allowed her daughter to grow up without parents. Could she let go of the past? She had to; her destiny beckoned. Pen and paper in hand, she began to make plans for her journey to Stratford Hall.

Lying beneath her blanket a moment later, Dani tried to find words to begin a new relationship with her Creator. But they just wouldn't form on her lips. Cold fear struck her. Was it too late? Not according to Bill Pendergraff. He maintained that God waited patiently for his children to call on His name. She relaxed. Somehow she'd find a way to have faith in Him again.

The next day during breakfast, Dani informed the Pendergraffs of her intention. They didn't have to share their thoughts. Lucille's pallid complexion and the clatter of Bill's coffee cup against the saucer spoke volumes.

"Well, I see your mind is made up," he said after several moments. "When do you plan to leave?"

"Tomorrow morning. But don't worry, I promise to take every precaution. Deep inside I know this is the right course for my life."

Lucille brushed away a tear. "Dani, I've never known you to take the easy way out of anything, but I guess that's one way God keeps me on my knees. We're here if you need us."

Dani pushed back from the table to hug them both. "I love you more than words can tell. And now I have something for you. I intended to give you the gift for Christmas, but I want you to have it now. Don't move. I'll be right back."

"Oh, Dani, what a wonderful surprise! You couldn't have given us a more thoughtful gift," Lucille said as she held up the portrait to admire. "Come on. I know the perfect place to hang it."

Dani followed the couple into the living room where she replaced the landscape painting above the fireplace with Dani's portrait, reminding Dani of a similar pose above the hearth in the formal parlor at the hall.

⁂

"Well, Percy, it's now or never," Dani said to her pet the next morning as she belted his carrier to the seat in her car. She laughed. "It's not exactly the road trip Valerie and I planned a few weeks ago." Dani sighed. She hadn't needed the holiday after all. The image of Justin floated into her thoughts. "At last I'm free of Lance." The cat looked back at her, meowed as though in agreement with his master, and then settled down upon his towel. They were on their way to Georgia at last.

# THE HOMECOMING

O n the morning of the second day into her journey, Dani discarded the disposable dishes into the container provided in the Hampton Inn breakfast room and then hastened to collect both Percy and her luggage from her room. Just a few more hours and they'd be at Stratford Hall. Halfway down the corridor, she paused, making an about-face to return to the café to retrieve the cardigan she'd left behind. In doing so, she almost collided with a tall, robust gentleman clutching her sweater in his hands.

Startled, Dani stepped back a pace to view the stranger dressed in Western clothing, taking in everything from the Stetson resting on his thick, chestnut brown hair cropped an inch or so below the neckline to his boot-shod feet. She suppressed a smile at the contrast between his rugged handsomeness and the femininity of her garment he held. Her mind occupied with thoughts of Justin, she hadn't noticed his presence during breakfast.

Like a magnet, his dark brown, vibrant eyes required complete attention. For a moment she seemed suspended between time and space. Sensing familiar warmth in her cheeks, Dani tried to look away, but his bold, incessant stare held her captive. She struggled inwardly. Why did she feel that the deepest depth of her soul lay bare for his scrutiny alone? At last, his soft, full lips tilted upward into a generous smile, breaking the spell.

"Excuse me, ma'am. I believe this belongs to you," he said, his words slow and entwined with Southern vernacular.

"Ye…Yes. I just remembered I left it in the breakfast room. Thank you." She reached for the wrap, hiding her trembling fingers beneath its folds.

"Any time, ma'am."

"Well, if you'll excuse me, I need to be on my way. Thanks again." Dani turned toward her original destination, flattening her palm against her fluttering midsection. She drew a deep breath, frowning. What had come over her of late? It seemed her attraction to men these days had unlimited boundaries.

She glanced backward. The cowboy put his fingers to the brim of his hat. "Good day to you, miss. Enjoy your journey."

The gesture sparked a memory in Dani's mind. Was this the cowboy who'd showed up in the parking lot during her confrontation with Lance? She shrugged. Possible, she decided, but not probable. Her eyes narrowed with concentration. And why did his identity seem so important to her anyway? A smile lifted the corners of her mouth. She'd had her fair share of rescuers of late. Perhaps modern-day knights preferred denim and buckskin over clanking, metallic suits of armor. Without another thought of the man, Dani gathered her belongings and checked out of the hotel.

Needing a break a couple hours later, Dani drove into a rest area located off the interstate in the secluded Georgia countryside. Fastening Percy's leash to his collar, she carried him to the jogger's trail where she could exercise her pet and take a brisk walk around the picnic site.

At the far end of the walkway, she felt a tug on the leash. Turning, she laughed. Percy had decided to take time for a playful romp in a nearby pile of leaves. A moment later, she reached down to pick up her kitten; they needed to resume their travel.

Dani's smile faded when she heard quiet, stealthy footsteps approaching from the rear. Abandoning her intention, she stood. Her breath caught and held at the sound of a gravelly, male voice near her ear.

"Well, pretty lady, you don't take advice very well, now do you? We thought your recent hospitalization might convince you to listen to reason, but I see you need a little more persuasion to keep you away from Stratford Hall. That pretty face won't look so good after I practice my carving lesson for the day."

She whirled around. Her fingernails dug deep into her palm as her grip on the leash tightened. "Davenport!" A quick look toward the visitor's center revealed no help in sight. What could she do? Helplessness stole over her like a shroud.

A sharp *swish* in the deafening silence immobilized an urge to yell for help. She glanced toward the sound, freezing at the sight of the switchblade knife poised in Davenport's hand. Dani's mind screamed for her to run, but her body refused to cooperate, her legs as wooden as the pines nearby. All of a sudden, a voice sliced through the air.

"Excuse me, ma'am. Is this man bothering you?"

Dani's gaze darted upward, her mouth dropping in surprise at who stood a few feet behind her assailant.

At the same time, Davenport threw a look over his shoulder, the blade snapping back into its case just before he sprinted toward the parking lot. Soon afterward, they heard the sound of an engine roar and tires squeal as he drove away.

"You!" Dani said to the captivating cowboy she'd met at the hotel earlier that day. "Once again I find myself in your indebtedness," she said, aware that this act of kindness yielded a much higher rate of gratitude than a forgotten sweater. "I think you just saved my life." Smiling, she reached to shake his hand.

"You're more than welcome," he said, removing his hat before he grasped her fingers with his large, powerful-looking hand. Dani noticed that his wavy hair shone in the sun like burnished copper. "It appears we're traveling in the same direction," he continued. "Stopping for a break myself, I recognized you when I stepped out of my truck. You seemed frightened, so I came to investigate. By the way, my name is Blake Spencer."

Eyeing his smile which seemed to dampen the brilliance of the sun, her insides crumbled like hot cornbread. She stiffened as though to bolster her reserve. "I'm Danielle McKinnon. And this"— Dani scooped up the kitten huddled near her feet—"is Percy." Dani moved a few paces forward, hoping Mr. Spencer hadn't detected the slight tremor in her voice. "Sorry to rush off like this, but I don't want to be late for a luncheon engagement."

He nodded. "Do you want me to contact the authorities about the incident?"

"No thanks. I'll see to that when I reach my destination."

"Well, maybe we'll meet again sometime."

"Perhaps so," she said, puzzled at the hope mingling with her words.

After Dani fastened Percy in the kitten carrier, she watched Blake step into a late model pickup truck through the side mirror on her car. Could this valiant champion be an angel in disguise? She frowned. "Really, Dani McKinnon, you're losing it."

On the road once more, she glanced heavenward. "Thank You, just in case."

Just short of the noon hour, Dani drove onto the lane leading to Stratford Hall, thankful the GPS system in her car had proved accurate in its direction. Although a virtual foreigner to the South, she marveled at the sensation she felt—that she had just arrived home from a long, tedious expedition.

Stepping from the car, Dani noticed an older African-American man standing on the porch, doing his best to calm the excited collie greeting her arrival. She smiled as he came forward.

"Hello, Miss Danielle. I'm Clive Morgan. Miz Annie said I should be here to welcome you to your new home."

"I'm glad to make your acquaintance, Mr. Morgan," she said, waiting while he first wiped his hand on his trousers before clasping her outstretched hand. "Justin Harcourt has told me of your fine reputation as a landscape artist"—Dani made sweeping motions with her arm—"not to mention the beauty of your skill I see all around me."

Clive bowed his head. "Thank ya' mos' kindly, Miz Danielle. I do enjoy using the talent the good Lord gave me to care for his foliage."

At that moment Mrs. O'Brien threw open the front door. "Miss Danielle, 'tis wonderful to see ye at last."

"Hello, Mrs. O'Brien. It's great to be here." The housekeeper took the suitcase Dani pulled from the car and extended it toward the gardener. "Now don't ye worry about yer luggage. Clive will take care of it. Ye just come right on into the house. The master suite is aired and ready. I'll put the finishing touches on your lunch while ye freshen up a bit."

"Thank you," Dani said once inside the foyer. "I'll be down in a jiffy."

During the following days, Dani became acquainted with Stratford Hall. She loved to congregate with Mrs. O'Brien in the gathering room after dinner and listen to the housekeeper's stories about previous owners of the hall.

On warmer days she roamed the estate with Percy and Lad, Mrs. O'Brien's dog, at her heels, their path ending at the gazebo where she'd feed the ducks parading near the riverbank. Although no further incidences occurred to threaten her peace, Dani noticed that Clive seemed to be nearby during her jaunts about the grounds.

On one particular afternoon outing, while romping with Lad on the south lawn, Dani glimpsed what appeared to be the entrance to a trail leading into the dense forest. A strong urge to explore the pathway overcame her, but Justin's warning the previous night to stay near the house held her in place. The thought of his remarks reminded her of their telephone conversation earlier. A possible lead had been found in her case.

In his search for Thorndike relatives, Phillip had come across the name of Silas Thorndike's stepsister, Rosemary Davidson. Observing Mrs. O'Brien's arrival from town, Dani wondered if the housekeeper knew anything about the woman in question. She rushed up the hill to help unload the supplies.

After the groceries had been tucked away in the pantry, Dani and the housekeeper sat at the kitchen table taking their afternoon tea. "Mrs. O'Brien," Dani said, using her napkin to erase a fingerprint from the smoke-colored, glass tabletop. "Justin phoned me while you were in Evansville and told me his father had found some information about Mr. Thorndike's sister, Rosemary Davidson. Did you know the woman?"

"Hump! She 'twasn't me master's sister at all, only the daughter of that heartless woman Mr. Silas' father, Adam Thorndike, married late in his years back in Pittsburg, Pennsylvania, the home of Thorndike Steel Mills. Why, the old man tottered on the threshold of death when he wed the money-hungry floozy. All she and her uppity child wanted was a paved road into Pittsburg society. After Mr. Silas's father died, he 'twasn't yet cold in his grave the day Rosemary's mother marched another wealthy victim down a church aisle."

Dani smiled within. "Did Rosemary or her mother ever visit Stratford Hall?"

The housekeeper nodded. "Fraid so. Not long after Mr. Silas refurbished the hall, Rosemary showed up on our doorstep with her no-good husband, Maury Davidson. I couldn't believe the nerve of the man. Just prior to their visit he'd been fired from Thorndike

Steel, having been caught red-handed embezzling funds from me master's company. It was all I could do to hold me tongue when I learned that Mr. Silas refused to prosecute. But Miss Mathilda said he didn't want to cause a family scandal.

"Once they arrived, you'd have thought Rosemary was mistress instead of milady—always changing things around, contradicting me orders. But at last Mr. Silas set the pair down a notch or two, instructing them as to who was in charge of things around here. A few hours later, they packed their bags and left, Rosemary acursing and acarrying on like a crazy woman. She even vowed revenge, but as far as I know, the Thorndikes never heard from her again. 'Twas good riddance in me mind.

"Why, I'd even caught that Maury asnooping around in the attic. I'd gone to me apartment to rest a spell after lunch and hearing a noise overhead. I decided to investigate, finding him aplundering Miss Mathilda's things. I told him he had no business there and threatened to fetch Mr. Silas if he didn't leave right then. He shoved the papers he'd been reading back into an old trunk and brushed past me, muttering words I don't care to repeat."

Dani looked puzzled. "I don't understand. Why didn't you tell Justin about this the day he asked you about Thorndike relatives?"

Mrs. O'Brien lowered her head toward the floor. "Well, Miss Danielle, I guess I just plumb forgot about the greedy upstarts. I thought Mr. Justin had only Miss Mathilda's blood kin in mind. I hope I didn't cause ye any trouble."

Dani slipped her fingers into Mrs. O'Brien's hand. "Of course not. The information may be useless in finding Davenport and his presumed accomplice anyway."

The next morning, Dani stepped out onto the second-floor balcony overlooking the front lawn. She shivered as the damp, cool air remaining from the thunderstorms of the night before shook the drowsiness from her eyes. Lad's consistent barking had kept her from sleep most of the night. Close to dawn he'd settled down, giving her a few hours of undisturbed slumber.

Her gaze toward the trees bordering the front lawn, she spied the collie lying near a lilac bush. After a moment Dani's eyes narrowed. With a sharp intake of breath, she whirled around. *Something was wrong*. He lay too still.

Back inside, she descended the stairs two at a time, pausing only long enough to grab a jacket from the coat tree in the foyer. Rushing outdoors, she scampered down the slope. When she neared the dog, a cry of alarm escaped her lips when she saw his blood-splattered, rain-soaked fur.

Dropping to her knees, she called to him. A slight whimper echoed into the frosty air as he tried to raise his head. Dani breathed easier. She shed her coat, placing it over the animal. "Hold on, Lad. I'll get help."

Dani ran to the house, yelling, "Mrs. O'Brien, Clive, come quick!"

"Miss Danielle, whatever is the matter with ye?" Mrs. O'Brien asked, as she hurried onto the porch. "I could hear ye a-shouting clean back in the kitchen."

Dani turned when she heard Clive's approach from the side of the house. A pruning tool still clasped in his hand, he hurried to her side. "Yes, Miss Danielle? What is it?"

"It's Lad. He's hurt bad."

Wringing her hands, Mrs. O'Brien turned to the gardener. "Lord, aliving. Bring him into the house while I call the vet."

A few hours later, Lad recuperated on a rug near the hearth in the gathering room. Percy, seeming to understand the calamity, curled up beside the bandaged dog. The three adults sat silent, staring at the scene in stunned disbelief. According to the veterinarian, Lad had been stabbed several times with a sharp instrument.

Mrs. O'Brien rose from her chair and knelt down beside the animals. "Me poor pet," she said, rubbing Lad's head. "How could anyone do such a thing to me faithful friend?"

Dani's eyes filled with tears as she reached for the phone. "Hello, Justin."

The lawyer's expletive rang in Dani's ear after he heard the details of the devious act. "Look, Dani, I know you don't expect me until seven, but would you like me to come now? I'm about finished for the day anyway."

"That would be wonderful. Maybe preparing dinner for us will take Mrs. O'Brien's mind off the tragedy for a while."

"Does the vet think the dog will recover?"

"We won't know for at least twenty-four hours. The doc said if he lives through the night, he stands a good chance for survival."

"We'll hope for the best. In the meantime, I'll phone Hagerman. Make sure the doors and windows are secure, and ask Clive to stay with you until I arrive, will you?"

"Yes. I'll see you soon."

***

Dani strode into the kitchen the next morning, afraid of what she might find. But to her amazement, she saw a joyous Mrs. O'Brien spooning scrapes of meat into Lad's food bowl, the dog lapping at the morsels while Percy snatched up the crumbs that fell his way.

"'Tis a beautiful sight, isn't it, Miss Danielle? Me pup's agoing to make it after all. Somehow I knew the good Lord wouldn't let me down. I prayed till me old eyes wouldn't stay open another minute."

Dani stroked Lad's head. "Yes, it's wonderful. I said a prayer or two for the old fur ball myself," she said, laughing.

Late that night, following her date with Justin, Dani nibbled on a cookie from the tray she'd known would be waiting for her in the gathering room. Curling up on the sofa, she recalled her evening. Her attraction for Justin became stronger each time she saw him. Although not yet declaring his love, he seemed to care a great deal for her. *At least if his kisses are any indication*, she thought, smiling.

Gathering up her coat and shoes, she blew out the candle in the warmer beneath the pot of hot chocolate and then climbed to her rooms. Pulling back her bedspread a few moments later, she reached to fluff her pillow. All at once a scream tore through Stratford Hall, causing Mrs. O'Brien to sit straight up in her bed.

# NEW BEGINNING

*W*ithin moments, Mrs. O'Brien burst through Dani's bedroom door. There she found her young mistress collapsed beside the bed, staring straight ahead, her fist muffling the wretched sobs erupting from her throat. Mrs. O'Brien lifted Dani from the floor and eased her into a chair and then scanned the room with troubled eyes, at last identifying the cause of Dani's distress.

The housekeeper picked up the phone. "Hello, Sheriff?" she said seconds later. "This is Annie O'Brien. I believe 'tis necessary for ye to come to Stratford Hall right away. Please bring Doc Bedford too."

Less than a half hour later, Mrs. O'Brien ushered Sheriff Wilson and the doctor into the master suite, pointing to the open switchblade covered in dried blood setting atop the pillow. The words, "You are next," were printed on a scrap of paper attached to the knifepoint.

"How is she?" the sheriff said when Doctor Bedford had completed his examination.

"She's had quite a shock, but if you go easy, she can answer your questions."

"Miss McKinnon, I'm Sheriff Wilson. I realize how frightened you must be. Would you please tell me what happened?"

Dani raised her head, her eyes the color of faded army dunga-rees. "The bed ... I pu ... pulled back the covers and ... and I saw that wretched knife!" Fresh tears spilled down her cheeks. "Oh, please! Find the despicable creature that put it there, please." She slumped forward, hiding her face in her hands.

Realizing that it would be best to question Dani another time, the sheriff excused himself to search the hall for other evidence. After his exit from the room, Mrs. O'Brien helped Dani to bed, waiting until the doctor administered a sedative to her mistress before escorting the physician downstairs. Just before the gentlemen departed the hall, the sheriff placed the plastic bag containing the knife inside his red plaid jacket.

"I should have a report from the lab by noon. If my hunch is right, this is the weapon used on your collie. Do you have any idea how the intruder gained entrance to the hall? While the Doc tended to Miss McKinnon, I checked the locks on the doors and windows, but I couldn't find any signs of illegal entry."

"I know Clive made sure all was secure before he left the hall to go home." Mrs. O'Brien moved her head from side to side. "'Tis a mystery, indeed.

"Did you or Miss McKinnon entertain any visitors today?"

"Only Mr. Justin. He arrived in the early part of the evening to escort Miss Danielle to an art show in Atlanta."

"I assume you're referring to the lawyer Justin Harcourt. Sergeant Hagerman told me about him."

"Yes. I suppose I should phone him about what's happened tonight."

"I'll do that since I have to ask him about his visit to the hall last evening."

The sheriff gazed at the floor for a moment. "Did Mr. Harcourt go upstairs for any reason?"

"Not that I can recollect, but of course he 'twasn't in me sights at all times." Mrs. O'Brien paused, surprise lighting up her eyes. "Why,

Bobby Wilson! You're not going to stand there and accuse Mr. Justin of such an evil deed. I've known him as long as I have yeself."

Sheriff Wilson held up his hand. "Please, Mrs. O'Brien. I have to examine all the facts when investigating a crime."

"Well, ye just look elsewhere. I know that as a lad he 'twas a source of anxiety for Mr. Phillip, but these past weeks he's been a devoted companion to Miss Danielle."

Doctor Bedford laid his hand on her arm. "Now, Annie, the sheriff is only doing his job." The housekeeper turned to the sheriff. "I'm sorry. 'Tis just the plight of me mistress that's arresting me mind. I promised Mrs. Thorndike I'd take good care of her niece."

A shock of the doctor's stark white hair fell onto his forehead as he leaned forward to squeeze Mrs. O'Brien's shoulder. "I can't think of anyone more qualified to fill that position. Now, if you need me, you know my number."

"Likewise," the sheriff said, opening the door. "I'll keep in touch."

Dani stared out the window while Mrs. O'Brien flicked the feather duster back and forth, tidying the bedroom, her eyebrows knit together in a frown.

"Miss Danielle, why don't ye take a walk today? The fresh air will work wonders for ye mulligrubs. Clive will accompany you if ye'd like. It's been days since ye've been outdoors or eaten more than a bite or two."

Ignoring the invitation and Mrs. O'Brien's light scolding, Dani made a mental appeal to the birds flitting from limb to limb in the maple tree outside her room. Surely they must realize how rash she'd been to leave a safe, secure world to live in an environment oozing with obscurity and danger. Was that mocking laughter she heard in their twitters? Dani reached for the phone. She needed a one-way ticket to Connecticut. Today!

"Miss Danielle. Please listen to me!" With a start, Dani obeyed. Mrs. O'Brien's expression softened. "Forgive me, lass. But I can't abide ye wasting away to nothing. I've something to say, and I won't rest till I've spoken me mind."

Dani looked up. She could at least hear the woman out, although it wouldn't make a difference; her mind was set.

"'Twas a grand day for me the moment I heard ye'd been found. I walked down to Miss Mathilda's graveside and spilled tears of joy that me darling mistress's dream had come true. And since your arrival at the hall, I've seen in you similar qualities that made your aunt one of the most loved people in the county.

"Of course it can't be pleasant knowing ye might be killed, the good Lord forbid, for hanging on to what belongs to you, but, Miss Danielle, ye've got too much of your aunt's grit aburning inside ye to allow them chicken-killin' weasels to clean out your hen house!"

With that, the housekeeper turned and marched out the door. Eying the rigid, retreating figure, Dani's mouth fell open in amazement. She winced at the sound of the housekeeper's labored walk down the hall. Apparently Aunt Matilda had shed some of her tenacity and stamina onto Mrs. O'Brien as well.

A short time later, Mrs. O'Brien stood by the kitchen sink peeling vegetables. She looked up to see Dani enter the room and pull a chair from the table. "What's for dinner, Mrs. O'Brien? I'm starved."

The housekeeper picked up a towel, drying her hands a mite longer than necessary, not bothering to wipe away the tear that splashed onto the counter. She lifted her face toward the ceiling for a second before she withdrew a cup and saucer from the cabinet. "Pot roast in short of an hour. But for now ye can munch on a tea biscuit or two." With a joyous smile, she picked up the simmering kettle.

At that moment Lad lumbered into the kitchen, Percy swiping his paws at the dog's wagging tail. Mrs. O'Brien laughed. "Would ye look at that? It seems ye aren't the only one acraving the likes of me cooking."

The following week, Dani accepted an invitation from Mrs. O'Brien to accompany her into Evansville, a quaint village a few miles west of Stratford Hall. While the housekeeper drove, Dani became absorbed in the dazzling foliage aligning both sides of the highway. The frost-spattered leaves sparkled in the morning sun, their brilliant hues—topaz, amber, fire opal, and bronze—shimmering like gems. Stately pines wove in and out the resplendent hardwoods, creating a tapestry only nature could weave.

Every few hundred yards, a clearing would reveal a farmhouse, the dormant, fallowed field in the background holding its peace until the first breath of spring. Topping a hill, Dani's breath caught at her first view of the town sunk deep into a small valley, the rolling hillsides aflame with color as though ready to sweep down on the picturesque village and extinguish it forever.

Once they completed their shopping, the ladies seated themselves on a park bench in the town square to enjoy the unseasonably warm day. They watched children play on the covered bandstand across from a massive brick building located in the midst of the park, the Greek revival architecture revealing its age.

Noting Dani's interest, Mrs. O'Brien nodded toward the structure. "That old courthouse housed the Carroll County Offices until they changed the county seat to Carrollton in the middle eighteen hundreds. Evansville's City Hall and the town library occupy the space now, thanks to a county-wide campaign a while back to keep the landmark from being torn down."

"That would have been a terrible shame," Dani said, turning her head to search for the owner of the eyes she sensed upon her. At once she noted the blond, shaggy-haired man leaning against one of the Victorian street lamps in the park. He held her gaze for sometime before he sauntered across the street.

Facing the housekeeper, she observed the crease in Mrs. O'Brien's brow. "Don't worry, Mrs. O'Brien. It's nothing." Yet Dani couldn't repress the shudder that raced down her spine. Would she always react this way when looked upon by an unfriendly man with a wiry build similar to Davenport's?

❧

One morning a few days later, the housekeeper stood near the fireplace in the formal parlor arranging seasonal greenery around the mantle. She turned to Dani, a gleeful smile in her eyes. "'Tis hard to believe Christmas is just around the corner. I tell ye, Miss Danielle, I can't remember how long 'tis been since the hall bore the earmarks of holiday cheer.

"When Miss Mathilda became confined to her bed, I decorated a small tree for her bedroom that year. Although it seemed to boost her spirits, I just didn't have enough heart to spread the gaiety to the rest of the house."

Dani looked up from the box of ornaments she was sorting. "Mrs. O'Brien, you were my aunt's companion for a long time. May I ask how you and she became acquainted?"

"Well, 'tis quite a tale, me lass."

"I'd love to hear it, if you'd care to tell me."

Abandoning her chore, Mrs. O'Brien stepped toward one of the blue satin chairs. "If ye don't mind, I'll rest me bones while I recall the details."

Dani nodded and then settled back into the sofa.

"When I 'twas but a lass in Ireland, World War II raged throughout Europe, the United States entering the war soon after me fifteenth birthday.

"One day while on an errand for me papa, a friend and I peddled to the village, the both of us gleeful like peacocks in spring. Just before we reached the shops, we decided to race our bicycles the rest of the way.

"A winning the contest, I looked back to give Elisabeth a smug grin, but she stared beyond me, a look of horror on her face. To me despair, I turned around just in time to see an American soldier step into the path. Before I could brake, me cycle plowed right into the young man, knocking him to the ground. I 'twas afrightened out of me wits, thinking I'd killed the fellow.

"When I jumped down beside him, I saw that I'd only jarred him a bit, hurting his pride more than anything else. Looking into each other's eyes at that moment, we both sensed that destiny had brought us together. Our love became as strong as the legend of the little people in me homeland.

"Michael O'Brien and I saw each other whenever the military would allow, at last saying our vows in the old parish cathedral just before he shipped out to France." The housekeeper pulled a hankie from the pocket of her apron. "But to me grief, the marriage ended a few days hence when German gunfire struck him down soon after his squadron landed on the banks of Normandy.

"Some months later, I received a letter from Michael's mother inviting me to live with her in Pittsburg, Pennsylvania. When I arrived in the USA, I learned that me mother-in-law had died from pneumonia just days before.

"Knowing I had to find work, I answered a newspaper ad for a position as a lady's maid at the Thorndike home. Miss Mathilda took a liking to me right away, asking me to join them when they moved to Georgia years later. I've been overseeing the care of Stratford Hall since that time."

Dani dabbed the corners of her eyes with her fingertips. "It's so sad that you lost your husband at such a young age."

"Yes, but I've no complaints about me life. The Lord's been good to me. But I've never forgotten me husband. I've often wished... I mean... if..." Mrs. O'Brien fidgeted with the hem of her apron. "Perhaps if we'd had a child, his passing wouldn't have been so hard to bear. But the Lord knows best how to direct our lives."

Dani wasn't sure she could agree with the housekeeper. Did God's best have to be teemed with tragedy?

Pushing her thoughts aside, Dani gave Mrs. O'Brien a warm smile. "Thank you. You've given me a better understanding of your regard for the Thorndikes."

A faraway look appeared in Mrs. O'Brien's eyes. "I've never known anyone like them," she said, rising from the chair. "Well, Miss Danielle, what say ye to a bite of lunch before we finish this task?"

"Great idea."

❧❧❧

"Justin, look at this," Dani said the following day.

Discarding his attempt to select the right Georgia pine to chop down for a Christmas tree, he propped the ax against a tree.

"What is it?" he asked, bending to crouch beside her.

Dani brushed away the red pine needles so he could get a better view of a boot print indenting the damp earth. "Do you think Davenport might have made this impression or his partner? It couldn't be Clive's. He wears a different type shoe."

"I suppose it's possible."

Dani stood up and walked a few paces beyond. "Here's more." She moved toward the entrance to the trail she'd seen often from the distance but hadn't yet investigated. "They lead into the woods." Her face brightened. "Maybe the culprits are hidden nearby. Let's go see."

Justin studied the original imprint a moment longer. "Uh, Dani, I really don't think that would be a good idea."

Dani, tilting her head to the side, frowned. "Why not? If we found their hiding place, we could call Sheriff Wilson, and this whole mess would be over. I don't know about you, but I'm tired of playing cops and robbers. It would be nice to know that I stand a chance of reaching retirement age. Come on."

She turned toward the trail. It wasn't just a mere longing to end her nightmarish existence that urged her on, but an urgency much more powerful—a strong perception that echoed with each of her heartbeats declaring that her life would never be the same should she risk the venture into the forest.

"Dani, stop!"

Jutting out her chin, she spun around, her lips drawn into a thin line. Standing transfixed, her hands on her hips, she pondered his words. What had prompted such a reaction? Fear? She glimpsed the set of his jaw. No. Just stubbornness. Why did he object to her intention? Did he know more than he'd confided in her?

Stepping forward, he latched onto her upper arms. Suddenly the memory of her brutal attack lurched into her thoughts. She tried to twist out of his painful grasp. All at once she felt color drain from her complexion. Was her previous inclination about him feasible after all? Could he be the person responsible for the mercenary acts against her? *No! No! No! Oh, please don't let it be so.*

Watching her eyes grow wide with fear, Justin relaxed his hold, pulling her close to his heart. "Dani, I'm sorry. I didn't mean to frighten you, but I'd never forgive myself if we did something foolish that could result in your injury or worse," he said, the fight in her corralled by his not so gentle kiss.

When he released her, she glanced down at her sneakers, the rapid rise of heat in her cheeks changing to a slow burn. She couldn't bring herself to raise her head. What man could kiss her like that and want to kill her at the same time?

Justin walked over and picked up the ax. "Besides, we don't want to damage any efforts the sheriff has engaged to capture these men. In fact, one of his deputies may be watching us right now." Dani glanced all around her, her porcelain like skin turning a shade lighter than usual. Justin laughed at the expression on her face. "Just kidding, Dani. But if you still plan to find the perfect tree before dark, we'd better get cracking."

With a wistful glance back at the trail, Dani donned the pair of work gloves Mrs. O'Brien had handed her before they left the hall. "Lead on, mighty hunter," she said, breathing a sigh of resignation.

That evening, seated in the gathering room, Dani and Justin admired the tinseled tree, its colorful baubles twinkling in the glow from the fireplace. She snuggled closer to him in the semidarkness, her heart melting like warm honey when he showered her with kisses a moment later. His lips became more demanding as he seemed to sense her fervent response to him. Breathless and trembling with passion, Dani forced herself to move away from his embrace, aware that a different type of jeopardy hovered in the shadows of her soul, ready and willing to accost her moral convictions at the first given opportunity.

# FAMILY TIES

"*D*ani, sweet Dani. Please say I don't have to return to Atlanta tonight," Justin whispered in her ear, again enfolding her into his arms.

She stiffened. The romantic illusion shattered as a sense of cheapness stole over her. Dani tried to twist away from him, but he held her tight against his chest. "Justin, please! You're hurting me." His face the epitome of frustration, he dropped his hands. Massaging her upper arms, Dani scooted toward the corner of the sofa, her eyes lowered.

Drawing a labored breath, Justin allowed a slight smile to soften his expression. "Come on, Dani, it *is* the twenty-first century, you know." He leaned over and kissed the tip of her nose. "It's not like I'm trying to seduce a girl fresh out of high school. Besides"—Justin placed his hand over her heart—"I think you want me to stay more than you're willing to admit."

At the sound of his words, heat crawled from Dani's neck to her hairline. Although appalled by his suggestion, she swallowed the accusation leaping to her lips. She couldn't lay all the blame at Justin's feet. If she'd used more restraint while in his arms, perhaps a happier ending would have crowned the evening. Rising from the couch, she drew a long sigh. At their age, you'd think maturity would come into play to trump the state of affairs. She stepped toward the foyer, forcing a glance his way. "I think it would be best if we called it a night, don't you?"

He held her gaze, his lips thinning. "Okay, Dani. You win."

"Sweet dreams, Justin. I trust you can see yourself to the door." A moment later, Dani paused at the top of the stairs, flinching. She hoped his lack of care in closing the door hadn't disturbed Mrs. O'Brien's slumber.

Once inside her room, Dani turned on her bedside lamp, her thoughts jumbled. To date no one had convinced her to break her self-made promise to remain chaste until her wedding night, although the vow had come with a high price—the loss of the few potentially marriageable men she'd allowed in her life through the years, Lance Carter the most recent. In fact, just as in past relationships, problems began to occur the moment Lance had realized that *no* to Dani meant *never* until she sported a wedding band.

Although some would think her a fool, she'd never regretted her decision to stand firm in her conviction. With satisfaction she recalled that she hadn't experienced too much difficulty overcoming temptation. Dani's next thought wiped the hint of smugness from her face. *Yes, but that was prior to meeting Justin.* With a slight shake of her head, Dani dismissed the niggling doubt. In the future she'd just have to enable extra precaution and exercise her fortitude in order to avoid the modern trend in romantic relationships.

Late the next morning, Dani entered the dining room and stopped short, her mouth dropping open in surprise. She watched while Justin helped himself to generous portions of bacon and eggs from beneath silver covers spread along the top of the buffet.

Straightening her shoulders, Dani moved forward to pick up a delicate-looking cup from among the china placed near the serving platters. The clatter of the dish against the matching saucer clamored in her ears. She examined them with a critical eye, sighing with relief when she found no evidence of breakage.

"I...I didn't think I'd see you today. Has Mrs. O'Brien left for church?" She took in his winsome smile, unable to disregard the plea for forgiveness in his eyes.

"Soon after I arrived," he said, munching on a slice of bacon.

Dani took a plate from the sideboard. Holding it in midair, she seemed to forget her intention to appease her appetite. She waited, holding her breath. Deciding a moment later he didn't seem eager to discuss their previous evening, she relaxed, ready to broach a safer subject. "I worry about Mrs. O'Brien. I offered her an extra day off, but she refused. Although we both do our best to keep things in order, the hall is an awesome responsibility. If you hadn't volunteered to stay with me on Sundays, she'd be guarding my every move right now instead of taking a day of rest. Maybe I should hire someone to help with the work around here."

Justin chuckled. "Do what you think is best, but it's my guess you'll have a fight on your hands. Stratford Hall is like a child to Mrs. O'Brien. Her nurturing touch is visible in every room, giving life to the place. But more important, the necessity of its care breathes strength into her. To take that away would, I believe, be more harmful to Mrs. O'Brien's health than the work itself."

Dani stared at Justin, her face crinkling into a smile a moment later. "If I should ever need a defense lawyer, you'll be the first one I call."

Justin set a crystal goblet brimming with orange juice aside and then took her chin in his hand. "The only crime you've committed, Miss Danielle McKinnon, is the theft of my affection." Raising his head, he stared off into space. "It's too bad we didn't meet a few years ago."

Dani turned away, a slight tremor in her fingers as she spooned the edibles onto her plate. "Why?"

Before he could answer, Justin's cell phone rang. "Excuse me." he said, placing his plate on the table before removing the phone from his shirt pocket. He glanced at the caller ID before answering the call. "Hello, Dad. Yes, I'm at the hall. What's up?"

Dani's heartbeat quickened. Why did she feel both anticipation and dread at Justin's words?

He seated himself at the table next to Dani several moments later. She leaned forward, awaiting the disclosure of his conversation with Phillip. She'd heard enough to know the call concerned her.

"Sergeant Hagerman thinks he has discovered something important to the case."

Her food forgotten, Dani's eyes brightened. "Good news, I hope."

Justin referred to the notepad in his hand. "The Sergeant asked a friend of his in Pittsburg to look into the life of Rosemary Davidson, the research including a visit to a penal institution in Massachusetts."

"She's in prison?"

"No, she never served any time, just her husband. Following his termination at Thorndike Steel, Davidson found employment with a competitive firm in Boston. A year or so later, soon after the birth of his daughter, the state of Massachusetts prosecuted him for embezzlement. Henceforth, Rosemary and the child returned to Pennsylvania to live with her mother."

"Maury's plight is not too surprising, considering what we learned about the Davidsons from Mrs. O'Brien."

"It's too bad the penalty outweighed his crime. "

"What do you mean?"

"A guard found his body stuffed in a trash dumpster just days before his sentence ended. The warden never discovered a reason for his death or who murdered him."

Dani's eyes widened. "That's terrible, of course, but how does that affect me?"

"None. But the friend's interview with Maury's former cellmate might. Although quite aged, the man remembered Davidson well."

She held up her hand. "Wait. How could a chat with this man aid the investigation?"

Justin sighed, his patient smile restraining her. "If you'll give me a chance, sweet Dani, I'll explain."

A teasing look tweaked her features. "Sorry. Please continue. I'll try to contain myself."

"Thanks. Knowing that cellmates often develop close friendships, the officer hoped the elderly prisoner might recall something pertinent that would benefit our search."

Dani leaned closer. "And?" She slunk back at the threatening gleam in Justin's eyes.

"Davidson told the prisoner that Rosemary felt she'd been cheated out of her share of the Thorndike fortune, which she thought included Stratford Hall."

"But that's impossible. The hall belonged to Aunt Mathilda."

"We know that, but Rosemary believed that the property belonged to her stepfather. And as his adopted heir, she assumed she had as much legal claim to the hall as Silas." Justin studied his notes. "But this is the clincher. When Maury looked into the matter, Rosemary refused to accept your aunt's title of ownership. Later, the two planned to steal the Thorndikes' valuable antiques once Maury was released from prison, their strategy due to a discovery he'd made during their one time visit to the premises."

Dani's senses sharpened. "What kind of discovery?"

"Unfortunately, Davidson didn't disclose that secret." He glanced at the Van Gogh painting above the century-old teacart stationed near the far wall. "Thank goodness his demise prevented the fruition of their plans."

Dani followed his gaze, agreeing in silence. "Are you saying then that Sergeant Hagerman suspects Rosemary in this evil hounding me?"

Justin looked away. "I wish it were that simple. Further research revealed that she died about fifteen years ago."

A sigh of disappointment lingering on her lips, Dani rose from the chair to pace back and forth. "I don't understand Sergeant

Hagerman's line of thought, how this information could lead anywhere. I'd say we've reached a dead end. And I do mean dead!"

Justin stood and then placed his hands on her shoulders. "Not necessarily. Think about it."

Dani didn't try to hide the look of irritation that crept onto her face. "Think about what? The fact that my hopes of this nightmare coming to an abrupt end were slaughtered moments after their birth?"

He winced. "No, the possibility of the daughter having learned of Mrs. Thorndike's death and plotting to carry out her mother's mission."

Contemplating Justin's words, Dani refilled their cups from the silver coffee urn. "That's right. You did mention the birth of a child. But don't you think the idea of her involvement is a little farfetched?"

Justin shrugged his shoulders. "Maybe. I guess time will tell."

Seated once again, she slowly stirred cream into her coffee, lines of concentration carved into her brow. Her former exasperation subdued, she asked, "What do the police know about the daughter?"

"Just that she met and married an Italian winemaker from California, moving to the Napa Valley years ago."

A wry smile crooked her lips. "Do you suppose the sergeant's list of friends includes someone on the western seaboard?"

Justin smiled. "It's possible. However, a private detective service might be more apt. And I know just the one. In fact, the owner and I were buddies in our years at Harvard. But he decided to enlist in the armed forces after graduation, his stint in our country's service initiating a major career change for him."

"Really. What kind of change?"

"His work in army intelligence, he claimed, was far more interesting than a dull courtroom. Soon after his return to the good old red, white, and blue, he formed a detective agency. I can't complain though. Our firm has often counted on his expertise to solve difficult cases."

"If you think this is the best approach, then by all means, pursue it."

Standing once again, Justin bowed low. "Your wishes are ever my constant command, Lady Danielle." Taking her hand, his voice took on a grave tone. "I know this whole affair is trying, but be patient. Justice is oftentimes slow, but the system does work."

"I don't doubt your word, but can my sanity survive the wait?"

His eyes full of tenderness, he chucked her chin with a gentle fist. "What say we forget all this for the time being and nab a couple of Clive's horses for an afternoon ride?"

"I'd love it. Just let me grab a coat."

Late that afternoon following Justin's return to Atlanta, Mrs. O'Brien opened the library door. "Miss Danielle, I've a favor to ask of ye."

Laying her book aside, Dani unwound her legs curled beneath her on the leather couch. "Sure. How can I help you?"

"I told Mr. Justin I wouldn't leave ye alone, but the lady who takes me place at the organ when I'm unable to attend church has taken ill. I hate to put me pastor in a bind, so I thought ye might consider attending the evening service with me?"

Hesitation shadowed Dani's face. "Well, I ..."

The housekeeper took a quick step forward. "There's to be a fellowship after the meeting, you know, sandwiches, cookies, hot cider, that sort of thing. 'Twould be an excellent opportunity for me to introduce ye to the people hereabouts. They so loved Miss Mathilda, and they're all anxious to meet you." Untying her apron strings, Mrs. O'Brien awaited Dani's answer.

Dani stretched her arms toward the ceiling, yawning. "I guess I can't be a hermit forever."

"Ah, Miss Danielle. Ye've made me day."

With the sun setting beneath the purplish-orange horizon, Mrs. O'Brien drove into the church parking lot. "Miss Danielle, an ancestor of yours, a Reverend Mordecai Gladstone, founded Pleasant Valley Community Church in the late 1830s. Influenced by the teachings of Evangelist George Whitfield, a missionary to America from England, Mordecai gave his heart and service to the Lord, spreading the gospel of Christ throughout the colonies, at last settling in Carroll County soon after its establishment."

The housekeeper pointed beyond the church. "His remains lie in the churchyard yonder. Many of those who now attend Pleasant Valley are descendents of its charter members."

Her interest piqued, Dani eyed the quaint red brick building situated in a cozy setting near a county crossroads. Mrs. O'Brien never ceased to amaze Dani. What other intriguing tales were bound in the woman's memory? Did others of Dani's ancestry also lie within the quaint cemetery?

She shivered as the image of Jules Davenport's countenance appeared in her mind. Would the time for her to be covered by this colorful earth arrive sooner than expected? Dani shook off the wearisome thought and then followed the housekeeper through the whitewashed double door.

"Now, Miss Danielle, ye just slide right into this pew while I attend me duty. I'll sit with ye shortly," Mrs. O'Brien said about halfway down the aisle.

A moment later, Dani listened in surprise as the housekeeper played a familiar melody on a large organ occupying a good portion of the stage. At once the words to the song drifted into her head, along with a vision of herself in childhood sitting between her parents, a hymnbook in her hands.

Standing with the congregation, Dani sang the words in her heart.

All hail the power of Jesus' name!
Let angels prostrate fall;
Bring forth the royal diadem,
And crown Him Lord of all;
Bring forth the royal diadem,
And crown Him Lord of all!

The next verse flooded her memory.

Ye chosen seed of Israel's race,
Ye ransomed from the fall,
Hail Him who saves you by His grace,
And crown Him Lord of all;
Hail Him who saves you by His grace,
And crown Him Lord of all!

Dani glanced at the hymnal with amazement. Why, she'd remembered each stanza of the song. She blinked back the loneliness that washed over her. How she longed for the peace and contentment she read on the faces around her.

Had bitterness and her refusal to forgive carved too large an idol in her heart for God's love and mercy to shatter?

Not according to the Pendergraffs. She remembered the times they'd spoken to her regarding the subject. Dani's skin tightened across her face, fresh resentment chafing her heart like sandpaper. Since God had turned a deaf ear to her childish pleas, how could she expect heavenly attentiveness now?

The worship service at an end, Dani moved over to make more room for Mrs. O'Brien who settled herself on the pew beside Dani. Eyeing the minister as he stepped toward the podium, Dani at once became captivated by the love and tenderness displayed in his eyes. She gave him her full attention.

"Dear friends, our text tonight begins in the book of Isaiah, and then we'll move to the books of Luke and John in the New Testament. Normally, I use these passages of Scripture to preach a salvation message; however, this evening I'd like to articulate from a different perspective."

Mrs. O'Brien switched the position of her Bible so that Dani could read along with the reverend. "Beloved friends, let's turn in our Bibles to Isaiah, chapter fifty-three, verse six: 'We all, like sheep, have gone astray. Each of us has turned to his own way, and the Lord has laid on Him the iniquity of us all.'"

Dani felt her face grow warm as his gentle voice penetrated her heart. "Beloved, although we've all sinned and come short of the glory of God, we're not destitute. The gospel of John, chapter ten, verse, fourteen tells us that God sent His Son to be our Good Shepherd, a shepherd willing to give His life for the sheep, 'that we should not perish, but have everlasting life,' as stated in John, chapter three, verse sixteen.

"Likewise, in Saint Luke, chapter fifteen, verse four, we read, 'Suppose one of you have a hundred sheep and loses one of them. Does he not leave the ninety-nine in the open country and go after the lost sheep until he finds it?'

"Friends, all of us have suffered heartbreak, misfortunes that have made us feel lost and alone, calamities that have suppressed all hope. While many turn to God in these times, others allow tragedy to devour their love for Christ like wolves nipping and tearing at the flesh of innocent sheep. But remember God is not the one who steals, kills, and destroys, according to Saint John, chapter ten, but rather Satan, the enemy of our souls.

"If these circumstances have befallen you, then, beloved, I'm here to tell you that the Good Shepherd is standing at the door of your heart, eager to restore your relationship with Him. I urge you to answer His call. He turns every tragedy into a triumph when we're willing to forgive those who have caused us sorrow or pain."

Dani grappled with the stab of conviction piercing her heart. Hadn't Uncle Bill expressed similar words when she lay in the hospital recovering from the attack in the parking garage? But like the dawn that appeared every day, a lack of trust in the Father's love had risen each morning since her parents' death to sever the Savior from her life. Although fear had provoked an earlier interest in spiritual rededication, she'd let that slip away once she'd settled into her new life at Stratford Hall, focusing on the protection of men rather than God's safeguard.

The minister's voice broke into her thoughts. "Friends let's look at verse five and six of Luke, chapter fifteen: 'And when he finds it, he joyfully puts it on his shoulders and goes home. Then he calls his friends and neighbors together and says, 'Rejoice with me; I have found my lost sheep.'"

Dani lowered her head to brush aside a tear. Maybe she could forgive Lance, her grandparents, even the drunk driver who'd destroyed her parents' lives, but how could she forgive God for refusing to answer her prayers at the most crucial moment in her life? Dani's composure crumpled. She searched for the packet of tissues she carried in her purse.

The pastor spread his arms wide. "Do you feel like a lost sheep tonight? If so, the Good Shepherd is waiting with His arms outstretched to welcome you once again into His fold, a haven of rest for the weary soul. Come forward, dear one. Let me reintroduce you to the King of kings and the Lord of lords."

Dani couldn't resist the Savior's appeal any longer. Standing, she made her way to the front of the church, realization burning in her soul like a flaming torch. It wasn't God who needed forgiveness but herself. He hadn't rejected her; she'd turned away from Him. She may never understand the why of her parents' demise, and perhaps she hadn't experienced the greatest of childhoods, yet God had not abandoned her. He'd placed the Pendergraffs in her life to nurture and love her as their own child.

Dani's eyes widened. And God in His infinite mercy had allowed her to become a triumph for their tragic state of affairs—barrenness of womb. Dani cringed inside. Why couldn't she have perceived this years ago? But thank God she did now. With His help, she could start fresh again. Also, because of Christ's faithfulness to forgive, Dani had the assurance of reunion with her parents one day in heaven. Dani smiled through her tears. Aunt Mathilda, too.

Returning to her pew a few minutes later, Mrs. O'Brien greeted Dani with a teary smile. Her eyes filled with gratitude, she hugged the housekeeper, savoring the joy she felt.

The service dismissed, Mrs. O'Brien guided her mistress down a flight of stairs to the fellowship hall where she introduced Dani to various church members milling about the room.

Later, while in conversation with Pastor Anderson and his gracious wife, Sarah, a tall, thin woman appeared at Dani's side. "Miss McKinnon, I'm Helena Radcliffe. I suppose you've heard of me."

Smiling, Dani turned to the dour-faced individual whose hazel eyes exposed more curiosity than friendliness. "Well, actually no. But I'm pleased to meet you nonetheless."

"Miss Danielle, Mrs. Radcliffe is the president of our town's most influential organization," Mrs. O'Brien said, the hint of wariness in her eyes not lost on Dani. "Before your Aunt Mathilda took to her bed, she devoted herself to their charitable causes."

Mrs. Radcliffe's drawn expression broke into a thoughtful smile, her cunning eyes sizing up the niece of their organization's late benefactor. Taking Dani's arm, Helena propelled the newcomer a short distance away from the group.

"Miss McKinnon, perhaps you'd like to join our little society. We meet each Tuesday at a local restaurant where we enjoy a pleasant lunch before discussing our projects. With the shortage of volunteers, your patronage would be of great value."

"Your luncheon sounds delightful. And too, I'm not a stranger to community service. I donated several hours a month to various Hartford organizations."

The lines in Mrs. Radcliffe's face deepened when her smile broadened. "Wonderful, Miss McKinnon. I just knew I could count on you. This week we begin our annual Toys for Tots drive, which provides toys and clothing for children at the county orphanage as well as other underprivileged youth of the county."

"It will be a pleasure to serve our community any way I can." Dani glanced back over her shoulder. "Perhaps Mrs. O'Brien can be persuaded to join us."

Dani felt rather than saw Mrs. Radcliffe grow rigid.

"Miss McKinnon. Housekeepers seldom attend our meetings."

Facing the woman again, Dani's smile faded. "Mrs. O'Brien isn't just the caretaker of Stratford Hall; she's my friend. Besides, if volunteers are indeed as needful as you stated, it seems another pair of hands would be welcome."

The older woman's nostrils flared. "I see you have a lot to learn about *Southern* ways, Miss McKinnon."

Dani bristled. *What impertinence!* "Mrs. Radcliffe, if my participation is of the importance you implied, I suggest you find *two* available seats at your prestigious affair."

Her eyes narrowing, Mrs. Radcliffe spun around on her heel, tossing a reply over her shoulder. "I'll see what I can do!"

Taking a deep breath, Dani turned, her cheeks reddening at the sight of Pastor Anderson.

He smiled. "I'm sorry. I couldn't help but overhear your conversation with Mrs. Radcliffe. Although apt at seeing to the poor, she must have forgotten the scripture that says, 'God is no respecter of persons.' Dismissing the issue, he reached out to draw Mrs. O'Brien to their side when she drew near. "Mrs. O'Brien is much more at peace now that you've arrived at Stratford Hall. And speaking for our congregation, we welcome you to the community." He nodded toward Mrs. Radcliffe. "Don't be too hard on Helen. She'll come around to the Lord's way of thinking in time."

Dani laughed. "The sooner the better, I hope."

Later, on their way home, Mrs. O'Brien turned to Dani, the dim light from the dash of the car just glimpsing the sparkle in the housekeeper's eyes. "Whew, whee, Miss Danielle! Ye sure singed the feathers right off Mrs. Radcliffe tonight. I haven't seen her that mad in a coon's age."

Dani turned to stare out the darkened side window, clasping her hands together in her lap. "Sometimes I let temper get the best of me. Perhaps a course in Christian Love 101 might be in order for this babe in Christ."

"Now, don't ye worry yer sweet self about Mrs. Radcliffe. I can't excuse her actions, but if ye'd known her before the hunting accident took the life of her son a few years ago, ye'd have met a different person. She needs our prayers in the worst way. Once she allows God to heal her inner woes, she'll change back to her old self. Ye just wait and see."

Dani's thoughts turned backward in time. Yes, she'd seen how anger and bitterness at the loss of a son had affected her father's parents. Their orphaned, coltlike grandchild, so much the image of their offspring, became a burden instead of the pleasure she'd been to them before the accident. Unable to bear the agony often observed in their eyes, she'd grown up finding ways to make herself scarce in her grandparents' sight, eager to accept the love and understanding the Pendergraffs had offered to her.

Dani shuddered. Until tonight she'd been traveling down a similar road. But God's mercy and grace had forestalled the inevitable: another Helena Radcliffe thrust upon the world. However, there were at least two who stood in the woman's corner. Dani decided she could be a third.

"Well, me young lass, what about a cup of hot chocolate before ye retire? It will take the chill out of our bones in no time at all."

With a start, Dani turned to the housekeeper. Caught up in the past, she hadn't realized they'd arrived at the hall nor been aware of the single tear that trickled down her cheek. With a crooked smile, she opened the car door. "Just the antidote I need."

# PARTY DEBRIS

*I*gnoring the flutter in her stomach the following Tuesday, Dani donned the dark green woolen business suit she'd chosen after careful consideration, concluding that its chic lines were perfect for the charity luncheon. Adjusting the multicolor silk scarf at the neckline, she dismissed the temptation to ignore the invitation, the children's welfare worth whatever she might have to endure from Mrs. Radcliffe.

Positioned in the foyer a few minutes later, Dani watched Mrs. O'Brien descend the stairs, aware that her friend's gray-speckled mahogany tresses swept high in a classic Victorian style crowned her brown and navy-patterned ensemble with just the right touch of elegance. "Why, Mrs. O'Brien, you've changed your hairstyle. I like it."

Dani reached toward the wispy curls framing Mrs. O'Brien's face. "I swear, Mrs. O'Brien, you look twenty years younger. It's a good thing this is ladies only or Stratford Hall might be short one loving matron by nightfall."

Mrs. O'Brien giggled. "Oh, Miss Danielle, do go on with ye now. 'Tis nary a soul that could make me renege on the promise to look after ye as long as I'm able." The housekeeper laid her hand on

Dani's arm. "'Twas love for your aunt that spurred me intention at first, but now I find me heart sings a similar melody when I cast me old eyes upon your face."

Her voice choked with emotion, Dani threw her arms around Mrs. O'Brien. "Mrs. O'Brien, I shall treasure our friendship forever."

Mrs. O'Brien pulled a lace hankie from the bosom of her dress to wipe the tears from her cheeks. "Mercy, lass. Look what ye've gone and done. I must grab me wits about meself before we arrive in town or all those women will think I've been a dipping into Clive's private stock of medicinal brew."

Quaking with mirth, Dani took the housekeeper's arm to escort her out the door. "Both of us may need a drink of his potion before this day is over."

Within the hour, she and Mrs. O'Brien stood outside the restaurant that hosted the weekly event. Dani chuckled. "I feel like I'm about to enter a den of lions."

Mrs. O'Brien's cerulean blue eyes twinkled. "I've known these women for years. 'Tis true some will act like pickled pears when they see us come in together, but most are God-fearing women who have the community's best interest at heart. And too, they will swallow some of their Southern pride in hopes ye'll part with a portion of your inheritance to aid their cause. Hold your head high, lass. Ye come from as good a stock as can be found in these ancient hills."

Taking a deep breath, Dani opened the door. When they entered the meeting room, a hush settled over the audience, every eye cast their way. Recognizing the newcomers, Mrs. Radcliffe started toward them, her face pinched and drawn with disapproval. At once Dani had the distinct impression of an eagle swooping down to snare sighted prey into its perilous talons.

But before Mrs. Radcliffe could verbalize her thoughts, Sarah Anderson intercepted the newcomers. "Miss McKinnon, I'm so glad you and Mrs. O'Brien decided to join us. Please sit by me. They're about to serve the meal."

Earlier concerned with how Mrs. O'Brien would fare at the meeting, Dani soon tabled her anxiety. By the time the dishes were cleared, the ladies seemed pleased to accept the housekeeper, Mrs. O'Brien's unique charm winning them over in no time. Dani grinned. Even Mrs. Radcliffe had turned cordial toward Mrs. O'Brien before the meeting ended. The housekeeper and her mistress returned home with both a certificate of membership in hand and a grudging respect for the president's adept presentation of the club's agenda.

The next weekend, Dani viewed her calendar with awe; days had turned into weeks with Christmas near at hand. Would her luck hold? It had been close to a month since she'd suffered at the hands of Davenport or his accomplice. Could it be they'd ended their tirade against her at last? "Dear God, please let it be so!" she whispered.

Although thoughts of the evil they might be conspiring disturbed her, she refused to let it affect the happiness she'd experienced since her conversion. Her trust in God had flourished, the devotions Mrs. O'Brien presided over in the evenings building her faith at a rapid pace. And with each attendance at Pleasant Valley Church, she'd grown to love the people more, their love for Christ inspiring a deeper commitment in Dani.

Recalling her telephone call to the Pendergraffs to announce her new life, a smile touched her lips. "No more than I expected," Bill had stated in a matter-of-fact tone. "I'm just thankful you saw the light before my knees wore out."

She glanced over at Justin's photograph, a touch of sadness in her eyes. She'd hoped for similar happiness at her news from him or at least polite interest. But he'd just shrugged his shoulders, saying, "Religion is okay for some people, but personally, I've never seen the need for it." Nevertheless, their relationship progressed. She felt that soon he would ask that important question.

Dani laid her date book aside, resuming her task of balancing the estate accounts. Finishing the chore sometime later, she glanced at the clock, realizing she had just enough time to dress before Justin arrived to take her to see *The Nutcracker* in Atlanta. Following the performance, they would attend a Christmas party at the Harcourt home, where she was to be the guest of honor.

After a last glimpse in the mirror, Dani met Justin at the bottom of the stairs. He beamed with pleasure as he admired the black, beaded sheath lightly draping her body.

Her heart pounded when he raised her hand to his lips, kissing her fingers one by one before he led her out into the crisp, ebony night.

Dani glanced upward, the canopy of twinkling stars adding jeweled magic to the air of romance encircling them. Enchanted, she watched their reflections pirouette atop the shining Cadillac, a youthful laugh catching in her throat. *A night for lovers*, she thought. She flashed Isaac a smile before he aided their entrance into the car. She felt as though the world stood at attention, ready to grant her every request.

Later that evening, Phillip greeted Dani with an affectionate hug. "How nice to see you again. It's been far too long. I hope country life isn't tedious for you."

Dani laughed. "On the contrary. Mrs. O'Brien sees to that." Dani looked away. *Not to mention other heart-stopping adventures now and then.*

Phillip leaned forward. "Dani, are you okay?"

She brightened. "Why, yes, thank you. And you? Justin tells me you've been working on an important case. I hope everything is going well."

"Yes, but let's don't discuss work. Come meet our guests. Justin and I have looked forward to this evening for some time."

Once inside their spacious den, Justin escorted her toward a group of merrymakers in the center of the room. A lady, seeing their approach, stepped forward to greet them.

"Hello, Aunt Claudine," Justin said, bending to hug a petite, well-dressed, older woman.

He pulled Dani forward. "May I present my aunt, Claudine Beaumont. Auntie, Miss Danielle McKinnon of Stratford Hall, Carroll County, Georgia."

Claudine smiled. "Yes. Phillip told me about you. I'm pleased to meet you."

"It's nice to make your acquaintance as well. Justin didn't tell me he had such a charming aunt."

Mrs. Beaumont turned to Justin, a teasing smile on her lips. "Shame on you."

He looked repentant. "Sorry, Auntie. The subject just never came up."

She patted his cheek, sneaking a glance toward Dani. "You're forgiven. After meeting your Miss McKinnon, I can understand how you might be prone to a memory lapse in her company."

A few minutes later, Justin propelled Dani toward the other guests, Phillip staying behind to chat longer with his sister. While engrossed in conversation with George Paine, Phillip's other partner, Dani and Justin turned at a familiar voice, both pleased to greet the owner with a smile.

"Hello, Mr. Van Buren. What a pleasant surprise." Dani nodded to his daughter standing beside him, noting that her attractive features appeared to be carved in stone.

"Hello, Marguerite. Glad you and Albert could make it after all," Justin said, slipping a martini from a nearby tray of drinks.

Mr. Van Buren took Dani's outstretched hand. "I must say the pleasure is mine. I understand you've made Georgia your home. When we first met, Justin failed to mention your relationship to my dear departed friend Mathilda Thorndike."

"Having heard of her prestige from many of her friends, I'm sorry I missed the opportunity to know my aunt."

"Father, we shouldn't monopolize Miss McKinnon and Justin. I'm sure he wants to give all his guests the opportunity to make her acquaintance," Marguerite said, running her hand along Justin's arm.

"We can always count on you to provide your guests with a variety of entertainment." She lowered her voice. "However, your guest list could be updated to include more quality of style." She threw Dani a sideways glance. "We'll talk again sometime. I'm sure of it."

Dani's smile paled. *Not if I can help it!*

The Van Burens moved away, Mr. Van Buren frowning at his daughter. "Why, Marguerite, what's come over you? Phillip has out-done himself tonight." Dani, having overheard his remark, couldn't help but smile.

Justin downed his drink, finishing a second one before he spun Dani into the midst of dancing couples. They didn't speak for several minutes, Dani's thoughts matching the dark look on Justin's face. Seeming to resolve the issue within himself a moment later, he pulled Dani close to finish out the waltz.

Later, Justin having left her side to refresh his drink, Dani moved to the side of the room to enjoy a moment away from the guests. She rubbed her temples. She couldn't remember the last time she'd breathed so much smoke. Or was it the confrontation with Marguerite that had set her nerves on edge? Fanning away a puff of cigar smoke with her cocktail napkin, Dani looked at Justin, grateful that he didn't use tobacco products.

However, disquiet of a different sort drew her attention. She flinched at Justin's loud, boisterous laugh. What had come over him? Her eyes narrowed as he received yet another drink from the man tending the bar. How many drinks had he consumed tonight anyway? Confusion filled her eyes. He'd never partaken of more than two drinks while in her company.

Departing the room, she climbed the stairs in search of a place where she could get a breath of fresh air. Entering the formal living area, she collapsed onto the sofa, not bothering to flip on a light, the glow from the fireplace adequate for visibility.

Suddenly the gaiety she'd enjoyed earlier dissipated, discontent shadowing the holiday cheer. It hadn't to do with the guests; they'd been receptive and cordial—Marguerite, the only exception. Dani drew her hand across her brow. Why did she feel like a stranger in a foreign land? She'd looked forward to social events like these in the past. Maybe her feelings had to do with her recent conversion. All at once a portion of Scripture Pastor Anderson had used in his message on Sunday came to mind. "Ye are in this world, but not of this world."

The sound of Justin's voice interrupted her thoughts. "Dani, is something wrong?"

She frowned at the slur in his words. "Just a headache. I'm sure I'll be fine shortly." She took the glass of ginger ale he offered and took a sip. "Thank you. This will help."

"Maybe this will too." Justin began to massage her neck.

"Mm, that feels good. You're right. The pain is beginning to subside."

A moment later, he took her into his arms, his kisses gentle at first and then deepening until they both were breathless.

"Dani, sweet Dani." Again, he touched his lips to hers.

As his embrace intensified, a vague sense of warning tolled in her thoughts. She tried to retreat from his arms, but he held her secure. Pushing with all her strength, she broke his hold.

Catching a glimpse of his face in the firelight, she shrank back from the look of fierce determination in his eyes. She attempted to stand, but he grabbed her, forcing her back against the arm of the sofa.

"Justin! Stop! We need to return to the party."

"Not so, sweet Dani. I need another kiss."

Before she could stop him, Justin placed his hands on the sides of her face, pulling her toward him. She grabbed his hands, trying to twist out of his grasp. As she lifted her hand to claw at his cheek, a voice from the doorway startled them.

"Well, now. Isn't this a cozy scene? What's wrong, Miss McKinnon? Justin's animal instinct too much for you?"

Justin faced Marguerite. "Get out! This is no concern of yours."

Dani sprang toward the fireplace, the heat no match for the flame of shame and disgust that rose to consume her self-respect. She tried to straighten her falling hair and rumpled clothing, wishing she could drown out the conversation across the room.

Marguerite's lips curled in anger. "Unless I'm mistaken, illicit behavior toward a woman without her consent is a criminal offense. You of all people should know better. Or were you so overwrought with passion that the thought of your profession slipped from your mind?"

"I don't need you to remind me of my occupation," Justin said, standing to face his opponent, his stance unsteady. Brushing Marguerite aside, he left the room without a word to Dani.

A long moment passed while both women stared at each other. At last Dani spoke. "I suppose I should thank you."

Marguerite held up her hand. "I don't need your gratitude or want it. Your safety is no concern of mine. Alcohol always brings out the worst in Justin. Let's just say it heeded my interest to curtail this little romantic liaison."

She turned to go and then again faced Dani. "How long did you think you could hold out on a virile man like Justin anyway?" A scathing laugh broke through her lips at the look of horror crossing Dani's features. "Oh, yes, I know all about your virtuous ideas.

"Justin and I were friends long before you entered the picture, little Miss Rich Girl. If you are waiting for a proposal, forget it. He soured on marriage a long time ago."

Dani straightened to her full height. "Excuse me, Miss Van Buren! I hardly think my relationship with Justin is any of your business. Furthermore, if I find it necessary to ask for lovelorn advice, you can bet I won't come knocking on your door. Observance of a barnyard in spring would yield a loftier expertise."

Marguerite's face turned ashen. She opened her mouth as though to speak, but threw Dani a venomous glower instead, stalking through the door a moment later.

Dani's shoulders slumped. She lowered herself into a chair near the fireplace. How could she ever forgive Justin or herself? Tears surfaced and rolled down her cheeks. How could she have said those awful remarks to Marguerite? *Oh, God! Please forgive me.* After what seemed like hours, her tears spent, she glimpsed a maid in the foyer, the same one who'd earlier taken her wrap.

"Excuse me."

The woman, her eyes squinted, peered into the dim room, her hand on her heart. "Oh. Miss McKinnon. I had no idea anyone was nearby."

"Would you please collect my things and call a taxi? I need to go home." The woman skittered away to heed Dani's request.

Within a few moments, Dani heard a step in the foyer. She glanced up, expecting to see the maid. Instead Phillip Harcourt entered the room. Worry creasing his brow, he switched on the light. "Dani, Nancy thought you might be ill. Should I phone a physician?" He took in her disheveled appearance, the fine lines around his eyes becoming more prominent as a questioning look covered his face.

Fearful of what he might read in her eyes, Dani lowered her head. "No, that isn't necessary. I've just developed a wicked headache. Please convey my apology to the others. You were so kind to host this party for me." Dani struggled to keep the tears out of her voice.

"Whatever you wish, Dani." He turned to leave. "I'll tell Justin he needs to escort you home."

"No!" Dani lowered her voice when she detected a knowing look on the elder Harcourt's face. "I mean, Justin shouldn't leave his guests. I'd be lousy company anyway. Besides, a taxi should be here any moment."

"Nancy said you'd requested one, but Isaac will see you home. I'll call him now."

Once on the way to Stratford Hall, Dani huddled beneath her cloak, the pain in her heart more agonizing than the throbbing in her head. Why had Justin been so crass in his behavior toward her?

And for Marguerite Van Buren to witness the affair! She'd never be able to face either of them again.

When the limousine taillights disappeared around the bend in the lane an hour later, Dani clipped along the cobblestone pathway toward the gazebo, relishing a few moments of solitude. Once inside the structure, she faced the shimmering silver brook, the soft ripple of the water soothing her torn emotions. She covered her face with her hands. In spite of what had taken place, she still cared for him. *Oh, Justin!*

Her gaze resting on the forest beyond a few moments later, a movement near the edge caused her pulse to quicken, the disastrous evening shriveling in significance as other possibilities formed in her mind. The hem of her cape flapping about her knees, she ran toward the hall, pausing just long enough to unlock the door.

She mounted the stairs two at a time, her heart pounding like winter surf rumbling against a cliff. Her hands shaking, she secured her bedroom door. Calmer, a few moments later, Dani tried to convince herself she'd just witnessed an animal watering near the thicket. She closed her eyes, reliving the scene in her mind. No. The bright light from the full moon had revealed a two-legged creature looking her way just before his form disappeared into the dense undergrowth.

A shiver streaked down her spine. What additional abuse did her hostile foes have planned? Would she live to tell it?

Dani knelt beside her bed. "Oh, God, help me trust You. Please lead the authorities to my tormentors soon." She glanced upward. A shaft of moonlight parted the curtains, highlighting Justin's smiling face in the photograph beside her bed. She turned it face downward onto the nightstand. If she never saw him again, it would be too soon. Pulling back the bedclothes, she dismissed the still, small voice inside her heart echoing Mark 11:25: "And when you stand praying, if you hold anything against anyone, forgive him, so that your Father in heaven may forgive you your sins." *I'm sorry, God. You're asking too much of me this time.*

# TWIN DILEMMA

*L*ate the next morning, a knock woke Dani from a sound sleep. "Come in," she said, peering at the door through half-closed eyes.

Mrs. O'Brien entered the room. "Miss Danielle, Mr. Justin is on the phone. I told him ye hadn't arisen as yet, but he asked to speak to you anyway."

Dani's eyes narrowed, her gaze lingering on the cordless phone in the housekeeper's hand. "I can't talk to him now." Glimpsing the surprised look on Mrs. O'Brien's face, Dani slid deeper into the bed, ignoring the red blinking light on her cell phone, which she'd keyed to silent ring hours earlier.

"Whatever ye say," Mrs. O'Brien replied. She studied her young mistress a long moment before exiting the room.

Unable to resume her slumber, Dani tossed back the covers and soon appeared in the kitchen. Ignoring Mrs. O'Brien's curious glances, Dani seated herself near the window, feigning interest in the landscape while she sipped her coffee in silence.

"Well now, how about eggs Benedict this morning?" Mrs. O'Brien said with strained pleasantry in her tone.

Dani acknowledged Mrs. O'Brien with a halfhearted smile then resumed her outdoor vigil. "No thanks. I'm not hung—" The phone rang, startling them both.

Mrs. O'Brien pulled the receiver from the extension. "Hello?" Mrs. O'Brien threw a glance toward Dani. "Just a moment. I'll see if Miss Danielle is available." The housekeeper cupped her hand over the phone. "It's Mr. Justin again."

Dani observed the squabble between a pair of sparrows beneath the thunderous gray sky. What luxury to have such few quandaries. She mulled over the past few weeks. The problems she'd faced previous to receiving Phillip's letter a lifetime ago seemed paltry now.

Sighing, she rose from the table, taking the phone from Mrs. O'Brien's outstretched hand. The housekeeper stepped into the pantry, her face bathed in curiosity.

With a grateful smile cast toward Mrs. O'Brien, Dani spoke into the phone. "Yes?"

"Dani, we need to talk."

"I'm sorry, Justin, but I can't think of anything you might say that would inspire even my remotest interest."

An eternity seemed to pass before he spoke again. "Dani, you have every right to be angry with me, but please try to understand. I had too much to drink. I swear it won't happen again."

Dani felt her throat constrict. "Whatever gave you reason to believe I deserved your roguish manhandling?"

"Lord, Dani. Nothing. Nothing. Won't you please forgive me? I can't bear the thought of never seeing you again."

Warfare raged inside Dani. How could she do as he asked? He'd insulted her in the worst way. She closed her eyes, trying to still the words within her heart: "Forgive us our trespasses as we forgive those who trespass against us. The scripture reminded her of the verse God had spoken to her in the wee hours of the morning: "And when you stand praying, if you hold anything against anyone, forgive him, so your Father in heaven may forgive you your sins."

Tears mushroomed in Dani's eyes and then cascaded down her cheeks. She stuffed the back of her hand against her lips to stay the mournful cry yearning to break her silence. Seconds seemed to elongate into minutes.

Words from the book of Joshua arose from her innermost being. "Choose for yourselves this day whom you will serve. But as for me and my household, we will serve the Lord." *Yes, Father, just as the people of Israel said to Joshua, 'we will serve the Lord our God and obey him,' so will I obey you.*

"Dani, are you still there?"

Dani's grip on the phone tightened. "Yes," she said between ragged breaths.

"Please, Dani. Again, I'm sorry."

She pulled several tissues from a box nearby. After a moment she spoke in a voice just above a whisper, "Yes, Justin, I forgive you." Dani felt a surge of peace sweep over her. She breathed a prayer of thanks. As Mrs. O'Brien often stated, "'Tis always best to follow the Savior's example. He always rewards those who diligently seek His ways."

Justin's voice jolted her back to the present. "Thank you, sweet Dani. You won't regret it. I promise. Now, what about an afternoon of Mozart at the College Center and then dinner at the French Connection later on this evening?"

To forgive was one thing, to forget quite another. "Not today, Justin. I have other plans."

Dani refused to be swayed by his sigh of disappointment. She just couldn't see him this soon. She needed time for her wounded spirit to heal.

"Okay, we'll get together another day."

Replacing the phone into its holder, Dani greeted the housekeeper with a smile when she returned to the kitchen. "Mrs. O'Brien, what do you say to a trip to Atlanta this afternoon? I need a bit of cheering up, and I've thought of something that will do the trick."

"'Tis not a problem at all. What did ye have in mind?"

Once inside the car and driving toward Evansville instead of eastbound to the capital city, Dani laughed at the baffled expression in Mrs. O'Brien's eyes. "I need to make one stop before we head to Atlanta. Here's what I hope to do."

Within minutes, a friendly employee of the Carroll County Children's Home ushered them into the administrator's office.

"Why, Mrs. O'Brien what a delight," Fred Coons said, rising to greet the couple.

Mrs. O'Brien shifted her attention to Dani. "Fred, I'd like ye to meet Miss Mathilda's niece, Miss Danielle McKinnon. She'd like a word with ye about the children."

"Of course, of course. Please sit down." Mr. Coons waved to the two chairs opposite his desk, his gaze fixed on his new acquaintance. "How can I be of service?"

A short time later, Dani followed Mrs. O'Brien out the orphanage door armed with the information the director had been more than willing to supply.

Fastening her seatbelt, Mrs. O'Brien's eyes sparkled with mirth. "I thought Fred's eyes were gonna pop right outta his head when you handed him that check. Ye talk about cutting red tape."

"Now that I've met Mr. Coons, I hope the police never find any reason to indicate the orphanage's involvement with Davenport. As the newest member of their volunteer office personnel, I'll keep an eye out for evidence in that direction."

The housekeeper's eyes grew wide. "'Tis the home they be suspecting? Why, the bobbies must be daft in the head!"

"Well, you know the clause in my aunt's will. The board of directors, along with orphanage staff, will be under suspicion until the criminals are apprehended." Mrs. O'Brien shook her head, disbelief written upon her face.

Desiring to change the topic of conversation, Dani glanced at the stack of letters to Santa Claus on the seat between them. "This is the most exciting day I've ever known!"

A moment later, a look of doubt shadowed her anticipation. "You don't think my aunt would disapprove of our plans, do you?

Mrs. O'Brien smiled. "Nay, lass. I've seen Miss Mathilda concoct similar undertakings meself. I remember one such occasion milady happened to be in the kitchen when the egg woman appeared at the back door. When she'd gone, I explained her recent widowhood, the passel of younguns she had to support, and how the bank intended to foreclose on her property within days.

"The next morning your aunt asked me to drive her to the bank in Evansville. Within minutes she'd paid off the mortgage, presenting the deed to the dear, God-fearing lady a few days hence." Mrs. O'Brien winked at Dani. "It seems to me ye be awalking along the same path."

Dani reddened at the look of pleasure she read on her elder's face. "I'm not sure I can compete with that kind of selfless generosity."

The housekeeper smiled. "Miss Danielle, 'tis not hard at all to share God's goodness with others when we take into account Christ's love for us—His life for ours."

Just after dusk the ladies arrived home, Dani's car filled to capacity with toys for the orphans. To their delight, they'd found everything the children had requested. The two women spent the rest of the evening wrapping the items, which would be taken to the orphanage to be packed in Santa's bag and remain out of sight until his scheduled arrival during the annual Christmas party. The Charity Club would host the event.

Close to midnight, they climbed to their respective rooms. Although weary from their excursion, their hearts overflowed with joy.

A few minutes past 3:00 a.m., Dani awoke to Lad's insistent barking. Grabbing her robe, she slipped into the hall, easing along the wall to the stairs. Creeping down one step at a time, Dani labored to hear the source of the dog's disturbance above her pounding heart.

Halfway down the stairs, Dani froze. A loud swish and thud waylaid her ears in between barks. A moment later, a hand touched Dani's shoulder, releasing a cry of alarm from her lips. She turned, her shoulders slumping forward in relief when she realized that it wasn't an intruder who stood on the step above, only Mrs. O'Brien.

"I'm sorry, Miss Danielle. I didn't intend to frighten ye," Mrs. O'Brien said softly. "What has upset me collie?"

"I...I think intruders. It sounded like they left through the back door."

In the dim light, Dani saw Mrs. O'Brien lift her head. "You're right. I smell tobacco smoke. We'd best call Sheriff Wilson."

At the bottom of the stairwell, Dani switched on the hall light, her eyes widening at the object in Mrs. O'Brien's hands. "Mrs. O'Brien, where did you get that rifle?"

"It belonged to Mr. Silas. When all this trouble started, I had Clive take it out of storage—thought it might come in handy sometime." Her eyes narrowed. "Ye never know when a coyote or jackal might come asnooping near the hall. I used to be a fair shot in me younger days, if I do say so meself."

Dani shuddered at the possibility of Mrs. O'Brien having to shoot an intruder.

At the gathering room entrance, she glanced at the housekeeper, her face contorted with confusion. "I don't remember closing Lad in here last night."

"I didn't shut the door either. It must have been the intruder."

Lad's barking ceased to a whimper at the sound of his mistress's voice. The collie rushed to their side when released from the room. Sniffing the floor, he trotted toward the dining room, the *click, click, click* of his toenails against the wooden floor sounding ominous in the early morning hours.

The ladies followed close behind the dog, Mrs. O'Brien raising the gun to a firing position. To their disappointment, Lad seemed to lose the scent. Abandoning his search near the china hutch, he returned to Mrs. O'Brien's side, his demeanor seeming apologetic. "'Tis all right, me pet. Ye did fine," the housekeeper cooed.

When they neared the kitchen door, they stopped short, their eyes fixed on the lock. They looked at each other, their faces revealing like expressions of awe. The deadbolt was still secure.

A silent question buzzed in the air like a bee swarming a hive. How had the intruder entered and departed the hall? Without wasting another moment, Mrs. O'Brien grabbed the phone and dialed the sheriff's number. The light of dawn on the horizon, Sheriff Wilson shook his head at Dani's quizzical look following his search of Stratford Hall. "Does anyone other than Mrs. O'Brien and Clive hold a key to the hall?"

Not for one second did the implication in her answer bypass Dani's thoughts. Swallowing a gasp, she met the sheriff's direct gaze. "Only Justin Harcourt, my lawyer. His father is executor of my estate. I wanted them to have accessibility to the hall in case of an emergency."

"I see."

Although he verbalized none of it, Dani detected the suspicion in the officer's eyes. Lying in bed later, she recalled a similar feeling the night she'd discovered that despicable knife lying on her bed. Justin had been at the hall that night. But she had thrust the thought aside, not believing him capable of the horrible act. Should she now consider the possibility? Sleep evaded her as seeds of doubt concerning Justin's innocence began to sprout and grow in her mind. Wincing, she recalled that he'd gone upstairs to refresh himself just before they'd left for Atlanta that night. Perhaps she should ask Clive to change all the locks in the house. But of course, as executors of the estate, Phillip and Justin would still need access to the house in case of an emergency. However, changing the locks might narrow the list of possible suspects. Deciding she would speak to Clive about the matter first thing tomorrow morning, Dani forced herself to relax, sleep overtaking her a short time later.

Late that morning, rejuvenated by several hours of sleep, Dani marveled that she'd allowed the sheriff's unspoken criminations to sway her trust in Justin. During their phone conversation that afternoon, he'd expressed genuine concern for her well-being following her account of the early morning occurrence. Again, he assured her that he would see to her protection, but when questioned as to how, he had become evasive, causing doubt to surface once more. She decided to do as Mrs. O'Brien had suggested: "Cast all your care on the Lord." However, Dani found it much easier to say than do.

Only two days till Christmas, "and all through the house...." Dani uttered as she glanced about the lower foyer just before she and Mrs. O'Brien walked out the door for their scheduled appearance at the orphanage. "It's a shame no one else will be here to enjoy these decorations," she said, eyeing the cedar boughs entwined along the banister.

A sudden wave of homesickness swept over Dani. Even the heavy aroma of pine saturating the crisp evening air added to her misery. She'd planned a trip to Hartford for the holidays, but Lucille had reported that she and Bill would spend Christmas out of town. Dani swept aside the urge to weep. It would be the first time the three of them hadn't celebrated the holiday together in years.

Inside the car, Mrs. O'Brien faced her mistress, her ruddy cheeks alive with excitement. "'Twill be a glorious site to see the young lasses and lads open their gifts. Their reactions will be enough to melt the heart of the nastiest Scrooge in town."

Dani brightened. "That *is* what it's all about, isn't it? Christmas, I mean. Everyone should experience the joy that giving brings to a soul."

"Agreed, and the Good News is that no one can ever out give God. The reward for His children's generosity is 'pressed down, shaken together, and running over' with their benevolence given back as 'some thirtyfold, some sixtyfold, and some a hundredfold,' according to the Gospel."

Her mood lightened, Dani hugged Mrs. O'Brien. "It pays in many ways to serve Christ—the initial peace and joy when we first accept Him as our Savior and then the additional promises we find in his Word. I'm glad I chose Him to be the Lord of my life. Just last night I read in the third Epistle of John that God's desire for His people is for them to be prosperous and healthy just as their soul is prospering."

Mrs. O'Brien nodded. "'Tis true. But some fail to realize the key to receiving those gifts is 'as the soul prospers.' We must first be willing to do as Matthew instructed, 'But seek first his kingdom and his righteousness, and all these things will be given to you as well.'"

Once they arrived at the orphanage, the children's gaiety soon infected the adults milling about the gathering, a trill of laughter from across the room surprising Dani when she realized the voice belonged to Mrs. Radcliffe. *Maybe there's hope for her after all*, Dani thought. Her smile vanished when she noted the somber expressions on twin boys about four years of age standing close together in a corner of the room, watching the other children. Wondering at their lack of participation, she made her way toward them.

Kneeling, she said, "Hi. I'm Dani. What are your names?"

They looked at her but didn't answer. She tried again. "Wouldn't you boys like to join the other children? Soon Santa Claus will arrive with candy and gifts for you."

One of the boys turned to her. "No, he won't," he said, his expression alternating between anger and sorrow.

Dani looked stunned. "Why, of course he will. He brings presents to all the boys and girls."

Tears began to stream down the other boy's face. "He didn't see our letters."

Dani pulled a tissue from the pocket of her trousers and wiped the boy's eyes. "Santa reads all his letters."

"Not ours. Mommy and Daddy died before they mailed them. I know, 'cause I saw them on the table before we came here. Grandpa is sick and can't keep us."

Dani hugged the boys, blinking to relieve the pressure behind her stinging eyelids. "I'm sorry you lost your mother and father."

"They're not lost. A drunk driver ran over their car, and they got killed," the first boy said, his eyes filling with tears. "The policeman said so."

A stab of empathy bolted through Dani. She glanced around the room and then grabbed a pen and notepad from a table nearby. "Maybe I can get a message to Santa Claus before he arrives here. But I have to let him know who you are." She looked from one twin to the other, waiting.

His face shadowed by wariness, the first boy stepped closer to Dani. "I'm Alex, and he's Andy." Andy gave her a shy smile.

"Good. Now, what would you like Santa to bring you?"

Dani recorded their wishes, whispering a thankful prayer in her heart that their requests were few. Giving them a quick hug, she motioned to Mrs. O'Brien. Leaving them in the housekeeper's care, Dani hurried from the room. Throwing reluctance aside, she sought the one person she felt could solve the problem. She located Mrs. Radcliffe in the kitchen arranging a tray of holiday treats.

Dani explained the situation to Evansville's First Lady of Charity. She examined the list and then asked Dani to point out the twins. When they entered the living room, Dani smiled, thankful that Mrs. O'Brien had persuaded the boys to join the other children.

After a moment of observing their activities, Helen turned a friendly smile upon Dani, startling her. "I know just the merchant to phone. He won't like opening his store at this hour, but the old buzzard owes me a favor," Mrs. Radcliffe said, clutching Dani's arm. "Make sure Santa doesn't appear until I return."

Dani nodded, staring after the woman in astonishment.

Dani's most rewarding moment of the evening came when she watched the twins' eyes light up with both amazement and happiness as they opened their gifts. Lifting her eyes, Dani spied a wrinkled, half-hidden handkerchief in Mrs. Radcliffe's hand, the frequent, discreet dabs at the corners of her eyes a pleasure to witness.

Their eyes met and held a moment before they each turned their gaze toward Alex and Andy. *Were they common ground on which she could begin a friendship with Mrs. Radcliffe?* Dani wondered.

Noting Dani's glance, Mrs. O'Brien leaned forward. "Fred told me they arrived this morning. Their only relation, a grandfather, is dying with cancer. 'Tis a shame about their folks."

"Yes. I wish I could do more to ease the pain I understand so well."

Dani watched Mrs. Radcliffe's interaction with the boys throughout the evening. Just before their departure from the party, Dani faced the housekeeper, eyes twinkling with inspiration. "Excuse me. I need to discuss something with Mr. Coons."

Late in the afternoon on Christmas Eve, Dani paced back and forth across the kitchen floor, peering over Mrs. O'Brien's shoulder more than once, seeming unaffected by the sights and smells of the approaching traditional dinner.

Mrs. O'Brien laughed. "Land sakes, lass. Ye're as nervous as a cat about to spawn her first litter of kittens."

With a sigh, Dani popped a piece of peanut brittle into her mouth. When she'd swallowed the tasty morsel, she said, "I must be insane! My only excuse is the anguish I read in Mrs. Radcliffe's eyes at her marked interest in Alex and Andy during the party. But her readiness to accept our spur-of-the-moment invitation may just mean success for our conspiracy." Dani glanced at the clock on the stove. "What time did the matron at the orphanage say she'd bring the boys?"

"Any minute now. Don't worry, lass. The good Lord will work out what's best for all concerned. We just have to rely on his judgment."

At that moment, the various bowls and platters scattered about the kitchen seemed to draw Dani's attention. "How shall we ever consume all this food?"

A sly look framed the housekeeper's features. "'Tis my guess none of it will go to waste."

The ringing door chimes forestalled Dani's questioning response. Expecting the twins' arrival, she quickened her steps to the entry-way, her arms ready to encircle them with a welcoming embrace. Throwing open the door, Dani's cheerful greeting froze on her lips, the shock of the callers' identity leaving her breathless.

# YULETIDE BLISS

Dani found her voice at last. "Aunt Lucille, Uncle Bill, Valerie! Oh my goodness. How wonderful!" Dani's gaze drifted to the man beside her best friend, the happiness aglow on Dani's face changing to frightened concern. "Is something wrong?"

Lucille stepped inside, moving into Dani's arms. "Of course not, darling. We just wanted to surprise you."

"Yes," Valerie said, giving Dani a tight squeeze. Momentarily, she faced the man at her side. I brought along my fiancé. I hope you don't mind."

Dani's mouth opened in surprise and then widened in a smile. "Mind? I should say not. Welcome to my home, Lieutenant Masterson. Please come in." Dani took hold of Bill's hand, pulling him inside. The others followed.

Lucille wrapped her arm around Dani's shoulder. "It's so good to see you. We just couldn't stand the thought of spending Christmas without you."

Dani looked at her guests, her eyes overflowing with tears. "Neither could I." Sniffling, she took their wraps and then ushered them into the gathering room where Mrs. O'Brien stood waiting, her eyes twinkling with mischief. Observing the look, Dani pretended to scold the housekeeper. "Now I know why you cooked all that food. You knew they were coming and didn't tell me. Shame on you, Mrs. O'Brien."

"Now, lass, you wouldn't have wanted me to spoil the surprise, would ye?"

Before Dani could answer, the doorbell rang again, Mrs. O'Brien bringing the twins, Alex and Andy, to meet the newcomers a few minutes later. Once the housekeeper had settled the guests on the second floor of the hall, they returned a short while later to catch Dani up on all the news from home while Mrs. O'Brien put the finishing touches on the evening meal. The twins, in the meantime, enjoyed playing near the adults with the toys Dani had purchased for the occasion.

Late that night, just before the party retired to their rooms, Dani gave her friends a tour of the hall, soon afterward tucking the twins into their bed. Entering the quietness of her room, she padded to the window to observe the brilliance of the stars shining forth in the midst of the cold, Southern night. Although aware of the slight draft seeping through the panes, it couldn't penetrate the warmth in her heart. "Thank you, God, for this special gift," she whispered to the sky. What more could one ask for than precious friends to help celebrate the joys of Christmas?

Wrapping her arms about herself, she swirled about the room as giddy as any child on Christmas Eve. Whisking on her nightclothes a few moments later, Dani hurried across the hall to her sitting room to await the earlier planned late night chat with Valerie.

"My word, Dani," Valerie said, breezing into the room. "I can hardly believe this place. What do you do all day long—wander from room to room?"

Dani laughed. "Sometimes. However, I do manage to find ways to keep busy. You know about most of them from our telephone conversations."

"Yes, as well as the not so pleasant events. Any news on the identity of your recent late night caller?"

Dani sighed, the thought of that experience dampening her spirits. "No. The sheriff still believes the intruder used a key to enter the hall. Unless I'm to suspect Justin or his father, the theory isn't plausible."

"By the way, Dani, you haven't said a word about Justin all evening. I just assumed he'd arrive at some point."

Dani stood to stir the coals in the fireplace and then placed more wood on the fire, not daring to look at her friend. "I'm sure he had family obligations this evening," she said in the cheeriest tone she could muster. Silence hung in the air for a brief moment before she continued. "What about you? Have you and Charles set a date for your wedding?"

"Yes. We've planned a small wedding for this summer at the beginning of his vacation. You will be my maid of honor, won't you?"

Dani smiled. "I'd love to."

A grin nipped at the corners of Valerie's lips. "Any marriage plans in the making for you and Justin?"

Pretending to stifle a yawn, Dani lowered her eyes. "Our relationship hasn't progressed that far. Nor will it ever if certain misgivings aren't laid to rest."

Valerie leaned closer to Dani, her eyebrows raised. "Such as?"

Dani rose from the sofa and stood by the small, dated secretary nearby. "I know it sounds crazy, but it haunts me day and night like a playful pup chasing an elusive rabbit."

"For heaven's sake, Dani, whatever are you talking about?"

"Just this nagging suspicion that Justin might be involved with Davenport."

Valerie looked horrified. "I can't imagine it! What reason do you have to suspect him?"

"When thinking about all that's happened since I first heard of Stratford Hall, there've been several instances when Justin could have engineered the event or taken part in them. I believe the sheriff is concerned about him as well. I've tried to think otherwise, but circumstantial evidence keeps pointing to him."

Dani returned to position herself beside her friend. At the astonished look on Valerie's face, Dani spoke the thoughts she'd previously refused to acknowledge. "He even fits the description of Davenport's accomplice seen after I was attacked."

"Have you confronted Justin about your suspicions?"

"No way. What if I were wrong?"

"It's hard to believe that Justin could be involved in a murder plot. As a successful attorney, what could he possibly want with Stratford Hall?"

"I've asked myself the same thing more than once."

Her eyes full of compassion, Valerie took hold of Dani's hand. "Something else is wrong, isn't there?"

Dani crumpled against the sofa. "You don't know the half of it."

Entering the gathering room the next morning, Dani heard a childish shriek of delight behind her, the sound dislodging the gloominess she'd incurred during her conversation with Valerie the night before. Alex and Andy hurled themselves into the room to land on their knees beneath the Christmas tree. "Can we open our presents now? *Please!*" they said in unison.

Dropping to the floor beside them, Dani enclosed them in her arms. "Not yet. We need to wait until the others are awake."

A sly grin broke over Alex's face. "Andy and I could go knock on their bedroom doors."

Dani laughed. "I don't think that's a good idea. Instead you can help Mrs. O'Brien and I make them something scrumptious for breakfast. What do you say to that?"

Eyeing their downcast expressions, Dani ruffled the boys' hair. "It won't be that long before we open the gifts, I promise." Dani led her young charges to the kitchen, where Mrs. O'Brien quickly put all three of them to work.

Just past midmorning, the guests, having given the breakfast "staff" their due for the delicious meal, congregated in the gathering room to the delight of the twins. Soon the air was filled with the crackle of crumpling paper and other sounds of holiday cheer.

Late that afternoon, while Mrs. O'Brien added the final touches to the Christmas meal, the doorbell rang. Dani introduced the new arrival, Mrs. Helen Radcliffe, to her friends. At first she seemed reserved, but soon Mrs. Radcliffe begin to respond to the warm, hospitable atmosphere within the walls of Stratford Hall, her pleasure with the twins' antics a source of encouragement for Dani and Mrs. O'Brien.

"Maybe the woman isn't such a hard nut to crack after all," Mrs. O'Brien whispered to Dani in between bites of sweet potato pie following their delicious Christmas fare. Dani sniggered, grabbing her napkin to smother a gale of laughter.

Bill leaned back in his chair, patting his stomach. "Dani, you'd better keep a close watch on Mrs. O'Brien, or I might steal her away from you. I can't see the harm in a king housing more than one splendid chef in his castle." Lucille smacked her husband on his tummy, causing him to groan. "Some women are just too narrow-minded," he said, grinning amidst the laughter of the others.

Early that evening, as Dani and her company prepared to depart for Pleasant Valley Church, she hurried to answer the door while the housekeeper retrieved their coats. Dani swallowed her surprise and then allowed the caller to enter the foyer. "Hel... hello."

"Hi. I hope you don't mind the intrusion. I...uh..." Justin handed her a small gaily wrapped box. "Merry Christmas, Dani."

She took the gift from his fingers, the lump in her throat constricting the words of gratitude forming on her lips. "Thank you." She took him by the arm. "Please come in and greet my friends. We're about to leave for the candlelight service at church. Would you like to join us?"

He paused in their stride to the gathering room. Dani held her breath, praying. Justin turned to gaze into her questioning eyes. "For you, I will."

Once seated inside the church, Dani gave Justin a sidelong glance, the look on his face so like her own in times past when she'd sat in church with the Pendergraffs, trying to gracefully shade her boredom. She marveled at the difference in her life now. The Christmas drama she now observed, so artfully portrayed by members of the congregation, had once meant no more to her than a fairy tale.

During the candlelight service, she sneaked a peek at Valerie and Lieutenant Masterson. They too looked uncomfortable in their surroundings. *Oh, God*, she prayed within, *please let all of them come to realize their need for a personal relationship with Your Son. How blessed they would be.*

Later, back at the hall, Mrs. O'Brien served them wassail and a tray of holiday treats fit for a king. Her labors weren't in vain. Not a morsel remained on the antique silver tray when everyone except Dani and Justin climbed the stairs close to midnight.

Alone with Justin, a sense of awkwardness came over Dani, similar to what a teenage girl might feel on her first date. To screen her nervousness, she offered him another cup of cider.

"No thanks." He watched her fiddle with an ornament on the Christmas tree and then patted the sofa cushion beside him. "Dani, please sit down. You don't have anything to fear from me. I need to talk to you. It's important."

Dani turned. Sensing the urgency in his voice, she obeyed his request. "Yes, Justin, what is it?"

"We have a report from the detective agency we hired to locate Rosemary Davidson's daughter, Emily."

Dani held her breath. Was this the beginning of the end to the grisly existence she'd known since she first heard of Mathilda Thorndike? "What did they find?"

Justin looked away from the expectation he read in her eyes. "The woman is wasting away in a mental institution near San Francisco.

Dani's shoulders slumped forward, her vision blurring. "I thought we'd finally reached the climax of this ghastly tale I'm living."

Justin traced his forefinger along the side of her cheekbone. "Don't give up yet. The agency hasn't. We have Rosemary's grandchildren to consider."

Dani raised her head to search Justin's face, a glimmer of renewed hope settling in her moist eyes. "Grandchildren?"

"Yes. Emily had a son by her husband, Antonio Davitello. They named him Julian."

Dani's eyes widened, the wind of understanding blowing the clouds of disappointment away from her face. "Justin! Do you realize what this means?"

She watched the corners of his mouth curve into a knowing grin. "That Julian Davitello could be our own Jules Davenport?"

"Exactly." Dani jumped up from the sofa and faced Justin, her hands on her cheeks. "A break at last. Thank God!"

"When my detective friend gave this information to Hagerman, the sergeant ran Julian's name through NCICC." Justin noted the blank look on her face. "The National Crime Information Center Computer to see if he had a criminal record. And he does."

Dani repositioned herself on the sofa, a facetious glint in her eyes. "Now, why am I not surprised about that?"

Justin grinned and then continued. "Julian was released by mistake a few months ago from an institution for the criminally insane. The man has a genetic mental instability, which caused outbreaks of violent behavior all his life. A judge ordered him institutionalized after he killed a college dorm buddy following an argument with him over a part in a college little theater drama. At his trial he pleaded not guilty by reason of insanity, thus his commitment to the asylum."

Dani pondered Justin's words, a moment later turning a thoughtful gaze upon his face. "I just remembered. You said grandchildren."

Justin nodded his head. "That's another story in itself."

She smiled. "I'm game. Let's hear it."

"When Julian was eight or nine, his father traveled to France to familiarize himself with the methods used in producing a strain of wine new to the market. While in the country, Emily developed an *affaire de coeur* for another man, becoming pregnant with his child. Upon his return to California, Davitello discovered his wife's indiscretion and divorced her but maintained custody of young Julian, Emily receiving only visitation rights to the child."

"What happened to Emily?"

"She moved to San Francisco, where she raised her illegitimate son. A former neighbor revealed that Mrs. Davitello was a real antisocial type, never leaving her apartment for weeks at a time. However, the neighbor did notice that a gentleman visited on occasion but never knew his name. When her son moved back East to go to college, Emily moved away from the apartment complex and became lost in the concrete jungle. The circumstances that accounted for her presence in the mental institution are anybody's guess."

"Did the detective learn the name of her son?"

"No. The neighbor couldn't recall it, claimed she rarely saw the boy or his mother."

"Do you think Julian's half-brother could be the one who attacked me in Hartford?"

"We have nothing to support the idea. However, we'll keep searching until we get the right answers." Leaning close to Dani, he covered her slender fingers with his hand. "Dani, I've missed you." Without another word, he took her into his arms.

Dani closed her eyes, her body responding to his touch, betraying her strength of mind to remain aloof. When his lips became more demanding, she withdrew from his hold. "Justin, it's really late. My friends' flight leaves before noon, and I want to be up early to give them a proper sendoff. But before you go, I have something for you." Dani left the room, returning moments later with a Christmas gift in her hands.

When Justin had finished admiring his cashmere sweater and gold cuff links, he stood, Dani walking him to the door. "Thank you again for this lovely necklace. I shall wear it often." She touched the emerald and diamond pendant that Justin had clasped around her neck just before they'd left for the church.

Justin linked his finger through the gold chain. "When I saw the emerald, it reminded me of the color of your eyes, although no jewel can compare to the loveliness of you. Good night, sweet Dani. We'll talk soon."

A knock on her bedroom door early the next morning roused Dani from a deep sleep. Valerie slipped into the room. "I'm sorry, Dani, but I wanted a few minutes alone with you before everyone gets out of bed."

Dani yawned. "Sure. Is anything wrong?"

Valerie shook her head. "No." She looked doubtful as though unsure of how to proceed. "I've been sort of watching you the last couple of days...I mean...there's something different about you. You seem so calm considering the trauma you're experiencing, and your face has a certain glow about it. Does it have something to do with religion? I noticed how much you enjoyed the church service last night."

Dani pulled herself up from the bed to rest on her elbow and smiled. "Yes. There's been a wonderful change in my life, but, no, it doesn't have a thing to do with religion. However, it has *everything* to do with the reason we celebrate the joy of Christmas, the birth of my Savior. I've been born again."

"I see. Lucille talked about the plan of salvation while we sat together in the emergency room at the hospital waiting for you to regain consciousness. But you know I've never given much thought to spiritual things." Valerie traced the pattern of the quilt atop Dani's bed. "But after witnessing the peace I see in you, despite all you've been through lately, I think I might give them more consideration. Life has always been pretty much okay for me, but I've always felt that something was missing inside me. For all my inward searching,

I've failed to distinguish what that something is or how to attain it…" Valerie looked over at Dani's bedside clock. "Oh, my. If I don't get a move on, I'll cause us all to miss our plane."

At that moment, Dani's alarm began to ring, startling them both. Dani hugged her friend. "I tell you what. I'll mention your interest to Aunt Lucille and tell her to give you a call. She can explain it better than I can anyway. Christian living is still new to me, but it's a wonderful experience of love, joy, and peace available to anyone. Val, all you have to do is believe that Christ loves you and be willing to accept his gift of eternal life, beginning the moment you take Him as your personal Savior and Lord. Should you choose to accept His freely given gift of salvation, I believe you'll discover, as I did, He is that something you are missing in your life."

Valerie grew thoughtful. "Maybe…Thanks, Dani. I promise I'll think about it." She smiled. "And I'll expect a call from Mrs. Pendergraff soon.

Dani sat up alongside her friend, laughing. "If I know Aunt Lucille, she'll get right on it once you're home and settled. Thanks for coming, Val. I wish the best for you and Charles."

"Thanks. The same goes for you and Justin."

After Valerie had gone from the room, Dani lay for a few minutes, mulling over her relationship with Justin. Would they find the same happiness witnessed in Valerie and Charles? *Oh, Justin, if only you'd give your heart and life to God. Then I could love you without reservation. But what about the growing suspicion regarding his involvement in the crime against her?* Dani shoved the thought to the back of her mind. With the information he'd provided the evening before, how could he be involved? She struggled with the sense of wariness beleaguering her. Sighing, Dani threw back the covers. She didn't have time to figure it out now.

Later that morning, Dani stood on the porch, waving good-bye to her friends, promising to visit them in the spring. When she could no longer see their rental car, she walked inside, determined to help Mrs.

O'Brien restore the hall to order. Although Mrs. O'Brien had tried to disguise it behind a cheery smile, Dani had seen the lines of weariness on the older woman's face when she'd served them breakfast. However, their plan to give Mrs. Radcliffe more time with the twins had blossomed. Offering to return the boys to the children's home, Mrs. Radcliffe had mentioned she might plan some weekend outings with them for the near future. Dani smiled. The boys had been delighted by her unique way of telling stories. Dani could hardly wait to see if part two of their plan unfurled in the coming weeks.

The hall spiffy by late that afternoon, Dani helped the housekeeper prepare a light dinner. The kitchen duties performed, they adjourned to the gathering room to relax before bedtime. Lad and Percy, following in their footsteps, joined the ladies, curling up on their favorite spot near the hearth.

Once settled on the sofa, Dani picked up the afghan Mrs. O'Brien had been teaching her to crochet, handing it over to the housekeeper for further instruction.

"Now this is the way to bind off the edge of your work," Mrs. O'Brien said, slowing her nimble fingers so that her mistress could learn the necessary stitch.

At that instant, the collie raised his head, a low growl in his throat. Dani and Mrs. O'Brien turned to stare at the dog, Mrs. O'Brien reaching for the .30–30 rifle near the couch.

"I wouldn't do that if I were you, old woman."

Uttering a loud cry, Dani jumped to her feet, the sight in the doorway yanking the retort from her lips.

# THE FLIGHT

*J*ules Davenport crept forward like a determined, deadly reptile inching toward its victim. Eyeing the steel blue pistol in his hand, stark-naked fear seized Dani, rendering her speechless. She gulped for air. *Dear God, don't let me faint.* She tried to move, but her feet seemed bolted to the floor. Dani gritted her teeth, the canine's ferocious barking pounding in her ears like a relentless drumbeat. Wary of the dog's intention, she glanced at their invader. *If Lad lunges at Davenport,* she thought, *the dog will surely be killed.* As if reading her mind, the man aimed the gun at the collie.

"No!" Mrs. O'Brien yelled, shielding Lad with her body.

"Then keep the mangy cur quiet."

While Mrs. O'Brien silenced her pet, Davenport fixed his gaze on Dani. "Now, pretty lady, you and I are going to take a little stroll. There's someone anxious to see you."

Dani started to utter a refusal, but the murderous gleam in Davenport's eyes stripped the words from her lips. She felt blood drain from her face. A silent plea for help nestled in her eyes; she glanced toward the housekeeper, who stood next to Lad, toying with the afghan she'd held throughout the ordeal.

Davenport followed Dani's gaze, snarling. "Maybe you'd better figure on joining our little party, old woman. Shall we go, ladies? Let's find out what Santa has left over for a little girl that wasn't so good this year."

"Wait," Dani shouted, her fear for Mrs. O'Brien's safety liberating her vocal cords. "Please. Don't harm Mrs. O'Brien. She's no threat to you." Dani's heartbeat gathered momentum as she waited for Davenport's response.

He studied the housekeeper with dark, foreboding eyes. "I suppose the old baggage would slow us down."

Mrs. O'Brien bristled with rage, the look in her narrowed eyes sizzling like a Fourth of July sparkler. Lad, sensing the heightened tension, growled. Fresh alarm spread through Dani. "Mrs. O'Brien, don't—"

Dani's warning unheeded, the housekeeper took a step forward. "Old baggage, ye say. 'Tis ye that be the garbage to be disposed of in this house."

Before Davenport could react, Mrs. O'Brien slammed into him, stuffing the afghan into his face. He plummeted to the floor, his gun falling beside him. Regaining her balance, Mrs. O'Brien booted the pistol across the carpet, blaring, "Run, me lass, run."

Dani gaped at her friend and then Davenport. Any second now his struggle to disentangle himself from the throes of the blanket and Mrs. O'Brien's hands—which slapped and pushed till the intruder was as far away from Dani as possible—would be history. Again, Mrs. O'Brien shouted. "Go, lass. Go!"

A force she couldn't explain compelling her forward, Dani bolted through the door, turning in the direction of the veranda. Precious seconds were wasted while she fumbled with the lock, the patio doors at last swinging free. At that instant, Davenport's voice reverberated through the air. "Hold it, lady!"

Ignoring his command, Dani scuttled into the garden, choosing the cobblestone path that led to the south lawn, hoping the dense foliage would shield her. She streaked across the yard, the image of the trail she'd desired to explore foremost in her mind. If she could make it to the woods, then maybe she'd be safe.

Voices from the rear bellowed at her to stop, ear-splitting footsteps droning in her ears. Dani lowered her head and ran with all her might, her lungs burning in her chest. Just before the trees closed in around her, a sound like the crack of a whip penetrated the night. Seconds later, acute pain surged through her left shoulder. She stumbled, breaking her stride. Dear God! She'd been shot!

Righting herself, Dani fled into the timber. Ribbons of moonlight floating among the trees guided her way. Her perpetrators' footsteps growing louder, she swerved off the trail, cutting into the thicket, slapping at the low-hanging branches and underbrush that scratched her face and caught at her clothing. A few minutes later, breathless and wracked with pain, she collapsed against the base of a huge oak. A moment later, the sound of angry voices drew near. Frantic, she scrunched closer to the ground.

"I know I hit your lady friend," Davenport said. "She's got to be here somewhere."

"Jules, you idiot! I told you no gunplay yet. We were to get rid of her in the cave, remember? The body would rot before anyone found it there."

Dani shuddered. They'd intended to kill her all along. Suddenly her head begin to spin. No! No! She couldn't pass out now. She had to hear what they had to say. The sound of crackling leaves and snapping twigs grew louder. She held her breath.

Davenport laughed. "Maybe she's dead already. As next of kin, we can claim Grandmother Davidson's inheritance. I bet the Thorndike fortune is worth a bundle."

Dani fought against the ringing in her ears. *Lady friend. Oh, God, Justin. It can't be you.* The stranger's voice began to sound far away.

"The initial plan, dear brother, was for her to disappear, never to be heard from again. Then in a few months I would claim the estate. No one would suspect me. But now, you trigger happy fool, we'll have to redesign our strategy. If a search party finds the body, we'll know soon. The news will travel like a roadrunner. Hey, listen! That's a police siren, and it's headed in our direction. Let's get out of here."

Dani shook her head to clear the mist swirling in her brain. Justin. Davenport's brother? It didn't make sense. Dani's teeth began to chatter as the frigid night air settled on her. But the voice … so familiar … she couldn't think about that now. She had to return to the hall. *Please let Mrs. O'Brien be safe.* Dani reached upward, immediately drawing her hand away from the sticky mass coagulating on her sweater. Nausea rose to her throat as the odor of blood invaded her sense of smell. The sound of disturbed brush nearby rallied her consciousness. She slowly raised her head. A tall, robust figure loomed above her momentarily and then crouched beside her. Her next thought too heavy to bear, she slumped against him, obscurity enveloping her senses.

Dani thrashed about the dark hole, fire nipping at her heels. She had to flee the cave or be burned alive. She rushed toward the opening of a tunnel just ahead, but a noise from behind broke her pace. She threw a glance over her shoulder, her worst fear emerging from the midst of the deafening blaze—Jules Davenport and his faceless brother, their bodies human infernos. She sought to increase her speed, but all of a sudden her legs refused to cooperate. She looked down. Her lower limbs were melting before her eyes. At that moment they grabbed Dani, their torched arms singing her flesh. Demented laughter ricocheted in her ears like rebounding bullets in a boxed canyon.

With a start, Dani awoke. Her erratic heartbeat quelled upon realization she'd roused from a nightmare, only to discover, after a quick look around, that the daylight might hold a reverie more chilling than her horrendous dream. Recalling the previous hours, however, she concluded that no delusion, day or night, could compare with the reality of her narrow escape from death.

The smell of frying bacon filled her nostrils. Desiring to become more acquainted with her ambiguous surroundings, she attempted a sitting position but fell back against the pillows, the throbbing in her shoulder too excruciating to complete the task. A sense of doom washed over her. Her efforts to hide from her assailants had been in vain. Why had they let her live?

Dani surveyed the room bordered by log walls. She lay on an old brass bed, handmade quilts keeping her warm. A single hurricane lamp decorated the crude bedside table on her right, while a cane rocking chair occupied the opposite side of her bed, silently awaiting its next occupant. Homespun curtains adorned the only window, the pane covered by weighty black fabric. An old dresser near the entrance to the room completed the furnishings.

To her left an open door revealed a rustic bathroom. She locked her eyes on the closed entrance separating her from Davenport and his brother. *How long will it be before they comprehend I'm awake?* Dani thought. She gasped as the door swayed inward at that moment.

"Not you!" Panic-stricken, she observed Blake Spencer's approach to her bedside. She cowered from his touch when he placed his hand on her forehead.

"Good. You're much cooler now." He sat down on the edge of the bed and smiled. "Please, Miss McKinnon, don't be afraid. I won't hurt you. I'll bet you're feeling plenty hungry about now. I put more bacon into the skillet when I heard your movements.

Dani recoiled from his fingers when he pulled back the covers to check her bandages. She almost choked on her next breath, her face roaring with color. She had on a man's shirt!

Blake seemed to sense her chagrin. "Sorry about the sweater. You lost a lot of blood. You're a lucky girl. If the bullet had struck an inch lower..." Blake pulled a long, deep breath. "But your fever has broken; that's good news." He wrung out a cloth from a pan of water atop the nightstand and washed the perspiration from her brow.

Still wary, Dani stared at him, her eyes full of questions. "Is Mrs. O'Brien okay? Where am I? How did I get here? I thought ... I ... Are you Davenport's half-brother?"

Blake chuckled deep in his throat. "No, thank goodness. And your housekeeper is fine. I guess I'd better explain things.

"I'm a private investigator. I'd just completed an assignment in New York the night Justin flew to Albany to ask my assistance in solving your situation. He thought he could wring a yes out of me faster in person than by phone. And I quote, 'The case means a lot to me.' Knowing Justin, it didn't take long for me to understand his motivation." Blake smiled. "You're a beautiful woman. I knew your identity already, having had three previous encounters with you." He grinned as confusion lined her brow, seemingly understanding her thought that she knew of only two incidences of which he spoke. "I'm the detective Justin's father employed to locate your whereabouts."

Dani's face brightened with perception. "Uh." She lifted her hand to point at him. "The cowboy in the Pendergraff parking lot the afternoon Lance and I quarreled."

He chuckled and then nodded. "Yep. I'm the guilty one. And all this time I thought you hadn't noticed me. Yes, I'd planned to introduce myself that day but decided a more appropriate moment might be in order. And too, I knew Mr. Harcourt had written to inform you of your inheritance. You'd soon know about it anyway."

Dani winced, remembering the public spectacle Lance had subjected her to that day. "As a matter of fact, I received the notice when I arrived home that afternoon."

A look of compassion materialized on Blake's face. "To continue, I was in Justin's hotel room when his father phoned about the assault." Blake grinned. "Desperate conditions call for desperate measures." He shrugged his shoulders at the look of chastisement on her face. "So I took the assignment." His expression sobered. "Justin and I flew to Hartford the next day."

Relief flooded Dani's mind. Justin wasn't the one who'd attacked her. She searched Blake's face. He could be lying. No. She determined after a moment. Too much honesty dwelled in those deep-set, warm brown eyes. Listening to his Southwestern drawl, her apprehension subsided. She didn't have to be afraid of this man.

Blake studied his patient for a short time and then continued the conversation. "I got my first look at Davenport in the rest area the morning you arrived in Georgia."

Dani felt coldness on the back of her neck. A shiver skittered up her spine at the memory of his switchblade only inches from her heart. "I'll never forget that day."

Blake nodded and then placed the quilt higher on her shoulders. "Justin and I agreed that an incognito approach would be the best way to handle your case. It would put me in a better position to discover the identity of the culprits, plus keep an eye on you at the same time. But I have to say they're a slippery pair. I can't for the life of me determine how they've obtained entrance to the hall all this time. But I will eventually."

Blake sniffed the air. "That would be the biscuits. I hope you like sausage gravy."

Dani placed her hand on his arm to stop him before he rose from her side. "But wait. Where am I?"

He stood up, smiling. "Let's get some food into you first; then we'll talk." Soon he returned carrying a tray of steaming food in his hands.

A few minutes later, Dani handed the dishes back to Blake. "I'm sorry. The food is great. I just couldn't eat more than a few bites."

Blake nodded his understanding and then aided her maneuvers to arrange a more comfortable position. Watching his movements, she marveled that a man with such large hands could be so gentle.

Checking the time on his watch, Blake took a prescription bottle from the nightstand. Shaking a couple of tablets from the container, he handed them to Dani, along with the glass of orange juice from her breakfast tray. "Take these. You'll feel better in a few minutes." He picked up the tray. "While I take care of this, you get some rest."

Dani yawned. "But you haven't told me where I am."

"I will. I promise."

When Dani awoke hours later, Blake sat in the rocking chair, a book in his lap. He gave her a crooked smile. "Welcome back."

She did her best to look cheerful. "Thanks." She looked around the room and then sent a penetrating glance his way. "Now will you tell me where we are?"

"We're in a hunting cabin in the southeast corner of your property. Mrs. O'Brien suggested—"

Dani looked stunned. "My housekeeper knows about you?"

"'Fraid so. She said this place would be perfect for my headquarters. And rightly so. Located in a well-concealed ravine, it's a virtual fort. The rock wall just beyond the stream behind the cabin stands at least a hundred feet high. The other three sides are corralled by heavy timber. And the beginning of the path that leads to the cabin is secluded behind some large rocks near an old logging road that runs through the backside of the estate. Nevertheless, I keep the windows covered so that anyone snooping around at night won't spot the cabin from afar by way of the lights."

Dani gazed at him in wonderment. "When I get home, remind me to give my sly Irish friend an Academy Award."

Blake smiled at her glum expression. "Aw, don't be too hard on her. Like me, she has your best interest at heart."

Something in the tone of his voice caused Dani to give him her full consideration. His eyes revealed that theirs could be more than a mere guardian-client relationship.

Suddenly she felt as though she'd swallowed a bowl of butterflies, similar to the experience she'd had the morning he'd rescued her sweater from the hotel restaurant.

What was happening to her? Turning away from his face, she observed her bandaged shoulder. "Did Doctor Bedford take care of my wound?"

"No, I did."

She looked aghast. "Are you saying you have medical training?"

"No, just some experience. Working in South America a few years back, I learned quickly how to take care of a person who'd been gunshot. In my business it pays to be prepared, so I carry medical supplies wherever I go on assignment. By the way, I talked to Doctor Bedford while you were napping and told him all I'd done and"—Blake threw her a sideways grin—"he assures me that you are in good hands."

Weak as she was, she couldn't resist his charm. "Well, I'm glad to know that," she said, her lips curving upward. She studied his broad shoulders. "I'm assuming it was you who found me last night just before I blacked out. How did I get here?"

Blake leaned forward and fastened his hand on his back, groaning. "I carried you every step of the way."

Dani laughed when she detected the teasing glint in his eyes. "I see. How did you find me?"

"I was on the far side of the trail leading to the hall when I heard a gunshot. Believing the sound came from the south lawn of the estate, I made my way up the trail as quiet and fast as I could. Gaining ground, I heard the voices of two men, but before I could get close enough to hear their words, they scampered out of the woods.

"I'd started toward the hall to see if you and Mrs. O'Brien were okay when a movement near a huge old oak tree caught my eye. I crept toward the spot, the moonlight just bright enough to recognize you." Blake lifted a strand of Dani's hair. "Your hair shone like silver threads." Blake seemed taken aback for a moment and then continued. "I smelled blood and knew you'd been hit. After finding the location of the wound, I decided the cabin would be the safest place for you to hide."

She sent a look of appreciation his way. "I'd probably be dead if you hadn't stumbled onto my hiding place."

He nodded. "Close to it anyway. Oh, I forgot. The sheriff would like to speak with you when you're up to it."

Dani yawned. "Yes, I will. Later."

Blake glanced at his watch and then stretched. "Guess I'd better mosey out to the old chuck wagon. We don't want you to starve to death. I'll cook up something while you nap. Then I'll phone the sheriff after you've eaten."

Dani watched his slow gait as he crossed the room, his well-proportioned muscular frame no less than to be admired. Curious, she glanced at the book he'd been reading when she awakened, her eyes widening in surprise. An open Bible lay on the floor beside the chair.

# CABIN FEVER

*B*lake entered Dani's room the next day, a smile on his lips. "Well, Sleeping Beauty, did you plan to sleep until the handsome prince came to rouse you from your slumber?"

Dani returned his smile. "I'm afraid the prince would take one look at me and move on to the next castle," she said, her glance teetering toward his mouth and then sliding away. A kiss from those sensual lips would certainly qualify him for the role of the male lead. *Now, what generated that thought?* A disgruntled sigh escaped her lips.

Blake frowned. "Is something wrong, Miss McKinnon?"

"I ... no ... uh ... since we're going to have to spend several days in these close quarters, don't you think we could be on a first-name basis? Most people call me Dani."

He smiled. "Excellent idea."

"Whatever you say, Blake," she replied, grinning.

She eyed the tray of bandages and other medical paraphernalia he carried in his hands, a pink tint shading her features. He set the tray down on the table, his eyes glittering with mirth.

"Your days of commanding your kingdom from your throne are over. Today I have enrolled you in Gunshot Recovery Therapy 101, education in bandage changing for openers, and then a short hike to the next room for our lesson tomorrow."

Dani looked away, her face flaming. When he pulled back the quilt, she sneaked a glance at his countenance, thankful that he seemed geared to tackle his task in a professional manner.

"Well, that does it for now," he said some minutes later, applying a last piece of tape to her shoulder. A twinkle appeared in his eyes. "I think you'll be an exceptional student with time."

"Thank you, Professor Spencer. It's good to know you have such confidence in my ability."

Blake tilted his head to one side. "Now let's not get snooty, Miss McKinnon, or I might be tempted to forget about your surprise."

Dani eyed him warily. "What are you talking about?"

He turned toward the bedroom door. "You can come in now." Mrs. O'Brien and Clive Morgan popped into the room with bathing supplies and fresh linen, Clive toting a box that contained several pairs of pajamas, a robe, and Dani's favorite toiletries.

Dani gave the housekeeper her brightest smile. "Oh, Mrs. O'Brien, I'm so glad to see you. I was afraid Davenport would go back to the hall and hurt you, even kill you." Dani shuddered.

Mrs. O'Brien dropped her load onto the bottom of the bed. "No, lass. I called the sheriff as soon as that barbarian left the house. By the time Bobby and his deputies arrived, no trace of ye or them shameless cutthroats could be found. We tried to contact Mr. Blake at the cabin, but no answer. I about wore me vocal cords out praying for your safety. I didn't know ye'd been shot until Mr. Blake phoned sometime after midnight informing me of your circumstances."

"I heard the phone, but I was tending to Miss McKinnon's injury at the time and couldn't take the call," Blake said to Mrs. O'Brien. "When I talked to Sheriff Wilson later on, he assured me they're doing everything possible to apprehend those characters."

Dani turned to the gardener. "And you, Clive, are you watching out for Mrs. O'Brien?"

"Shore nuff, Miss Danielle. Me or my older boys are nearby night and day. But I've been most worried 'bout you." He smiled. "But Miz Annie tells me you'll be jest fine."

"Yes, thank God."

Clive patted her hand. "We have been, Miss Danielle, we have been."

Mrs. O'Brien sorted the items she'd brought with her, placing some of them in the dresser before she started toward the bathroom, a large metal bowl in her hands. "'Tis baffling how that infidel managed to get into the hall," she said above the noise of running water.

"It is a mystery," Blake agreed, determination replacing his thoughtful expression. "However, mysteries were made to be solved. And we're getting closer all the time to finding the answers to this one."

"It won't be too soon for me," Dani said, eyeing Mrs. O'Brien's return to the bedroom.

"Now, Mr. Blake, ye and Clive just scoot right on outta here while I take care of me mistress's needs."

Blake raised his hands in mock fear. "Right away, Mrs. O'Brien." He grinned at Dani. "Maybe we should have signed you up for How to Tame a Tiger in Forty-five Minutes or Less first." Dani giggled.

Mrs. O'Brien paused, looking bewildered, and then frowned. "Out, I say," she said, shooing him out the door with her hands. They walked out the door, laughter rumbling deep in their chests.

Later, after Mrs. O'Brien and Clive left the cabin with a promise to return daily as needed, Blake administered Dani's medication, leaving her to rest while he occupied himself with paperwork in the other room. She closed her eyes but couldn't fall asleep.

What was it Davenport had uttered that had been so disturbing just before Blake appeared at her side in the forest? She tapped her forefinger against her lower lip, her brow wrinkled in concentration. All at once her eyes lit up. He'd made reference to her as his brother's friend. Yes, that was it. *Lady friend!*

Dear God! Were her suspicions about Justin true after all? Was it his voice she'd heard that night? But if Blake had been truthful, Justin couldn't have been the assailant in Hartford. He'd been in New York. But what about the turmoil she'd endured since moving to Georgia? Was it possible he was responsible for that? Dani tossed her head from side to side. It just didn't make sense. And Justin, Davenport's brother? How could that be? Come to think of it, Justin had never discussed his mother. Had Blake lied after all? Were Mrs. O'Brien, Phillip Harcourt, and Justin all involved in the plot to steal Stratford Hall?

*Dani McKinnon, stop it! You'll drive yourself insane.* If only she could talk to the Pendergraffs. Dani lay awake for what seemed like hours, mulling over possibilities before slumber finally overtook her thoughts.

Late that afternoon, refreshed from a long nap and Blake's tantalizing beef stew satisfying the hungry lion in her stomach, Dani blamed the strong painkillers for her earlier wild thoughts. However, medication had nothing to do with the fact that Davenport had had her in mind when he'd referred to his brother's "lady friend." The image of Justin's handsome face appeared in her mind. *Dear Savior, please don't let Justin be a murderer.*

Dani put her distressed thoughts aside when Blake peeked around the edge of the door. "Like some company?" he asked, smiling.

"I'd love it. By the way, where did you learn to cook? That stew was awesome."

"In my business it's a matter of necessity. I never know where I'll be from case to case. A nearby eating establishment isn't always available, so between jobs I go home to Texas and stand over my mother's shoulder in the kitchen, gleaning all the knowledge I can. In my opinion, she's a gourmet chef par excellence."

Blake started to say more, but his cell phone began to ring. He pulled it out of his shirt pocket, giving it to Dani a moment later. "It's Justin," he mouthed at her perplexed expression. Blake picked up her empty dishes and carted them from the room.

She put the phone to her ear, Justin's voice sending a tingle along her arms. "Hello, Justin."

"Hi, sweet Dani. I just had to talk to you. I'd like to come see you, but Blake thinks it unwise. Davenport might be following me, hoping to find you. Much as I want to be with you, he's right. We don't want to endanger you further. I suppose Blake has told you of his part in all this."

"Yes. And thanks to God and Blake, I'm still alive."

"That is great, considering what's at stake."

Deep lines formed on her brow. "I don't understand what you mean."

Justin's breath caught and held, a cough catching in his throat. "First and foremost, you're a special person, and any guy would be a fool not to notice, not to disregard how important it is to Dad and me that your interests remain intact." His voice grew husky. "And heaven knows how much I enjoy holding you in my arms."

Dani swallowed hard. How could she care so much for him and mistrust him at the same time? "Oh, Justin. I'm so scared. I know I act brave in front of Mrs. O'Brien and Blake and all, but sometimes I wish this whole affair would be over, no matter what takes place. This not knowing what's going to happen from one day to the next is so disconcerting. If this mess doesn't end soon, I'll be rooming with Emily Davitello."

"Dani! How could you consider such a thing? You have to admit we're closer than ever to solving this case. Please don't make any impulsive decisions."

A pain shot through her shoulder. She winced. "Well, to be sure, I won't be able to do anything for a day or two... uh... Blake just walked in, and by the look on his face, I've talked long enough."

"And he's probably right. You take care, sweet Dani, and obey his orders. He can be pretty vicious when crossed," Justin said, chuckling.

"I know what you mean. He's standing with pills in one hand and in the other a glass of water tipped at a precarious angle over my head. Good-bye, Justin."

"So long, Dani. I'll phone you tomorrow."

Dani eyed her surrogate doctor, nurse, and chef. Noticing his muscles straining against his shirtsleeves as he lifted her to a sitting position, she realized it wouldn't be smart to challenge Blake Spencer. He rounded the bed and dragged the spindled rocking chair close to her side.

"Have you known Justin long?" she asked when he seemed ready to chat.

"We met in college, becoming best friends soon afterward. He helped influence my decision to become a lawyer."

"I'm a little confused. You studied to be an attorney, yet you're a private investigator. May I ask why you changed careers?"

"Sure. After I passed the bar exam, I decided to give four years to Uncle Sam. Meanwhile, Justin went home to Atlanta, married, and set up practice with his father, promising me a place in their firm when I came to my senses.

"But while in the armed forces, I applied for Special Forces training in military intelligence. After I graduated, they shipped me to South America, my stint in the service ending soon after I returned to the States. That training and experience under my belt, I chose a career in investigative work rather than a life locked behind a desk or in a stuffy courtroom. I'm not saying I won't practice law someday, but for right now I'm satisfied with my decision."

"You chose an exciting life, to be sure."

He shrugged his shoulders. "Sometimes, at other times boring." A faraway look filled his eyes. "It gets lonely at times too." He turned to stare at Dani with that same penetrating gaze that had unnerved her twice before. Her insides seemed to turn to jelly. Why did she react this way when he looked at her like that?

He laughed, breaking the spell. "Justin keeps after me to give up this 'perilous job,' as he calls it, and form a partnership with him, but since he and I don't see eye to eye on things as we did in college, I'm not sure it would benefit either of us. In fact, it might ruin our friendship altogether."

Blake eyed Dani's inability to smother a yawn, his lips lifting as her pastiness heightened with color. Blake rose from the chair. "I think, young lady, we've reminisced enough for now." As though without thinking, he leaned over and kissed her on the cheek. Her eyes meeting his, Dani's heartbeat quickened. His warm gaze told her he'd sensed the chemistry too.

She looked away, troubled by a sudden intensity to know and understand this man. *Why?* She had no idea. Her past romantic attractions had been toward the suave—men with sophistication and style. She grew puzzled. Had her desires changed? If so, when?

❧

Strong enough the next afternoon to get out of bed, Dani allowed Blake to help her into the other room of the cabin, the inviting rock fireplace with its roaring fire a welcome sight. A number of pillows stuffed behind her, she studied Blake while he prepared their dinner on the other side of the room.

"You know a lot about me. Tell me something about yourself. You mentioned Texas. Were you born there?"

He turned to give her a smile. "Yes, central Texas. My folks and older brother still operate the family cattle ranch."

"Do you have an aversion to ranching as well as the practice of law?"

"No. I just like to be on the move. My mother abhors my lifestyle. She wants me to find a wife and give her more grandchildren. However, the right woman just hasn't come along yet, as they say."

Dani's eyes twinkled. "And what kind of woman could wear the title Mrs. Blake Spencer? Maybe I know someone among my friends who would fit the description."

He stopped peeling potatoes and turned a thoughtful look her way. "Well, I've never put the requirements in black and white. I suppose number one she'd have to be attractive and have a pleasant personality. Two, a sense of humor would be great . . . uh . . . three, she would need to be of reasonable height, so I wouldn't break my neck when I wanted to kiss her, and four, she'd have to love children." He grinned. "My mother, you know."

He grew quiet for a long moment and then looked deep into her eyes. "Most important, she'd have to love God with all her heart and soul, even before she loved me."

It was Dani's turn to stare. "Are you saying you're a Christian?" *Could that be the reason he and Justin no longer see eye to eye?*

"Yes, about ten years now. Just before I joined the army, a girl I dated at the time invited me to her church. The minister's message inspired me to accept Christ's love, and I've served God since that time. As a result, my whole family has accepted the gift of salvation."

"I've had a recent conversion myself."

Blake nodded. "Mrs. O'Brien told me about it. You know, that woman dotes on you."

Dani laughed. "I've grown to love her too. In my book she rates a close second to the Pendergraffs." Her face sobered. "Do they know what happened to me?"

"Mrs. O'Brien thought it best to let you decide when to tell them."

Dani's expression turned bleak. "I think I'll wait a few days. I don't want to upset them."

"I under—" Blake wiped his hands on a dishtowel and pulled his BlackBerry from the case clipped on his hand-tooled leather belt. "Yeah, Justin, she's doing great. In fact, she's out of bed for a change. Sure." Blake handed the phone to Dani.

Dani wondered at the stab of resentment she felt. It was as though a clap of thunder had shattered the intimacy of the peaceful setting. "Hello," she said, frowning at the brusqueness in her tone. Justin didn't deserve to be treated that way.

Blake turned toward the stove. She didn't see the scowl on his face that reflected his own thoughts.

"Hello, sweet Dani. Blake indicated you're much better, but I'm not so sure you sound like it."

"Yes. I'm sorry if I sound cross," she said, mandating cheerfulness into her voice. "Is everything going well for you?"

"Mostly. But you don't want to hear my woes. I hope to have things straight before too much longer. Has Blake said when he thinks you can return to the hall?"

"The subject hasn't come up. But I'm sure my prison guard will let me know when he'll free me from my cell." She winked at Blake.

"I hope it's soon. I don't want to leave you in his clutches too long. He might try to steal my girl right out from under my nose."

All of a sudden, Dani's breath caught and held momentarily, her expression hardening. "Justin, I don't recall any news broadcast reporting that I belonged to anyone." No matter how she longed for him to declare his love for her, she wouldn't be taken for granted.

"Hey! I didn't intend to offend you. However, I did think we had something going for us."

A sense of remorse gripped her. "I'm sorry. Just chock it up to cabin fever."

Later, when Dani tired of her position on the sofa, Blake came to aid her retreat to the bedroom. Just as they neared the doorway, she stopped to look into his face. He touched the side of her face with gentle fingers. The tenderness she saw in his expression evoked feelings in her too new to interpret. "Thank you, Blake, for the good care you've given me. I hope we'll be friends for a long time to come."

Dani's heart reeled at his searching, probing eyes. A moment later, the breath-taking moment passed as he spoke. "I'd best get you back to bed now. We don't want your healing to regress."

Following Blake's return to the living room, she heard a loud thump, as if something had been hurled against the wall. She called out to see if he was okay, but he didn't answer. Dani knew he'd wanted to kiss her—she felt the familiar heat in her cheeks—and that he was aware she expected it. Dani whipped the quilt aside, desiring the coolness of the room. He probably assumed her to be the most wanton woman alive. She recalled the look in his eyes. *You weren't so innocent either, Blake Spencer.* Dani flinched. But that didn't excuse her behavior. Dani shook her head. A lifetime ago she'd led a rather simple life. If only she could turn back the clock.

The days seemed to grow longer. Dani's shoulder healing in record time, she begged Blake each morning to let her return to the hall, the tension between them like a pressure cooker about to blow from too high a flame.

She discouraged the memory of Blake's caress by keeping Justin current in her thoughts. She noticed that Blake kept his Bible close at hand, often reading for hours.

One night she paced back and forth. She threw the magazine she'd read from cover to cover into the fireplace, the flames licking up the pages in no time. Blake looked up, reading her expression before he closed his Bible.

He chuckled. "Something bothering you, Dani?"

She collapsed onto the sofa, throwing him a look that showed her lack of appreciation for his humor. "I want to go home, Blake. You told me yesterday no sign of the perpetrators have been found near the cabin or the hall. For all we know, he and his brother may have skipped the country."

Blake shook his head. "Not likely. Stratford Hall is too big a prize." He smiled. "However, the topic of your return to the hall came up when I spoke with Justin earlier today. We'll grant your wish on one condition."

She scooted toward the edge of the couch. "Anything!"

"You can go home tomorrow if you agree to let me move into the hall so I can keep a closer eye on you."

Dani brightened. "Agreed."

The teasing glint in his eyes vanished. "Yes," he said. "It's time for you to go. The longer we stay here, the greater the risk." Dani discerned at once that he referred to more than just the probable danger of her assailants discovering that she still lived.

The following afternoon, Dani stood amidst the timber, observing her home for the past two weeks, the height of the bluff behind the cabin causing it to appear smaller than its actual size. Dense woods swallowed up the tiny clearing. Although thrilled that she'd be at Stratford Hall in a matter of hours, a sense of regret stung her soul. Her time alone with Blake had come to an end. She stared at him against the backdrop of nature that surrounded them, swallowing hard, hoping to diminish her attraction for him. As she returned his encouraging smile, his expression seemed to reveal similar thoughts of loss.

She turned for a last look at the cabin, aware his physical allure was minute compared to the respect she'd developed for him while in his care. She knew he had more than friendly feelings for her— she observed it each time he glanced her way—yet he'd refused to act on them, the exact opposite of Justin who'd pursued her from the moment they'd met at the airport. Dani sighed deeply. Her thoughts so confused of late, she wondered if her world had tilted too far off its axis, never to find balance again. Breathing in a breath of fresh air, Dani began the climb that would take her back to civilization and Mrs. O'Brien's sustaining presence.

Later, her shoulder aching from the exertion, she paused. Blake, sensing she wasn't behind him, turned and walked back down the incline. Motioning with his hand, he steered her toward a large rock where she could sit awhile.

Dani rubbed her upper left arm. "How much longer before we reach the hall? I'm sorry I've had to stop and rest so many times."

Blake encouraged her with a smile. "You're doing fine, Dani. No need to apologize. Just a few more yards and we'll be at the old logging road I told you about the other day. Our trek will be easier from there. Another half mile and we'll be at the hall."

She threw a look back over her shoulder. "I don't know how you thought the murderers would find me. Only a mountain goat could discern this trail."

Blake laughed. "You have a good point."

Just before they topped the ridge near the road, Dani slipped on a bed of wet pine needles. She let out a yelp, Blake catching her in his arms before she fell to the ground.

All of a sudden, heaven and earth stood still. Not even a breeze disturbed the moment as their lips melted together. They clung to each other, a sense of desperation in their embrace. When they stepped back from each other, Dani beheld his remorse and then silenced his apology with the brush of her fingers against his mouth. "No, don't. Let's just forget it, pretend it never happened."

Dani proceeded up the path, refusing to cast a look in Blake's direction. *Forget?* She could still feel the warmth of his embrace. How could she forget something that had felt so right? She glanced around her. Perhaps the ambiance of their surroundings had stolen their senses momentarily. Nevertheless, she knew the memory of that kiss would lodge deep in her heart, never to be forgotten.

A few minutes later, they came to the entrance to the well-worn path that beckoned them toward Stratford Hall. Dani stood transfixed, reluctant to traipse near the place where she'd stared death in the face.

Blake, noticing her hesitancy, squeezed her uninjured arm. "You're alive now. That's what counts, isn't it?

"Yeah," she said, gazing heavenward. "That's what counts."

# TRUSTWORTHY COMPANION

*E*merging from the forest onto the south lawn of Stratford Hall a short time later, Dani saw Clive standing at the edge of the garden, a rifle tucked under his arm. Spotting the couple, he hurried toward them, a smile of greeting on his lips.

"You're a welcome sight, Miss Danielle. You too, Mr. Blake. I sho is glad you're gonna be around to look after things from now on." He turned back to Dani. "Now maybe Miz Annie will be her ole self again. She's been as cross as a she bear 'bout to lose one o' her cubs to a lioness."

Dani gave the tall, gangly man a hug. "Maybe things will be back to order before too much longer." Dani looked at Blake, her pain and tiredness reflecting in her eyes. Freedom from chaos couldn't come too soon for her.

Observing her pale features, Blake scooped Dani into his arms, ignoring her protest. When they reached the fountain, the veranda doors burst open and Mrs. O'Brien clattered onto the patio, a jovial smile on her face. Opening wide the entryway, she ushered Blake and Dani inside, speaking phrases that caused Clive to exhale a sigh of relief.

"Jest lik' a mother hen cooin' and cluckin' over a wanderin' chick now safe under her wings," he said under his breath, his glance taking in the garden before he locked the door behind them.

"Now ye be careful climbing those stairs, Mr. Blake. Miss Danielle's room is on the right," Mrs. O'Brien cautioned, huffing her way toward the master suite. "I swear, if I get my hands on that varmint, I'll tear him from limb to limb. He'll rue the day he came into this house."

Dani viewed the gallery from Blake's arms. "It's wonderful to be home, Mrs. O'Brien. Please don't worry about Davenport. He may appear to be as elusive as the Loch Ness monster, but he and his partner will be caught eventually. And too, Blake is here to protect us now." He tightened his hold on her as though to confirm her words. Her heartbeat quickened. Refusing to look at him, she decided this attraction for him would reconcile itself once Justin held her in his arms.

Inside her bedroom, the scent of fresh flowers from the conservatory greeted them, the aroma a far cry from the smell of wood smoke and pine she'd inhaled for the past two weeks.

Mrs. O'Brien arranged the covers on Dani's bed to accommodate her mistress. "Ye can put Miss Danielle right there, Mr. Blake. I'll show ye to your room just as soon as I see to me lass's comfort. I phoned Doctor Bedford earlier to tell him what time we expected your return. He should be here shortly."

"That's good," Blake said when he'd placed Dani on the bed. "In the meantime, I'll send Clive's boys back to the cabin to retrieve our things." Smiling, he took off his Stetson, swept it outward, and then replaced it on his head. "She's all yours, Mrs. O'Brien."

When they were alone, Mrs. O'Brien fluffed Dani's pillows, shaking her head in despair. "I should have known that Rosemary Davidson's kin would be mixed up in these doings. All this proves she meant no good the first time I cast me eyes on her. Now she's passed her evil ways on to her grandchildren. It's all I can do to keep me old bones from aquivering and aquaking with anger when I think about it.

"I plan to sleep with one eye cocked open until them polecats are caught and caged. I know God expects us to leave revenge to Him, but 'tis hard for me to stand aside to let the Lord settle the score with that little weasel all by Himself."

Following the doctor's visit, Dani, refreshed from a long shower, waited on the daybed in her sitting room for Blake's return, a cup and saucer in her hand. Soon he strode into the room at her invitation.

"At least you look like you feel better," he said, removing his Stetson. "What did Doctor Bedford say?"

"A lot of hmms and uh huhs. Then he wanted to know if you'd like to take over his practice when he retires." She sighed, giving him a sidelong glance filled with mock disgust. "You'd think I'd be used to probing and prodding by now."

Blake laughed. "Now, Miss McKinnon, surely you realize that all noteworthy physicians gained their notoriety by their extensive study of patient anatomy." His eyes traveled down the length of her reclining body at a slow pace. "I can't believe you'd want to deprive me a chance at a future Nobel Prize." His gaze moved upward to rest on her wounded shoulder, a display of emotions crisscrossing his features.

"Blake, please don't blame yourself that you weren't here to prevent Davenport's attempt on my life." "It's taken me a while to grasp this knowledge, but God didn't promise that bad things wouldn't happen to us, only that His grace is sufficient to see us through them. And like you said earlier today, I'm alive. That's what's important. All we are assured of is the present, but if we do our best to follow His commands today, He'll take care of tomorrow." She paused to take a sip of tea. "We just have to trust God for a breakthrough in the case."

Blake formed his hands into the shape of a strangle hold. "But when I think of what you've suffered, I can't wait to meet these guys face-to-face. Just give me five minutes alone with each of them."

A cold wave slithered down her spine at the cloud of anger she viewed on his face. All at once he relaxed his hands at his sides, a guilty look on his face. "There have been times in my work I could have forgotten which side of the law I represent."

She glanced at his muscular torso and then smiled. "I'm glad I'm not your enemy."

He picked up his hat from the Pembroke table where he'd placed it moments before. "If you'll excuse me, I need to set up a portable office in my new quarters. We'll get together later. Be careful that you don't do too much too soon."

Dani saluted. "Yes, Captain Spencer. I shall follow your orders without exception." When he left, she took the phone in hand and dialed a familiar number. The Pendergraffs had to know the latest in the inheritance saga. She'd avoided the issue too long.

❧

Early that evening, Dani sat in the library reading one of the family journals she'd found among the other leather-bound titles. She looked up at the knock on the door. Expecting to see Blake, she called to him to enter then uttered a glad hello when Justin walked into the room.

"Gosh, sweet Dani, it's good to see you," he said, leaning forward to brush her lips with a kiss. "Blake tells me you're recovering at a rapid rate, but I had to see for myself. I hope you don't mind that I came without telephoning first."

"Not at all. I'd have been disappointed if you'd stayed away. How is your father?"

"Busy with a new case, as usual. Are you still in a lot of pain?" he asked after seeing her flinch when she changed positions on the sofa so he could sit beside her. "I'm convinced Blake did his utmost to give you the best of care. But he's not a doctor."

She smiled. "You couldn't prove it by me. He seemed to know just what to do. Even Doctor Bedford praised his work."

"Well, he did receive a Medal of Honor from the president for his outstanding service in South America, although he's too modest to tell anyone. It had to do with Blake's performance in saving the life of a visiting American senator who was gunned down during an outburst of guerrilla warfare in the country."

Dani grew thoughtful. "You've known Blake for some time. Are you acquainted with his family too?"

"I've visited their home a few times. His folks are hardworking, also a pleasure to be around."

"Have they been in the ranching business a long time?"

Justin nodded. "As the story goes, Blake's great-grandfather bought the ranch in the early 1900s from a cattleman who'd been forced to sell his property after losing a fortune in a poker game at the Stockyards Hotel in Arlington. Within a few years, the ranch became a prosperous enterprise from both cattle and oil."

When Dani heard the word *oil* she thought of Lance Carter, wondering if his new job was going well. She hoped so.

"Dani? Yes or no."

"What? Sorry. Something you said reminded me of someone, causing my mind to wander for a moment."

"I asked if you'd like to be my date for the upcoming Sweetheart Gala at the country club in a few weeks," he said, his tone perturbed.

She ignored his disgruntled expression. "I'd love to, that is, if Doctor Bedford has released me to a normal life by then." All of a sudden the complexity of those words struck her. She laughed as the sounds of skepticism tumbled into her throat. "Normal life, indeed!" She hadn't known what to her had been normality for weeks. And who knew when it all would end?

Sobering, she cast a troubled gaze toward Justin. "Any report from Sergeant Hagerman or the sheriff?"

He shook his head. "Nothing. With the number of Davenport's composites floating around the state, you'd think someone would have seen him by now. However, they did find a car fitting the description of the one Davenport drove the day he showed up at the hall. Remember? Someone reported to Atlanta PD an abandoned car in one of the suburban neighborhoods. Turns out the car was stolen and wiped clean of fingerprints."

Dani rolled her eyes toward the ceiling. "How could I forget?" She looked up to see Blake step into the room after a light tap on the door.

He looked apologetic. "Sorry to barge in on you like this, but Mrs. O'Brien asked me to look in on you two. And I quote, 'Mr. Justin is a fine young man, but I don't want him to tire me lass. So would ye mind taking a peek while I finish dinner?'" He grinned. "So naturally I agreed; the odor of someone else's cooking convincing me not to do otherwise."

Laughing, Dani turned to Justin. "Would you like to stay for dinner? You know Mrs. O'Brien always prepares enough food for a battalion."

"Thanks but no thanks. I have a dinner engagement with a business partner. I think I mentioned my partnership in a small Mississippi company to you before."

All at once Blake began to cough. They both stared at him, Justin scowling at his friend. "Are you all right, Blake?" Dani asked, her face marked with concern.

When the spasm subsided, he gave Dani a reassuring smile and then turned to Justin, a dark look passing between the two she failed to comprehend. Justin stood to his feet.

"I'd better leave before Mrs. O'Brien throws me out on my ear. I'll take a rain check on that invitation though."

Dani's eyes lit up. "Say, Justin, why don't you plan to spend the weekend at the hall. I'm sure Blake could use some male company for a change." When she saw him hesitate, Dani continued, a flirtatious grin preceding her words. "I know I'll feel much safer with two bodyguards about the place, at least if they're as handsome as the two of you."

"Or if you have other plans, Blake, I could keep vigil on Dani," Justin said.

Blake drew a deep breath, his gaze focused on Dani. "No plans." He smiled at Justin. "You can tell me all about this new enterprise of yours."

"Perhaps." The men squared off, their annoyance with each other quite visible.

Puzzled at their behavior, Dani stood, lifting her face to receive Justin's kiss. "Good. It's settled then. We'll see you Friday night."

Blake clapped Justin on the back. "Be sure and tell your *partner* hello for me."

Justin threw Blake a scathing look over his shoulder. "Yeah, sure."

Following Justin's departure, Dani sat back down, motioning Blake toward an overstuffed chair beside the deceased Mr. Thorndike's desk. "What was that all about?"

"Nothing. Just a private joke between friends."

"I didn't hear any laughter."

He removed his gun from its shoulder harness and placed the weapon on the desk. "If you don't mind, I'd like to skip it."

"Sorry, just curious. Did you find your room satisfactory?" she asked, dismissing the incident from her mind. "Mrs. O'Brien said you wanted a tour of the place."

"Yes. I'd like to inspect the security system."

"Sure. And please understand the hall is at your disposal. If life here becomes too monotonous"—she swept her arm out from her side—"as you can see, the library is full of interesting books and other material." She showed him the family journal she'd been reading before Justin had entered the room. "There are several diaries similar to this one, each written by various members of my ancestry." Smiling, she glanced about the room. "I spend a lot of time in here."

"I'm an avid reader myself." Blake rose from his chair and took a seat beside Dani, taking her hand. She felt her face grow warm from his bold stare. "As for the other, I don't think for one moment that tediousness will be the conflict I'll have to battle where you're concerned, Miss Danielle McKinnon."

Stunned, she couldn't utter a word. After a moment, he stood, his face bathed in a knowing smile. "How about that tour after dinner?"

The air crackling with unspoken emotion, she watched him exit the room. "Sure thing, Blake," she said, the quiet-spoken words barely audible above the sound of her drumming heartbeat.

❧

One morning a few days before Valentine's Day, Blake stood waiting by his pickup truck to drive Dani into Carrollton, Georgia for a shopping trip. Soon she appeared at the front door, twirling across the porch before she ran down the steps. She lifted her head, sniffing the outdoors. "Oh, Blake, what a gorgeous day! If I didn't know better, I'd have to say spring is just around the corner."

He laughed. "Not according to the weatherman."

The door slammed, causing them both to look up. Mrs. O'Brien hurried to the edge of the porch with Dani's coat in her hands. "Miss Danielle, ye forgot your coat. They're predicting an uncommon eight or more inches of snow today in the Atlanta area. We can't have ye catching your death of cold just when Doctor Bedford has given ye a clean bill of health after weeks of convalescence."

"But, Mrs. O'Brien, the temperature is in the fifties. I think my jacket is sufficient."

"Now don't argue with me, lass."

Mrs. O'Brien smiling her approval, Dani took the coat from the housekeeper and then climbed into the truck humming a cheerful tune.

"You're in as good a mood as you are lovely today. Is it the thought of a new dress or the evening with Justin prompting your good spirits?"

"Both, actually," she said, thanking him for the compliment with a smile.

Seated in the vehicle a moment later, she waited until Blake started the engine before she spoke. Her eyes twinkling, she pointed in the direction of their destination. "Onward, Sir Blake. I must find a dress that guarantees I'll feel like the belle of the ball at the country club dance."

Dani turned to gaze out the window, smiling. Justin had been more than attentive to her in the weeks since the night she almost died, a perfect gentlemen in all respects, even when she'd been tempted to let down her guard during those passionate moments he'd held her close in his arms.

Her attention on Blake once again, Dani's smile eased off her face at the look in his eyes.

"In my opinion, Miss McKinnon, you'd fit that description whether you wore an evening gown or jeans and a sweatshirt."

Dani felt the heat rise in her cheeks, his slow, honeyed Texas dialect causing a sweet shiver to race along her arms. Although pleased by the compliment, she didn't know what to do about his often less than subtle attempts to show his attraction to her. She cared for Blake a great deal, no doubt about it. *More than you're willing to admit.* Dani brushed aside the inner thought. He's a wonderful friend; he'd proven that. But Justin—her heartbeat quickened. Justin made her feel alive, vibrant, as though she were the most sought after girl in the whole world. Now that she no longer had to be confined to the estate and could give her full attention to her relationship with Justin, she was sure any attraction she might have for Blake would diminish soon.

Dani grinned. "Thanks. I'll try to remember that the next time I'm in my grubbies, helping Clive repot flowers in the conservatory," she said, determined to keep their conversation light.

He lifted his shoulders. "I just call things as I see them. For instance, to some people a cow is a cow. To me, there are Texas Longhorns,

Holsteins, Jerseys, and Black Angus, to name a few. Each breed has its own unique quality of excellence, no matter how they are dressed on the outside. Of course, that's not to say I don't prefer some breeds over others." He took his eyes off the road a few seconds to look her up and down, his gaze lingering on her limbs. "And then there are horses, in your case, most definitely a Palomino thoroughbred."

Laughing, she held up her hand. "Okay, okay. I get the picture and thanks again." She frowned. "I think."

Blake grinned. "You're welcome."

Later, when they drove past the Morgan cabin, Dani's light-hearted mood changed to a serious one. "Has your man in California been able to secure an interview with Mrs. Davitello?"

"No. The doctor said that her mental condition has improved some lately, and he's afraid that questions about the past will cause his patient to digress."

"Doesn't he understand that my life is at stake?"

"Yes, but he wouldn't change his mind, nor allow Abe to scan her biographical records." Blake observed her long face. "Don't look so glum. We're not licked yet. There are other channels we can turn to for help."

Dani's lips softened into a smile. "By the way, thanks for offering to drive me."

Blake tipped the brim of his hat toward Dani. "Just doing my job, ma'am."

"And great at it you are," she said, taking a moment to read the expression on his face. She felt sure that he'd do everything in his power to protect her, even at the risk of his own life. Before she had time to sort her feelings about the sudden revelation, Blake parked in front of the boutique.

"Dani, while you shop, I'll go visit the sheriff," he said as he assisted her onto the pavement. A slow grin spread across his features. "If you're anything like my sister, I hope Sheriff Wilson is up to a mighty long discussion."

Dani tried to look miffed. "You're so funny." The corners of her mouth twitched. "I tell you what. If I get bored before you return"—she glanced toward the drugstore, her attention drawn to the pink flashing sign in the window that read ice cream parlor—"I'll just help myself to a soda while I wait for you to finish your little gab session."

As Dani sifted through the various styles and colors of evening gowns a few moment later, thoughts of Justin filtered through her mind. Would she soon become his one and only valentine? All at once her breath caught and held. She lifted a quality copy of an Armani original from the rack of designer look-a-likes, holding it next to her while she viewed its potential in a nearby full-length mirror. A smug smile of success on her lips, she walked toward the dressing room. What should she order—strawberry or cherry soda?

# VALENTINE
# EXTRAVAGANZA

*D*ani paid the clerk for her dress and matching accessories and then emerged from the store. Blake's truck not in sight, she set a quick pace for the drugstore, snuggling deeper into her jacket against the sudden significant drop in temperature. Crossing the street, she scanned the quaint business section, glad for the recent revival of yesteryear sweeping the nation, a nostalgic view the perfect remedy for effects from the fast-paced, survival-minded, technology-influenced lifestyle of today.

Dani approached the drugstore, allowing the stooped, elderly man just ahead of her to open the door. A word of appreciation on her lips, she froze when she looked into his eyes. The gray hair and mustache couldn't disguise the murderous evil in those familiar orbs.

"Davenport!" she screeched, grabbing her throat.

Intimidating laughter spilled from his mouth at her recognition of him. He let go of the door, the tinkling, attached bell resonating in Dani's ears like the gong of an Oriental drum.

"Hello, pretty lady. We meet again. I see you've recovered from your ... ah ... little accident." His eyes narrowed to thin slits. "I followed you today hoping for a chance like this. Take warning, sister, you survived this time, but you won't be so lucky in the future." At that he sprang from sight around the corner of the building, Dani standing statuelike on the sidewalk.

Within minutes, Blake stood at her side, lifting the packages from her grip. Eyeing her ashen complexion, he took her arm. She began to tremble. "Dani, get into the truck; then you can tell me what happened."

The warmth from the heater soon drove the chill from her body but not her soul. "I just saw Davenport masquerading as an old man. He said I wouldn't survive a future attempt on my life."

Blake pulled her against his shoulder, a parade of emotions traipsing across his features. He snapped his fingers. "Of all the ... Why didn't I think of that before?"

Dani raised her head. "What?"

"Driving to the dress shop, I saw you talking with that man, picking up right away that something was amiss. You stood too still. Just as I parked, he ran. Observing his flight, I thought he had remarkable agility for one so old. Now that I know it was Davenport, something just occurred to me I hadn't thought important before. Do you remember what Davitello and his college roommate argued about before Julian killed the guy?"

Dani frowned then brightened. "Yes. A college drama."

Blake nodded. "I never dreamed Davenport would use his interest in theater to escape capture. It would be my guess he has a number of disguises available for his subterfuge, along with a different identification for each one."

All at once Dani recalled the blond, shaggy-haired man that had ogled her from the old courthouse lawn in Evansville a few days before Christmas. No wonder he'd reminded her of Davenport. "I bet you're right. You'd think these small town police who are well-acquainted with their townsfolk would notice two strangers in the area."

Blake shook his head. "It's hunting season. Sportsman from all directions flock into the county each year to seek game." He backed the truck away from the curb, turning toward Stratford Hall. A minute later he had his BlackBerry in hand, speaking to the sheriff.

Dani huddled near the door of the truck, wondering if the word *safety* would ever intersperse with her vocabulary again. When they reached the edge of town, she spoke her thoughts. "It's hard to believe those two could find a place remote enough to elude the authorities this long.

Blake waved his hand toward one side of the truck and then the other. "Look around you. These Appalachian foothills are full of places to conceal the worthless pair. Legend has it a ring of horse thieves used this area for their hideouts in the late 1800s, some places so obscure it took several years to capture the bandits. According to the sheriff, other than additional populace, not much has changed in this environment since that era." Blake reached over and squeezed her hand. "I'm sorry Davenport spoiled your outing. Do you feel like lunch? I'm starved."

She drew a deep sigh. "Why not? I'm still breathing. Besides, I never did get that ice cream soda."

Late that afternoon, Dani soaked away her tension in a steaming bath, the image of Blake from the top of his white Stetson to the toes of his black boots foremost in her mind. The girl that won him for her own would be blessed indeed. Would she qualify as a candidate? Frowning, she shook off the idea. It seemed of late her thoughts had developed a mind of their own. Yes, she was attracted to his brawny good looks, but she *loved* Justin. Meditating on her dashing beau, all thoughts of Blake dissolved. Soon Justin would arrive to whisk her away to his country club for an evening of dance and romance.

Just before his expected appearance, Dani eyed her image in the dressing room mirror, studying her reflection. The marquis-cut ruby earrings dangling from her ears matched the full-length, red satin dress to perfection. She made a slight adjustment to the gem-studded bodice and then orchestrated the jeweled hair ornament into place, her simple French roll now a sophisticated coif. Giving her likeness a thumbs-up, she slipped into her shimmering ruby red satin pumps and then glided toward the stairs.

Entering the formal parlor a couple of minutes later, a surprise greeted Dani. Blake, magnificent in formal attire, stood looking out the window at the light snowfall. Her eyes widened. "Good heavens!" she breathed. A girl would have to be dead not to notice his appeal.

Hearing a sound, he turned and moved to her side, his smile reflecting the admiration in his eyes. "Good evening. Has anyone told you how stunning you look?" The overpowering magnetism between them caused Dani's breath to sharpen. He leaned close to her face, so close she thought her heart might stop beating. "If not, then let me be the first."

Dani backed away, his spicy scent nerve-wracking, to say the least. Why, if she weren't so taken with Justin…

"Thanks. You clean up great yourself. Justin didn't tell me you planned to attend the dance."

"I didn't, but he phoned earlier this afternoon saying he'd been detained and asked if I would escort you to the country club." Blake grinned. "How could I say no when the feat includes such charming company?"

She laughed. "The feeling is mutual, kind sir." Concern dragged the mirth from her eyes. "That's odd he phoned you instead of me. Did Justin give a reason for the delay? I hope nothing is wrong."

Blake averted his eyes. "Nothing specific, just that he'd meet us there, indicating he didn't have time to explain." He crooked his arm then bowed. "If mademoiselle is ready, your limousine awaits."

Dani smiled. "I'll get my wrap."

She turned to leave the room, her intention suspended by the entrance of Mrs. O'Brien toting a large box. "I thought ye might need this, lass. Miss Mathilda wanted ye to have it."

Lifting the lid, Dani gasped. She pulled an exquisite, full-length black sable from the carton and held it to her cheek, closing her eyes.

A moment of silence passed before the housekeeper again spoke. "Land sakes, lass. Let Mr. Blake help ye into it. If ye don't hurry, ye'll miss the entire doings."

Blake took the coat from Dani's hands and wrapped it around her shoulders. "Mrs. O'Brien is correct. We need to be on our way. Your suitor is waiting."

Luxuriating in the feel of the coat about her, Dani turned to stare at Blake, the hint of sarcasm in his words a surprise. She glanced at Mrs. O'Brien, noting her raised eyebrows. Blake, his back to their reaction, stepped into the foyer, his face somber as he slid back the deadbolt on the front door.

"After you, *mon chéri*." The words were lost on Dani as she bade Mrs. O'Brien good night. "Now, Mrs. O'Brien, don't wait up for me. I'm sure I'll be later than usual."

Once outside, Dani drank in the fresh, clean air, laughing when a snowflake tumbled onto her nose. Just before Isaac opened the car door, something made her look back at Blake. Their eyes locked. She resisted the urge to lift her hand to his cheek, at last tearing her eyes from the bold unspoken words etched on his face. Inside the automobile, they kept their conversation light, ignoring the explosive electricity that danced between them.

Arriving on time, Justin greeted them, taking Dani's arm to escort her into the country club, his eyes brimming with pleasure at Dani's appearance. When they'd checked their coats, he led them to the center of the festivities. To Dani, it seemed they'd attracted the attention of the whole assembly, especially the eyes of the ladies. *Well, who could blame them*, Dani surmised, feeling that the two most handsome men for miles around stood at her sides. Even Cinderella couldn't boast that status.

Soon Dani found herself in the midst of several couples she'd met at the Harcourt Christmas party, Justin's aunt Claudine giving her the warmest welcome of all. Within a few moments, she'd apprised Dani of the latest happenings in Atlanta and then scooted away when Mr. Beaumont appeared to claim his wife for a dance.

A familiar voice in her ear, Dani turned and smiled a hello to Phillip Harcourt. "How are you?"

"Just fine, thank you." He took her hand in his and held it close to his lips momentarily. "You are absolutely gorgeous this evening, my dear," he said, releasing her fingers. "Don't forget to save a dance for me."

"Thank you, Mr. Harcourt. You're quite debonair yourself, as always." She passed her dance card to him.

He glanced at the list, smiling as he added his signature to the last available dance. "From the looks of this card, you'll be on your feet the whole evening. Oh, excuse me," he said, acknowledging the woman at his side. "I'd like you to meet Ms. Charlotte Gilmore. Charlotte, Miss Danielle McKinnon of Carroll County, Georgia."

Dani smiled at the pleasant-faced woman. "Great evening, isn't it? Did you know my aunt, Mathilda Thorndike?"

Charlotte shook her head. "No, although I've heard of her generous exploits."

Dani nodded. "I hope I can live up to her reputation."

"From what I understand, you're doing just that," Phillip said, smiling at the blank look on Dani's face. "I'm referring to your generosity to the children's home."

"Oh, that," she said waving away his praise. "I've always had a heart for underprivileged children. I wouldn't trade the hours I spend at the orphanage for anything. There's nothing like the laughter of a child to melt away your own troubles."

At that moment, Justin took her arm, retrieving her dance card from his father. "Come on, Dani. Let's have some fun," he said, leading her into the throng of twirling couples.

While they danced, Dani felt someone's eyes on her. She glanced about, at last catching the eye of Marguerite Van Buren across the room. Dani gave a slight nod to address the woman, but she looked away.

Dani stiffened. Justin pulled back from his embrace to observe her countenance. "Is something wrong, Dani?"

She forced herself to relax. "No, I'm having a wonderful time."

Later on, following numerous dances with various gentlemen attending the function, Blake cut in on her current partner. "I believe this is our waltz." She hesitated a few seconds before she walked into his arms.

"No. You picked a later one."

A lazy smile smoothed his rugged features. "I guess I made a mistake. Forgive me?" He laughed at her expression that stated clearly she didn't believe him for one second. He pulled her close, his embrace too snug to constitute mere friendship. His hold reminded her of when he'd last held her in his arms. She could almost smell the pine trees. The temperature in the room seemed to escalate.

She struggled to loosen his arms, but his grip tightened. Betraying her will, her heartbeat quickened, her mouth drying like harvested cotton beneath a blistering August sun.

Blake glanced down at her, his lips curving into a grin. "A little too warm, Dani? Would you like to step outside for a breath of fresh air? However, as beautiful as you are tonight, I might be tempted to kiss you."

She decided to play along. "And what if I don't want to be kissed?"

His face softened. Flecks of gold frolicked in his eyes like a sparkling topaz gem. "Dani, I think you want me to kiss you every day for the rest of your life, but you're not ready to admit it—not to yourself, nor to me."

Eyes flashing, Dani jerked away from him, her face turning crimson. She clamped her lips together to keep her thoughts at bay. Had they been elsewhere at that moment, her reaction to his overt display of affection would make an eruption from Mount St. Helens seem like a Sunday stroll in the park. "And just what inspired that notion, may I ask?" All at once she realized the music had ended and people on the crowded dance floor were staring at them. She breathed a sigh of relief when Justin walked up beside her.

"Hey, Blake, ole buddy. You're not trying to steal my girl, now are you? I recall something like that taking place a few times when we were in college."

Blake laughed. "For the moment I believe she's all yours. But there's always tomorrow, you know."

Dani stepped into Justin's arms, her face flushed and grim. "Can we dance now?" she said tartly.

"Sure, sweet Dani." Justin glanced over his shoulder at Blake, mouthing, "What did I do?"

Blake, a look of innocence stamped on his face, just shrugged his shoulders and then strode across the room to their table.

At the close of their dance, Dani and Justin climbed into the limousine to keep their dinner reservations at an exclusive French restaurant. "Isn't Blake coming?" she asked when Justin had settled beside her. Dani smoothed a loose tendril of hair, her expression becoming stolid. Of course, she didn't care if Blake accompanied them or not.

"No. He offered to drive my car to the hall so I'd have transportation back to Atlanta later on. I hope you don't mind that I'm inviting myself to bed and breakfast."

Dani turned toward the window. As a matter of fact, she did. She wanted to be alone to sort through the havoc in her heart.

Justin placed his arm around her shoulder. "It is okay, isn't it?"

She faced him, observing his self-confident pose in the light of the streetlamp. She glanced away, her eyes narrowing. "I can't imagine you thinking otherwise." Dani flinched when she felt Justin grow rigid. He had done nothing this evening to deserve her peevishness. To show her remorse for using him as a target for her irritation with

Blake, she slid close to him, disregarding Blake's good-bye wave from outside the car.

Still, she couldn't release Blake from her mind. Who gave him the right to toy with her heart? *You did.* Her breath caught and held. She recognized the voice of the One who knew her better than anyone. At that moment, Justin took her in his arms. She gladly received his affection; it delayed the inescapable outcome—dealing with the truth of her feelings for Blake.

Soon after they'd ordered their meal in a corner of an elegant establishment designed for lovers, Justin leaned forward, caressing her cheek with his fingertips. The glow from the candlelight deepened the color of his eyes to violet. "Dani, sweet Dani, you have to be the eighth wonder of the world."

She cocked her head gracefully, forcing a cheeriness she didn't feel into her manner. The corners of her lips tilted. "Is that so? And what may I ask prompted your summation, Mr. Attorney at Law?"

"With all that's transpired since we've met, I've never known a woman with such fortitude. While recovering both physically and mentally from a murder attempt, with minimum complaints, I might add, you've managed to carry on your responsibilities and continue your work at the orphanage in lieu of the imminent danger oppressing you daily."

She held up her hand, laughing. "That doesn't take tremendous bravery, considering that Blake drives me wherever I need to go. One look at his biceps would discourage anyone from thoughts of evil. At least it didn't take Davenport long to hightail it from that rest area where he pulled a knife on me."

Justin planted a gentle kiss on the tip of her nose. "That's one of the reasons he's on your payroll. Now, back to why I'm spending a fortune in this gilded den of romance." The look in his eyes intensified. "I've often dreamed of someone like you—you're beautiful, vibrant, resolute." He grinned. "Albeit, your moral strength *has* taken a toll on me."

He raised her hand to his lips. "What I'm trying to say is … will you marry me?"

Dani raised her eyebrows. "Justin?"

"Yes, sweet Dani. I'm asking you to become my wife." With that he extracted a jeweler's box from a side pocket of his dinner jacket. "Open it," he said, noting her startled reluctance.

Her hands trembling, she lifted the hinged lid. She gasped at the sight of the large twinkling diamond encased in a circle of emeralds. Her mind whirled. "I don't know what to say."

Justin lifted the ring from the box. "How about yes?"

She withdrew her hand from his clasp, preventing his attempt to slip the ring on her finger. "I didn't expect this, I mean … it's not that I haven't entertained the idea of a marriage between us, but you've never once expressed that you're in love with me."

Annoyance circled his features. "I thought we had an under-standing. I just assumed you knew how much I cared for you."

Her voice softened. "A girl likes to hear love declared now and then." Dani cradled her head against his shoulder. "Justin, you've been wonderful to me. But marriage is a lifetime commitment, and a wrong choice would be disastrous for us both. Since you've suf-fered from a broken marriage, surely you can understand my reserva-tion." She caressed his cheek, trying to assuage his disappointment. "I promise to give you my answer soon."

Justin nestled the ring into its satin coffin and then snapped the lid in place. "I hope so. I can't wait too much longer." Puzzled by his state-ment, she picked at her salad in silence, her appetite dissipating rapidly.

Later, on their way to Stratford Hall, the distance between them grew with each mile, Justin's attitude as frosty as the dense snowfall. All of a sudden, the car swerved, startling them both.

"Sorry, sir," Isaac said, scrolling down the privacy shield. "It's a virtual blizzard out there. Stratford Hall is just ahead though." Within a few minutes, the chauffeur slowed the car to a halt on the circle drive.

When Justin helped Dani from the vehicle, he gazed upward, brushing away the moisture from the large snowflakes melting on his chin. "Dani, I believe I shall return to Atlanta tonight. I can't afford to become snowbound and miss court proceedings on Monday."

She nodded. Dani lifted her hand to stroke his cheek. "Do drive careful," she said, a touch of guilt intermingling with the sense of relief that overshadowed her. A moment later, they reached the sanctuary of the porch, where Justin unlocked the door and returned her key, his goodnight kiss brief. *No more than I deserve,* she thought, hating that she'd spoiled the evening for him. When Justin turned to go, she called to the chauffeur, who stood waiting until Justin entered his car. "Isaac, please take extra care in the trip back to Atlanta."

The chauffeur tipped his hat, smiling. "Yes, Ma'am. I shall indeed."

Surveying the grounds, Dani admired the majestic scene in childish delight. The beams from the flood lamps stationed at the corners of the house offered a magic all their own, spiraling the estate into a semblance of Camelot in winter. "Breathtaking," she uttered.

Following the men's departure, Dani climbed the stairs, bypassing her room to stand a moment later at one of the large conservatory windows. Spellbound by the icy flakes bombarding the roof of the gazebo, she withdrew from the room after several minutes to hurry downstairs. Within seconds, she traipsed across the ballroom floor. Unlocking the French doors, she entered the courtyard, the lighted cobblestone pathway guiding the way to her favorite spot on the estate. She looked around, knowing she shouldn't be out here alone. But no sign of Davenport or his accomplice had been discovered anywhere near the hall since her escape with death. She could almost believe they'd given up their intentions against her. Glancing around again and not seeing anything out of the ordinary, she moved cautiously toward the gazebo.

Stepping onto the planked floor a moment later, she brushed aside the moist white powder to clear a seat on the bench overlooking the creek. Huddled deep into her fur coat, she reflected on the previous hour.

Justin had finally proposed. Her utmost desire lay snuggled in the palm of her hand. But did she have his love? Loving someone and caring for someone were two different categories in her view. She watched the greedy brook gobble the snow from the air without mercy. According to fictional romance, this should be the happiest moment in her life. Sighing, Dani brushed away the inexplicable tears seeping from the corners of her eyes. Maybe she'd put too much reliance on romantic fantasy.

The sound of a voice caused her to spin around. "Blake! You frightened me."

"Sorry. I heard you descend the stairs, and when you didn't return right away, I grew concerned." He smiled. "It wasn't hard to trace your steps. The ballroom doors are wide open." He grew serious. "Dani, it's dangerous for you to be out here by yourself."

She sighed. "You're right, I know." She held out her hand to catch a few flakes of snow. "It's so beautiful and peaceful out here. I couldn't stay away."

In the predawn light, he scrutinized her water-stained shoes with a critical eye. "Don't you think you should come inside? Mrs. O'Brien will have my hide if you catch a cold. I can just imagine the trial your taste buds would have to endure from her countless home remedies."

Dani couldn't hold back her laughter, in spite of her contention with him over his conduct at the country club. "You're right. It would be terrible." She threw a glance over her shoulder. "This is a wonderful place for soul searching."

He put his hand on her arm, beholding her features in the light from the flood lamp attached to the house. "Would you like to discuss what's troubling you?"

Dani looked down, the sight of his fingers on her coat causing her pulse to quicken. "No. Thanks anyhow. Although I will take your advice and return to the house."

How could she tell him about Justin's proposal and her hesitation in accepting it? How could she disclose to Blake Spencer that each time he came near, she responded to him like a teenager enthralled with her first crush? How could she explain her attraction for two men at the same time when she couldn't comprehend it herself? Justin was sophisticated, resourceful, and handsome. Wasn't he the kind of man she'd desired as a husband? And too, once she concluded that Justin was the man for her, wouldn't the infatuation she had for Blake be discarded by the wayside? Mrs. Justin Harcourt. How could she go wrong?

Taking her hand, Blake guided her down the snowy gazebo steps. Turning to thank him, her breath slowed at his proximity. All at once the storm faded into oblivion as he buried his hands inside her coat to gather her against his broad chest. When he lowered his face, his hat brim shaded her face from the soft glow of dawn rising on the horizon. She closed her eyes, anticipating the touch of his mouth, conscious of another battle lost to Blake in the war of love brandishing her heart. No matter how much she wanted to deny the fact, he meant more to her than she cared to admit. To her chagrin, God knew it and so did Blake.

# THE SNOWSTORM

"*N*ope. I was wrong," Blake said, shattering the early morning stillness. Dani stepped back from his arms, startled. "Wh … What?" she said, her sudden movement dislodging the thin layer of snow draping her shoulders.

At her blank look, Blake tapped the end of her bright red nose with his forefinger. "It's not frozen yet. I thought old Jack Frost might have played another one of his tricks. Now scoot along, Miss McKinnon, before we turn into icicles."

"But I thought …" She glanced at the twinkle in his eyes. "Oh, just forget it."

Dani flung away from him, her weather-reddened cheeks deepening several shades in color. She carefully stepped toward the house, losing her foothold just before gaining security on the canopied courtyard. Righting her balance, she stared down Blake's offer to help, clinching her fists at the sight of the tall Texan's huge grin.

*Of all the nerve!* How dare he tamper with her emotions! Stomping the snow from her shoes, she sidestepped the sleeping rose arbor and entered the ballroom. Not about to face him again, she left the securing of the doors to Blake.

In staccato time, Dani's high heels tapped a rhythm on the parquet tiles, the sound grating on her ears like sandpaper. She looked down. Her motley-stained shoes aped her thoughts, remorse splotched with anger and—she winced—disappointment. She kicked them from her toes, vowing never to look at them again.

She streaked up the stairs, pausing on the gallery landing to catch her breath, stretching to her full height at the sound of Blake's cordial "good night" from the bottom of the staircase. Her lips straightened to near nothingness when she heard his muffled chuckle.

Inside her room, Dani tossed her clothes aside and turned on the shower. But she found that no amount of scrubbing could rid the guilt pouncing on her mind. Moments later, she threw on her nightgown and crawled into bed, pulling the covers close to her chin, moaning with shame. How would she ever be able to look Justin in the eyes again?

She'd wanted—Dani recalled how her arms stole around Blake's neck—yes, she'd almost begged for that moonlight kiss. And she on the verge of marriage to another man! Shaking her head, she prayed. *Heavenly Father, I need your help in the worst kind of way. Where is the sense of all this?*

When she awoke early that afternoon, the memory of her tryst in the snow with Blake charged into her thoughts. Following her morning ritual, she paged the housekeeper on the intercom. "Mrs. O'Brien, I think I'll just have juice and coffee in my room."

"Of course," Mrs. O'Brien said, a twinge of concern in her voice. "You're not feeling a bit under the weather, are you, lass?"

"No. Just too late a night." She heard Mrs. O'Brien's sigh of relief.

"I'll have it to ye in no time."

While Dani waited, she poured over her correspondence, thankful that she owed several letters to her friends in Hartford. Answering them would require the rest of the afternoon. She might join Mrs. O'Brien for dinner, that is, if Blake had plans to dine in his room.

Dani contemplated her decision. She wondered if the person who'd coined the term *yellar* had known someone like her.

Dani carried the letters across the hall to her sitting room, giving a silent thank you to Clive for laying a fire in the fireplace. She stoked the embers until it blazed once more and then walked over to the window to view the deluge of the storm. A good eight inches covered the grounds, plus, to her amazement, large flakes continued to pepper the earth at a rapid rate.

When she heard a knock on the door, she pasted a sunny smile on her face, ready to greet Mrs. O'Brien. However, her face quickly sobered at the sight of Blake bearing her breakfast tray. Her neck muscles grew taut, cutting off her cheerful salutation.

"Good afternoon, Dani. I volunteered to bring up your meal. Hope you don't mind," he said, placing the silver platter on a nearby table. "I'm sure Mrs. O'Brien appreciated the reprieve from the climb."

Blake shifted from one foot to the other. "Well, I promised Clive I'd help him shovel snow this afternoon." He gave her a heart-stopping smile. "Gotta earn my keep, you know. Not that it will do much good. The weatherman is predicting another six inches by nightfall." He surveyed her uninviting expression, a hint of mirth lighting up his eyes. "I guess an afternoon trek in the snow with me is out of the question?"

Anger flashed in her eyes. She opened her mouth to speak, but the phone rang, slicing the retort from her lips.

Giving her a salute, Blake disappeared down the hallway, whistling a popular love song. Closing her eyes, she drew the deepest breath she could muster before she picked up the phone.

"Hello, Justin. How are you surviving this weather?"

"Fine. And what about you?"

Dani glanced toward the door. "Everything is just great now. How is Atlanta fairing?"

"Not so well. The city doesn't have the equipment or the manpower to handle dense, unprecedented snowfalls. However, the noon news reported that the mayor has called in crews from farther north to help mobilize the area. Say, Dani," he said, his tone softening. "Have you decided to marry me?"

Dani felt the receiver slip in her fingers. She strengthened her grip, glad that he couldn't see the guilty flush stealing across her features. "Please, Justin." Would he be as ready to escort her down the aisle if he knew about the early morning escapade?

"Okay, Dani, I can take a hint," he said, chuckling, his laughter slightly strained. "I won't pressure you, although I've never been known for patience."

"Maybe I just want to keep you in suspense," she said, her teasing lilt sounding much loftier than she felt.

"In that case, I might have to jump on the nearest sleigh and steal you away tonight, holding you captive in my arms until you say yes."

The phone hid her half-smile as she thought, *That might solve his problem, but what about my feelings for Blake I can't seem to resolve?* To Justin she replied, "When can I expect you?"

Justin's laughter mingled with her own. "I'll be there when I finish preparing these briefs for court. Duty first, you know."

Their conversation spent a few minutes later, Dani settled back against the couch to ponder her circumstances. The problem with Blake had to be dealt with before she could give Justin an affirmative answer to his proposal. But the one situation that bothered her most was Justin's lack of a personal relationship with Jesus Christ. She'd avoided the problem until now in hopes it would correct itself. Could she marry someone who didn't live according to the standards of God's Holy Word? She darted a glance toward her Bible. Would their love be strong enough to endure whatever dilemma might arise from such a relationship?

Rubbing the creases from her brow, Dani reached for the phone and then drew back her hand as Blake's image filled her mind. No need to discuss it with the Pendergraffs now. They were too perceptive. Dani rose from the sofa, the room seeming to diminish in size. Maybe Mrs. O'Brien had some input that would aid the decision-making process. She found the housekeeper in the kitchen preparing their afternoon tea.

"'Tis good ye've decided to join the rest of the world." Dani threw Mrs. O'Brien a suspicious look. She shook her head. "No need to try to fool the likes of me. What's ailing ye, lass?" Mrs. O'Brien said, pausing in her task to brush a wisp of hair from Dani's forehead.

"Justin asked me to marry him last night."

Mrs. O'Brien returned to the stove to switch off the burner beneath the whistling teakettle, her eyebrows drawn together in thought. "'Tis no more than I expected. What did you tell him?"

Dani wondered at Mrs. O'Brien's lack of enthusiasm. "That I didn't want to do anything rash."

"Aye, 'tis good ye felt that way. I've heard that Mr. Justin is a good bargain in the marriage mart, although he cost his father many a sleepless night. Boyish pranks, ye know, plus some gambling predicament he got himself into while in college. Miss Mathilda felt that these scrapes would have been prevented had his mother lived to raise him. 'Tis so hard for a man to be both mother and father to his children. But the lad seems to be sowing a crop of good oats now."

Dani brightened with relief. "His mother died?

"Yes, poor soul. Leukemia, I believe, when Justin was but a babe. 'Tis a shame his first marriage failed. There's talk that he and his childhood sweetheart, Marguerite Van Buren, would go before the altar." Mrs. O'Brien sighed. "But I guess that ye're the one that's set his heart to spinning."

Again puzzled by Mrs. O'Brien's downcast look, Dani opted to forego the temptation to inquire about the illustrious Marguerite. "It would appear thus. But you know what it's like for me now—a completely new world from my orderly existence in Hartford." A sound of distorted mirth escaped her lips. "The phrase 'till death do us part' has a whole new meaning for me. Who can say how many months we might have as man and wife with Davenport and his brother still at large?"

"Now, Miss Danielle, ye mustn't ride that wave. God won't let us down. His faithfulness will see us through."

"But something else concerns me." Dani caught a glimpse of Blake and Clive out the kitchen window, shovels swinging high above their heads. "I...I think I'd say yes without hesitation if Justin would become a Christian. But he won't even talk to me about it anymore."

"'Tis well ye are concerned. God's stand on the subject is clear in His Word. If we yoke ourselves to an unbeliever, we're asking for troubles."

At that moment the kitchen door swung open. Followed by the collie, Blake and Clive walked in the room, their shoes depositing puddles of water onto the floor. Mrs. O'Brien shooed them into the pantry to take off their wet outer garments. Dani rose from the table to search for a mop. Soon they were all settled, enjoying the housekeeper's fare.

Dani showered Clive with attention, careful to make sure she didn't give the slightest hint she enjoyed Blake's company. "How are you, Clive, and your family?"

"We're jest fine, Miss Danielle, though my missus has had quite a time corralin' those youngins. They're sure enjoyin' the outdoors. I can't 'member when we've had this much snow."

Dani laughed. "I can't blame them. As a child, my friends and I had hours of fun building snowmen, snow forts, and the like. An ample supply of ammunition stored nearby, we'd soon be pelting one another with snowballs. I was a tomboy at heart; my grandmother worried that I wouldn't be much of a lady when I grew up."

Blake grinned. "I'd say she wasted her time," he drawled before consuming another scone.

Dani ignored his comment, directing her attention to the cook. "Delicious, as usual, Mrs. O'Brien, but I still have some correspondence that needs attending. Give my regards to your family, Clive." With a slight nod to Blake, Dani exited the kitchen, ignoring Mrs. O'Brien's quizzical glance.

When the dinner hour rolled around, Dani couldn't bring herself to go downstairs. She informed Mrs. O'Brien of the fact, claiming a lack of hunger and a desire to retire early as her reasons—anything to prevent silent cat and mouse games with Blake.

When she'd sealed and stamped her last letter, Dani drew up her legs and propped her feet upon the edge of the sofa, resting her hands and chin on top of her knees. She stared into the fireplace, observing the flames that seemed to compete for superiority in the grate. She could almost visualize the quote "Hell hath no fury like a woman scorned" in the leaping inferno.

She cringed as guilt consumed her mind for her childish behavior toward Blake. It hadn't been his ardent display of affection that had disgruntled her but his rejection. Why, she'd all but thrown herself into his arms. Not to discount the fact that she'd blamed him for her betrayal of Justin's trust. The truth be told, she felt more ire at herself than Blake.

A swooshing sound preceded by a light knock broke into Dani's musings. She darted a glance toward the sitting room door, startled by the intrusion. Blake stood there, his muscular frame filling the open doorway, his hand on the doorknob. "I guess you didn't hear my knock. May I come in?" He ran his hand down his blue jean-clad leg, his gaze hesitant to meet her eyes. "I'd like to talk to you for a minute."

She studied his expression. "Is something wrong, Blake?" she asked, a touch of alarm singeing her thoughts.

He smoothed back his hair, letting his hand rest on the back of his neck. "I just want to apologize for last night and this morning. I upset you, and I'm sorry."

Dani raised her hand to switch on a lamp to lighten the room and then let it fall to her side. The shame visible on her face would no doubt be sufficient effervescence. She bowed her head. "I've come to understand what a fool I made of myself. Please forgive me."

Within seconds, Blake stood before her, lifting her chin. "Dani, look at me. You did nothing for which to be ashamed. I'm the one who should wear that brand." He took both her hands in his, lifting Dani to her feet. "I acted like an ogre at the dance, and this morning, well, I humiliated you, and there's no excuse for that.

"When I came near the gazebo and saw you gazing out across the brook, you looked so forlorn, as if you bore the weight of the world on your shoulders. As I stood watching you, the memory of a female deer I came across one afternoon while on a hunting expedition came to mind. There she stood, wary of me yet not about to leave the grazing fawn at her side. She licked the top of the fawn's head and then turned soulful eyes upon me. She seemed to be pleading for the chance to care for her baby. I tell you, Dani, I wanted to run and throw my arms around her neck and beg forgiveness for the cruelty of this world, swearing allegiance that I'd protect her till my dying day.

"From the first moment I saw you outside Pendergraff Accounting, I've wanted to spend the rest of eternity loving you, protecting you, caring for you like no other before me."

Blake turned aside, mopping the sheen of moisture from his forehead with his shirtsleeve. "It used to be a game with me to steal Justin's girls, but not with you, Dani."

Blake walked to the door. Facing her once again, he opened his mouth to speak and then pressed his lips tightly together. After a moment, he seemed to find the words he desired to speak. "I didn't intend to say these things, but I'm glad it's out in the open. Unless you give me a sign that you desire to hear more of the same, as far as I'm concerned, the subject is closed. But just so you know, about this morning, it took every ounce of strength I possessed to resist your loveliness."

The door whispered shut. Dani sank to the rug near the hearth, tears cascading down her cheeks.

Later, her composure intact, Dani descended the stairs, seeking solace in the peace that often radiated from Mrs. O'Brien. She found her friend in the gathering room with Lad tucked at her feet, eyeing Percy's warfare with a ball of yarn. When Dani perched on the sofa, the cat jumped to her side, content to feel his mistress's hand upon his head. Percy's loud purring ceased at the sound of the phone.

"Probably that wrong number again. The same man has called several times today," Mrs. O'Brien said, starting to lay aside her latest needlework to reach for the phone.

"Let me get it," Dani said, motioning for the housekeeper to stay seated. "Hello? Dani McKinnon speaking."

"Well, now, Dani. I wondered how many calls it would take to get you on the line. You best tell your buckskin bodyguard he won't be any help when I'm ready to give you what you deserve. The day of reckoning is at hand for you."

Before she could respond to the muffled voice, the caller rang off the line. Dani stood dead still, the phone cradled in her hand. Seeing Dani pale, Mrs. O'Brien came to stand alongside.

"Who was it, lass?"

At that moment, they heard Blake calling her name as he clamored down the stairs. Seconds later, he took the receiver from Dani's hand, replacing it before he led her back to the sofa. "I heard every word on the extension upstairs."

Her eyes large with fright, she gazed across the room. "It wasn't Davenport—someone else, someone who knows me well enough to call me Dani." She knotted her hands into fists. "On days like today, I think dying would be preferable to a life hounded by stalkers."

Mrs. O'Brien threw up her hands to clasp Dani by the shoulders. "Nay, Miss Danielle, ye must not speak so."

"I can't imagine anyone harboring hate so vile. What could I have done to cause such loathing?" She sank onto the couch, heart-wrenching sobs pouring from her lips, the housekeeper rushing to comfort her mistress in any way possible.

Blake's face contorted with rage. "Those two reprobates deserve to hang from the highest tree in Georgia," he said, jerking his BlackBerry from its case.

A short time later, Dani stood in the foyer gazing upward, her focus on the second-floor landing. If the heaviness in her heart drifted to her legs, she'd never find the strength to climb to her room.

Late the next morning, following fitful sleep, Dani entered an empty kitchen, save for Lad and Percy taking a sunbath in the rays streaming through the windows. She'd just popped a couple of slices of bread in the toaster when Blake entered from the outside. Bundled in warm clothing, his cheeks ruddy from the exposure, he greeted her with a wave of his gloved hand.

"Good. You're up. You need to come with me. Although the roads don't allow our attendance at church today, I think God might have sent something that will cheer you anyhow," he said, his sparkling eyes twin displays of excitement. "Don't dawdle now, or you'll miss what Clive and I have to show you."

Dani caught his eagerness. "Okay. Okay. I'll be out in a jiffy." Forgetting her breakfast, she rushed from the room to throw on a coat, hurrying to comply with his request.

# NEW DISCOVERY

W ithin five minutes, Dani zipped through the veranda doors. Blake, standing by the courtyard fountain, seemed unaware of her presence, his attention absorbed in the construction of the colonnade.

"I didn't realize private investigators held such an avid interest in colonial architecture," Dani said, nearing the fountain.

Blake returned her smile and then continued to study the base of the Grecian statue. "While waiting for you, I felt warm air gush from these bricks. That's odd since the temperature is below freezing. I've been indulging my curiosity. See for yourself."

Dani leaned over to inspect the area. "You're right. I can feel it too."

Blake pointed to a series of slits in the patterned design. "The draft is coming from those. All four sides are constructed the same way."

"Hm. I never noticed them before. Do you suppose the statue serves as a vent for the old wine cellar that Mrs. O'Brien told us the Thorndikes closed off when they remodeled the kitchen area?"

"Could be."

Dani begin to shiver. "By the way, what's the surprise you were so fired up about a few minutes ago? It's hard to believe you dragged me from a warm house to look at a pile of bricks." She grinned at the look on his face.

"Oh, yeah. Come on. I hope we're not too late," Blake said, grabbing her hand to pull her onto a shoveled path.

When they reached the outskirts of the garden, Dani saw Clive and his three older children in the distance sitting atop a horse-drawn wagon loaded with bales of hay and sacks of feed corn. They were engrossed in some diversion near the woods.

Taking Dani's arm with one hand, Blake slowed their steps, approaching the wagon as quietly as possible. Clive and his children greeted the two arrivals with a smile and then nodded toward the forest. "Oh, my," Dani breathed when she took in the splendor of the winter panorama before her.

Below the knoll, a small herd of deer feasted on strewn hay atop the crested snow. The does guarded their fawns with wary eyes while they partook of the provision. Dani held her fingers to her lips to stifle a chuckle when a young buck used his antlers to nudge a wandering fawn back into the herd. Too soon, something spooked the deer, and they bolted into the timber.

Dani felt Blake's eyes upon her. She glanced his way, thanking him with a smile. He removed a piece of straw from between his lips and then leaned back against the wagon. "Would you like to accompany us, Dani? We want to supply the animals with enough food to tide them over until the snow melts."

Dani observed the eager faces awaiting her answer. "I'd love to help." For just an instant, she regretted her decision when Blake lifted her into the wagon. Their eyes came together, the magnetism between them sparking feelings that best be forgotten.

Clive whistled, and the mare plodded forward, high stepping the powdery glaze. At one point, the movement of the wagon jostled Blake against Dani, the strength of his muscular touch taking her breath. She saw him grin from the corners of her eyes. What she'd give to swat that ridiculous smugness from his face.

Late that afternoon, Dani descended the stairs and strolled toward the library, intending to spend the evening curled up with an exciting novel. Opening the door, she found Blake, to her surprise, pouring over one of her ancestor's journals.

Blake acknowledged her presence with a smile. "I hope you don't mind that I took you up on your offer."

"Certainly not. Did you find something interesting?"

He nodded. "Were you aware that one of your progenitors, Nathan Kingsley, a converted Quaker, smuggled runaway slaves during the era of the Underground Railroad?"

"No. I haven't read that particular diary. If I remember my history, the Underground Railroad functioned as an escape network to help Southern slaves flee to the North before and during the Civil War."

"That's correct. According to Nathan, unknown to his family, he used Stratford Hall as a temporary station to host fugitive slaves en route to Indiana and Ohio. Levi Coffin, the infamous Quaker known as the president of the Underground Railroad, mentored Kingsley's activities. It is reputed Coffin aided and abetted over 3,000 slaves to Northern freedom." Blake replaced the journal with an old family Bible. "According to this record, Nathan died at Gettysburg fighting for the Union.

Dani cocked her head to one side, a look of astonishment on her face. "And to think one of my forebears participated in the Underground Railroad. Does his journal indicate where Nathan hid the runaway slaves?"

"Yes, in a cave on the plantation."

Dani's eyes widened. "Did you say a cave?"

Blake smiled at her intuitive look. "My thoughts exactly when I stumbled onto this information. The cave had a tunnel that led to a bank of the Chattahoochee River, which borders the northeast side of the estate. At night the slaves would travel in canoes to the next station near the headwaters of the river on their way north. This could be the same cave Davenport spoke of to his brother the night you were shot."

"Maybe that's where they've been hiding all this time," Dani said, turning to leave the room. "I'll go ask Mrs. O'Brien if she knows the location."

Blake reached out to stay her departure. "Don't bother. When I discussed it with her earlier, she said if Mrs. Thorndike knew of such a place, she never voiced it to her."

"But how would Davenport know about the cave? Lucky find?"

Blake rubbed the slight stubble on his chin. "I think it had to do with someone's good fortune all right, but not Davenport's." Blake pulled a stack of papers from his briefcase. "This is a copy of Sergeant Hagerman's report on your case. There's a summary of an interview his friend had with an elderly prisoner who bunked with Maury Davidson while he served his time."

Dani nodded. "Justin shared that information with me some time back."

"If I were a betting man, I'd say the cave is what Davidson referred to when he told his cellmate about a discovery that would aid his and Rosemary's plan to pillage the hall. It would be the ideal place to stash the valuables until they could be sold."

"But that still doesn't explain how they'd enter the hall in the first place to—and I quote—'steal the antiques right out from under the Thorndikes' noses,' as Davidson told his prison friend."

Blake centered his gaze on the globe across the room, his eyelids dropping half shut as though in deep concentration. "I'm still working on that. An idea or two keeps cropping up, but so far nothing concrete to justify them."

"Oh?" she said, raising her eyebrows.

Blake squeezed her nose. "Don't be so curious. All in good time." He rose from the desk. "If you'll excuse me, I'll go phone the sheriff. He needs to know this information right away. Also, Mrs. O'Brien suggested I inquire as to his knowledge of the layout of the estate. It seems he was one of the few people your aunt allowed to hunt for game on the estate. Perhaps he knows about the cave."

Blake paused at the doorway to stretch. At the sight of his taut muscles straining against his shirt, Dani felt her throat constrict. Directing her eyes toward the leather-lined shelves, she began to run her fingers across the book titles, the memory of the feel of him making her knees go weak.

Later at the dinner table, Blake informed Dani that Sheriff Wilson knew nothing about a cave on the estate. Noting her crestfallen expression, Blake squeezed her hand.

"Don't give up yet. We intend to start a search for the cave just as soon as this weather breaks."

By the next weekend, a warming trend had dissipated the last of the snow from the storm. The thought of roaming about the estate at her leisure lifted Dani's spirits. Today, however, insisting that Mrs. O'Brien accept her help in her yearly mission to clean the ballroom, Dani strode into the room, finding that the housekeeper had begun the chore already. Believing the task would be more agreeable with music in the background, Dani plugged in a CD player and loaded one of the discs she'd brought with her, thinking Strauss apropos for the occasion.

Having polished the balustrade in front of the orchestra box until it sparkled, she paused, circling the gilded room with her eyes, recalling the valentine dance she'd attended with Justin. How wonderful it would be to experience the pageantry the hall boasted in bygone days. All at once her eyes glimmered with excitement. Maybe the idea wasn't too farfetched after all. Dani stood stock-still, her thoughts in a tailspin. Could she pull it off?

Mrs. O'Brien, observing her mistress's faraway look, discontinued her cleaning and hurried to Dani's side. "Is there a problem, lass?"

Dani leaned forward, her eyes widening with inspiration. "What do you think of the idea of us hosting a spring cotillion? It would be a pleasant way to reciprocate the kindness my new friends both here and in Atlanta have extended to me since my arrival in Georgia."

Mrs. O'Brien grew thoughtful, her eyes beginning to twinkle. "Aye, lass, 'twould be a glorious occasion, no doubt. I'm sure we could count on Clive's missus and oldest daughter to help with the preparations."

"And I know the perfect theme for the ball—nineteenth century, period costumes and all." She put her forefinger to her chin. "Let's see. How does the end of April sound? Spring flowers should be at their peak by then."

"Aye. The estate will be afoxed with dogwood, camellias, azaleas, hyacinth, and the like, not to discount the tulips and iris asporting their colors as well."

Dani grabbed the mop and danced around the floor. "Just think, the cotillion, the quadrille, the waltz; we'll have a grand time."

Shaking with laughter, Mrs. O'Brien returned to her task, saying, "Ye'd best not forget the Virginia Reel if ye want to remain in good graces with the Southern folk."

❦

One evening a few weeks later, Dani joined Mrs. O'Brien in the gathering room for their nightly devotions. She plopped down on the sofa, exhaling a deep sigh. Mrs. O'Brien surveyed Dani with a discerning eye.

"Ye look a frightful tired tonight. Are ye still busy with the plans for the ball?"

"I've finished most of the arrangements. I hope the outcome of the event will justify my extravagance."

Mrs. O'Brien smiled. "I've been in the South long enough to know that it will tickle your guests' fancy like nothing else could. Pomp and circumstance is a trademark of Southern culture. So ye just bury your fret."

Dani jumped up to hug her friend. "Thanks, Mrs. O'Brien. You always seem to say the right thing to encourage me when I'm down." Dani resumed her position on the couch and reached for her Bible on the end table, opening it to a chapter in Proverbs. "I believe it's my turn to read tonight."

The following morning, Dani searched for Blake, finally locating him near the Grecian statue in the midst of the garden. "What are you doing?" she asked, eyeing his critical, calculated examination of the brickwork.

"Still working on a hunch. Have you ever considered that there might be a secret entrance to the hall? That would account for your perpetrators' uninvited presence inside the house."

Dani's eyes widened. *Of course.* Why hadn't she thought of that before? The age of the estate alone endorsed the possibility. "Do you think there's a hidden door in the base of the statue?" She watched his trek around the fountain.

"That warm air has to be coming from somewhere. I'd say a concealed room or passageway. This statue is too far west of the kitchen area to be the old wine cellar Mrs. O'Brien mentioned. But I've scrutinized every inch of these bricks, and nothing is forthcoming."

"Is this the idea you referred to earlier in the library?"

"Yes. However, I'm back to square one." He watched Dani check the time on her timepiece. "What are you up to this morning?"

"Well, since you still won't let me go anywhere alone, I thought you might drive me to the print shop in Evansville to pick up the invitations for the ball."

"Sure. When?"

"Right away, if you don't mind. I've got some other shopping to do as well, and I want to be back to the hall before Justin arrives." Dani watched a flicker of sadness wash across Blake's features. She stood on her tiptoes and kissed his cheek. "You're a wonderful friend, Blake."

All at once he turned to her, his face contorted with anger. "That's great, Dani, but I am human." For a long moment, his eyes held her startled gaze, a look of silent appeal for forgiveness replacing his tortured expression. He brushed past her, throwing soft-spoken words over his shoulder. "I'll go start the truck."

All the way into town, Dani agonized over her guilt. She hadn't meant to hurt Blake. For that reason alone she'd disregarded Justin's constant pressure for her to marry him. She'd hoped in time that Blake's feelings for her would subside, but they seemed to grow stronger. She saw it each time their eyes met. An engagement announcement would cause him even more pain. How could she do that to him? Nonetheless, the longer she put Justin off, the more Blake would think he had a chance with her. She wasn't being fair to either one of them, much less to herself. But did she have a right to marry Justin when he might have to bury his new wife soon after she said I do? And what about his lack of interest in Christianity? Could they not be one in spirit and be happy just as soul mates?

When Dani and Blake returned to the hall early that afternoon, they were surprised to find the sheriff's car parked in the driveway. Their eyes asking similar questions, they hurried into the house, finding Sheriff Wilson and one of his deputies conversing with Mrs. O'Brien in the formal parlor.

When the housekeeper saw Dani, she rushed to her side. "Oh, Miss Danielle, 'tis awful, just awful." She dabbed her eyes with the tissue in her hand. Someone has stolen the Danielle tea service and the Louis XIV candlesticks."

Dani shot a glance toward the fireplace mantle and then shook her head in amazement. "When? How?"

Sheriff Wilson stepped forward. "This morning, maybe. As to how, we can't be sure. There's no sign of forced entry anywhere in the hall. Mrs. O'Brien discovered the theft close to an hour ago."

"Aye. Awielding me dust cloth about the room earlier, after I returned from me visit with the Widow Grayson, I noticed the items were gone. At first I thought ye had taken them to your sitting room, but after searching the whole house in vain, I phoned the sheriff."

"Did you find any prints?" Blake said, watching the deputy put away his fingerprint dusting equipment.

The sheriff shook his head. "Just the expected ones." He faced Dani. "I suggest you and Mrs. O'Brien take inventory of the furnishings and then let me know if anything else is missing. In the meantime, I'll contact area antique dealers to see if anyone has tried to sell the items."

"Do you think Davenport is responsible for this?" Dani asked, her face still drained of its color.

"Possibly. However, there's another group that might be involved. We've had several burglaries in the county in the past few weeks, and our leads indicate gang activity. Members of the Titans, a gang from Atlanta, have infiltrated some of our county's troubled youth, inciting them to take part in the crimes. We'll soon know if Stratford Hall is one of their targets. There's always at least one gang member who likes to brag about their misdeeds. Hopefully, he'll talk to one of our undercover deputies."

A look of compassion flitted across the sheriff's features. "Miss McKinnon, I'm sorry about these additional troubles. We'll do our best to recover your valuables."

Later, when the authorities had taken their leave, Mrs. O'Brien left the room to fetch them some refreshment while Blake stood at the window, his eyes glued to the red sports car approaching the house.

Dani, seated on the piano bench, remarked to no one in particular. "This harassment has to stop, or we'll all go crazy."

"You're right, more than you know. If something doesn't break soon, we'll both suffer a great deal of agony."

Dani stared at him, a puzzled frown on her brow. Before she could inquire further, the sound of the doorbell took the words from her mouth.

"I'll get it, Mrs. O'Brien," Dani called from the foyer.

A sound of irritation escaped Justin's lips when he saw Dani's casual dress. "I was hoping we could leave earlier than usual."

"I'm sorry, but a crisis has just occurred."

Justin's expression turned to one of concern, his gaze questioning when Blake stepped from the formal parlor into the hallway.

Dani headed for the stairway. "I'll let Blake explain while I go change."

Once they arrived in Atlanta, Justin drove her to his house. His father out for the evening with Mrs. Gilmore, Justin surprised Dani with a meal he prepared and cooked himself. Following dinner with soft music and lights surrounding them, they relaxed on the leather sofa.

"Justin, you never cease to amaze me. Have you dabbled in gourmet cooking long?"

He grinned. "How do you think I've managed to remain a bachelor all this time?" He pulled her close to him. "A circumstance I'd gladly change if I could sway a certain beautiful young lady to cooperate." He leaned forward, touching his lips to hers. After a moment, he raised his head. "What's wrong? You seem a bit distracted."

Dani, too, wondered at her lack of response. "I . . . I guess I have a lot on my mind, the cotillion and all."

"I thought you had that all arranged."

"I do. I'm just nervous about it."

Justin smiled. "No need to be. You'll be a great hostess." He pulled her back into his arms for another kiss.

When their lips met, Blake's winsome, crooked smile appeared in her mind. She broke the hold. "Justin, would you mind taking me home? Tonight I'm lousy company for anyone, including myself. I think the robbery has upset me more than I realized."

He frowned. "If you insist. Let me get your things."

In the dash light of the car, Dani winced at the hard set of his jaw. She started to give him some sort of explanation but tightened her lips. How could she define the miserable end to their evening when she didn't understand it herself? They arrived at the hall in record time, Justin leaving her after a brief good night kiss and a promise to call before his car roared out of sight.

"Well, you're home early," Blake said, opening the door.

Anger flared in her eyes. "Don't even talk to me, Blake Spencer." She raced up the stairs two at a time. He caught up with her in the gallery.

"Dani, what's wrong?"

She twisted out of his grip. "Nothing." Tears trickled down her cheeks. "Please leave me alone." She started down the narrow hallway leading to her rooms and then turned around, laying her hand on Blake's arm. "Just blame it on my complicated life." A smile of apology on her lips, she proceeded to her bedroom.

Close to noon the next day, Mrs. O'Brien drove Dani to Evansville for her luncheon engagement with Mrs. Radcliffe. Recalling the urgency in her voice when she'd phoned yesterday to confirm their appointment, Dani hurried into the restaurant, Mrs. O'Brien promising to return after she'd finished her shopping.

# CHARITABLE REQUEST

*D*ani slid into the booth opposite Mrs. Radcliffe, a little short of breath. Taking a menu from the hostess, Dani smiled at her benevolent comrade in arms.

"Miss McKinnon, I heard about your horrible accident. Poaching for game on posted property has always been a problem in the county."

Dani threw her companion a suspicious look. "Poaching?"

"Yes, the term for people who hunt illegally, for instance, out of season, spotlighting on private property, that sort of thing."

Dani pretended to study the menu. "I see." *How did that rumor get started?* Dani smiled within. The hazard of living in a small community, no doubt.

Mrs. Radcliffe glanced at Dani, an apologetic look on her face. "I'm sorry, Miss McKinnon. I can see it bothers you to talk about it. I've been praying for your speedy recovery."

Dani breathed easier. "Thank you. That must have been difficult for you. Mrs. O'Brien told me of your own loss in a similar incident."

Mrs. Radcliffe took a drink of water and then wiped a tear from the corner of her eye. "Yes, a tragic affair, one that I didn't handle too well. But God has sustained me, along with the forgiveness of my friends for my deplorable actions at times. By the way, I wasn't at all kind to you when we first met. I've never asked your forgiveness. Would you please accept my apology?"

Dani reached across the table and squeezed Mrs. Radcliffe's hand. "By all means. Since we've become friends, I've never given our first meeting a second thought."

Mrs. Radcliffe smiled. "Thank you."

When the waitress took their order, Mrs. Radcliffe continued. "Until recently, I blamed God for taking my son from me, but like the Scriptures say, 'God doesn't kill, steal, or destroy. He came to give us an abundant life.'"

Dani nodded. "I came to that knowledge too not long ago. I grew up feeling the same as you when I lost my parents in an automobile accident at an early age."

Compassion for Dani settled in Helen's eyes and then she brightened. "God has turned my grief into joy. I believe you and Mrs. O'Brien will be pleased with the news as well."

"Oh?"

Mrs. Radcliffe leaned forward, her face illuminating her excitement. "I'm adopting Alex and Andy. Just this morning I signed the papers. I pick them up tomorrow."

Dani beamed. "That *is* wonderful news."

"I fell in love with those blond angels the minute I saw them during the Christmas party at the orphanage. Then after spending the afternoon with them at Stratford Hall on Christmas Day and other times since, I had to have them for my own sons. I can't thank you enough for that holiday kindness."

Dani laid her hand on top of Mrs. Radcliffe's fingers. "I'm delighted for you. I can hardly wait to tell Mrs. O'Brien."

Helen stared off into the distance. "It wasn't the easiest project I've tackled. I had two strikes against me from the beginning—my age and widowhood. Even after badgering a political friend or two for their approval, I wasn't sure the boys would be mine until a couple of days ago. To me it's a miracle."

"You're not that ancient," Dani said, grinning. "Besides, single parent adoptions aren't the rarity they used to be."

"That's true. Although most people prefer infants, the adoption agency held out until the last minute, hoping a married couple would ask for the boys."

Dani smiled at the waitress delivering their salads and then resumed her conversation with Mrs. Radcliffe. "Have the boys been told yet?"

"Mr. Coons is to do that today. Then tomorrow the boys and I go before the judge to finalize the procedure. They've been ecstatic about the idea of living with me."

Dani again congratulated her friend and then changed the conversation. "Now what is this emergency you spoke about on the phone?"

"State funding, as always. The Health and Welfare Department is cutting back their support for the orphanage, and it's up to the citizens of the county to rally and undergird the orphanage budget."

"You know you can count on me for a donation."

"Yes, but the whole county needs to participate. I have something in mind where they can do just that. At the last meeting of the Charity Club—sorry you missed it; we all we're praying for you—while we were tossing ideas back and forth on how to raise the extra money, one of the ladies suggested we have a charity bazaar and all agreed. The problem is where to hold the event."

Dani smiled. "I'm beginning to understand."

Mrs. Radcliffe returned the smile. "Mrs. Thorndike often allowed people to tour the estate grounds in the spring to admire Clive's handiwork. We thought this would be a good calling card, not only for vendors but customers from Carroll County, even the state, once the word is out."

"I agree. What date did you have in mind?"

"The second week in May, if that isn't too soon after the cotillion. By the way, thanks for the invitation. I plan to be there."

"You're welcome." Dani pulled a date book from her handbag, taking a few minutes to study the calendar. "I think we can work that out."

Relief smoothed the worry lines from Helen's brow. "Thank you." She grew thoughtful. "I just heard yesterday that vandals broke into the hall and stole some valuable antiques. Those of us who share like heritages empathize with you."

Dani's countenance turned sad. "I wish I could deny it. I've come to realize that I didn't just inherit property, but a legacy of love, which has woven its pattern into my heart, binding me to all its charm and lore in just a matter of months."

Mrs. Radcliffe held up her glass of lemon water. "Hear! Hear!"

As their glasses touched, they heard Mrs. O'Brien's chuckle. "Now what do ye ladies be celebrating?"

"Several things. Just wait till you hear," Dani said, scooting over to allow room for Mrs. O'Brien to sit alongside. "But most of all our friendship."

Mrs. Radcliffe nodded, a wide smile showing her pleasure.

The day prior to the ball, Dani entered the conservatory to confer with Clive about the floral decorations. She spied him pruning ivy that hung between two of the windows. "Good morning, Clive."

"Mornin,' Miss Danielle. This here ivy got too uppity for its britches—thought it could take all the sun for itself."

Dani laughed and then looked around. "You treat these plants like they were children."

"Yes'm. Some, like those violets over there, have to be pampered with gentleness; then others, like this vine, you have to keep a strong hand on them or else they'll bully the rest into keeping their beauty 'neath their leaves."

Dani looked at Clive as though she were seeing him for the first time. "My guess is that you understand that concept even more than I do. In fact, our ancestors were part of the bloodiest war in history over that issue."

"Miss Danielle, there's not a man alive that wants to feel he's controlled by another gentleman's fancy. The good Lord meant for all his people to be free to use every opportunity available to live life the way they sees fit." Clive scooped up a handful of dirt from a flowerless pot nearby. "It's like this fine soil. Left to itself, it will always be jest dirt, but ya put some seeds in it, water it now and then, pretty soon ya will have a beautiful flower to admire and enjoy." He grinned. "Course, some people, no matter what their station in life, prefer to yield a crop of weeds. That's jest the way it is."

A smile of resignation appeared on her face. "I'm afraid you're right," Dani said, the image of Davenport's face coming to her mind. "Clive, you're a fine man. I'm glad we share the heritage of Stratford Hall."

A broad smile covered his coal black features. "Me too, Miss Danielle, me too."

"Before you leave today, I need to talk to you about some last-minute decorations. Also, I was wondering if you had plenty of help to arrange the conservatory for the dinner tomorrow night. I don't want you to overtax yourself."

"I've got plenty of help. My boy Toby will be here soon after school is out, and Mr. Blake offered his services not an hour ago. All we need is ya here to direct our efforts. I took the chairs and tables out of storage this mornin.' My missus is cleaning them now."

"Good. I knew I could count on you."

Before she left the room, Dani took a quick look around the conservatory. It would be the perfect place for their midnight dinner. The huge windows would reflect the candlelight, creating a lovely atmosphere.

Pondering the long day ahead as she descended the stairs a few moments later, Dani debated whether to call Justin and cancel their concert date for that evening. A moment later, she rejected the idea, not wanting to upset him again. Instead she made a mental promise to make it up to him for the less than enjoyable evenings they'd spent together in the past couple of weeks, the blame hers alone.

"Can't get enough of Stratford Hall history, huh?' Dani said to Blake following her entrance into the library. "I thought I'd find you here. What are you looking for anyway? You don't seem the scholarly type somehow."

"You might be surprised, Miss McKinnon, at the wealth of knowledge I own." He gave her a roguish grin. "Care to find out?"

She couldn't help but smile. "No thanks. Seriously, what do you hope to discover?"

"A clue to the location of the cave. With several of the sheriff's deputies assisting me, I've covered most of the estate and can't find an entrance to a cave anywhere. But we did see fresh tire prints on that old logging road that runs across the property. However, the marks didn't seem to lead anywhere."

"I hate to tear you away from your study, dear old bodyguard of mine, but I need to collect the table decorations from the florist. Could you give me a lift into town?"

Blake stood up, a glint of mirth in his eyes. "Old, am I?" He unbuckled his belt and whipped it from his jeans in a flash. "It sounds like you need a lesson in how to respect your elders. And I'm just the one to teach you."

Dani instinctively backed away, laughter bubbling in her throat. "You wouldn't dare!"

"Oh, no?" He reached out and grabbed her, wrestling her into a position to be spanked. His belt high in the air, he laughed. "Ready to apologize?"

"Okay, I'm sorry," she said, her laughter making it difficult to pronounce the words.

"You don't sound like you mean it."

She had trouble catching her breath. "I do. I swear."

Blake let her stand erect, rethreading his belt a moment later. "I believe you've learned your lesson well."

She marched over to the door, an indignant gleam in her eye. "I'll meet you at the truck, Sir Brute." At his look that promised retaliation, she chuckled and then scampered into the hall.

Dressing early for her date with Justin, Dani left the house to seek a few moments of solitude in the gazebo before his arrival. She touched some of the tiny rosebuds forming on the vines covering the latticed walls. Soon red roses would burst forth in full bloom, the perfect backdrop for the antique auction she planned to stage in the gazebo the day of the bazaar. The three days she and Blake had scoured the countryside for saleable antiques, they'd found county residents to be generous in their donations for the children's home. After the ball, she intended to raid her own attic as well.

Mrs. Radcliffe reported that the whole community had responded well to their project. Even the Atlanta newspapers had given free advertising to announce the charity fair, and the Evansville squire printed up leaflets to be distributed throughout the county. The whole club felt the event would be a huge success.

Dani started at the sound of Justin's voice. She greeted him with a kiss. "I didn't hear you arrive." She pointed out the antics of some baby ducks bathing in the brook. "They had my attention," she said with a chuckle.

"They don't hold near the fascination you do, dear sweet Dani. You look lovely. I hope it's due to anticipation for the evening ahead with me." He took her hand in his, bringing it to his lips. A moment later, arm in arm, they watched the Georgia sunset.

Blake's voice broke the spell. "Oh, excuse me." They both turned startled glances his way. "Mrs. O'Brien thought you might need this."

Dani took the light stole from Blake's hands, the brush of his hand sending a bolt through her like jagged lightning. His dark, smoldering eyes told her he'd experienced a like sensation. Her complexion turned the color of the setting sun. "Th...Thank you. Please tell Mrs. O'Brien I appreciate her thoughtfulness." Steeling her spine, she smiled up at Justin. "Shall we go?"

"Have a good evening, you two," Blake called later from the porch, directing his gaze at Dani.

She hurled an explosive look over her shoulder when she noted his smug grin, aware that only Blake saw it. "Absolutely."

Once in the car, Dani tried in vain to put aside thoughts of Blake. Even when Justin stopped the car at the end of the lane to shower her with affection, it was Blake she kissed with all her heart, not Justin. The realization struck her like a bucket of ice cubes thrown onto a sidewalk on a blazing summer day. Feeling like a traitor, she moved closer to the door, forcing a smile. "We'll never get to the concert at this rate."

Justin grinned. "Would that be so bad?"

Returning to the hall late that night, Dani and Justin sat in the convertible, gazing at the stars overhead. "Dani, please say you'll marry me," Justin pleaded after a long, passionate kiss. Dani resisted his attempt to take her in his arms again. "I'm sorry, Dani. You know how hard it is to keep my hands off you. Just say the word and we'll be married in a week."

Dani pulled in a deep breath. "Okay, Justin, I'll marry you, but not in a week. When this thing with Davenport is behind us then we'll set a date. Deal?"

He looked stunned and then smiled, the moonlight reflecting his look of relief. "Deal."

He sealed his promise with another kiss.

Opening the glove box, he withdrew the familiar jeweler's box. "I've kept this close at hand, waiting for you to make up your mind." Lifting her left hand, he placed the ring on her finger.

Dani stared at the sparkling cold stones. Along with the moonlight, they seemed to reflect the sudden chill in her heart. "I hope

I've made you happy," she said, wondering if all women felt such sadness when given an engagement ring.

When Justin walked her to the door, he gave her shoulders a gentle shake. "Dani, you don't know how much I would have suffered if you had said no."

Later, after he left for the city, Dani sat in a chair next to her bedroom window staring out into the night. She couldn't see the moon, but its beams lit up the sky. After a while she dressed for bed but couldn't sleep. At last she rose from the bed, donning her robe and slippers. Within another moment, she padded through the doorway and down the stairs.

Lad by her side, the moonlight aiding her sight, she climbed into the gazebo, heavy of heart. The tree frogs singing their love songs, she fell onto the wrought-iron bench, unleashing the tears she'd held back all evening.

The collie laid his head on her lap, whimpering as though he understood her plight. She stroked his head. "Oh, Lad, I've really got myself in a fix this time," she said when her sobbing had subsided. "Not even Uncle Bill or Aunt Lucille can get me out of this one."

Shortly thereafter, Dani sensed rather than heard Blake enter the gazebo. "I see I'm not the only one with insomnia."

"I've been checking out the grounds." All at once Blake lifted her left hand, a sound of dismay on his lips. He stared at the brilliance of the ring caught by the moonlight and then dropped her hand as though it burnt his flesh. The next moment, Dani found herself standing erect, her body pulled into Blake's arms. "Dear God, Dani. How could you do it? You know how I feel about you. Look at me." She lifted her eyes. "Why is it so hard for you to admit you love me?"

Fresh tears sprang to her eyes. "I just couldn't turn him down. It would hurt him too much. He's been so good to me, his father so kind to help with Stratford Hall. You said yourself they refused to give up looking for me."

Blake shook her. "You agreed to marry Justin out of obligation?" She tried to turn away from his stricken look, but his bold, hard stare held her mesmerized. "You'd sacrifice the love that's between us because of *obligation*?"

He gripped her shoulders so tight, she cried out in pain. "Blake, you're hurting me!"

"Not near as much as Justin will. He'll make your life miserable. You'll never be happy with him."

All of a sudden, Dani took on new strength. She twisted out of his arms. "And just what knowledge do you have on which to base your theory?" she said, glaring at him.

Blake's eyes bore into hers. "I've known Justin a long time. He'll have you swooning with undying love for him. Then when you've outlived your usefulness, he'll put you out to pasture and go looking for a new mare to breed."

With all the force she could muster, she slapped him across the mouth. "How could you of all people say such a vile thing? You are Justin's best friend."

All at once the anger left Blake's eyes, a look of gentle appeal softening his features. "I deserved that. I just don't want you to become a pawn in his game of life. Because I'm the man you love, not Justin."

Dani felt the ire drain from her soul. "Even if that's true, it's too late."

Before she had time to resist, Blake crushed her body to him, his lips seeking and then finding fulfillment. No longer holding back, she curved her arms around his neck, savoring his touch.

All of a sudden, the moonlight seemed to clothe her with its softness as wave after wave of sweet delight washed over her. She felt safe in his arms, secure in the knowledge that nothing could ever hurt her again.

Blake, reluctant to release her, held her another long moment. "Dani, it would be wrong in both God's sight and man's to marry someone you don't love." He ran his finger along her cheekbone. "Why are you afraid to love me?"

Dani turned her back on him, aware he spoke her heart. "I'm promised to Justin. I can't, and won't, hurt him." Without a backward glance, she ran toward the house.

Blake reached out to stop her and then let his hands fall to his side. Sitting down on the bench, he hung his head in his hands, a groan escaping his lips. It was his turn to be comforted by the compassionate collie.

Standing with her back to her closed bedroom door a few minutes later, Dani squeezed her eyes shut when she heard Blake's steps on the gallery floor. She jammed her fist against her mouth to keep from crying out his name. She sank to the floor. *Dear God, what have I done!*

# SPRING COTILLION

*H*er tears spent, Dani climbed into bed, only to toss and turn. She tried to crush the memory of Blake's tortured expression when he'd discovered Justin's ring on her finger. Just before she entered the house, she'd watched him from the sanctity of the rose arbor. The image of his silhouette doubled over beneath the weight of a broken heart would be etched in her memory forever. *Oh God, You said you wouldn't put more on a person than he could bear.* Dani winced, realizing that God had nothing to do with the pain she'd brought on both Blake and herself. Streaks of daylight crowded into Dani's bedroom before she managed to drift into an exhausted sleep.

Waiting for her cotillion guests to appear that evening, Dani stood alone in the formal parlor, studying the portrait of Mathilda Thorndike. "I hope the first McKinnon Ball will do your memory justice," she said in a low voice.

"If my backbreaking labor has anything to do with its success, then it will no doubt be the most talked about sensation of the season," Blake said from the doorway.

Dani faced him with a touch of dismay. Dressed in past century magnificence, he covered the space between them momentarily. His black coat complete with tails offset by gray pin-stripped trousers heightened his virile physique. She drew her feathered fan close to her face to hide her quickness of breath.

"Why, Mr. Spencer," Dani drawled with honeyed words. "I do declare I've just worked your body till you're nothing but skin and bones. How can I ever expect you to forgive me?"

Blake picked up her hand and bowed over it. "My dear madam, how could I not forgive your indiscretion when your loveliness puts to shame the famed beauty of Marie Antoinette herself? Oh, wretched I am to think that someone other than I may possess you for his own."

Dani glanced at her engagement ring and then back at Blake. His dark eyes seemed to develop a magnetic force. He turned her hand over and kissed her palm, closing her fingers over the caress. Dani took hold of the mantle to steady her jellied legs.

At that moment, the doorbell rang. Clive, standing poised in butler's garb ready to answer the door, peeked into the formal parlor. Taking a deep breath, she nodded to him and then allowed Blake to escort her to just inside the ballroom to make ready to receive her guests.

Having lost count of the previous times, again she smoothed the sheer gold overskirt shadowing the full-bodied, emerald green satin billowing from her tiny waist.

All of a sudden, the fitted bodice seemed to hinder her breathing. Blake reached over and squeezed her hand.

"Dani, don't worry. You'll be the perfect hostess." He grinned. "And if anyone should disagree, just let me know."

She thanked him with a smile. After a quick glance around the ballroom, a satisfied smile appeared on her features before she turned to greet the first arrivals.

"Ms. Charlotte Gilmore, Mr. Phillip Harcourt, Mr. Justin Harcourt of Atlanta," announced Clive from the ballroom doorway just before he stepped aside to allow the guests to enter the room.

Dani brightened. "Good evening, Ms. Gilmore, Mr. Harcourt, Justin. I'm glad you came early. I need moral support."

Charlotte smiled. "How delightful. I've looked forward to this night." She looked around. "Stratford Hall is quite a landmark. Thank goodness it was off course for General Sherman's burning march to the sea."

"Yes. However, the plantation didn't go unscathed, according to family history. Both the Civil War and Reconstruction took their toll on the hall."

Ms. Gilmore's face brightened. "I'd love to hear the stories sometime."

"It would be a pleasure," Dani said, turning to receive Phillip's affectionate hug.

"Justin tells me congratulations are in order."

Dani looked down, her face paling. Lifting her eyes, she forced a smile. "I assume you're referring to our engagement." She felt the heat from Blake's gaze but didn't dare look his way.

Phillip took her hand to admire her ring. He gave a whistle and then grinned at his son. "Justin, you do know how to please a lady."

When Charlotte and Phillip moved on to greet Blake, Justin leaned over to give Dani a hello kiss. "You look exceptionally beautiful this evening, sweet Dani."

"Thank you." She eyed his apparel. "I don't think you'll have to beg for a partner this evening."

Justin gave her a quick kiss and then turned to Blake. "Ah, my favorite private investigator."

Dani saw Blake's tanned complexion turn a shade of pink. Could he be remembering his comments about Justin the night before? While Blake discussed the latest developments in her case with Ms. Gilmore and the Harcourts, she listened to the names of her next guests. Her nervousness faded as she caught the blossoming excitement of the cotillion.

A short time later, taking advantage of a lapse between arrivals, Dani scrutinized the happenings in the room. Clive's two daughters, dressed in appropriate apparel, served Mrs. O'Brien's famous punch.

Mrs. O'Brien wasn't to be seen, but Dani knew the housekeeper could be found in the kitchen presiding over the final preparations for the midnight supper with the aid of Mrs. Morgan.

The sound of Clive's voice interrupted her surveillance. "Mrs. Helen Radcliffe, Mr. Clifford Bradbury of Evansville. Mr. and Mrs. Harold Beaumont, Atlanta."

Dani greeted the first couple with a slight raise of an eyebrow. "I've been seeing him for some time," Mrs. Radcliffe whispered in Dani's ear as she greeted her with a hug. "He'll make a wonderful father for the boys."

Dani introduced the couple to Justin, hiding her surprise well. She knew Mr. Bradbury from church, but it had escaped her notice that Mrs. Radcliffe saw him socially. While Justin pointed them in the direction of the refreshment table, Dani turned a smile upon the Beaumonts. "Welcome to Stratford Hall."

"Spectacular!" Claudine said, taking in the grandeur of the ballroom.

"I agree," her husband said.

"Hello, Auntie, Uncle Howard," Justin said, kissing his aunt on both her cheeks before shaking hands with her husband. "Miss McKinnon has honored me by saying she'll become my wife."

"Your father phoned me with the news just this morning," Claudine said. "Congratulations to you both. May you enjoy the best of the goodness offered in life."

Justin smiled, looking around. "Thank you. We intend to do just that."

Guilt ate at Dani, stealing the pleasure from the moment. Receiving a hug from the Beaumonts, her eyes met Blake's. She swallowed hard. If only she could erase the last twenty-four hours from her life.

Clive's voice averted Dani's attention. "Miss Marguerite Van Buren, Mr. Albert Van Buren of Atlanta."

Dani propelled her features into a pleasant expression, recalling her dilemma whether to invite the Van Burens to the cotillion. Her desire not to slight Mr. Van Buren winning over her reluctance to ask Marguerite to the occasion, she'd mailed them an invitation the following day.

"Good evening," Dani said to them both, her smile warming when she extended her hand to Albert for his usual chivalrous greeting.

"So wonderful of you to think of us, Miss McKinnon," he said. "It's been years since I've visited the hall. You must save at least one dance for me."

Dani smiled and then removed her dance card from around her neck to give to him. "It will be a pleasure."

Once he'd signed his name to his preference and handed the card back to Dani, she turned to speak to Marguerite. At the look on the woman's face, a twinge of compassion gripped Dani. Marguerite's face chalk white, she stared at Dani's ring.

"Are you okay, Miss Van Buren?" Dani asked, her concern for Marguerite overriding any dislike Dani had for her adversary.

Marguerite peered first at Dani and then at Justin. She straightened her shoulders, her expression one of denial. "I'm just fine. Why do you ask?" she said, throwing Justin a murderous look.

He shifted from one foot to the other, his face clouding over with anger. Leaving Dani to greet the next guests, he escorted the Van Burens to a row of chairs near the wall. Dani hid her perplexity behind a smile for the next couple.

Soon, Clive appeared at her side. "Miss Danielle, all your guests have arrived."

"Thanks, Clive." She looked over the fifty or so names he'd checked off the list. "You did a superb job. I'm sure Mrs. O'Brien could use your help in the kitchen."

"Yes'm. I'm on my way there now."

Blake's voice at her ear caused her to turn around. "I see the illustrious Marguerite is up to her old tricks. Anything to get Justin off to herself. She's had her talons locked in him for years. He blames his divorce on his ex-wife's infidelity, but he drove her to it by his constant trips to Marguerite's apartment."

Dani's lips tightened. "Blake, I never figured you for a gossip. If you're trying to discredit Justin, thinking I'll fall into your arms, forget it. Just leave me alone!" Realizing her voice had raised a notch at the last, she looked around to see if any of her guests had detected her discomfiture. Everyone seemed to be engrossed in conversation. Relief flooded her at the sight of Justin strolling toward them.

"Say, Blake, old man," he said, coming alongside. "I haven't heard you congratulate me yet. You did notice that rock on Dani's finger, I presume."

"I noticed. If you both will excuse me, I promised the opening dance to Miss Mason."

Justin watched him walk away. "Well. Talk about unfriendly."

"I'm sure he just wanted to collect his partner before the music starts," Dani said swiftly.

A moment later, Dani nodded to the orchestra leader and then put her arm through Justin's. "Shall we open the ball?" He led her to the center of the room where they danced to the melody of the "Blue Danube Waltz," the guests giving them a few minutes alone on the floor before they joined their hostess.

As the evening progressed, Dani became absorbed in the dazzle of the moment, her confrontation with Blake forgotten. However, when he approached for his first turn on her dance card, she stiffened. She looked for Justin, locating him amid the dancing couples with Marguerite in his arms. Frowning at her discovery, she allowed Blake to lead her onto the floor.

"Dani, I shouldn't have said those things about Justin. I just don't want you to do something you will regret the rest of your life. Had I believed he'd ask you to marry him, I'd have warned you earlier of his inconsistencies. I know I promised you days ago that I would resign myself to this marriage, but I'm not handling it too gracefully, am I?"

Dani found it hard to resist his apology. So she granted him absolution in the best way she knew how. "I forgive you, Blake. After all, I prefer to end this dance without any broken toes."

His relief showed in his smile. "Ah, come on, Dani. I'm not that bad of a dancer." For the next few minutes, he proved his point.

However, she soon realized it had been a mistake to waltz with him, his arms around her stirring all kinds of feelings within her.

He grinned. "Uncomfortable, Dani? I hope so."

"You're despicable."

His smile widened. "The last I heard, all is fair in the battle to win the love of a man's heart."

At that moment, she spotted Justin and Marguerite in a shadowy corner, noting how difficult it would be to slide a thin-bladed knife between them without drawing blood. When he bent to give Marguerite a quick kiss after she whispered something in his ear, Dani blanched, causing her to miss a beat. Blake pulled back at once, observing her stricken look. He then danced them a half-turn to see what had caused her misstep. The look in her eyes warned him not to say a word. She wasn't ready to admit that Blake's prediction of the night before might be in the embryonic stage. Nonetheless, she didn't resist when he held her a fraction too close, his embrace discounting proper nineteenth century etiquette for dancing.

Shortly thereafter, the orchestra began playing the final number prior to the supper hour. A moment later, Justin appeared at her side, ready to take her into his arms. Shoving her misgivings aside, she planted a smile on her face. She'd discuss his actions with Marguerite another day.

"I haven't heard other than good comments about the McKinnon Ball," Justin said when they climbed to the conservatory for the evening meal.

"Yes. They all seem to be enjoying themselves."

Once she and Justin were seated at their table, the man on her right leaned over to speak to her. "Miss McKinnon, I daresay I'm having a jolly good time. You've bloody well outdone yourself."

She smiled at Justin's British-born friend, recalling the Capwells' charming company when she and Justin had dined in their home a few weeks back. "Thank you, sir. I hope the other guests share your opinion."

The sound of a chuckle from Blake caused Dani to look across to the next table.

Susan Mason, an attractive brunette, gazed up at him, an adoring expression coloring her features. Dani rejected the sudden thought that it might have been a mistake to put her sanction on the pair. She sat up straight. It wasn't any of her business whom Blake entertained. Then what accounted for the sinking feeling in her stomach?

Ignoring the couple, Dani spoke to Mrs. Radcliffe on her left. "How are the twins adjusting to their new home?" Blake's laughter, mingled with Susan's titters, drowned out Mrs. Radcliffe's reply. Dani's lips curved downward. She marveled at her sudden desire to strangle a certain private investigator.

"That's wonderful," Dani said, hoping she'd uttered an appropriate response. "Your earlier announcement about Mr. Bradbury took me by surprise."

"Cliff asked me to marry him a few days ago, and I said yes. He's besotted with Alex and Andy." She laughed. "It's a toss-up whether he's marrying me or the boys."

Again, the sound of Blake's voice rattled Dani. She lifted her chin a little higher, turning toward Mr. Capwell, who vied for her attention. Smiling, he lifted his wine goblet to peer at the sparkling water. "I must say I never thought I could enjoy a delectable meal without the accompaniment of an appropriate wine. Perhaps the beautiful and charming lady at my side has something to do with the softening of my bias."

From the corner of her eye, Dani caught the look of hurt that passed over his wife's face. Dani backed away, heat rising in her cheeks. "Sir, it would be an irrefutable challenge to me if I served my guests a beverage that caused a drunk driver to slam his vehicle into my parents' car, killing them instantly," she said, her tone ice cold.

Mr. Capwell cleared his throat. "Yes, well, uh, I can understand your aversion to alcohol."

While Dani constrained her emotions, Mrs. O'Brien placed a slice of raspberry torte before Dani. "'Tis a splendid affair, me lass," the housekeeper whispered.

Dani gave Mrs. O'Brien her sweetest smile. "Not near as delightful as the food. You outdid yourself." Mrs. O'Brien moved about the table, her eyes sparkling with pleasure as various guests complimented her efforts.

When Dani's friends began to migrate back toward the ballroom, she excused herself and slipped into her bedroom a few moments to freshen up before she joined the others. Later, emerging into the gallery, she met Marguerite face-to-face. The regal brunette stood alone, gazing at the portraits of Dani's ancestors, turning at the sound of footsteps.

"Well, if it isn't Little Miss Get-Rich-Quick Girl," Marguerite said, her words sodden with scorn.

A vague smile tilted the corners of Dani's mouth. "Careful, Miss Van Buren. Your claws are showing."

Marguerite's lips curled back. "You think you've won, don't you? That's what the first Mrs. Justin Harcourt thought too. They were hardly back from their honeymoon when he called on me." Spiteful triumph worked its way into her eyes at the shock on Dani's face.

"Miss Van Buren," said Dani in a low, restrained voice, "for the sake of your father, I won't ask you to leave. But should you ever decide to pay me a social visit, you'd best change your mind, because I'll never be home to you." Her head high, she descended the stairs, Marguerite staring after Dani in slack-jawed amazement.

When Dani entered the ballroom, Phillip stood nearby waiting for her. "You almost missed our dance, young lady," he said with a scolding smile.

"I'm sorry. A brief interlude with Miss Van Buren detained me."

He sighed. "If I know Marguerite, the subject focused on Justin. To be honest, if she could have her way, they'd be married by now."

Dani's brows came together. "It's obvious they were involved in the past..." Dani hesitated then spoke her mind. "Why do you suppose they never married?"

Phillip took a moment to consider her question. "Having watched her grow to womanhood, I couldn't help but discern her personality. Marguerite is like a tropical flower—beautiful yet void of an alluring fragrance to entice a man's soul into a meaningful relationship."

Before she could voice a reply, the dance ended and Mr. Van Buren approached to claim the next one. Dani squashed the seed of guilt that tried to plant itself in her thoughts when she took the elder gentleman's arm to participate in the Virginia Reel. Momentarily, Stratford Hall came alive with one of the favorite pastimes of the South.

Who would have thought her frail-looking partner could be so spry?

At the end of the dance, Justin materialized at her side, a look of concern on his face at Dani's withered appearance. "You're not overdoing it, are you?"

She smoothed back the escaped tendrils of hair from her upswept hairdo, wiping perspiration from her brow with Justin's handkerchief a moment later. "No. I hope the guests aren't too uncomfortable. All the windows are open, but not a breeze is stirring. It's getting muggier by the minute."

Justin nodded. "A storm is brewing, that's for sure. Would you like to accompany me to the courtyard?" A faraway look in his eyes, he grinned. "Do you recall our first kiss beneath the rose arbor?"

His winsome smile capturing her former miff, Dani laughed. "Yes, and it's my guess Mrs. O'Brien does too," she said, remembering how Mrs. O'Brien had happened into the courtyard at that moment.

Just as they started toward the doors, Blake walked up from behind and touched her on the arm. "Hold on, Miss McKinnon. I believe this is our dance." He took in her less than agreeable expression, his eyes filling with mirth. "I hope you're not thinking of turning me down. Only a couple more dances before they play the final waltz. I believe Miss Mason is my partner for that one." The deceptive innocence in his voice didn't fool Dani for one second. The cad! He'd known about her jealousy all along.

Her look turned defiant. "Justin has just invited me to take a stroll with him. Perhaps you and Miss Mason would like to join us."

A woebegone expression formed on Blake's face. "Surely you wouldn't begrudge your faithful guardian angel a last dance?"

Dani looked up at Justin, who shrugged his shoulders. "He does have a point, Dani."

She gazed at the two coconspirators. "I guess we'll take our walk after the dance, Justin. Come along, Blake." The two men winked at each other. In two strides, Blake caught up with his exasperated partner.

Once on the floor, Dani couldn't resist the comfort of Blake's arms. She closed her eyes, letting him lead her where he wished. She knew she should move farther away from his embrace, but something impelled her to want to remain in this position forever. She felt a stroke of guilt a moment later as she watched Justin depart the ballroom through the French doors.

Halfway through the song, she slowed their steps. "Blake, could we please go outside? I need some fresh air."

Blake searched her face, his tender eyes speaking words that made her heart reel. "I could use a breather, myself." He danced her toward the door.

Entering the courtyard, they found they weren't the only couple seeking relief from the sultry ballroom. Nearing the pavilion, they stopped, unwilling to disturb the couple inside the gazebo having a heated discussion. They turned to go. All of a sudden, a loud, angry retort transfixed her to the lawn. Blake pulled her tight against him when she staggered from the blow of the daggerlike words severing her heart.

# THE ATTIC

*D*ani ached to cover her ears, the sound of Marguerite's voice droning like angry swarming bees. But her hands remained clasped at her breast as though she could shield herself from the verbal abuse.

"It's not necessary to marry the Yankee chaff, Justin."

"Where else am I going to raise enough money to pay for our floating casino? Your so-called lucrative business venture has depleted both our finances."

"How was I to know the economy would take a downswing? Besides, you're the one who said you could incite investors in the riverboat."

"Well, I was wrong."

"You're her lawyer. Can't you think of a way to extort the funds we need from her holdings? If not, then borrow the cash from the orphaned angel of mercy."

"That's enough, Marguerite. You've gone too far. Dani's not like you and me."

Seeing their bodies melded together, Dani slumped against Blake, gasping.

"Look," Justin continued, "Drake won't wait forever for his money. If you recall, he's got hard-nosed associates who mean business when they come calling. I've managed to stall him a while longer, explaining to him I'll soon have my hands on a considerable amount of cash."

"And just what plan do you have in mind to extort funds from your little bride?" Marguerite said, her words soaked with sarcasm.

"Community property, of course." His voice softened. "The bottom line is I either marry Dani or you read about my disappearance in the newspaper some morning. Which do you prefer? I admit it will be hard to witness her desolation when I ask for a divorce soon after our marriage vows. I am rather fond of her."

Dani wanted to scream, to curse, to choke the breath from Justin's throat with her bare hands, but she stayed rooted to the ground, a strangled cry ripping from her chest. The shadowed figures in the gazebo whirled around.

"Oh my God!" Justin said, pushing Marguerite out of his way to race to Dani's side. A powerful fist streaked out of the night to land square on Justin's jaw, knocking him to the ground. Marguerite rushed to him, falling on her knees beside her unconscious lover. "What have you done, you barbarian?" she said, shaking her fist at Blake.

"What I should have done years ago," said a voice behind them. They all turned to see Phillip Harcourt alongside Ms. Gilmore, glaring at his son. A few of Dani's guests, hearing the commotion, began to gather as well.

When Justin had regained consciousness, he glanced at the crowd, his guilty gaze coming to rest on his father.

Phillip held out his hand to his son and then let it fall to his side. "Justin, at this moment, I'm ashamed to be your father. I think perhaps you should phone for a cab and take Marguerite back to Atlanta. I'll make excuses to Albert and then bring him with me later."

Dani stepped forward, her face a portrait of disgust as she faced Justin. "Since you seem to be a little short of cash, maybe this will make a deposit on the taxi fare." She slipped Justin's engagement ring off her finger, handing it to him. He stared at it a moment before he took it from her outstretched palm.

Turning, she addressed those around her. "If you'll excuse me, I have a cotillion to attend." With Blake supporting her, Dani walked toward the ballroom without a backward glance, bidding each guest farewell a short time later. Insisting that Mrs. O'Brien and the Morgan family leave the cleanup until they'd all had sufficient sleep, she climbed to the second floor.

A few minutes later, she threw her robe over her nightclothes and then treaded across the hall to her sitting room and tumbled onto the sofa. In the distance, thunder rumbled, the sound not unlike the roaring in her ears. She rubbed her hand across her jaw to relieve the ache from the pasted-on smile she'd worn the last hour. If only she could cry, maybe the scalding tears would melt the wall of ice encircling her heart. How could she have become so deceived?

Dani knew the answer to that before the thought had time to clear her mind. Pride! Stubborn, rebellious pride! She'd refused to admit what she'd felt for Justin had been nothing more than infatuation and that his feelings for her was affection, at best, intertwined with lust—of that there wasn't a doubt. Let's see, what had been his term? Oh, yes. Fondness! Dani felt her stomach twist with disgust. How could she have been such a fool?

The signs of his real interest in her had been visible, but she'd ignored them—his guarded concern in her financial affairs, his evasiveness when she questioned him about his personal life, his fear of mishandling a lucrative client's case, not to mention his obvious involvement with Marguerite. *Oh, he wined and dined me to perfection*, Dani thought with disgust, but not a word of undying love. She cringed as knowledge of the truth sank deep in her mind. In fact, now that she'd allowed herself to see their relationship for what it had been, he'd exhibited more devotion for Stratford Hall than for her.

Dani blinked back the tears that begin to fill her eyes. To think she'd fallen into his arms time after time. What if... what if? Thank

God He'd given her the strength to keep her moral wits intact. And God, He was yet another matter. She'd been so sure she could win Justin over to her spiritual beliefs. If he hadn't been willing to serve Christ to date, what had made her think a marriage license would prompt a change of heart?

She swallowed hard, turning her face to the wall. If only she'd listened to Blake. Had she not overheard Justin and Marguerite's degrading remarks, no doubt Dani McKinnon would have been the next name plastered on the wall of the Fools' Hall of Fame. Dani slumped forward, drowning her face in her hands. She would have deserved the distorted recognition, every jot and title etched into the brass plaque.

A knock sounded at the door. Blake entered the room without an invitation. Flashes of lightening illuminated the self-scorn depicted on her face. With a groan on his lips, Blake sat next to her, taking her into his arms to cradle like a small child. She buried her face in his shoulder, unable to meet his gaze.

At that moment, a loud clap of thunder rattled the windows, the clouds beginning to spew their pent-up deluge onto the Georgia soil. However, the lashing rain failed to muffle the choking sobs that spilled onto Blake's shirt, his whispered words of love torn from his lips by the storm that besieged his beloved.

Awaking hours later, her robe twisted about her body, Dani brushed the dampness from her eyelashes, the moisture from tears shed in her sleep. The memory of the previous evening's events came crashing down on her. She pulled the blanket Blake must have thrown over her when she'd fallen asleep to her chin, sinking deep into the sofa. Maybe she could lie here forever. No mornings to face, no people to intrude into her small, safe world, just sweet, sweet oblivion.

All too aware her new responsibilities called for a life other than indifference, she opened her eyes, an alternate remedy for survival shaping her thoughts. Someone once stated that hard work would cure a broken heart. Well, today she had the perfect opportunity to prove its worth.

Dani tossed the bedding aside and rose to her feet. How wonderful it would be if she could trash her heartache within the amount of time it would take to clear the cotillion refuse from the hall.

When Dani walked into the kitchen a few minutes later, neither Blake nor Mrs. O'Brien was anywhere to be seen. Opting to skip breakfast, Dani hurried to the ballroom, finding the two in question busy at restoring the room to its normal existence. Observing Mrs. O'Brien's expression, Dani knew the housekeeper had been told of the broken engagement.

"It's about time you showed your face," Blake teased from his position on a tall ladder. "We could use some help around here."

"If you were just a little more observant, Mr. Spencer, you would have noticed that I'm not dressed for a ball," she said pulling at her tee shirt and jeans.

Blake grinned and then tossed an azalea bough toward her. "Oh, I noticed all right."

"See what I have to deal with, Mrs. O'Brien? Casanova was a saint in comparison."

"Well, me lass, no real harm can come from admiring a beautiful specimen of God's creation.

"Admiring and ogling are quite different in my mentality," Dani said, frowning. She raised an eyebrow as she observed Blake's villainous grin. "I guess that's a matter of opinion."

Mrs. O'Brien glanced from one of her companions to the other, scrutinizing their features before a grin brightened her eyes. "I suppose it does depend on how each of ye view the issue in question."

Dani rolled her eyes toward the ceiling. "If you two confederates don't mind, I'll go put the conservatory back to order. At least I'll have peace while I work," she said, her smile at last reaching her eyes.

"No need to bother, lass. Mr. Blake and Clive carted the table and chairs from the room hours ago after we disposed of the debris. I'm surprised you slept through the noise."

Dani looked stunned. "I didn't hear a thing." She dropped her eyelashes at the compassionate expressions on her companions' faces. "Thank you both for all you've done. Since I don't seem to be needed here, I think I'll go to the attic to search for saleable items for the bazaar auction."

Blake sidled by with the last load of flower swags in his arms. "I'll be up to help you soon as we're finished here." He turned toward Mrs. O'Brien. "That is, of course, if Mrs. O'Brien doesn't have an additional chore for her humble servant." Blake bowed in Oriental fashion, smiling.

"Oh, be off with ye," the housekeeper said, motioning them to exit the room. "I've got better things to do than stand around gabbing all day." A twinkle in her eyes, she switched on the electric sweeper, the noise drowning out Dani and Blake's laughter.

After Blake discarded the swags, he found Dani at the bottom of the stairwell leading to the attic. Noting her woebegone look, he clasped her hand in his. "Are you okay?"

She looked away. "Please, Blake, I can't talk about Justin now. No offense, but I can't see you in the role of objective confidante."

He nodded in understanding and then opened the door. Soon they were knee-deep in treasures from bygone eras.

After they'd sorted through the furniture, Blake toted the saleable furnishings to a cleared area close to the door to be carried downstairs later. Wiping the dust from a Victorian perambulator, Dani found she couldn't bear to part with it. The two of them carried the baby carriage down the steep stairs and placed it in the nursery.

While there, Dani walked over to the handmade cradle, lifting an infant's quilt from inside the bed. She held it to her breast, a far-away look in her eyes. At moments like this, she ached to know the joys of motherhood, the urge often so strong she'd spend her entire afternoon at the children's home in the baby wing.

Blake stood to one side, his gaze filled with tenderness. He reached out and touched her cheek. "You'll make a wonderful mother someday, Miss McKinnon," he said, his voice beginning to break at the Madonna likeness in her complexion.

"I like to think so," she said, replacing the blanket in its original position.

Their mind on the business at hand when they returned to the attic minutes later, Blake moved the half dozen or so trunks they'd found scattered among the odds and ends to a more accessible area of the top floor.

"I have my Grandmother McKinnon to thank for my knowledge in yesteryear. Sometimes on rainy days, we'd plunder through an old hatbox filled with pictures of deceased relatives. After a half dozen or so stories, she'd say, 'Danielle, never forget your heritage. You are who you are because of those who lived before you. I will always treasure those times. It was at those moments I felt loved and wanted. As I grew older, I gained a world of knowledge in antiquity by hours spent in my grandparents' antique shop on Saturdays and school holidays." She removed a priceless Tiffany lamp wrapped in an old knitted shawl and held it toward the ceiling. "This should bring a tidy sum. In fact, I might have to bid on this myself," she said, turning to smile at Blake.

She studied him for a moment, realizing he hadn't heard a word she'd said, his attention captured by a sheaf of papers he'd found in a large tin box he'd taken from an old wooden, leather-strapped trunk.

At that moment, Mrs. O'Brien's voice could be heard from the bottom of the stairs. "Yoo-hoo, Miss Danielle, telephone. 'Tis Mrs. Pendergraff awanting to chat with ye. Should I tell her ye'll call her back?"

Dani started to say yes and then recounted. "No, I'll be right there." Halfway down the stairs, she heard Blake yell. "Hey, Dani, I found it."

Puzzled, she turned to quiz him but decided not to keep Lucille waiting. Returning less than thirty minutes later, she discovered

Blake had fled the attic. When the dinner hour rolled around and he hadn't returned to the hall, Dani grew worried.

"Did Blake say where he was going or when he'd be back?" Dani asked Mrs. O'Brien when they'd sat down to their meal.

"No, just muttered something about ferreting out a rattlesnake den."

"That's strange. I wonder what he meant."

Mrs. O'Brien shrugged her shoulders. "Are ye planning to continue your search in the attic this evening? I'd be glad to help ye when I finish my chores in the kitchen."

"No, I think I'll turn in early tonight." The sympathetic look in Mrs. O'Brien's eyes nearly swayed Dani to confide in her trustworthy friend. But the memory of Justin's words still chiseled away at her self-esteem. Just before she left the room, Dani gave the housekeeper a hug. "Just pray for me, Mrs. O'Brien. That's all that can help me right now."

Mrs. O'Brien sniffled. "I have been, lass, all day long."

About to become a waterspout for tears, Dani gave Mrs. O'Brien another quick hug and hurried to the master suite.

❦

Several days passed before Dani had the opportunity to ask Blake about his comings and goings of late. He usually left before she arose in the morning and returned after she'd retired. Mrs. O'Brien, too, had no clue to his mysterious disappearances.

But to her surprise, on the day before the charity fair, he stood in the foyer, waiting to drive her into town to meet with Mrs. Radcliffe to finalize the plans for the bazaar.

Noting his tired expression and reddened eyes, she frowned with concern. "Blake, what is going on? You look exhausted."

Seeing her anxiety, he smiled. "Don't worry, Dani. It's all part of the job. But I can't discuss it. You'll just have to trust me."

"Sorry, didn't mean to pry. I…I've just missed you. After all, you've practically dogged my every step until the last few days."

He smiled. "Let's just say I've been involved in an alternate method of keeping you safe. Will that satisfy your womanly curiosity for now?"

She eyed the set of his jaw. "I can see I have no other choice."

"That's my girl. I promise you'll know all about it in good time."

When they parked near the old courthouse square, all of a sudden, Dani grabbed Blake's arm. "Look! See that old man talking to that teenager in the black leather jacket? That's Davenport wearing the same disguise he wore in front of the drugstore in Carrollton. What do you suppose they have in common?"

Blake scrutinized the situation. "They seem to be discussing that paper Davenport is clutching in his hand."

She focused on the sheet of paper. "Why, that looks like one of the handbills for the fair. What would be their interest in a charity function?"

"I'd say they're more intrigued with the happenings at the hall," he said as they watched the two part company in opposite directions.

When Davenport had disappeared down a nearby street, Blake helped Dani from the truck and walked her to the café to keep her appointment with Mrs. Radcliffe. Once he'd seated her next to Mrs. Radcliffe, he looked as though he couldn't leave the tearoom fast enough. *Who could blame him?* Dani thought, glimpsing the admiration on women young and old seated throughout the establishment. She laughed within. He must have felt like a well-fed antelope locked in a cage full of hungry female lions.

Once the waitress had cleared the dishes from their table, Dani pulled the itinerary of the charity fair from her oversized handbag. She smiled at Mrs. Radcliffe. "Shall we begin?"

Late that afternoon, with a broom in hand, Dani trotted toward the gazebo. She wanted to make the pavilion attractive to display her antiques for tomorrow's auction. She'd had a number of calls from several individuals desiring more information than had been printed in the bazaar advertisements. She had a feeling the auction would go well.

She slowed her steps, knowing it wouldn't be easy to complete her job. Harsh words echoed in her memory. She stumbled as she climbed the steps. What gave her the idea she could do this simple chore without suffering repercussions from a fortnight ago?

Dani swiped at the leaves and dust, her eyes filling with tears. She kept her back to Blake when he entered the gazebo a few moments later.

"Hey, what's the holdup? You've been out here long enough to have the place immaculate by now."

She pushed the broom faster. "I do hope this weather holds," she said in a husky voice. "It will make all the difference."

Before Dani had time to finish her sentence, the broom was lifted from her fingers, Blake standing it against one of the latticed walls. "Dani, look at me."

She turned to reveal swollen, red-rimmed eyes. Anger replaced by helplessness a second later flashed in his eyes. "What I'd give to take that night from your memory."

He wrapped his arms around her. "All I want to do is love you." He drew a long sigh. "But you won't let me near your heart."

Dani stepped backward, reaching for the broom. "It will be dark soon."

Blake started to leave, pausing at the doorway. "Dani, it's dangerous to keep all that hurt bottled up on the inside. You need to let someone help you deal with it. Our Father, God, would be the perfect someone, in my opinion."

When she didn't answer but just stared at him with that haunted look in her eyes, he walked away, his shoulders hunched forward as though hoisting a heavy burden.

The next morning, Dani opened the doors to the second-floor piazza, delighted that it promised to be a warm, sunny day. For a few minutes, she watched Clive and Blake direct the fair vendors toward the west lawn of the estate and then hurried downstairs to grab a bite to eat. She'd promised to help Mrs. O'Brien set up her bakery booth and didn't want to keep her waiting long.

Dani sniffed the air in the kitchen. "I know where I intend to spend the biggest part of the day," she said, snatching a chocolate chip cookie from a plate on a nearby countertop.

For the first time in days, the housekeeper detected a sparkle in her mistress's eyes. "'Tis good to see ye have a bit of bounce back, lass. I'm excited meself. If the talk in town is correct, we have a passel of folk ready to spend their hard-earned dollars on the wee ones."

As Dani poured a glass of milk, the memory of Davenport with one of the bazaar advertisements in his grimy hands rushed to her mind. She hoped buyers were the only people the fair attracted.

Late that morning, when time drew near for the antique auction, Dani and Blake stood talking with the auctioneer she'd hired to sell her wares. "Well, Miss McKinnon, it appears your organization has accomplished its goal," the auctioneer said, looking around at the large crowd enjoying the fair. "It looks like the whole county and then some have turned out for the festivities."

"Yes, we're grateful for the concern the people have shown for the orphans."

Dani looked at her watch. As cashier for the auction, she walked to a table close to the gazebo where she would sit and record the sales. Sensing someone's eyes on her from behind, she turned, gasping when she recognized the familiar face. She felt her stomach clench into angry knots. "What are you doing here?"

# Disobedient Damsel

"Hello, sweet Dani," Justin said, his face a mask of remorse. "Could I have a word with you, please?"

Dani looked over her shoulder. Blake, assisting the auctioneer, hadn't noticed Justin's arrival. To avoid a scene, she allowed Justin to lead her toward the brook. When they reached the water's edge, she faced him, her manner stone cold, like fine Italian marble. "I don't believe we have anything to discuss. Your performance with Marguerite the night of the ball spoke volumes to me."

He reached as though to take her into his arms. With an angry shake of her head, she stepped backward, her eyes pools of resentment.

He ran his hand through his hair and then down the side of his neck. "I know how upset you must be, and I can't blame you. No one knows what a fool I've been more than I. Can you find it within yourself to forgive me? I *swear* I'll never go near Marguerite again."

His words chafed her heart like dry, brittle sand gnashing within the eye of a desert whirlwind. "Upset, Justin? I overhear you plotting with your lover to extort money from me, make a sham of our marriage, jerk my home right out from under me, and you think I'm just *upset*? You make it sound as though we had a mere misunderstanding that can be patched with a few apologetic words. I admit the strategy worked for you in the past, but not this time. Even if I believed you, how could I trust you? I'd always wonder if you loved me or Aunt Mathilda's estate."

"Please, Dani, I was desperate. I've exhausted all my financial resources and was too ashamed to ask Dad for help. I didn't know where to turn, and you landed in my lap, so to speak. Marguerite and I thought you'd be the perfect solution to our problem. I…I just didn't realize how much you would come to mean to me. I should have sought Dad's advice in the first place. He has a client who's an entrepreneur in gambling establishments, and after Dad shared my dilemma, the man decided to purchase the casino. Our"—he paused at the look in her eye—"I mean, my future looks great. I do love you, Dani."

She stared at him for several minutes. For months she waited to hear those words—had built her future on them. All at once her body grew limp, her fury wafting into the air like a piece of driftwood floating to waters unknown. Now, at last, she comprehended Justin Harcourt for the person he was. For all his sophisticated charm, he'd never outgrown his childish manipulation of others to his own advantage. A person couldn't help but pity him.

As for Marguerite, she'd fallen victim to his winsome ways early in life, and now trapped in her love for him, she'd paid the highest price a woman could give for his affection. "No, Justin. You don't love anyone but yourself." She took a deep breath. "But I forgive you." Turning, Dani retreated to the gazebo where Blake stood eyeing their movements. She wished it were as simple to forgive herself.

Justin hurried after her. "Dani, we can work this out. Give me a chance, please!"

Her heart deaf to Justin's plea, Dani smiled up at Blake when she reached his side, a peace she hadn't felt in days brightening her countenance.

"Is everything all right?" he whispered.

"Yes. Now."

Dani signaled the auctioneer to begin the sale. Later, when the receipts had been tallied and the auctioneer paid his fee, she had more than fifty thousand dollars to contribute to the children's home. She looked up to tell Blake the news, but he'd disappeared. Glancing around, she located him by one of the game booths, holding some sort of document in his hands, conversing with Justin. Dani sighed, thankful that only a flicker of pain remained from what was probably the shortest marital engagement in history.

While she stood waiting for Blake's return, Sheriff Wilson walked up to her, offering her a piece of homemade fudge. Taking the morsel from the sack in his hands, she thanked him and then asked, "What brings you to the fair, business or pleasure?"

"Both, actually. I came to make a contribution, plus handle any trouble that might arise on the premises. Have you seen Mr. Spencer? The office radioed to tell me he'd phoned after I'd left for the hall."

"Yes. He's right over there talking to Justin Harcourt," Dani said, pointing toward an oversized dartboard.

"Thanks. I'll go see what he needed." With a tip of his hat, he walked away.

Meanwhile, Dani decided she would check on Mrs. O'Brien to see how she fared with the bakery items. She knew if the discussion with Justin or the sheriff concerned her, Blake would let her know soon enough.

"How did the auction go?" Mrs. O'Brien asked when Dani stepped up to the counter to order a croissant.

Dani pulled some money from her jean pocket. "Great." She leaned forward, speaking in a low voice. "And I've got fifty thousand dollars right here to prove it." Dani patted the canvas bag beneath her upper arm. "It looks like you did all right too. You're about sold out of goodies."

"Aye. I do have a few loaves of bread acooling in the kitchen. Clive's missus took them out of the oven for me earlier, but when her youngest became ill, she had to take the child home before she could bring them down to me. I didn't want to leave me customers to fetch them.

"I'll go get them," Dani said wiping her hands on a napkin. "Anything else you need?"

The housekeeper gazed beyond Dani in thought. "We still have an hour before the fair closes. Ye might fetch those cookies I was saving for Mr. Blake in the cupboard next to the stove. I'll make him another batch tomorrow."

Dani nodded. "Good as done." She turned to go, but at that moment she felt two pairs of small arms around her knees. She looked down into the shining, ketchup-smeared faces of Alex and Andy Radcliffe. They each held a portion of a hotdog in their hands.

Bending down, she gave them each a kiss on the forehead. "You two look like you're having fun."

"We sure are, Miss Dani," Alex said.

"Yeah," Andy echoed. "We got to ride the horse a long time."

Dani knew they referred to Old Suze, Clive's mare. He'd sold rides all day as his donation to the orphan fund. "Did either of you fall off the horse?"

"Miss Dani," Alex said in childish indignation. "We're big boys."

Dani winked at Mrs. Radcliffe standing near the boys. "That you are."

"Now, boys," their new mother said, "you mustn't speak unkindly to your elders."

They both hung their heads a moment and then finished their meal in silence, eyeing the cookies on Mrs. O'Brien's stand.

"I've been looking for you, Mrs. Radcliffe," Dani said, "to give you the earnings from the antique auction. I think you'll be pleased. Did your quilt sales go well?"

Helen smiled. "Yes. Better than I expected." She paused as loud shouts rose above the din of the crowd. Dani and those about her turned to focus on the commotion a short distance away. A ring of people had formed around what appeared to be a ruckus of some sort.

"We'd better see what that's about," Dani said to Helen.

"Yes," she agreed, instructing the boys to stay with Mrs. O'Brien.

Both Dani and Mrs. Radcliffe hurried to the scene. Once they'd wormed their way through the people, they found the sheriff, along with Blake and Justin, corralling several ruffians wearing black jackets involved in a fight with some local high school boys. Observing the disturbance, Dani realized that she'd seen one of the troublemakers the day before with Davenport in Evansville. She felt the offbeat flutter of her heart. Had they arranged this upheaval? If so, why?

A moment later, Blake caught up with her. "Dani, Justin and I are going to accompany the sheriff into Carrollton to take these hoods to the county jail. We shouldn't be gone long, but while we are, don't go wandering off alone. Stay close to Mrs. O'Brien until I return. Okay?"

Dani rolled her eyes toward the sky. "Yes, master."

Mrs. Radcliffe looked from Dani to Blake and then back to Dani, her expression puzzled. "What did you say Mr. Spencer did?" she asked when Blake had gone.

This wasn't the first time Mrs. Radcliffe had shown curiosity about Blake. Dani had wanted to confide in her new friend on several occasions, but both Blake and Justin had warned her against it. They believed the fewer people who knew of Dani's life-and-death situation, the better. Blake felt it would give the authorities an edge in their pursuit of her perpetrator.

"He's a private investigator by trade. To me, he's a wonderful friend who's accepted my invitation to spend a few weeks at the hall." Too late Dani realized that Mrs. Radcliffe had heard the softening in her tone when she'd spoke the word *friend*.

Mrs. Radcliffe smiled at Dani, a knowing glint in her eyes. "You're in love with him, Dani McKinnon. It's written all over your face."

"Really?" Dani said before they both burst into laughter.

When they returned to Mrs. O'Brien's booth, Mrs. Radcliffe and her boys took their leave to meet Mr. Bradbury, her fiancé. Facing the housekeeper, Dani snapped her finger. The bread. "Sorry, Mrs. O'Brien, I'll be right back with the bread and cookies."

Blake's warning popped into her head. She slowed her pace. Should she wait until his return? But the fair would be over by then. She'd be back in no more than five minutes. What could happen in that space of time? Brushing caution aside, Dani ran toward the hall.

Unlocking the front door, Dani paused, intimidated by the eerie silence greeting her when she stepped into the foyer. Uneasiness filled the pit of her stomach, but she laughed aloud, her voice shaky. "Next thing you know, I'll be seeing ghosts."

Gathering her courage, she padded across the dining room floor, about to enter the kitchen, when she heard a noise from behind her. Startled, she whipped around, her lips parting in amazement. The china hutch moved inward like the opening of a door. She stood frozen, the hair on the back of her neck rising as a bone-cold chill slithered down her spine. Too frightened to flee, she watched Davenport and one of the leather-decked youth emerge from the opening in the wall.

She opened her mouth to scream, but no sound came forth. She gaped at the pistol stuffed into the waistband of Davenport's trousers. His swarthy face broke into an evil grin when he noted Dani's presence, the gun instantly finding a new home in his palm. "Well, hello again, pretty lady. This looks like a case of perfect timing to me."

Davenport pulled a roll of money from his shirt pocket and handed it to the rough-looking youth standing alongside. "I guess I won't need you after all to find Pretty Lady and bring her to me. She has played right into our hands." Davenport pointed to the money in the young man's fingers. "Tell Mario that's enough to cover the gang's bail. They did a good job getting rid of the cowboy chaperone. I'll be in touch should we need them again." Pocketing the bills, the teen sauntered toward the foyer, walking out the front door after a cautious peek to the outside.

Amazed disbelief held Dani in check as she comprehended how Davenport and his brother had entered and left the house without detection. Clive's efforts in changing the locks on the house had been wasted. Was this the secret Maury Davidson had withheld from his cellmate?

All at once Dani recalled the day spent with Blake in the attic and his announcement as she was leaving to take a phone call from Lucille. Had he discovered the secret of the china hutch? Did she have a chance of rescue after all? *Oh, God, please let someone find me before it's too late!*

Davenport, his gun aimed at Dani's head, walked over to the buffet and lifted a silverware case from one of the drawers. Opening the lid, he smiled. "This should bring a nice sum to tide us over for a while." He snapped it shut again, his lips curling into a sneer. "Let's go, pretty lady. My brother is anxious to see you. He isn't convinced you no longer care for him."

A look of horror settled on her face. *Justin! No! Anyone but Justin!* A sob rose to her lips.

"What's wrong, pretty lady? Scared?"

"Just who is your brother anyway?" Dani said, spitting her words at him.

"You'll find out soon enough." With the silverware tucked under his arm, he waved his gun toward the gaping hole in the wall. "Let's go."

Dani's spine grew rigid. "And if I refuse?"

He looked down at the floor. "I sure would hate to stain this lovely carpet with your blood." His gritted his teeth. "Now move!"

Her legs wobbly, she stepped forward. She looked around, searching for a means of escape, realizing seconds later none existed. Blake, her one hope for rescue, had fallen prey to Davenport's plan. Justin must have made some excuse to stay behind at the last minute. How else would she be able to see him now? Repulsed, Dani swallowed the taste of bitter gall surging to her throat. He'd fooled them all.

Seeming to read her mind, Davenport laid the barrel of the gun next to her temple. "I wouldn't try anything foolish. Get going down those steps unless you want to drop dead at my feet."

With a sharp intake of breath, she remembered the bread. Mrs. O'Brien would realize that Dani should have returned to the booth by now. Would she think something was amiss and come to investigate or send someone? Dani's hopes plummeted as she stepped into the cavernous space behind the china hutch.

*Blake. Oh, Blake.* She'd never be able to convey her love for him. If only she'd paid attention to Sheriff Wilson's suspicions. When she came face-to-face with Justin, would he kill her right then or later? And how did Phillip fit into all this? She felt her stomach begin to shake. Too many questions, too many answers about to be divulged. And at what price? *Aunt Lucille, Uncle Bill,* she thought, tears flooding her eyes. She'd never see them again.

*Dear God, please forgive me. You tried to warn me and I wouldn't listen.* With one last glimpse into the dining room, she migrated toward the yawning darkness that sealed her fate.

# THE RECKONING

*O*nce they'd entered the passageway, Davenport motioned for Dani to stand aside. He grabbed the handle on the backside of the china hutch and pulled forward. She jumped when the spring-loaded lock snapped into place. A sensation of being buried alive swept through her. She gagged.

Davenport produced a flashlight from somewhere, its beam capturing the tiny beads of moisture speckling the walls. After a short jaunt down an uneven cobblestone walkway, a heavy door fashioned from thick planks and strips of iron suddenly loomed in front of them. Davenport brushed her arm when he stepped ahead to lift the iron latch.

Dani shrank back at his touch, her face shedding its color as a stream of nausea spiraled upward. She swallowed hard, the potent taste in her mouth causing her to wretch dry heaves. At that moment, Davenport pushed her forward into a chamber about the size of a small bedroom, the only source of light a kerosene lamp sitting in the middle of a rough-hewn table.

While Davenport slid a metal bar into place to secure the door, Dani glanced about, taking in the menacing shadows splattered onto the mortared walls. She sensed the death angel lurked nearby. The heat radiating from a space heater next to the table did nothing to curb the chill that crept through her cotton shirt. Coercing Dani into one of the Windsor chairs situated on each side of the table, Davenport tied her hands behind the chair.

The rope biting into her wrists, she surveyed her surroundings. In a corner to the right, she noted a darkened staircase. Trying to imagine its destination inside the hall, she became aware of a cave-like opening on her left that appeared to be the entrance to a narrow tunnel. Could that be the passageway to the cave Nathan Kingsley wrote of in his diary? Another quick look around and Dani closed her eyes, her lips moving in silent prayer. *Oh, God! Please help me.* But what if God chose not to keep her on this earth? No. She wouldn't think about that.

"Yea, though I walk through the valley of the shadow of death, I will fear no evil for Thou art with me," she muttered beneath her breath. "God will never leave me nor forsake me. If God be for me, then who could be against me?" Dani felt faith rise in her heart as she mouthed the familiar scriptures. Whatever she had to face, somehow she would find the strength to accept His will.

After checking the security of her bindings, Davenport fell into the other chair on the opposite side of the table. Lighting a cigarette, he opened the fifth of whiskey sitting beside the lamp. Taking a long swig from the bottle, he replaced the stopper, eyeing her with a vengeful smug. "No use wasting your breath on prayer." He laughed. "Nobody can help you now."

Dani stiffened. "What's going to happen to me?"

"Don't be so impatient. You'll get your due soon enough. My brother will return shortly from loading the car with the valuables we looted from the house earlier."

Dani leaned forward as far as the rope would allow. "How dare you plunder my home. The items you stole are part of my family's heritage."

Davenport slammed his fist on the table. Startled, she fell back against the chair. "For your information, sister, Silas Thorndike and his wife cheated my grandmother out of her share of the Thorndike fortune. Now it's payback time." He waved his arm in a circular motion above his head. "We have more right to this place than you. In a few months time, the law will see things our way too.

At that instant they heard a noise in the tunnel. They both turned toward the sound, Davenport retrieving his pistol from the table and aiming it toward the entrance. "It's just me," said a voice from the dark space.

Tears stung the back of Dani's eyes. How could she bear the sight of the man she'd loved and trusted all these months? Her stomach tightened with dreaded expectation. She turned her face away, cringing as he stepped close to her chair.

"Hello, Red. It's been a while."

Dani felt her arms and legs go numb at the sound of the voice. No! Stunned by the realization penetrating her thoughts, she hardly noticed her sigh of relief that the perpetrator wasn't Justin. "*Lance!* It can't be! You, you're somewhere in the Southwest."

A cunning smile distorted his clean-cut appearance. "My little fabrication worked like a charm." He pulled a gun from inside his sports coat.

Dani's heart lurched at the sight of the pistol in his hand. She shook her head, fear escalating at the demented look in his eyes. "Why, Lance, why?"

He leaned sideways to untie her hands. "It's really quite simple, Dani. You took away everything I ever wanted," he said, his soft, monotone voice unable to squeeze the hatred from his tone. "First, you landed the managerial position I'd dreamed of from the moment I went to work for Pendergraff Accounting; then you threw aside my love for you, treating me like a second-class citizen."

Dani straightened in her chair. "Lance, I never—"

He drummed on as though he didn't hear her words. "I often envisioned how it would be. Pendergraff would retire or maybe die, and you'd be in charge of the company. Then we'd marry, and in time I'd see that the leadership in the firm would be turned over to me.

Women have their place in business all right, but men need to be in control, not some frustrated, dominating female."

Lance jerked Dani to her feet. His grasp sparked the memory of a similar hold months ago. "You were the one who attacked me in Hartford," she said, dazed.

He cupped his hand around her chin, the evil smirk on his face contradicting his gentle hold. "You shouldn't be so haphazard about leaving your personal mail lying around your office for anyone to see or so stubborn about following orders." He tightened his fingers, causing her to cry out. "I'm referring to the letter from Phillip Harcourt, the one you left lying on your desk while you lunched with Sandra and Kristin. Remember, Dani? You flew to Atlanta to meet with Harcourt a few days later."

She managed to pull her face from his grasp, her eyes blazing with fury. How could she forget? From the moment she'd returned to her office until now, she'd lived in fear of her life. She glanced at his face. Every dark force in Hades seemed to march across his features as he continued to speak.

"When I saw the name Mathilda Thorndike, it stunned me, she being the one who'd cheated my grandmother, Rosemary Davidson, out of her inheritance."

Lance glanced away, a distant look in his eyes. "Each time my grandmother came for a visit in California, she'd talk about the secret room and the cave my grandfather discovered the one time they visited Stratford Hall. They'd concocted a plan to get even with the Thorndikes for shunning them, but my grandfather died before they could carry out their strategy."

Dani sighed, a plea for understanding replacing the anger in her eyes. "Lance, how could I have known about the association between your grandparents and the Thorndikes? I didn't even remember Great-Aunt Mathilda until I received that letter."

Lance didn't seem to notice that Dani had spoken. "When my grandmother would start to cry," Lance continued, his tone becoming childlike, "I'd throw my arms around her neck and say, 'Don't cry, Granny. When I grow up, I'll make those mean old people sorry they hurt you.'"

The clink of the glass stopper against the whiskey bottle seemed to knock Lance out of his reverie. His voice normal once again, a smile touched his lips but not his eyes.

"Of course, Jules doesn't remember too much about our Grandmother Davidson. He was only three when his father divorced our mother. And he only got to see her once or twice. But I told him about her during one of my visits to the sanatorium. It was a break for me when some office clerk processed the wrong file, releasing him to my custody while you were in Atlanta discovering our mutual inheritance. Jules proved more than willing to help me render payment to you for the misery you've dealt me."

"Yeah," Davenport said, wiping his mouth on his shirtsleeve. "I got out of that place just in time to cash in on our good fortune."

Dani touched Lance's arm, her expression turning compassionate. "Lance, your grandmother lied to you. Stratford Hall belonged to my aunt, who inherited it from her brother, Matthew Jackson, my great-great-grandfather."

Dani stifled a painful cry as Lance grabbed her hair and pulled her to him, his face only inches from her own. "You're the liar, Dani. Don't think for one minute we'll let you steal this estate away from us." Lance threw her into the chair.

Hot tears scorched Dani's eyelids. "Lance, please. You're ill. Let me go, and I'll see that you have the best medical care possible."

A sharp blow to her face relayed his opinion on the matter. Davenport rose from the chair and came to stand beside Lance as though ready to aid his brother in her torture.

Her hand clasped to her burning cheek, she gazed at the two men, eyeing the resemblance between them. Separated, she'd never have connected the relationship, but now, seeing them together, she couldn't doubt their kinship; their eyes the same gray hue, now dark with anger. No wonder she'd thought Davenport a past acquaintance she couldn't recall.

"The only help I need is good riddance to you." With one swift movement, Lance pulled her to her feet. "We're going for a walk."

Dani dug her heels in the stone floor. "Where are you taking me?"

"There's a cave a few hundred yards from here that will become your final resting place."

She fought to break loose from his hold. "No! You can't do this awful thing."

Lance wrenched her tight against him and then pushed her away. The lunge throwing her off balance, she fell to her knees. Dani looked up at the two men, her lips thinning. "I'm not going with you anywhere, not now, not ever. If you intend to kill me, you'll have to do it right here."

Davenport bent down and placed his arms under her shoulders and snatched her upward to face Lance. All at once in the misty light, Dani saw a hint of remorse crisscross his features. He drew her into his arms. "Dani, I really didn't want it to come to this. However, I forgot how stubborn you are. I'm sorry it has to end this way."

"It doesn't have to. You can have Stratford Hall. I'll go back to Hartford."

Lance shook his head. "It's too late. You know too much."

He bent forward as though to kiss her. She turned her face away, a look of loathing she couldn't hide contorting her features.

A sound that imitated a low growl erupted from his throat.

Her knees growing weak, she braced herself for the sound of gunfire when she felt the barrel of the gun against her temple. She tried to pray but couldn't find the words.

The sound of scurrying feet within the tunnel caused Dani and her assassins to turn toward the passageway. "Hold it, Carter!" yelled Sheriff Wilson. "You're under arrest, both of you."

Both Lance and Davenport fired their weapons toward the entrance to the tunnel. Following a flurry of fists, Dani's assailants were soon sprawled face down on the floor, their attempts to escape curtailed.

Dani cowered against the brick stairwell, observing the tussle, her prayers answered within moments as Blake, Justin, and the sheriff brought the culprits under control. The handcuffs secure, she released her breath.

A moment later, she gasped when Blake turned toward her. One of the bullets had found a target. She ran to him, horrified. The sheriff used the rope that had held Dani earlier on Blake's upper arm as a tourniquet.

"Don't worry," Blake said, pulling Dani to him with his good arm. "It's only a superficial wound. No real harm done."

Dani wasn't sure when the tears began to stream down her cheeks, but with the aid of the handkerchief Justin handed to her while he held the sheriff's gun on the prisoners, she wiped at them, thanking God for His merciful intervention.

"How did you know where to find me?" she asked Blake when Sheriff Wilson had finished with the emergency first aid.

Blake smiled at her, his relief for her safety visible on his face. "After we take care of these riffraff, you'll hear every aspect of the adventure. I promise. But right now, let's get out of this dungeon." He took Dani's arm to guide her toward the door, but she balked to stare at the shadowy staircase.

"I wonder where that goes."

Blake laughed. "Here you've just been saved from sure murder and now you want to go exploring." He again took her arm. "Come on, Miss Impatience, I'll tell you on our way out of here.

"This is the underground room George Kingsley built to conceal his family in case of an Indian attack. That staircase yonder leads to a cubicle inside that brick fountain in the garden."

"You're kidding."

"Nope. Remember those slits I showed you? You guessed right about them. Not only did they have ventilation purpose, they were useful as a means to view the Indians in case of a raid."

"May I ask how you became so well informed about all this?"

"The day we searched the attic for antiques to sell at the charity fair, I found the original blueprints for the house in one of those old trunks. The plans detailed both rooms, plus they had an explicit view of the secret door and its hidden mechanism. I started to show you the find, but you had to leave to take a phone call from Mrs. Pendergraff."

Dani nodded. "Yes, I remember. By the time I returned to the attic, you were gone."

Before she proceeded through the door of the cellar, Dani glanced over her shoulder. "I suppose the plans showed the tunnel to the cave as well."

"No, the tunnel wasn't carved from the earth until Nathan Kingsley participated in the Underground Railroad. He'd discovered the cave in his boyhood; then when he began hiding fugitive slaves, he obtained their help to dig the passageway to the cave and another tunnel to the river. Remember, I shared some of the account in Nathan's journal with you in the library. Before the slaves traveled on North, they fashioned barges inside the cave to float on the Chattahoochee River."

Dani laughed. "You're just a walking history museum, aren't you?"

She felt rather than saw him grin. "It was your idea to give me access to your library. In another of Nathan's diaries, I found directions to the cave and the tunnel leading to the river."

Dani drew a deep breath. "I'll be forever thankful that you did."

"Dani, the secret room had to be what Maury Davidson discovered when Mrs. O'Brien caught him pilfering the attic that time," Justin interjected while he waited for Blake to trip the lock on the back of the china hutch. "Remember? She said she saw him stuff some papers into a trunk."

Dani nodded, recalling Mrs. O'Brien's story. Once they all stood inside the dining room, Lance glared at Dani. "I'll get you for this someday."

The sheriff pushed the brothers toward the foyer. "I wouldn't worry, Miss McKinnon. Where these two end up, they won't have a chance to hurt you. By the time they get out of prison, they'll be too feeble to cause trouble for anyone."

Dani smiled. "Thanks, Sheriff Wilson. I can't tell you how wonderful it will be to wake up each morning without a death threat looming above my head. And just as soon as I can procure the workmen necessary to do the job, the tunnel to the cave and this secret entrance will no longer be a cause for worry either."

While Blake and the sheriff escorted the prisoners onto the porch, Justin held back to speak to her. "Dani, no matter what you think of me now, I'm glad the ordeal is over for you. We've suspected for days that Davenport had made plans for your kidnapping at some point during the fair, but we didn't know for sure until a couple of hours ago. That's one reason I came today. The other ... well—"

Dani lowered her eyelashes, unable to gaze at the naked regret she read in his eyes. "I'm grateful for your participation in Lance's apprehension. You helped give me back my life. I won't ever forget that." She stood on her tiptoes to brush her lips against his cheek. "And maybe in time we can be friends."

He chucked her on the chin and then grinned. "I'd like that, sweet Dani. I'd like that very much." Glancing toward the door, he shifted from one foot to the other. "Guess I'd better go aid the sheriff in getting those thugs to jail. Good luck to you and Blake. He told me how he feels about you. Give him a chance, Dani. He's a great guy."

At that moment, as though on cue, Mrs. O'Brien burst into the room. "Land sakes, lass," she said, eyeing her mistress's swollen face and soiled clothing. "What did those monsters do to you?" With a scowl, the housekeeper turned to observe the prisoners inside the sheriff's car before the vehicle sped down the lane. "Aye, the devil's next of kin. They deserve what's ahead of them and more in me opinion."

At that instant, Mrs. O'Brien spied the open space behind the china hutch. "Merciful heavens! Would ye look at that?" she said, stepping forward to examine the hidden walkway.

Dani laughed. "Come along, Mrs. O'Brien. While I freshen up, you can brew our favorite tea. Then I'll fill you in with all that's happened while we wait for Blake's return from Carrollton. He'll give us more information about the capture then."

Mrs. O'Brien's jaw dropped when Dani pushed the hutch back into place, the secret that had spawned surreptitious heroic events and incited criminal activity at Stratford Hall for two generations.

# THE LEGACY

*M*rs. O'Brien followed Blake into the gathering room upon his return from the Carrollton County Jail, critically eyeing the sling that held his injured arm. "What happened to ye, lad?"

He swept off his Stetson and tossed it onto a nearby chair. "I didn't move quick enough when Carter and Davenport started blasting away after we surprised them. No need to worry though. Doc Bedford says I'll be fine in a few days."

The housekeeper rolled her eyes toward the ceiling. "Ye two are going to be the death of me yet." Her merry eyes twinkled. "In case ye be interested, dinner is awaiting to be served."

Dani rose from the sofa, smiling. "That's wonderful. I feel like I haven't eaten in days. Following dinner, if Blake is up to it, maybe he'll share the missing details leading up to our exciting afternoon."

When the housekeeper had finished dishing up their meal, Dani waited until Blake had blessed the food to ask, "Did Lance or Davenport cause any other problems?"

"Not to speak of." Blake rubbed his hand along his jaw. "Lance did get in one lucky punch when the sheriff removed his handcuffs to be fingerprinted. Trust me. He got the worst end of it. A broken nose is tame punishment for what he did to you." A look of regret appeared on Blake's face. "I'm sorry to say I kind of hoped he'd pull something like that. I hope God hasn't become weary of all my pleas for forgiveness lately."

"Now, lad," the housekeeper interjected. "Don't ye be so hard on yourself. If I had me way about it, I'd have tarred those scoundrels with so many layers of feathers they'd be far into the next century apluckin' to rid themselves of me toil."

Blake roared with laughter. "Mrs. O'Brien, I plan to work over-time to stay in your good graces."

Wiping tears of laughter from her eyes, suddenly Dani grew quiet. After a moment, she put her fork aside. "I still can't fathom Lance hating me to the point of murder. If I hadn't accepted the promotion at Pendergraff, then maybe he wouldn't have toppled off the edge of reality."

Blake reached across the table and laid his hand over her fingers. "Now, Dani, you can't fault yourself for wanting to advance your career. Besides, there's no guarantee Mr. Pendergraff would have given the promotion to Lance anyway. It's my guess the discovery of the letter from Phillip Harcourt was the catalyst that exposed his instability."

"All the same, I pray he and his brother can be helped. It such a waste of human potential when mental illness destroys lives. Lance had so much going for him."

"Lass, ye just keep praying for them. God is still a miracle worker in spite of what some people believe. He's our present help in time of need, no matter what troubles come our way. All we have to do is call on Him."

Dani smiled at her two friends. "Well, He certainly proved Himself today. If I spend the rest of my life giving Him praise, it won't be long enough."

Her eyes filled with tenderness. "And, Blake, how can I express my gratitude for all you did? You've more than earned your wages, not counting other ways you might have suffered." Dani looked at his arm, but the look in his eyes revealed that he knew she meant otherwise.

All at once the silence in the kitchen seemed deafening, broken a moment later by the clatter of dishes as Mrs. O'Brien began to clear the table. "Well, me lass, 'tis best to look on the bright side of the coin. In the midst of the accursed wickedness ye endured today, the good Lord blessed the wee orphans. The money the charity bazaar earned will keep the little darlings in necessities for months to come."

Dani brightened. "Yes, God granted life in more ways than one today."

The kitchen back to normal, the three occupants of Stratford Hall withdrew to the gathering room. Once seated into a comfortable position on the sofa, Dani turned to Blake, her disgruntled expression offset by the teasing glint in her eyes. "Okay, cowboy. You've got some tall explaining to do. Why don't you begin with the events preceding my rescue, including what you learned about the case prior to today, you know, all those little tidbits of information you failed to mention to me?"

Blake lowered his eyelashes, shielding the hint of guilt in his eyes. "Well, as you know, Justin and I helped the sheriff curtail the disturbance caused by those gang members. As soon as deputies arrived from Carrollton to transport the gang to jail, Justin and I headed for Mrs. O'Brien's booth. We wanted to make sure you were safe."

Dani coaxed Percy into her lap, reveling in the kitten's softness. The cat circled a couple of times and lay down, falling asleep in Dani's arms. A line from the poem "Twas the Night before Christmas" came to mind: "We settled down for a long winter's nap." Dani focused on Blake's remarks, looking confused. "But I thought you and Justin accompanied the sheriff to the jail."

"That was our original intent. Just as we were to leave for Carrollton, Sheriff Wilson received a phone call from an undercover policeman who'd infiltrated the gang months ago. He'd learned of Davenport's plan to kidnap you during the bazaar. Immediately, the sheriff phoned for a backup. The moment they arrived, Justin, the sheriff, and I went straight to the bakery booth.

"Mrs. O'Brien informed us of your errand, stating she'd begun to worry since you hadn't yet returned. Aware that another of the gang's members had been instructed to lure you inside the hall while we handled the disturbance, we hurried to the house."

Blake stood up from his chair and began to pace back and forth. "Not locating you right away, we entered the secret passageway and slipped down the hidden corridor, our worst fears incarnated when we heard your conversation with Davenport behind that oak door. A moment later, we returned to the dining room, agreeing our best hope of rescue would be a surprise attack from the tunnel leading to the cave. Knowing it would take too long to reach the cave by car, we traveled on foot through the woods to the cave entrance a hundred or so yards from the river."

Dani held up her hand. "Let's back up a minute. Why didn't you or Justin tell me about the hidden room and the location of the cave before now?"

Blake grinned, winking at Mrs. O'Brien. "For one, we all know just how verbal you can be when riled and we didn't want you to accidentally spill our findings to Davenport or his brother should you have an encounter with them."

Dani rolled her eyes toward the ceiling. "Thanks for the confidence you have in me."

Blake laughed. "You're welcome. To continue, we had to have hard evidence to make an arrest. So we decided to give them an opportunity to carry out part two of their devious plot—steal several antiques from the hall for cash to live on until they could claim Mrs. Thorndike's fortune. The sheriff posted deputies at the cave site 24/7 to monitor the thieves' activity, hoping to catch them with stolen articles in their possession. He wanted them to be permanent house guests of the county before they could harm you in any way."

Dani threw her hands into the air. "And without suspecting a thing, I waltzed right into their evil plan. I guess it's too late to wish I'd obeyed your instruction to stay with Mrs. O'Brien. What happened next?"

"We worked our way around to Deputy Johnson's hidden place of surveillance where we witnessed Lance emerge from the cave and place the Ming vase from the main entryway of the hall into his car nearby."

Dani gasped. "Oh, the despicable cads! That vase is priceless."

"Don't worry," Blake said. "It will be returned after the trial."

"When Lance stepped back into the cave and didn't return after a few moments, we followed him, making as little noise as possible, arriving just in time to save the damsel in distress." Blake, grinning, shrugged his shoulders. "That's it. You know the rest."

A frown of concentration appeared on Dani's face. "This afternoon, right after the auction, I saw you discussing with Justin a document you held in your hand. Did that paper have something to do with all this?"

"That was a fax from my agent in California. A judge ordered Mrs. Davitello's doctor to release her family records. Justin and I could hardly believe the identity of her youngest son. Not wanting to upset you during the fair, we chose to wait until after the bazaar to inform you about him. I'm sorry you had to find out the way you did."

Dani shook her head. "And to think Lance knew about the hidden room all these years. Aunt Lucille and Uncle Bill will never believe it. I'm not sure I do myself."

Mrs. O'Brien nodded in agreement. "Who would have thought such a place existed at Stratford Hall?"

"Actually," Dani said, "such rooms aren't that uncommon in these old houses, along with hidden staircases and the like. But years of remodeling, refurbishing, and the death of those who knew about the concealments have taken their toll on historians. Lance probably speculated that no one else knew about the room or the cave. How else could he have thought he could get away with his hideous crime?"

Suddenly, Mrs. O'Brien's eyes lit up with remembrance. "Miss Mathilda once told me her old nanny often tried to frighten her young mistress into obedience with tales of ghosts who lived in a hidden room beneath the floors of the hall. But milady said she'd laugh, accusing the old nurse of listening to servants' fables." The housekeeper sighed deeply. "It seems the caretaker's tales were more truthful than me mistress realized."

Dusk drifted into the room as the three sat in silence pondering the afternoon events. After a while Mrs. O'Brien rose from her chair. "'Tis time I be agetting back to me duties. Clive and his boys should be about through with the cleanup from the fair. I want to send one of my good remedies for tummy aches home with him for his ailing lad."

Dani looked at Blake, suppressing a grin. "Tell Clive I appreciate all his family's efforts to make our bazaar a success."

"Sure thing, lass. And, Mr. Blake, don't ye keep me mistress up too late. She's had a rough day."

When Mrs. O'Brien had taken her leave, Blake stood to his feet. "If you'll excuse me, Dani, I have to finish my report. I'll catch you later."

She nodded. "I think I'll stroll down to the gazebo and watch the stars come out. I think a little solitude is just what Doctor Bedford would order for me right now."

A short time later, Dani stood gazing out over the brook, listening to the peaceful night sounds. She smiled as the full moon peeked over the horizon to embrace the encroaching black velvet. *A night for lovers,* she thought.

A hint of regret washed over her as Justin's smiling image poked into her thoughts. *If only . . .* But that was then. She prayed he would find happiness with Marguerite.

And besides, there was Blake—yes, Blake. A sudden rush of love for him tumbled into her heart. Was it too late for them now? Could it be possible Blake had lost interest in her?

The stars were high in the sky when he stepped into the gazebo and sat down beside her, sliding his arm along the back of the bench. They didn't speak right away, the silence too golden to disturb. At last, Dani turned to look at him, the satiny glow of the moonlight revealing the questions in her eyes.

"Blake, Justin told me right before he left the hall that you'd spoken to him about us. Is it true?" She looked away, afraid of what she might read in his eyes. After all, Justin couldn't be trusted.

Blake turned her face toward him. "Yes. I told him that I intended to do everything in my power to make you love me."

The thoughts of her heart filling her eyes, Dani caressed his cheek. "I promise you from now on your efforts won't be in vain."

For a moment, Blake looked stunned; then he touched his lips to her mouth, gently at first, as though to reassure himself he'd heard her correctly. Momentarily, he deepened the kiss, filling Dani with delight. In his arms, she discovered the devotion she'd longed for all her life.

Suddenly, Blake broke the embrace and descended onto the lawn. Dancing a jig, he threw his hat into the air, shouting, "Hey, world! She really loves me." Dani stood watching from the doorway of the gazebo, breathless with laughter.

All of a sudden, a sense of peace overwhelmed her, consuming every ounce of anxiety and alarm she'd suffered at the hands of Lance and Davenport. She sank to her knees, realizing with thankfulness that she could now live her life as God intended—sharing His love with others in the manner He desires, the legacy God bestows on all His children through the gift of His Son. *No earthly inheritance could ever compare to His righteous endowment*, she thought lifting her face heavenward. Somehow she knew Aunt Mathilda rejoiced with her niece.

A moment later, Blake pulled her into his arms. "Dani, you can't begin to know how happy you've made me this night." A cloud drifted across the face of the moon, severing the view of the grin curving his lips. "You do know how to keep a guy tied up in knots though. There was a time or two I thought I'd lost out for sure."

Dani turned away. "Oh, Blake. I'm sorry I caused you such misery. When Lance held that gun to my head, the thought of never seeing you again was worse than the actuality of dying. I understand more than ever the meaning of the proverb that says, 'Pride goes before a fall.' Thank God He gave me another chance to tell you how much I love you. Will you forgive me?"

"If anyone needs forgiveness, it's me. In my desperation to win you, I said hurtful things about Justin and acted in ways that didn't exactly correspond with a heavenly note. What I'm trying to say is I wasn't the Christian witness I could have been. I should have let God work out our relationship in His own time and fashion."

Dani put her fingertips to his lips. "Let's not waste this gorgeous night dredging up past mistakes. God has forgiven our sins and put them into the sea of forgetfulness to be remembered no more. Let's do the same. I'd rather talk about us."

Sweeping his hat from his head and laying it aside, Blake enfolded her hands in his. "Dani, just between you and me, I believe the future holds great things for us."

A slow smile formed on her lips." "I think you might be right."

After Blake pledged their destiny with a kiss, Dani lay her head on his chest, singing praises in her heart for his love. She couldn't begin to forecast where life would take them. But for the time being, they would face the future together arm in arm, encircled in the legacy of love God ordained before the beginning of time.